Editing: Susan Barnes Editing

Proofing, Formatting, Cover Design: Cruel Ink Editing and Design

Photograph: Artur Verkhovetskiy, Deposit Photos

To my sister Linda—
For always encouraging me to write down the thoughts in my head.

AUTHOR'S NOTE:

I have lived in the Midwest all my life. It was my first playground for telling stories, and I will always want to come back to it. With that said, though the metro of Des Moines, and the towns of Saylorville, and Ankeny are real and lovely places, the characters, businesses, products, and events that take place in this novel are entirely fictional. Any resemblance to real life places, people, or things is entirely a coincidence.

Also... Mom, relatives, and anyone else I interact with on a regular basis. This book has a lot of dirty words, phrases, and descriptive acts. You've been warned. Please don't give me heck at social events. Love you.

We were together.

I forget the rest.

- Walt Whitman

Playlist

Ocean Avenue—Yellowcard

Thiskidsnotalright—AWOLNATION

My Demons—Starset

Praying—Kesha

The Night We Met—Lord Huron

Self Control—Laura Branigan

Jenny (I Wanna Ruin Our Friendship)—Studio Killers

Tempest—Deftones

Dig—Incubus

*Ricochet—Starset

*Cardigan—Taylor Swift

Nothing's Gonna Hurt You Baby—Cigarettes After Sex

Leathers—Deftones

*Sweet—Cigarettes After Sex

Heat Waves—Glass Animals

Chapter One
Noelle

"CAFFEINE IS A SOCIALLY APPROVED ADDICTION."

Someone snorted on the other side of the divider between desks, and Elissa smirked as she slipped me the list of orders. "Didn't you used to work part-time in a coffee shop?" she asked.

"I always drank tea. Or hot cocoa."

"Tea has caffeine. So does chocolate." She passed me the office card I used nearly every day when I went to pick up coffee orders and grinned. "You're just as addicted as everyone else."

The implication of being addicted to something made me flinch, and I briefly thought of the parents I hadn't seen in almost ten years before pushing their faces out of my mind. Thankfully, Elissa missed my brief descent into nostalgic grieving, having turned her head back to her desk. She threw a smug look over her shoulder at me as I tucked the card into my purse and slung the bag over my shoulders.

The clack of keyboards and chorus of murmuring voices were my soundtrack as I exited the building and unchained my bike from the rack, frowning at the traffic that had already started to accumulate. I'd been at the office since 6:30 and it was now close to 8:00. Not only did I have to navigate through cars to get to the shop down the street, but I'd also have to wait in line and rush back to the office before the drinks got cold. There were plenty of days I thought *internship be damned, I'm staying in bed.*

But I never did. I hauled myself out of the covers, covered the bags under my eyes with foundation, and tried to stay awake as I coasted down the hill from my tiny apartment into downtown Des Moines.

Traffic aside, there weren't many people out in the residential areas I passed on the way to the shop. It was a little out of the way, but I used to work there and a few of the girls still gave me a discount. Probably the reason my boss sends me instead of someone else.

I'd just turned onto another side street that would let me avoid the busier areas around parking garages, along with branches and debris that had fallen during the storm the night before last. But when I rounded the corner, I immediately slammed on my brakes, almost falling off my bike as I tried to take in what I was seeing. There was a large tree branch hanging precariously over a cable that ran from a post to the apartment building. It swayed in the breeze, and the two guys on the ground were staring at it with worried expressions. A third man appeared, chainsaw in hand, and he started to climb onto a picnic table.

Then onto a card table.

Then onto a short stepladder stacked on top of the card table.

"Bryce, watch it," one of the guys on the ground cautioned, and I silently echoed him while unstrapping my backpack purse and digging around inside it for my camera.

A second later the chainsaw roared to life, and I watched with bated breath as the guy set to work on the branch. His friends on the ground shouted instructions up at him, trying to make the task a team effort. I positioned my shot and started to snap photos.

The chainsaw growled, cutting through the morning air and almost drowning out the sound of cracking wood and shouts from the ground. Finally, one of the guys below jumped up and snatched the end of the branch just before it came loose. He tugged it down, helping it narrowly avoid the wire as it came tumbling to the ground. Both guys dodged it as it fell, cheering, and I joined in before I realized what I was doing. They turned to look at me, three pairs of eyes fixing me with curious glances, and the warmth that had filled my chest turned to a tightness that made my breath hitch.

I swallowed through the tightness, lowering the camera as I tried to ignore the knot forming in my stomach. The sensation wasn't unfamiliar, but it hadn't been this bad for a few weeks. I took a deep breath, reminding myself that I was safe. No one was after me, and there was no reason to assume danger simply because people were staring at me.

"This," I gave them my best winning smile and gestured to their set up, "is crazy, but it's clever. I write for *The Journal*— do you mind telling me about what's going on here?"

I kept smiling when I finished, grateful my voice carried a confidence I didn't quite feel.

I had to get over this aversion to strangers. I couldn't be a journalist and not talk to people.

Interest lit up their faces and the two guys on the ground jogged over while the third started to climb down the MacGyver-esque set up. "We had to get that branch down after the storm," the first guy said, rubbing at his short hair. "It was gonna take down the cable line and that would have been on us. No one was going to be able to come out here for at least a week."

His friend nodded, his shirtless chest shining in the morning sun, distracting me a little. I wasn't sure if it was attraction or discomfort, but I wasn't going to stick around long enough to find out.

"You're not the only ones," I said as I jotted down their names on one of my notepads. "The storm downed branches all over the metro, and there's been talk about having to call out-of-state crews to come in."

Shirtless guy agreed and told me about how they'd called four places and hadn't gotten a call back. Hence, the unsteady platform.

"This only proves my theory that nothing good happens after midnight or before 8:00am," I joked as I tucked the pad away, smiling to myself at how all three of them laughed unnecessarily hard.

"You need our phone numbers or anything? In case you forget our names or want more information?" the chainsaw operator asked.

"Or want one of us to show you some of the fun things that can happen after midnight?" the shirtless guy teased, officially signaling that it was time for me to leave.

"I'm... good. But thank you," I said, tucking my things in my purse and grabbing my bike again.

"What's your name so we can look up the article?"

"Collins," I replied. "T.N. Collins."

"What's the T.N. stand for?" the shirtless one asked, as I put my feet on the pedals and started off. "Hey—"

"Thanks again!" I yelled over my shoulder, waving as I headed toward the shop. I had to go. This had taken up some of my precious time, and the line to get coffee would be even longer now. Plus, it wasn't like I would do anything with the phone numbers they gave me. I wouldn't call. I wouldn't text. I didn't go out, and I didn't have any interest in what went on after midnight.

That's what I told myself at least. There are a few popular bars and restaurants not too far from my apartment, and I could hear people laughing as they passed my windows nearly every night. There was a part of me that wanted to be out, doing the same. But every time I'd tried, I'd ended up a shaking mess; reminders of what happened when people got too close.

I hadn't tried in at least six or seven months, but the fact that I had to resort to deep breathing exercises on my ride to the shop told me nothing had changed. There was no point, and honestly, I was too busy to go out anyway. Maybe once I graduated things would be different.

As I expected, the shop was crowded when I arrived, people loitering in a line that stretched halfway down the block. I wrinkled my nose and parked my bike near a tree, securing it into place with a chain before I took my spot. I pulled my hair out of its ponytail, letting it fall to cover my face as I took out my phone and started making notes; I needed to gather my thoughts about the tree guys and their quest to remove the branch.

The line moved quickly, which I was grateful for as nausea swirled in my stomach. All I'd had to eat that morning was a slice of banana bread. Maybe I could also grab a sandwich with the coffee, or oatmeal. Anything to take this ache away so I could focus in class later.

I looked inside to count the people ahead of me, wincing at the amount of people in the shop sitting down at tables. There was a group of businessmen in one corner, another table full of what had to be college students in another. My eyes skimmed the crowd and landed on a girl with a messy blonde ponytail and scrubs. She was laughing at a guy with shaggy hair, another guy sitting beside her. He shook his head, running a hand over his short, buzzed hair. It was the same bright shade of blond as the woman beside him. I tried not to stare, but there was something familiar about them that made me do a double take.

The guy with the buzz cut and the girl in scrubs both had similar oval faces. The girl's nose was slightly up turned where the guy's was straight and sharp. They bore a resemblance to one another that said siblings or some relation. One they didn't share with the third man, who wore a scuffed-up leather jacket even though it was almost eighty degrees outside. He ran his hands through his hair, messing it up more as he grabbed a bike helmet and stood just as I was about to enter the shop.

When he pushed his hair back again, I noticed the black outline of a tattoo behind his ear. Black sweeping lines that formed a circle with horns.

A Taurus symbol.

Memories appeared unwanted and unbidden inside my head. I knew the two people still sitting at that table, and I knew the guy smiling down at them. I knew that dark, coffee brown hair. Knew those broad shoulders, that sharp nose, those full lips, and that wide smile

My hand involuntarily crept up to my neck, touching the Cancer tattoo behind my ear.

The one I'd gotten with Kellen Bishop holding my hand.

No. No, it can't be. There's... there's just no way.

The line moved again, and I stepped further into the shop, trying to figure out why in the hell Kellen would be here, in this coffee shop, at almost 8:00 in the morning. My throat felt dry. Constricted. Tight. I reached up, feeling nothing but my bare skin, but that assurance did nothing to still the rabbiting pace of my heart, the panting breaths I couldn't keep trapped behind my lips.

My hands started to shake, and I took one last look at the guy before I bolted out of line and ran toward the bathroom, shoving the door open and practically throwing myself into one of the stalls. I pressed my hand to my chest as my body sank to the floor and I tried to corral my stampeding thoughts. Tall guys with peachy skin and brown hair were as common as deer in the Midwest. That guy could have been anyone. It couldn't have been Kellen. Iowa was small, and the metro felt even smaller sometimes, but the odds were too great. Our town was over an hour away.

And even if he was here, it meant nothing. We had nothing to say to one another, or at least, I had nothing to say to him. We'd shared so much that last summer before I left Northshore, but he'd made it clear to me that it meant nothing. He'd pushed me away and left me alone...

Left me alone to face the same thing he'd tried to save me from.

Davey...

"You're going to regret this. God punishes those who defy him."

An involuntary, panicked noise slipped past my lips, bouncing off the sterile white walls of the bathroom. I clasped my hand over my mouth, the other pressed to my chest, and tried to force my breathing to slow down. It had been months since I had an episode this bad, and I'd forgotten how awful it felt. How weak it left me. How paranoid.

And all because the guy outside looked like Kellen, bringing back the memories I'd thought I'd buried long ago.

Apparently, I hadn't dug far enough.

I didn't want to relive the painful memories of a life I'd tried to forget. A life Kellen had made bearable before a storm tore us apart. Before Davey Adler tore us apart.

"I can't stop, Tatum. I won't. Why can't you love me?"

My throat bobbed, the taste of bile burning my tongue. *Get it together, Tatum.* I had to be logical about this. That couldn't be Kellen. The odds were too unreal. It would mean he lived in the metro, or very close to it. That he'd moved to the same city I had and we existed within miles of each other without ever knowing.

Impossible. Right?

It was... unlikely.

I shook my head, grateful my breathing had finally slowed. I was overreacting. Letting my imagination go crazy. It was the crowd. I'd never liked crowds and could easily blame that for putting me on edge. Not to mention talking to those guys earlier. And I hadn't slept well last night. And I was hungry. This was all just an overreaction.

I stood up on shaky legs, smoothing down my white blouse and the thin sweater covering it before taking a deep breath and exiting the bathroom.

The chaos in the shop had only ebbed a little, and I folded in on myself, keeping my arms tucked to my side, my backpack guarding my back. Thankfully the line had shortened as well, so I took my spot in it again, bracing when I turned to look at the table in the corner. All the tension in my body drained out when I found it empty, cleared of cups and chairs pushed in like no one had occupied it all day. Maybe the whole thing had been a figment of my imagination.

I got to the counter, ordered the coffees, took the boxes, and finally escaped outside. Breathing a sigh of relief, I looked around, then stopped in my tracks, the earlier relief draining out of me and onto the sidewalk.

About halfway down the block was a motorcycle—red and black, a Harley Davidson logo visible on the side. The guy from earlier, the one with coffee brown hair and the kind of smile girls went stupid over was grinning at the blonde girl and the guy standing next to her.

I could see the emblem of a police department on the blond guy's sleeve, and remembered that about a year and a half ago, when I'd logged onto my Facebook for all of ten minutes, I'd seen a single picture. Isaac Moore, Kellen's best friend, had been sworn in as a police officer in Lakeside. His little sister Hannah, who'd been the only person to keep me sane the last few months of high school, had posted the picture and announced that she'd show him up when she finished taking her nursing exams in a few years.

I looked at the girl's scrubs before I put the two boxes of drinks in the basket on my bike, and threw my leg over the seat, trying to get out of there before they saw me; even if I knew they wouldn't recognize me. My hair was longer, onyx black instead of light brown. There were rings in my ears and in my nose that hadn't been there three years ago, along with a few more tattoos. And the one thing everyone had always been able to recognize me by, the stupid spot of muddy brown that disrupted the pale blue-green iris of my right eye, was hidden behind contacts that made my entire iris a dark brown no one bothered to look at.

Including the three people on the sidewalk that looked far too familiar for my own comfort.

I put my feet on the pedals, turning around on the street and riding away before any of them had a chance to look in my direction, or I stared too long in theirs.

I was still a bit shaky when I arrived back at the office, hating that every loud clack or shout made me jump as I walked around, dropping off orders before finally making it to Elissa's desk. She looked up when I arrived, a curious look on her face as she took her drink.

"Was the shop busier than normal?" She glanced at the clock, frowning, then looked back to me. "You've gotta leave right away again, don't you?"

I nodded, trying to reign in my still rabbiting heartbeat. "It was packed, plus, I stopped to take pictures of this." I pulled out the camera and showed her the pyramid the tree guys had built, a smile coming to my face at how wide her eyes got before she started laughing. One of the other editors, Pak, looked up from his desk in interest, and I flipped the camera around to show him.

"Are you going to write a piece about it?" he asked.

"A small one. I thought it might be funny to put it in *Beat*."

Pak grinned. "Email it to me when you're done. Just so you know, Gina approved the extra piece you submitted on that school board meeting last week. She's running it in the opinion section."

I felt my eyes widened, hands splaying out as I bounced involuntarily on my toes. It had been so long since I felt excitement—real excitement—that I'd forgotten how akin it was to anxiety. It took me a moment to discern between the two. I took a deep breath and smiled. Pak nodded, and Elissa chuckled beside her desk.

"I told you," she said smugly. "That'll be the first article you'll have in print instead of just on the website, right?"

I nodded. "Yeah, but it'll just be in the back pages or—"

"Pfft." She waved me off. "Still counts. We should celebrate. A few of us are planning on going out downtown so it wouldn't be far for you to go. It will be fun."

"I told my neighbor I'd clean her apartment this weekend." I grimaced when Elissa groaned dramatically and Pak laughed. "She's eighty-two and her only family lives seven hours away. I don't want her to fall or something."

"Admirable, but you have to get out, Noelle." She waved her hand up and down in my direction. "You are twenty-two! You should be taking selfies, getting drunk on the weekends, and having bad hookups."

For the second time today, Elissa made me flinch. She didn't mean to, I knew that. No one I worked with knew enough about me to understand why certain words made my jaw flex, or my teeth clench. They didn't know how sometimes when I was alone, the litany of sermons I'd heard for four years flashed through my head. Lectures on purity and piety, and how if I gave in to my deepest desires, I'd find myself damned. That if I behaved like Elissa suggested I'd end up in a worse hell than I already was.

"You made me do this. You made me this way."

"I really have to go, I don't want to be late for my class," I said, interrupting Elissa's list of places she'd like to take me to. My shoulders tensed as I watched her sigh in exasperation, and I gave her a contrite smile before turning and grabbing the rest of the things off my desk and heading back outside to my bike. I shoved my purse into my backpack along with my laptop and sent a quick text to the professor for my first class, letting him know I'd be a little late. He wouldn't see it until after class most likely, but at least I'd tried.

By the time I got onto campus, I was calmer. My muscles weren't as tense, the exertion of pedaling as fast as I could across town had burned out the adrenaline pumping through my veins. Still, when I got off the bike and parked it, I flinched as one of the other students walked past me, a bit too close for comfort. My fight or flight response hadn't shut down yet, and part of my brain was convinced that at any moment, Davey was going to appear from behind a tree and come at me again.

Seeing Kellen's look alike had been a ghost I wasn't prepared for, and it made me wonder if there were others lurking nearby, lying in wait for a moment to strike.

Chapter Two
Noelle

THERE WASN'T A BIKE RACK OUTSIDE MY APARTMENT complex, so unfortunately, I had to drag my bike down the hall and into my apartment every afternoon when I got home from class. It wasn't easy, especially considering whenever I opened the door to my apartment I was greeted by a gray and white cat curling around my legs.

I shoved the bike inside as Haku pawed at my calves, alternating between eager purrs and agonized meows. He trotted along behind me as I walked into my kitchen and grabbed a scoop of his food from the container, bending down to pour it into his still half-full bowl.

"Spoiled brat." He arched into my touch when I ran my palm over his fluffy coat, a few strands of fur clinging to my fingers. "You lived on the street, my man. What happened to those hunter-gatherer skills you had to cultivate?"

Haku didn't offer me any sort of response as he folded himself into a bread-like shape and bent over his cat bowl, diving into the food like he'd been starved for weeks. My eyes rolled even as I smiled and stood to deposit my bag onto the table, still feeling shaky even after the ride home. There were too many thoughts in my head, and if I had any chance of focusing and getting that article done tonight, I had to clear them out. Stretch, or do jumping jacks. Scream into a pillow. Anything to exorcise the imaginary demons playing tag in my head.

I pulled out my laptop and set it on the table, pressing the button before walking away to make some tea. The thing was very close to taking its last breaths and took forever to fire up, but a new computer was an expense I couldn't afford just yet; not unless I absolutely had to. I had one more round of tuition to pay, and if I made it, I'd escape from school with minimal student loans. A smile crossed my face. My bank account was small, but it was well managed for someone who'd started with nothing and now had an apartment, clothes, food, and a cat. Some would think that was an unnecessary expense, but I'd loved Haku ever since he showed up on my balcony, knocking over my neighbors' plants and pawing at my window. He was worth the money I spent keeping his insatiable appetite satisfied. And once I made that last student loan payment, I would graduate from poor college student to starving journalist, but that didn't seem as daunting as it once did. Hopefully, the internship at the paper would turn into a job, and I could get a steady paycheck while I tried to establish myself so I could write what I wanted; human interest pieces. Specialized articles about whatever caught my attention, made my brain light up.

Tell the stories no one would hear unless someone gave them a voice.

I poured some honey into my tea and sat down, greeted by a picture of Haku on his back on my screen. The camera upload would take a bit to connect but as soon as it did, I could move the photos into the drive I shared with Pak and open them to use for inspiration. I opened a word doc and stared at it, trying to think of how to start this short little piece.

But there was only one thing on my mind. The guy from earlier. And how much he'd looked like Kellen.

I ran a hand through my hair as though I was trying to push him out of my head. It had been months since I'd thought about Kellen. Since I let the memories of that last summer, of him and I together, wreak havoc in my head, and I worried if I indulged myself now, I'd end up crying all evening.

But I couldn't just sit here and wonder either.

I bit the inside of my cheek, hating the way my fingers shook when I put them on the keys.

K E L L E N B I S H O P

I knew as soon as I hit the enter button, and the spinning circle in the corner of my screen started moving, that tea wasn't going to be enough to calm my nerves. I didn't have much in the way of alcohol, but I kept some on hand for when my neighbor Priest came over. His drink of choice was either whiskey or gin, so I grabbed the latter and poured a measured amount into my tea, stirring it as the results for my search popped up on the screen. The first few links made me frown. Social media links, a Facebook and Instagram I'd once been very familiar with. Following that were court records, where I found that he'd been released a little over a year ago. That seemed like such a short amount of time. Two years. Not that it bothered me. Truthfully, I was grateful. The thought of him behind bars had given me nightmares, so I'd tried just as hard not to think about it. Just like I tried not to think about what the two of us could have been if things hadn't gone so horribly wrong.

After taking a large drink of my now alcohol-laden tea to ease the tightness in my chest, I clicked the third link. It brought up a page for Bishop Builds and Autos, which had been in business for roughly eighteen months. They specialized in motorcycle repair and rebuilds, but also took auto repairs on a case-by-case basis. They had a four point five star rating, and the website was littered with quotes from customers. Outstanding, personable service.

I couldn't help but laugh, the images of Kellen scowling at people whenever we were out popping into my head. I never knew if he threw out glares like parade candy because he sincerely didn't like people, or if his dirty looks were a return of the scowls levied in my direction. For me and the few friends he kept, the smiles had been plentiful, but they cost more for the rest of the world.

Seemed that had changed, along with a few other things. There were several pictures of Kellen at events. Various auto shows, one where he'd put himself in a suit and slicked back his hair. There were images of him in a shop, too, where it was loose and shaggy, hanging a little past his ears. I swallowed, a twisted mix of emotions building inside me as I thought back to the guy I'd seen earlier. The slight wave in his hair, the ease in his stance. That smile.

It was him. He was here, so close to me, but so very far away.

I continued to click through the photos, taking another drink to try and push down the nostalgia laced cocktail of excitement and dread that coursed through me. Did I want to see him? No. No, that would just be a recipe for heartbreak, and God knows I didn't need more of that on top of everything else. Would he want to see me? Would it matter? Also no, because he'd been the one to end things. Not me. He'd told me loud and clear what we were, so there was no point in opening the box when I already knew what was inside it.

But still, curiosity was an itch I needed to scratch, so I kept clicking to see what his life was like now. More pictures came up on my screen. Kellen standing next to bikes he built, then shaking hands with a guy who'd won some motocross tournament on one of them. Most of the casual pictures featured him wearing the same clothes he'd worn whenever we were together.

Jeans in varying states of disarray, old band or anime T-shirts. There were a few pictures of him wearing a denim vest with a patch that read *Heartland Heathens*. I opened another tab and googled it, unsurprised to see that it was a local bikers club. I didn't click the link to see pictures though, choosing to down the rest of my tea and wince again at the burn of the gin going down my throat.

Kellen was doing well.

Really well.

He had a life again. A good one, it appeared, which meant everything he'd said the last time I saw him must have been true. Everything we'd had together... it meant nothing.

I frowned at my now empty mug and stood up, filling it with more tea from the kettle and a larger amount of gin this time. I didn't drink often, but sometimes it took the edge off sleepless nights or softened the bitterness that raced through my veins when I saw people living outgoing lives I knew I'd never share. I swallowed a large gulp, wondering if it would do anything to drown the confusion and anger swirling in my chest.

Anger was the last thing I should have been feeling, especially toward Kellen. He'd spent two years in prison and deserved a good life. This was exactly what he'd wanted, and he deserved it—truly. Kellen had always been harder on himself than he ever needed to be, and I was glad he'd moved on from that feeling.

Knowing that still didn't ease the ache forming in my chest, the tightness settling into my jaw as I clicked aggressively through more photos, finally going to his Instagram page, which he'd made public since it was mostly bikes. But the *really* irritating thing about all this was with every picture that confirmed his good life, it also confirmed that he looked good living it. Very good. Years of throwing around bikes and engines and doing God knows what else had made his already broad shoulders stronger, not to mention the toned arms and abs I could see even in the pictures.

He looked just the right amount of wild, too. Maybe even dangerous, with that slightly shaggy hair that was always a mess, his strong jaw, broad cheekbones. He had a more masculine appearance now versus the boyish one I'd known. The one I'd fallen for when I was way too young to fall for him. Back then he was cute, now he was the kind of hot girls went stupid for.

I looked down at my mug, frowning when I found it empty, and drummed my fingers on the table as memories bloomed like flowers that used to grow by the fence that surrounded his property—heavy peonies that always attracted ants, wasps, and butterflies; ones I used to stare at when I sat nestled in the large, exposed roots of an overgrown weeping willow. The only one I'd ever seen outside of pictures.

"What you reading?"

The voice startled me so much I nearly dropped my manga, and when I lifted my eyes, I was shocked to find a boy staring at me.

An older boy. He was broad, a slight shadow on his jaw which confirmed my suspicions. Maybe seventeen or eighteen. A senior?

The boy said nothing, and neither did I, but I still couldn't stop staring at him. He didn't look like any of the other boys I'd met since I moved here. The ones belonging to other families at the church Harvey and Marta had been taking me to. They all sported short, clean haircuts, and wore khakis or jeans with church camp T-shirts or ones that featured parent approved bands. It was that or button downs. There wasn't a lot of variety.

But this boy wore jeans that were dusty with dark, oily spots on them, and a Slipknot T-shirt. His hair was disheveled, shaved on the sides but long enough that when he pushed it back, it hung over his fingers. And he'd been tanned by hours in the sun. Almost sunburned—a dark contrast with the tattoos on his bicep and wrist.

"Death Note."

He laughed. "You're not reading Death Note."

"No, um… your tattoo." I gestured again. "I know that. It's Ryuk."

His eyes widened at the same time a grin spread over his full lips. My heart skipped a little at the sight, and I felt my cheeks flood with heat. He looked at the tattoo again, then back to me. "Yup. So, back to your manga…"

He hopped over the fence and folded himself onto the grass in front of me, holding out his hand. I didn't pass it to him, but I did turn it to hold up the cover.

"Fruits Basket," he read. "I haven't read that one, but you must really like it."

"What makes you say that?"

He reached out and tapped the cover. "Collector's Edition. That had to cost a shit ton of money."

My eyes widened at the curse. It wasn't like I hadn't heard it before, but it had been long enough, and Harvey and Marta would definitely have had something to say if they'd heard it. They'd probably have a lot of things to say about this particular boy if they saw him.

But for some reason, despite the effort I'd put into pleasing them, to finding my footing on what they called a path to salvation, in this moment I didn't really care what they'd think.

"It did," I confessed, turning the cover of the book back to face me. "I saved up forever. So many babysitting jobs."

So many nights where the parents of the kids I watched had dropped me off to an empty house, all of them assuming my parents were asleep. But it sure was nice they let me stay out as late as anyone needed, they always commented.

"So, what's it about?" the boy asked, tilting his head when I made a face.

"You wouldn't like it."

"Why not?" He gestured to my shirt. "I liked Sailor Moon. Sailor Jupiter is actually my favorite."

"Everyone likes Sailor Moon. You've got a Ryuk tattooed on your arm, and a Berserk *tattoo on your wrist. You're not going to be into this.*"

Thick eyebrows narrowed over round, dark blue eyes, and a smirk spread across his face. "*Are you gatekeeping me?*"

My mouth dropped open, but I snapped it shut when he started to laugh. "*No, I'm not… gatekeeping…you.*" I scoffed and he laughed again as I flipped the manga back around. "*It's about a family that's cursed. They turn into animals whenever anyone of the opposite sex hugs them. A girl finds out their secret and she has to keep it all through school. It's girly. Slice of life Shoujo stuff.*"

"*And Harvey and Marta are okay with you reading it?*"

It was my turn to tilt my head. "*How did you—*"

"*I saw you with them the other day at the bakery. It's a small town, word travels fast.*" His expression was calm, but his voice had dropped. "*How'd you end up with them?*"

My nose wrinkled, not wanting to tell him the whole story. My parents had decided to start getting high again. They'd left for a party that had turned into a full day. Then a week. Then a month. It wasn't the first time I'd been in foster care, but the fact that no one could find out where Chris and Noelle Ivers had gone told me that unless Harvey and Marta decided to put me elsewhere, I was stuck here.

The boy waited patiently, expecting some sort of an answer, so I offered him a shrug. "*It's a long story. But they're fine so far.*" I flipped the manga over in my lap. "*They haven't taken me to get any new books since I moved in last month, and the library here is lacking… so…*" I held it up again. "*I'm re-reading this.*"

"*I've got stuff you could read.*" He jerked his head toward the fence, standing up and dusting off his pants. "*Come on. You can read whatever you want. I sure as fuck won't police it.*"

I bit my lip, tucking the manga into my bag and getting to my feet, suddenly self-conscious about the messy pony tail my hair was thrown into; not to mention the fading T-shirt and the cut off shorts I had on. Part of me wished I was in jeans or a sundress. Something a little prettier.

But then I remembered that his boy was older, and there were probably a dozen other girls in town I could never compete against.

Still. It'd be nice to have a friend.

He jerked his head again and hopped over the fence, taking care to avoid the large flowers on the bushes surrounding the gate. His hand extended out in offering, but I narrowed my eyes.

"You're not gonna take me to your basement and murder me or something, right?"

That grin flashed on his face again and my heart stuttered. "Only if you ask nicely."

A laugh bubbled up out of my throat, and I threw my bag over my shoulder before hopping over the fence on my own, not wanting to take his hand and give away how badly mine were shaking. "What's your name?" I asked.

"Kellen." He pushed his hair back, starting to walk backward across a field toward a big white house with a large barn beside it. "Yours?"

"Tatum." I smiled back. "But everyone calls me Tate."

A knock on the door pulled me back to the present, and I tensed, slamming my laptop shut harder than necessary. No one ever came to visit me. No one even really knew where I lived, except my neighbors.

"Noelle, it's me." The voice was deep, a little gravelly, and it took me a moment to register the name—*Noelle. Not Tate. Not anymore.*

The knock came again, and even though I knew who it was the tension in my body didn't fade. It lingered, and I cursed my overreactive fight or flight response. *You're fine. No one is coming to get you.*

I opened the door to find Priest on the other side, his lion's mane of thick blond hair pulled back into a low ponytail that hung just above his shoulders. In his hand was an empty paper plate, a loaf-shaped grease stain in the center of it. I grinned and leaned against the door frame.

"That banana bread must have been good."

"You gotta stop giving me all this sugary shit."

"Yes, because obviously you hate it," I said, gesturing to the plate before stepping back and allowing him inside. I closed the door behind him, relieved I didn't have to explain to my co-workers why I didn't want to go out with them, but hanging out with a growly, six-foot-three man with a lion's mane of hair and a lumberjack's build was fine.

Priest was the only man–only person—I regularly talked with. It had started because we both hated our landlord and worried about Macy, the sweet eighty-two-year-old woman who lived in the last unit on our floor. I got her mail regularly. He fixed things around her apartment and got her grocery orders. When I moved in, he'd helped me with my couch. When he split with the girl he'd been seeing, I ordered him take-out when I got mine. I gave him the extra cookies and banana bread and anything else I baked when I was feeling anxious, and he kept me company when I got bored throughout the week. The guy looked scary, but he reminded me of a Great Dane. Terrifying bark and appearance, nothing but gentleness inside.

It also helped that Priest kept a brotherly attitude toward me, which fit since there were twelve or thirteen years between us. I'd teased him about his name when I'd moved in, after he'd assured me that yes, Priest was his given name. Then he said I couldn't talk because I was named after a Christmas song.

Noelle. That was my name. I'd changed it about six months after I moved here. Noelle Collins. Not Tatum Ivers.

I wondered if I'd ever get used to it.

"I'm serious, Noelle," Priest grumbled as he threw himself down on my couch. "I've put on ten pounds since you moved in."

I scoffed, looking up and down his stocky muscular frame as I sat down in the little wingback chair I'd found on the street a few months ago. "Where do you hide it? With the hair?"

He scowled and folded his arms. "Find a different hobby."

"No." I mimicked his petulant pose. "I'll just give everything to Macy, and she can take it to bridge night or wherever she goes every Wednesday."

He grimaced. "She'll just bring it to me."

"Not my problem."

He unfolded his arms and sighed, stretching his long legs out in front of him. "What's got you stressed?"

"I'm not stressed."

"The banana bread you made at 2:00AM says bullshit."

My mouth twisted to the side. Cheap apartment, thin walls. "Something going on?" he pressed.

"Yeah, life," I muttered, thinking about what had actually kept me up last night. My life, and everything in it. Things that had nothing to do, and would never have anything to do, with Kellen. "I've got exams coming up in a few months, and I've got another tuition payment coming due in a few weeks."

"You could take out loans."

I shook my head. "I have less than $20,000 left in student debt. If I can avoid getting more, I think I'll be okay. I can handle this. Unless," I gave him a look. "Are you gonna get pissed if I keep stress baking at 2:00am?"

Priest snorted and rubbed his scruffy jaw. "Depends. What are you making?"

I thought for a second. "Cinnamon rolls? Everyone likes cinnamon rolls."

His eyes flashed with interest, then he frowned. "Are baked goods all you ever make?"

"Just eat the carbs, Priest. Life is short, bread is good. Enjoy it."

"Why don't you eat it all then?"

"I'd get sick if I ate a dozen cinnamon rolls, or they'd go bad before I finished them. And why are you worried? They're homemade at least. You need to eat less take out."

"*I* need to eat less take out?" He turned and gestured toward my overflowing trashcan and the Styrofoam containers peeking out. "You stress bake, but you can't make yourself dinner. *You need to eat less take out. Think of all that sodium.*"

"I'm an overworked college student with stress levels the size of Everest. Sodium is the least of my worries right now." I smirked. "But you should be careful. Gotta worry about your heart in your advanced age."

"Oh, fuck you." He laughed.

"Maybe not, might hurt your hip or something."

He smirked, eyebrows raised, then narrowed them and jabbed a finger in my direction. "Don't start shit you can't finish, friend," he cautioned.

A flash of longing raced through me, settling into an ache in my chest. I reached up and cupped the side of my neck, covering the tattoo like it might broadcast the thoughts flashing through my head.

Kellen's perfect lips curled at the corners. "You're probably a bit too cute to be my friend."

My heart stuttered, but I stifled the ache and shrugged. "That's all right. We aren't... that close."

No, I said to myself. He only came home nearly every weekend and met up with you at that tree. You only spent God knows how many hours in his loft watching Anime and old cult horror movies in secret. You knew he was the only one you'd wanted to spend your eighteenth birthday with. The only time you didn't hang out with him was when you dated Davey, and you missed him all the time.

No, we weren't close at all.

He smirked, shrugging one shoulder. "Not really."

I started to reply, but the words got caught in my throat when Kellen leaned in, head tilted so he could seal his mouth over mine.

He was kissing me.

Kellen Bishop was kissing me.

His lips were soft, and warm. And so eager. There was a hunger in the kiss, one I'd felt for years, but I'd had no idea he'd felt the same way. Had no clue he'd been just as starved as I was. Kellen went to pull back, but I reached up, grabbing hold of his wrist, a silent plea for him to stay. Please stay...

"Yeah?" he asked, nose rubbing against mine.

"Yeah."

Then his arm was around my waist, tugging me against his body as he cupped my jaw and tilted my head, our mouths fitting back together as he used his thumb to coax my lips open. His tongue slid past them, licking against mine, urging me to mimic his movements. I had no idea what the heck I was doing. Davey had never kissed me like this. No one had. Kellen tasted like the birthday cake we'd shared. I closed my eyes, melting into the kiss as he pressed me into my car. He was steady where I was shaking. So hard where I felt so soft...

"You wanna catch up on *Castlevania*?"

Priest's voice shocked me out of the memory, and I swallowed, rubbing my palms along my thighs to try and steady them. "Yeah, sure." He nodded, reaching for the remote, and I was glad he didn't notice how shaky my voice was. "Got you hooked on it, huh?"

"Yes." He gave me a half smile. "Makes me want to replay the games."

"I never played them."

"They were a little before your time."

"Still. Video games weren't something I was allowed to do."

I stood and moved to grab my laptop, noticing Priest's frown when I returned and sat down next to him, propping my feet up on the table. "What?"

"I always forget you missed out a lot cause of your weird-ass foster parents."

"Well, the world can corrupt you. I mean, look at us." I gestured to his old shirt and dirty shoes and my messy ponytail and the bags under my eyes. "Overworked. Exhausted. Eating takeout every night. We're prime examples of what happens when you stray away from God's commands."

My self-depreciating attempt at humor didn't amuse him, and I elbowed him in the side as I pulled up the blank word document. "I didn't really miss out if I didn't know it existed, you know."

He frowned at me, then turned on my small TV, leaning back and putting his feet up on my water-stained coffee table. "I kind of want to corrupt you. Loan you my PlayStation and give you all the old games from the early nineties."

"I'm plenty corrupted," I assured him. "But I might take you up on that when I'm not so swamped."

Priest smiled and logged into his Netflix account, finding the episode we'd been on a few weeks ago. I'd seen the show before, so I was able to split my attention between the story on the TV and the one I'd promised to Pak. There wasn't much to it, just a short anecdotal piece to go along with the pictures, but when it was done, I didn't close my laptop. My fingers lingered on the keys as I thought about another name. One I'd avoided thinking about or saying because it might conjure him from thin air.

D A V I D A D L E R

I hesitated, stomach twisting so violently that I shifted on the couch before immediately erasing the name. I didn't want to face the fact that there was a high possibility he was down here too. Northshore was a little over an hour outside the Metro, so small people missed it if they blinked. But since it boasted few if any jobs in the town, people commuted or moved into the metro for work.

It was possible Davey could have moved down here. But it was also entirely possible he'd forgotten I existed.

Instead of typing in his name to see, I navigated back to Facebook and spent the next twenty minutes resetting my password. I'd abandoned my email and all socials after I kept getting harassed by Davey after I left town. It was never from his account. It was always random e-mails. Spoof accounts. Ones he'd created just to ensure that I'd never forget that I was damned. I'd tempted him, made him unable to control himself and if I wanted to be saved, I needed to repent and submit to his guidance and control.

I rubbed at my bare throat, reassuring myself that the tightness was imaginary, and thinking fire and brimstone would be better than what he'd done to me.

"Didn't think you were on social media."

Priest was looking over my shoulder, a frown on his face. "I'm not." I pointed at the high number of notifications and the messages in my inbox. "I haven't logged in since about a year ago. I should probably delete my account."

"Why don't you?"

I shrugged. "Journalists are supposed to be on social media to make connections, so I kept it open even though I never check it. I'd have to make new accounts anyway. Pen name and all."

He pursed his lips but accepted this reasoning, turning his eyes back to the TV. I waited until his attention was completely on the show again before clicking my inbox, curious who was still messaging me.

I wished I hadn't. The box was full of message requests from names I didn't recognize. Fake ones most likely, but the message was all the same. I needed to pay. I deserved to be punished. I'd abandoned God and his tenets and—

My hand shook as I closed the message box, not needing to see anymore. My chest was tight, stomach churning from the gin and tea sitting on top of nothing. I was about to log out again and close the browser completely when the main inbox caught my attention. There were a few messages from people I knew. Philip and Suzanne Zentu, both from their personal accounts and the bakery. My jaw clenched, trying to bite back the guilt as I looked at the others. A few random classmates, several from Hannah Moore.

And several from Kellen.

I couldn't read any of them. I had to forget that life if I wanted to live mine.

I logged out and practically slammed the laptop shut, startling Priest, who gave me a curious look. "You good?"

"Yeah." I wrinkled my nose and took a deep breath, putting the computer aside and turning my full attention to the show. This was my life now. Tiny apartment. Tiny TV. Old couch, old coffee table, secondhand chair.

I'd moved on. It was fine. *Noelle* was fine, and there was no point in digging into the past.

My life was full. Busy. And there was no room in it for Tatum's ghost. Or anyone else's.

Chapter Three
Kellen

THERE OUGHT TO BE A LAW PROHIBITING RADIO stations from declaring any song written in the last two decades a "classic."

I'd been excited about getting a Bluetooth headset for my rides. I could listen to the radio, take calls, or talk to one of the guys while we were out. Only now did I realize that changing the station was impossible, so I was stuck listening to some idiot DJ proclaim Yellowcard's "Ocean Avenue" a "classic we'd all forgotten about."

Not sure who the hell "we" is, but it was pissing me off to think of a song I latched onto as a kid a "classic."

I'm twenty-fucking-six. Nothing that's existed in my lifetime should be labeled a "classic."

A text pinged through the music, the monotone voice app drowning out the song as it read the message.

Message from Lane Bishop—Driving over this weekend. You owe me. I grew your portfolios ten percent last quarter, so you're buying all the drinks. And I'd better not hear about any drunken rampages or anything, dumb ass.

I cracked a smile and breathed a little sigh of relief. My

brother had managed my finances since I graduated high school. That was his job. Lane took money and somehow turned it into more money. It had gotten me a down payment on my house, the collateral I needed to start a business, and a decent sized savings. It made my life far easier than other people I knew, so I put up with him calling me dumb ass and hoped maybe next year when he turned thirty, he'd come up with a better insult.

Deep down, I knew it wasn't a good turn on the stock market that had made him decide to come see me. Lane didn't need a place to gloat about his financial prowess. He had plenty he of friends to do that with. He was coming because it was the end of August, and time for his annual little brother check-in. It was meant to be nice, time for us to bond or some shit, but it only reminded me that this was the month my life went to hell three years ago.

My phone pinged again.

Message from Rev—Gonna be late. Probably after nine. Tell Cas to have a drink for me and not to be stingy on the whiskey.

I rolled my eyes, cursing him out under my breath. Rev had seen me two hours ago, right before he kicked me out of the shop for the day. My name was on the business license, and on the sign, but he'd still kicked me out like he owned the place.

The bike engine gunned, and my jaw clenched, my irritation with Rev turning inward. Rush owned the space we rented for the shop, and even though everything was in my name it was both our asses on the line. I'd gotten pissed about a screw that wouldn't turn, had thrown the grips I'd been working with across the room, knocking a shelf off the wall. That's why Rev had called me "kid" and shoved me out the door, scowling as he told me to take a ride and get the "shitty attitude" out of my system. It was his way of looking out for me.

Same with Lane driving over from Chicago this weekend. Same with Isaac and Hannah insisting on meeting me for breakfast or coffee every day this week. It was a distraction. They were trying to keep me busy, trying to keep me from spiraling into regrets and memories.

I appreciated it in the way people appreciate healthy meals. You know it's good for you, and your body feels better when it eats fruits and vegetables and whole grains. But there's only so much you can take before the cravings kick in again.

And that's where I was now. I had a craving. The same one I'd had for three years—if not longer. I wanted something sweet. Something comforting. Something familiar.

Something I'd probably never have again.

The engine of my Harley turned from a growl to a purr as I idled into the parking lot of Styx. There were roughly ten bikes parked in the front row, patched in members whose spots were always saved. I pulled in behind them, taking one of the spots they saved for prospects.

It was just me right now, had been for a few months. Rush, Cas, and the rest of the Heartland Heathen's didn't pull in new members often. The club was small and tight knit, but I fit the requirements, and Rev had vouched for me. Inside the bar, I'd find a bunch of ex-cons who wouldn't question my shitty mood or glowering stare. They understood without me saying anything that this month was rough, and were more than happy to indulge me with enough liquor that I could forget things for a while.

I pulled off my helmet and hung it on the handlebars, then tugged my phone out of my pocket. A custom gold and black Fat Boy I'd rebuilt for a guy a few months ago stared at me from the lock screen, and I swiped it away, re-reading Lane and Rev's texts before I closed them out and opened my photos. Something to give me a hit that would make the pain bearable for a few weeks, maybe a month, before I needed another fix. Whiskey would kill the pain flitting through my head for a few hours, but tomorrow I'd resurrect the memories to suffer all over again. I refused to let them die.

I refused to let *her* die.

It took some navigating to get to where I wanted. I'd kept the folder hidden to avoid any questions. Most of my pictures were of bikes I'd worked on, parts I needed, the occasional meme. I never had pictures of girls on my phone, not in the main folder at least. There had been a few that had come and gone since I had been released, but they hadn't held my interest long enough for me to take a picture.

She had, though. Three years later, and she was still the only girl I wanted to look at.

I tapped the image and swallowed when it came up, running a finger along the screen; like I might be able to touch her if I thought about it hard enough. Wavy, honey brown hair sat just above her shoulders, the strands curling around her neck and over her face, like even they couldn't resist touching her. She was smiling, pink lips spread wide and parted in what looked like a soft laugh, and her eyes were focused on the distance, squinted against the sunlight. A picture didn't do them justice, but I'd memorized the way they looked, how the blend of blue and green reminded me of the sea, complete with an island on her left eye. A single spot of brown that diluted the blue. That spot always made people stare a little too long.

Tatum hated that.

Which was inconvenient, because whenever I was around, I had a hard time keeping my eyes off her.

It had been that way since the first moment we met, when I'd stalked out to the edge of our large yard to find a girl nestled in the roots of the weeping willow. It was like she'd been dropped out of the sky. Something new and exciting. Northshore had roughly two hundred residents and nothing was ever new or exciting. Everyone knew everything about everyone, and dating felt borderline incestuous when you'd been in diapers together.

But Tatum had been a novelty. Particularly to me. Most of the kids I went to school with were forbidden from watching most movies, reading most books, or listening to most music. There were select artists and writers that were approved. The church had weekly movie nights where they showed films that bordered on propaganda. The kids that snuck in "secular" movies and music were met with disparaging remarks, me included. It helped solidify the good kids versus bad kids cliques that always formed, and I always found myself in the latter.

Then Tatum had showed up, with her wide blue-green eyes, that shy but bright smile, wearing a faded *Sailor Moon* shirt and holding a manga. The cover of it had been innocuous enough, with a brown hair girl wearing a school uniform. I was sure her foster parents hadn't questioned it, or maybe they couldn't since they were just her foster parents and she later told me she got to keep all her personal belongings when they took her in.

Either way, Tatum had been a good kid. Straight A's, volunteered in the nursery at church, attended camp. But every weekend and summer we hung out together, I felt like I was corrupting her. She had been eager to get her hands on anything that pushed her boundaries. Cult horror movies, manga that would have made her foster mother clutch her pearls, and whatever music I shared with her. Her hunger for more—more stories, more life, more chances than she'd ever been given— was palpable, and I'd found myself jealous of her drive sometimes. I was going to college, but came home every weekend, sometimes to see her, sometimes to check and make sure my dad hadn't drank himself to death. I'd desperately wanted out of that place, but I'd made no moves to get there. I wasted the opportunity to go to a bigger college with no debt, thanks to my family's money, to get an auto-tech degree and scrounge around junkyards for motorcycle parts.

Meanwhile, Tatum had been getting scholarships, making plans to be a writer or a journalist. She kept the school paper running and talked constantly about wanting to give a voice to the voiceless. Sometimes I thought I clung to her because that energy rubbed off on me, it made me want more for myself. I was pissed when she started dating the Pastor's kid Davey, and he seemed to suck the life out of her. I'd heard rumors from Hannah that he was pushing her away from college, trying to steer her into the life of a homemaker. That's what role a wife should have, according to him, not one where she'd be taken away from her family.

I scowled, flipping through more pictures I had of her, trying not to think about how, when Tate had refused to cower to his demands, Davey turned her into a pariah over some stupid purity vow.

My free hand closed into a fist, but I took a deep breath, focusing back on the pictures because this was Tate when she was with me. When she'd blocked him a hundred different times and moved on. The pictures I had were of Tatum Ivers as I knew her. A little jaded, but still hopeful. I had pictures from when she'd gotten her first tattoo and I'd gotten one to match. Pictures of her sitting on my bike, begging for me to teach her how to ride it. Pictures of us together, cuddled under a blanket, her head on my shoulder, her lips on my cheek. Her in the back of my truck, shoulders and waist bare, her legs and hips covered by a blanket as she stared at the rising sun and the stars still clinging to life against its light.

That's how I wanted to remember her. Like this. Before my dirty fingers had ruined her shine. Before I'd broken her heart by telling her lies to get her to leave, to avoid having to see her when I was at my worst. Behind a glass wall, wearing a gray jumpsuit, stuck in a cage when she was free. It horrified me that she'd kept coming around, that she'd planned to stay around. So I lied. I lied through my teeth and told her it was a fling. That the hours we'd spent together, the touches, the kisses, the long talks... all of it was nothing. Sweet, yes, but nothing.

I flipped to the last photo I had of her. One of her at the

bakery where she worked. There was flour in her hair, just like there had been the last time she'd come to see me, when I'd told the guard to tell her to leave. I didn't want her there. She was just some random girl. No one important.

So she left, and I plead guilty a week later to aggravated assault for breaking Davey's jaw and two of his ribs. My lawyer had wanted to call her in for testimony, but he couldn't reach her. Not like it would have mattered. She was one of "those" girls to him. No "real" family. Tatum could have told the judge I had the cure for cancer and poverty and I'd saved a thousand orphans from a fiery death. None of it would have mattered. Davey's testimony, and the fact that he was a pastor's kid, a well-liked pastor's kid—one who spent summers at camp, played in state basketball tournaments, and was destined for seminary school—was damning even without my history of truancy and a few disorderly conduct charges that had been dismissed.

Another text from Rev came up, but I didn't read it, I was too lost in my thoughts. He had been inside with me, my bunk mate. Listened to hours of me talking about Tatum, how much I regretted lying to her. He was released a few weeks before me, and since Lane couldn't be there to pick me up, he came. The first thing we did was drive to Northshore and go looking for her. He'd said it was a long shot at getting her back, but I'd regret it if I didn't try.

I never got the chance to try.

I looked down at my phone, stomach churning at the thought of Tatum looking exactly as she did in this picture. Never aging. Forever eighteen and beautiful.

No one had heard anything from her in over three years. Philip and Suzanne Zentu, the only adults who ever really cared for Tatum, had no idea where she was. A missing persons report had been filed, and I added to it, but no one had done anything with it. There were never any updates to her social media, no responses from emails, no hits when I Googled her name. She left behind nothing. All I had were memories, a few pictures, and an old hoodie she'd left in my truck. Blue with a cat, a rat, and a rice ball on the front of it. I kept it hung up in my closet in case I ever saw her again.

Which seemed less likely with each passing year.

Isaac, Lane, and even Rev had told me it was a waste to keep thinking about it. To let regret and grief become a prison that prevented me from living now that I was free. To me, it was just more waste in my life, because I was here taking up space and she was gone. It was a waste that her voice, always so strong and sure, was gone. It was a waste that I was seeing things she'd love, but would never get to tell her about.

It was a waste I never got to tell her how I really felt. That I been so worried about holding her back, about dulling her shine, that I'd lied to myself and to her, about how much she meant. In the end, I was just another person who'd let her down. Like I always knew I would.

My fingers felt stiff as they swiped her picture away and opened the apps I'd reinstalled on my phone at the beginning of the month. I checked Instagram first, where nothing about her profile had changed since I looked a few months ago. Same with Twitter, and again with Facebook. Same picture of her smiling face, same lack of updates.

I opened the messenger app, the pang of disappointment making me flinch even though I knew what I'd see. Every single message I'd sent remained unread, waiting for an answer unlikely to come.

That didn't stop me from reaching out into the void to try and pull her back. I put my fingers against the screen, taking a breath before I started typing another message.

Hey Tatertot.

Yes, I'm still calling you that. I know it pisses you off, but who doesn't love potatoes?

I'm still in Saylorville. Ten minutes from downtown Des Moines. Phone number hasn't changed.

If you see this, text me. Or call. Send a smoke signal, I don't care. Anything to let me know you're okay. You don't have to see me if you don't want to. But let me know you're okay.

I twisted my lips, trying to think of how to end the message. There was really only one way to do it, since I wasn't sure if I'd ever feel this four-letter word again. Two years of girls passing in and out of my life, and not one of them held a candle to the one whose flame could have been snuffed out.

Love, Kellen.

Or Kellogg if you still have your phone and I'm in your contacts.

Just call me, okay?

I STUFFED MY PHONE IN MY POCKET AND HEADED inside the bar, finally ready to have this grief drowned out for a few hours. I wiped the back of my neck, the stickiness of the air making the denim vest I'd put on when I left the shop feel heavier than normal.

August really was the worst.

Chapter Four

Noelle

"YOU, MY FRIEND, STIRRED A POT I DIDN'T EVEN KNOW existed."

I looked up from the article I'd been editing, watching as Elissa took a seat on the edge of my small cubicle. I raised my eyebrows and she gave me mischievous smile. "Pak showed me some of the comments on your piece about the school board meeting. There are some doozies in there. I can't believe we're still living in a world where everyone gets up in arms about sex education."

"How up in arms?"

"*'Teaching kids about sex will make them want to have it.' 'I can't believe the paper is encouraging teenagers to have sex!'*" She laughed. "Yeah, that's what's happening. And crime reports make them want to be criminals."

"Was there any good feedback?" I pressed. "Like about my writing style or anything?"

Elissa wrinkled her nose. "You're not going to get that in a comment section, honey, sorry. Most of it's bad, and it'll always be mostly bad, but you had a few commentors thank you for bringing the topic up. That's all you can hope for."

I let out a long sigh and nodded, having expected as much. The public was more inclined to comment when they had negative feelings versus positive. Change was a bomb to some people, where to others it was a minor upheaval.

"I wouldn't worry about it, Noelle. That legislation has everyone talking, and there's some sort of ministry conference happening in a few weeks so people are paying more attention. It's a timing issue, not every article you post is going to get that much negativity."

"Yeah," I mumbled, drumming my fingers on my desk. "Maybe I should read the comments to see—"

"No, don't," she interrupted, shaking her head. "Don't do it. Pak will pass on any good ones or someone else will. It messes with your head."

"My professor did tell me that," I admitted. "He has a blog where we ran stories for one of my courses, but no one commented anything mean. It was all meant to be constructive."

"I can promise you there won't be anything constructive in the comment sections online. But that's what you have us for." She smiled, then bit her lip and handed me the office card, raising her eyebrows when I took it.

"Yes, that's what I have you for. And you guys have me for coffee runs."

I stood and grabbed my bag while Elissa hovered over me, a sympathetic look on her face. "Just for a few more months. Gina likes your work, and your work ethic, so I don't think you'll have the intern title forever."

She gave me a wink and turned back to her desk while I headed in the opposite direction. I might actually get myself some coffee today. I hadn't slept well last night. Priest didn't leave until around 9:30, and then I'd stayed up looking through the few photos I'd taken with me when I left Northshore. I had one album, and my yearbook from my freshman year. The other three were left behind in the apartment I'd lived in above the bakery, forgotten in my rush to get out of there.

The coffee shop wasn't as busy this morning, but it was later when I got there. I didn't have class until 1:00 today, which meant a longer day in the office, but that was good. It gave me a chance to get ahead on articles I wanted to write, got me in front of our main news director and the other editors aside from Pak and reporters outside of Elissa. I'd been interning for a few months and while I knew most of the names, not a lot of people knew me. Granted, interns came and went, but I was close to graduation and could potentially apply for a job if there was an opening.

I bounced on my toes while waiting in line, imaging what that would be like. To be paid to write articles and put my opinions into the world. My advisor knew about my desire to turn freelance eventually, and he encouraged me to scout out stories I could really sink my teeth into. The ones people often overlooked for larger, more dramatic headlines. It would give me a niche, and those human-interest pieces gained a lot of interest with larger online publications. Writing something for *the Times*, or a larger paper, would be great, but it wasn't the only way to get my name out there.

I started pulling my hair up when the line moved forward. It was hot today, and I was warm from the ride up the slope to get here. I wiped a hand over my neck, grimacing at the dampness I felt there when I heard a soft gasp behind me and turned around, my eyes locking with the girl standing behind me. Her blonde hair was tucked up in a messy knot, blue scrubs hugging her tall frame. She gaped at me, lips parted, round eyes wide and eyebrows raised. My body tensed, but I held my breath, trying to keep my expression passive. Beside her stood a guy whose expression was just as shocked, though his eyes were narrowed instead of wide. The pinch of his eyebrows highlighted a scar above his left eye. Isaac.

"Maybe if you would have showed up on time I wouldn't have been distracted, dick."

Isaac glowered, but Kellen only snickered and pulled me close, tucking me into his side and putting his arm around my shoulders. "It's not my fault you can't catch a ball."

"Fuck you." He rubbed at his cheek, taking care not to touch the black and blue ring that surrounded his left eye or the large gash that cut through his eyebrow. I counted two stitches in the cut, which ran halfway up his forehead. It was going to leave a scar, but I didn't say that out loud. Isaac already didn't like me because I'd basically monopolized Kellen all summer. I didn't want to give him more of a reason to hate me.

"Oh, my God."

Hannah spoke, drawing my gaze away from Isaac's face. She continued to gape, her brown eyes glistening before she stepped forward, head tilting to look at the side of my neck before her eyes flicked to my face.

"Tate? Is that... is it you?"

Lie, I thought as she kept looking at my tattoo. She knew it, so did Isaac. For some reason, me marking my skin with my zodiac sign had been interesting, but again Northshore was small. Rumors spread faster than a wildfire, and there had been several people who'd come into the bakery to see the artwork I'd put in a spot I thought wouldn't draw a lot of attention. Hannah had been one of them, Isaac another. She'd said she wanted one someday while he accused me of doing it just to impress Kellen, not realizing Kellen had been with me when I'd gotten it.

"Han, it's not her. The eyes..."

Isaac reached out and pulled her back, but his voice wavered like he wasn't fully convinced. I turned away, tossing my hair over the side my tattoo was on and folding my arms, tucking my wrist against my side. I didn't say a word as they mumbled to one another. I wasn't sure I could speak, even if I wanted to.

Hannah stepped forward, putting herself right in front of me to look at the tattoo on my neck again, then her eyes flicked down to my waist, then lower to my leg. Of all the days I decided to wear a stupid skirt. She saw the line of zodiac animals on my calf and gasped, eyes widening as she gestured, then turned to Isaac.

"No, it *is*. Because who else would... that sweater you had. That comic book or whatever. *Tate!*" She whipped her gaze back to mine, tears filling her eyes. "Oh, my *God*, Tatum."

Before I could react, she'd practically leapt forward and thrown her arms around me, squeezing so tight it was difficult to breathe. Her breathing was heavy, like she was trying to hold back sobs, and I tentatively put my arms on her back. It had been so long since I'd hugged someone, I think I'd forgotten how, but that wasn't the only problem. Our exchange had drawn the attention of a few people standing around, and they were all looking. They were all staring.

And all I could think about was how much longer I could keep manage to keep this costume on now that it had been so easily removed.

Chapter Five

Noelle Tatum

I GLANCED AT MY WATCH. I'D BEEN GONE FOR FIFTEEN minutes. Eventually they'd start wondering what held me up, maybe even call. But my phone was silent, and for the first time in three years, I wished more than anything it would ring.

"I can't believe you're here," Hannah said, holding a cup of coffee between her hands. She was dressed for work, or labs, or something she surely had to get to instead of sitting here with me. Isaac wasn't in uniform, but his eyes were pure cop. Her expression was warm and inviting, his was hard. Judgmental.

We hadn't had more than a few seconds of eye contact since ordering our drinks and sitting down. Well, they were sitting. I was standing, the boxes of drinks in my hands, trying to make it clear that I had to leave, and I did not want to be part of this conversation. Whatever it was. But midwestern tradition dictated I couldn't just walk out of there, not while they were actively speaking. Rudeness was a crime akin to theft. Or breaking a purity contract.

"Me either," I said, unsure if I was talking about myself or Hannah and Isaac. "But, I am, I guess. So… I've got to get—"

"How long have you been living here? Tatum, no one's heard or seen anything—"

"Noelle."

Hannah paused, and Isaac sour expression softened some. "Noelle," I repeated. "That's my name. I changed it."

"Last name, too?" Isaac asked, frowning when I nodded. He turned to Hannah, and she let out a heavy sigh.

"Well, that explains why nothing came up when anyone searched." Isaac rubbed his short hair and leaned on the table, fixing me with a cool expression. "There's a missing persons report out on you. Did you know that?"

I pulled the drink carriers closer to my chest, shaking my head. "No, I didn't. Who... who filed it?"

Isaac hesitated, then he crossed his arms over his chest. "Davey."

My stomach dropped, and I slid into the chair, hoping that sitting down would hide my shaking knees. I set the drink carriers aside and scrubbed a hand over my face, looking to Hannah first then to Isaac. "Can you tell me when?"

"Middle of September. When did you leave town?"

"September 8th."

"Why?"

I shook my head and Isaac frowned again.

Hannah's expression softened, but Isaac's remained hard. "Tate, I'm going to have to update it and—"

"You found me. I can assure you, I'm safe, I left of my own accord, and I don't want anyone to know where I am. Legally, you can't disclose that information." I folded my arms over my chest and glared at him when he widened his eyes. "I know my rights. You can't disclose my location unless I give you permission."

Isaac turned stoic again, and I looked to Hannah when she leaned forward, grimacing a little. "Davey filed the report, but Phil and Suzanne... they were looking too. And Kellen..."

"Doesn't matter. I don't…" I swallowed the guilt trying to claw its way up from my chest, taking a breath to steady my resolve. "I don't want anyone to know where I am. I would have thought the name change made that obvious."

"Name change, yes, but you couldn't expect us to not recognize you, Tate," Isaac said. "You don't look *that* different."

Hannah nodded. "Yeah, I saw the tattoo and then I started looking at your face and… you look different, but you still look like you."

I frowned, leaning back in my chair as I stared at my reflection in the glass. I'd put a lot into it. Grown my hair out to the point it was almost annoying to deal with. Dyed it black, kept a consistent dying schedule to cover my roots. I was a little more filled out than I'd been in high school. My legs were strong from the bike rides I took every day, and I had a bit of padding around my hips, too. My clothing style had changed, my personality had changed.

And they'd still been able to see through it.

Which meant if Davey ever found me, he could too, if he looked long enough.

"Kellen lives down here, too," Hannah said. "He's a mechanic."

"And he builds bikes," Isaac filled in.

"Yeah, right. But he's down here, and so are a few other people. You haven't run into anyone?"

"I don't go out a lot," I admitted. "I'm only here because I used to work at this shop and they give me a discount. And it's close to the office."

"Office?" Hannah asked.

"I…" I paused. "I'm an intern at *The Journal*."

Her eyebrows lifted, and a smile crossed her face. The corner of Isaac's mouth lifted too, and he pursed his lips as he leaned forward. "You're actually doing it then. The journalism stuff."

"I guess. But they are expecting me back, so I need—"

"Wait, Tate. At least let me take your phone number," Hannah said, digging into her purse. "I won't bug you. Shit, I'm in class or working half the time, but I want to see you again."

"Why?"

She lifted her head, expression slightly hurt at my question. "I... I mean... we were friends, right?"

I grimaced. Aside from Kellen, Hannah had been the one person I called a friend. Especially after I was exiled when everything ended with Davey. She was the only person who straddled the line between the church kids and everyone else and didn't shun me when the rest of them had.

"I might need your number, too," Isaac added, and when I gave him a confused look he glared back at me. "Your file is sitting on my desk, Tate. Even if you refuse to tell me why you ran, I need to close it out, and honestly, I have some questions."

I raised my eyebrows in challenge. "Like what? Should I address you as Officer Moore? Don't you need a warrant to question me?"

"I'm not questioning you. But if you want to be cagey about why you ran, can you at least tell me if you know anything about why Kara Marlan might have taken off? Or Tiff Manchester?"

Shock slammed into me like the bats Isaac used to swing around when he played in college. Those were names I could have gone a lifetime without hearing again. "No," I spat. "They were awful to me. Why would I know anything about where they are?"

"Because they went missing not too long after you did."

I stared, somehow tense, but also limp as I tried to process this. Missing. How? Why?

Isaac grimaced, then leaned over the table and fixed me with his gaze. "Kara was reported missing about a year after you were by a friend who hadn't seen her for a few months. Tiff about nine or ten months later after she didn't show up for work."

"I haven't heard anything about this," I said, the curiosity and investigative nature I'd honed in all my journalism classes kicking in, overriding my shock. "Was there a press release? A news article? Any stories run?"

"No," he said. "There wasn't for you either though, and by the time Kellen got out and came in to add more information, it had already been two years since the original report had been filed."

"I don't think anyone would have listened to him if you weren't on staff," Hannah added, frowning when she looked up at me. "He was pissed, Tate. Davey left off half the stuff on the report and Kellen filled it all in. Where your tattoo was, your birthmark. Weight, height, correct eye color. He had to explain what heterochromia was and that it wasn't always having two completely different eye colors." She laughed softly and gave me a warm smile. "I think he even knew your blood type."

"The only thing he was missing was the names of your parents," Isaac admitted as my stomach twisted, my jaw clenched so tight I worried I might never speak again. "Harvey and Marta—"

"I haven't spoken with them since they kicked me out after graduation," I said, looking up when Isaac made a noise and Hannah scoffed.

"Was that even legal for them to do? You weren't eighteen."

"I was less than a month away." I shrugged, then waved a hand to dispel whatever her next question was. "You're telling me Kara and Tiff *both* disappeared, and no one has sent out a press release or anything?"

Isaac grimaced, rubbing a hand over his short hair. "Department resources are thin. We have the reports and if we find anything we go through them, but no one is clamoring for their return." He fixed me with a pointed gaze. "Even you. Most of the assumptions were you'd gotten involved in drugs. Maybe moved states."

Bile burned in my throat, but I swallowed it back. I'd banked on this exact thing. No one would care that I was gone. A girl with no family, and seemingly no future. No money, few friends. It all worked in my favor.

"Kellen raised a fuss, though. Isaac says he calls the station once a month asking if there are updates to the file." Hannah looked at me. "You should let him know where you are, Tate. He's worried."

I blinked at her, the sickness I'd been feeling since sitting down giving way to bitterness. "Why does he care?" Both of them stared blankly at me, then Isaac scoffed.

"I don't know. You spent the entire summer fucking him, then didn't even bother to show up when he—"

"*Kellen.*" I cut him off, slamming my hand down on the table. "Kellen told me to *leave.* I went to see him, *several* times, and he told me to go away. Called me '*clingy.*' Said we were just a fling and none of it mattered. The last time I tried he wouldn't even come see me."

I glared between them. Hannah looked alarmed, Isaac confused, but he rallied and pressed on. "Still, if they called you to testify—"

"No one ever called me. If they had, I would have shown up."

"He ended up pleading guilty," Hannah said. "Maybe they tried but couldn't get a hold of you?"

"Or," I countered, "he plead guilty because he acted like a jackass and beat Davey senseless in the middle of the street. No testimony from me was going to get him off, and like I said, he all but told me to fuck off." I sat back in the chair, arms wrapped around myself to keep my heart from beating out of my chest. "I kept my phone active for six months after I left. I still have it. No one ever called me. No one except—"

This time I cut myself off, Davey's name on my lips. I didn't want to say it. It felt like if I did, he'd manifest and the hell would start all over again. I couldn't handle that. I could barely handle seeing Isaac and Hannah, and Hannah was a friend.

I didn't even want to think about what would happen if I saw Kellen again.

"Kellen is... Tate, he's upset. He's really worried. We all are. Were. I..." Hannah's voice shook, and she set her palms on the table and tapped her fingers. "I thought you were dead. I just... it's been so long with nothing and I really thought you might be dead."

I rolled my lips, exhaling a heavy sigh before I reached out and covered her palms with mine. "I didn't think anyone would care. And I... I couldn't stay around. I had to get out of there."

"Because you wanted to leave?" Isaac asked, his voice lowering and eyebrows pinching together. "Or did Adler do something?"

My hands slid back from Hannah's, and they only shook a little as I reached in my purse to pull out my phone. I passed it to her, watching as she took down the number and sent me a single text so I'd have hers before I looked at Isaac. His eyes widened and I matched his challenging gaze. "You want me to talk? Get a subpoena or something. Otherwise use those stellar investigative skills you've learned and figure it out, Isaac."

I offered him the phone, and he did the same, shooting me a text so I'd have his number and he'd have mine. He tucked it back into his pocket and gave me another look, this one softer, a little more concerned. "Did you file a report?"

A derisive laugh escaped me. It had to be that, or I'd scream. "Tried a couple of times. I couldn't prove anything, so they did fuck all with it."

Hannah scoffed, glaring at Isaac like it was his fault the cops up there were inept before turning back to me. "I saw you the day after Kellen beat up Davey. You had bruises on your arms, your face. They didn't—"

"They asked me if it was Kellen."

She blanched and I gave her a pitying smile. "I said no, but they didn't believe me. He had a 'pattern' and Davey didn't. Girls like me often make excuses for their abusers."

Hannah's face turned red, her nose scrunching up as she swore under her breath. My natural inclination was to offer her some sort of solace, but I had none to give. The officers in charge that week had taken one look at me and decided I wasn't worth their time and neither was Kellen. I was a pariah, and everyone was waiting for Kellen to screw up because he'd bucked against his dad's expectations. It was wholly unfair to everyone involved.

And now, possibly even to Kara. And Tiff.

And anyone else that Davey...

No. I couldn't think it. If he'd hurt someone else after me, because of me, because I didn't say anything or force them to listen...

I glanced down at my watch. 9:30. I'd been gone for half an hour. "Listen, I'm not gonna say this was fun, but I am fine. I have to get back to work."

I stood, two pairs of eyes following me as I pulled my backpack purse over my shoulders and grabbed the drink carriers. I gave Hannah a soft smile then turned to Isaac.

"I'm telling you again—I don't want anyone to know where I am. I know you have to inform them or something, but I do not permit you to disclose my location."

"Yeah, I got it," he muttered. "I won't tell anyone where you are."

"Or my new name."

"Or your new name." He paused, arching a brow. "What's the full name? I have to note you changed it, even if I don't reveal it to anyone."

I hesitated, then sighed, deciding it would be better to get it out now than deal with a phone call from him later. Isaac had never liked me, never liked Kellen and me together. And there was no sense in trying to rectify his opinion of me.

I wanted to forget this whole run in had ever happened.

"Collins," I said, watching him tilt his head. "It was my mother's maiden name."

"Noelle Collins." He smirked, then let out a soft laugh. "Smart girl. If anyone searched that, they'd probably find info on her before they would you."

"That was the goal," I confirmed, giving him a shrug before turning to Hannah. "It was good to see you, Han. I'm glad you're... doing the thing," I added, gesturing to her scrubs. "You'll be a good nurse."

Her smile was bright and eager. It reminded me of my fire before it had been doused in cold water. I'd never managed to warm it up again. "Thanks. I just got my ASN last year. I'm going back to start my bachelors in the spring so..." She held up her hands, fingers crossed. "I want to get into maternity care, so stick around here for if you ever end up pregnant."

I scoffed but didn't reply other than that. There was zero chance of that happening.

Just like there were no chances of me forgetting Hannah and Isaac now knew where I was. They'd seen through the mask, which meant other people could.

It was only a matter of time.

Chapter Six
Noelle

I GOT BACK TO THE OFFICE TO FIND A WORRIED PAK waiting for me, phone in hand. It was unlike me to take so long. I had no excuse, so I went with the truth. Or a shortened version of it. I'd run into an old classmate from back home. They hadn't seen me in a while, and we took a minute to catch up.

"Oh, that's fine. We were just a little worried." Pak took his drink from the carrier and followed me back to my desk. I looked over my shoulder, watching him as he stayed with me until I sat down, a sheepish smile on his face.

"You run into an old boyfriend, maybe? You probably have a few."

I blanched, rapidly shaking my head. "No, *definitely* not."

Pak's expression relaxed, and a playful smile tugged at his lips. I watched him take along sip of his drink, dark brows pinching together as he organized his thoughts before speaking again. "E told me she mentioned the comments on the opinion piece you wrote."

I shrugged. "I'm not worried. It's not like they said it to my face."

"Good. That's good. I don't want you worrying about it or letting that interfere with your work, Noelle. I know that opinion thing is the only piece Gina has approved for print, but I read all the pitches you turn in and they're good."

He looked at me, pressing his lips together before taking another drink, then setting the cup down. "I guess what I want to say is keep at it. Something will stick and you'll get noticed. I remember what you said during your interview. That thing about wanting to give a voice to the voiceless, right?"

Immediately, Kara Marlan popped into my head. And Tiff Manchester. Yeah, they'd hated me, but we had been the same. Different cliques, but the same story in many ways. And until today, I'd been just as forgotten as they were.

"That's the goal, right? Tell the stories no one else hears. Bring them out of the dark into the light?"

Pak beamed at me. "Exactly. So keep doing what you're doing. Don't let any comments slow you down. Write whatever extras you want and give them to me. I'll get them in front of Gina as often as I can, okay?"

"Thank you, Pak," I said, watching as he nodded, still smiling. He lingered at my desk, and I wondered if there was more on his mind. "Did... the story about the tree guys make it into *Beat*?"

"What?" He tilted his head, then snapped his fingers. "Oh, yeah. I sent it over. They're gonna run it with the pictures." He licked his lips, then jerked his head toward where Elissa's desk was. "Speaking of *Beat*, there's a concert happening this weekend in the East Village. Elissa got a bunch of extra tickets since she's covering it. She'll probably talk to you about going. I could give you a ride..."

His eyebrows lifted, dark eyes wide and hopeful while I kept a tight smile plastered on my face. "That sounds fun, but it's my weekend to help out my neighbor. Maybe next time."

The lie came so easily, which didn't make me feel any better.

Macy didn't need me for more than an hour or so, if that. And if I really wanted to go, Priest would have helped her out.

But I didn't want to go. Not after what happened today. It had only proved that going out was a bad idea. I wondered how much tattoo removal cost.

"Ah, gotcha," Pak said, and there was a trace of disappointment in his voice. It only made the knot that had been in my stomach since the coffee shop worse. I was sure it wouldn't unravel for several days.

Pak walked back to his desk, and I spent the rest of my day staring at a blank screen, thoughts running everywhere from tattoo removal, to changing my hair color, to worrying if Pak had developed some sort of a crush on me that would go unrequited. I knew how bad that felt, having lived it for four years with Kellen coming back on weekends and over the summers and giving me a thrill each time he found me under that stupid tree. Davey had never made me feel that way. Not when we'd went to homecoming together. Not when we'd kissed chastely after school or youth group. The only time there had been a flicker of desire was after prom when we'd skipped the sponsored after party to be alone.

That had been the night everything had started going wrong. When I'd given into my desire for connection, and tempted Davey too far. Not sex. Oh no, we couldn't have that. Not real sex anyway, just everything but. And after weeks of doing everything but, I questioned it. Guilt ate at me because when I'd wanted to stop, he insisted we couldn't. He had the desire now, and I was supposed to bend to it. When I put my foot down and we broke up, he told everyone what we'd done and how ashamed he was. How it was all my fault for steering him off the righteous path.

Saying no had cost me everything.

By the time I got home that night, my mind was spinning and I ended up making more tea and gin to try and calm my nerves. It didn't loosen the knot in my stomach, but it did have enough of a calming effect that I was able to focus my thoughts into something with purpose. I sat down on my couch, computer on my lap, cat curled up beside me, and started typing in names.

There wasn't much to go on with a direct search. Kara Marlan was reported missing by a friend who had posted a few times on Facebook about it but had since stopped asking. Tiff was reported by a co-worker, and several people had tagged her in posts on Facebook and shared images, but the search had gone no further. I was able to look them both up on the missing persons database, but the information was about the same.

Eventually I'd made my way to the state database for missing people, trying to compare if information on the national database was different than the local one. Kara and Tiff's names I had expected, but another name popped up that gave me pause.

Courtney Mackelson.

A flash of jealousy flared up inside me, which made zero sense because I didn't know this girl at all. All I knew of her was that she and Kellen had had a *thing*. A thing I was never aware of until I'd heard rumors he'd slept with her in a church. That had been a lie, but the basics of the act were true. He'd slept with her and a few other girls before I ever moved to town, and I shouldn't have cared, but I'd been jealous. I pictured a girl with curly blonde hair or dark raven locks with mysterious eyes that were the same color. Someone older and more beautiful. Someone he could have actually dated. It had faded when he kissed me and all but vanished that summer. Only the memory of it remained, and immediately searched her up, wanting to see what I could find. She'd gone missing before Kara. The February after I'd left town.

Randomly, I decided to search Nicole Parsons, another old flame of Kellen's who lived in Northshore and was around Courtney's age. Nothing much there. She was married and living in Arizona, so I went back to the database. The database only brought up one more name that sounded familiar and made me put my laptop aside to pull out my old yearbook.

Opening the book, I flipped through pages until I found the senior class that year. Kellen and Isaac's class. Their faces jumped out at me first, but after some scanning, I found the fourth name that sounded familiar. Rachael Jefferson, whose name was also in the state database after a co-worker had reported her missing from Lakeside about six months ago.

I stared at my open tabs, the four reports glaring back at me like misaligned puzzle pieces waiting for connection. I went ahead and opened my file, which Isaac had yet to close. My own face stared back at me and I looked for common features. There weren't any. We were all different ages. Different heights, different hair, different body shapes. The only connection was Northshore. Well, and one other small town nearby. Tiff hadn't actually lived there, but her parents had gone to Twin Valley Reformed Church, the same one I'd visited every Thursday and Sunday for four years when I lived with Harvey and Marta.

I flinched, recalling when Pastor Adler came to talk to my foster parents, and me, about how concerned he was for Davey.

"I hope you know Davey is still quite upset about the two of you split-ting up," he'd told me, a sad look haunting his hooded eyes. He wanted me to reflect on the choices I'd made, and wondered why after promising to my foster parents, to him, to Davey, and to God, that I'd keep myself pure in body and pure in soul, I'd broken my vows and made Davey break his.

"I didn't make him do anything. Davey chose—"

"Because you tempted him. You did not steer him away from his lustful thoughts, and from what he tells me, you encouraged them." Pastor Adler sighed, leaning forward on his knees and fixing me with a stern but soft expression. "As a young woman, it's important for you to recognize the responsibility you bear. You will be a wife someday and will support your husband and his role as the leader of your family. Submis-

sion, piety, and purity are key parts of this. It seems cruel to leave him alone now as he tries to navigate this, considering what you promised."

What I'd promised was that I would keep myself pure for God. Not for Davey. And God wasn't here. That was quite clear considering everything that had gone on in the last month. The torture I'd been receiving from my classmates and the humiliating lectures I'd gotten from nearly every adult in my life. God was nowhere to be found in all of that, and I only received silence when I asked why I was being punished for doing the right thing.

"Davey humiliated me by telling the entire school everything we did," I pointed out. Harvey and Marta blanched, and Pastor Adler frowned.

"He's struggling, Tatum. You two had something special. Both he and I believe God brought you two together, and I know at one time you felt the same. What changed?"

"What changed was I wanted to stop." I widened my eyes, pleading for understanding even though I knew I'd get none. Pastor Adler did not look impressed by my statement, and when he opened his mouth, I held up my hands, tired of this conversation

"I'm sorry, Pastor Adler, sir, but Davey is going to have to figure this out alone. I'm doing him a favor. If he's so tempted by me, it's best I stay away so I don't cause him to stumble again."

I rubbed at my throat, wincing when I pictured hands around it, Davey's sobs as he squeezed and squeezed. Is that what happened? After I left, did he get involved with someone else? Had they caused him to stumble, and this time it cost them more than humiliation?

Haku stirred beside me, nuzzling into my thigh as he rolled onto his back and offered me his belly. I scratched his fur, thinking. More than likely, these women had simply fallen off the radar. People quit work all the time without notice. Sometimes they leave town, or the state. Sometimes they leave the country. They all might have had their reasons. I knew better than anyone how true that was.

But none of them were coming forward to say what they were. And no one seemed to care.

I scratched Haku some more then dug into my jeans and pulled out my phone, staring at the text Isaac had sent me. I hadn't officially added him or Hannah in as a contact, but I knew which number was which just by the messages they sent. Hannah had greeted me with her name and an emoji. Isaac had just sent a text saying call if you want to talk.

Right now, I wanted to talk. Just not about me.

Isaac picked up on the third ring, his voice relaxed but a little wary when he picked up. "Hello?"

"You got a second?"

There was a pause and some shifting around. "You feel like talking? Let me get a pen."

"I'm not giving you a statement, Isaac. You said Kara and Tiff were missing, but did you know there are two other girls from Northshore that have gone missing, too?"

Isaac hesitated, then there was more background noise before he spoke again. "Who?"

"Courtney Mackelson and Rachael Jefferson. And those are just the names I recognized. There might be others I didn't from the same—"

"Whoa, whoa, hold on. Courtney and Rachael? They graduated with me."

"Yeah, I know." I adjusted the laptop and pulled up the windows with their open reports. "Courtney went missing in February after I did, and Rachael was reported missing about six months ago."

"How do you know this?"

"I was looking up Kara and Tiff on the state database and I recognized their names. It's all online, public record if you know where to look. Journalist, remember?"

"I know it's all online, but... Jesus." He made a noise, like he was thinking or frustrated. "Any connection between them?"

"Besides the fact that they're all from around Northshore? Not that I can see. But you might be able to. That's why I called." I hesitated, turning the words over inside my head. "Would you be okay with me writing something up on this? I might make some calls, see if I can get any more information. There's a lot of missing people who never get any press time. Maybe they deserve some."

"You don't need my permission," Isaac said, a hint of a laugh in his voice. "But if you find anything of value, will you let me know? Or at least put the number of the office in the article?"

"I can't even guarantee it'll end up in print, but yes. I'll call you if I find something that might be useful. You have channels that I don't, and I've got the time you don't."

There was a pause, then Isaac let out a heavy sigh. "You gonna be okay with this? Are you sure you don't want to give any sort of a statement?"

"What would I say?"

"You could tell me what Davey did for starters."

"It's not going to change anything, Isaac," I muttered. "The statute of limitations on stalking is three years, and I couldn't get anyone to listen to me the first time. Not even with a bruised face. I'm not going to try again."

There was a long pause, then Isaac let out a weary sigh. "I can't say I blame you, but giving a statement might help us if something comes up about another case. Or... something happens to another girl." He paused, letting out a heavy sigh. "You know I'd listen, right Tate?"

"Noelle."

"Yeah, sorry. Not calling you that. Don't expect Kellen to either."

"I don't plan on seeing Kellen, so it's not something I'm worried about."

Isaac was quiet, then he made a grumbling noise and the phone shifted again. "Fine. If you get anything useful, give me a call or shoot a text. If I find anything that might pique your interest, I'll do the same."

"Sounds good."

"And Tate?"

"Yeah?"

"If you do run into Kellen—"

"I'm not planning to, Isaac. End of discussion. Have a good night."

Silence, then Isaac sighed. "Yeah, night."

The line clicked, and I stared at the phone for a bit before putting it aside, fighting the urge to log in to Facebook again so I could look at Kellen's profile, but there wasn't any reason for me to snoop. Whatever we had, it was well over by now. I didn't want to see him and reopen old wounds for either of us. I was better off alone. I'd accepted that. Embraced it. That way, the only person who had the power to hurt me, was me, and I knew how to handle my self-inflicted damage. It would never tear me apart.

Letting anyone else in was too risky. I'd that the hard way. Never again.

Chapter Seven
Kellen

"YOU WANNA KNOW HOW YOUR LITTLE BROTHER GOT his road name?"

Rush flashed me a shit-eating grin before looking back to my brother, the neon lights of an old Pabst Blue Ribbon sign giving his face an almost ominous glow despite the smile he wore. I rolled my eyes, downing the rest of my whiskey before spinning on the stool to face him.

"He doesn't know what a road name is or what one means." I jerked my thumb at Lane only for him to shove it away. "This asshole only rides on the weekends."

"I ride during the week," he shot back, draining the last of whatever IPA he'd ordered. Cas had been giving him all kinds of hell since we walked in, riffing him on the designer jeans, his button-down shirt, the slicked back hair. He had on a jacket that probably cost at least five-hundred fucking dollars, and it clashed horribly with the rough aesthetic of the bar. But that was Lane. He liked expensive, unique things, and liked showing them off even more.

"You joyride during the week," I pointed out. "And it's a fucking crotch rocket, not a bike."

"Yeah, yeah," Lane said, waving off the teasing like he always did. My brother was unflappable, and it was always a quality I'd envied. He took another sip from his beer and smirked at me before turning back to Rush. "Now, tell me about this nickname. I'm expecting a good story."

Rush laughed while Cas grinned from behind the bar, placing another shot glass full of dark liquid in front of me. It was only 5:00, but I knew they planned on getting both of us wasted, so the drinking had started early. I hated being hungover, but tonight, I wanted the relief. This week had been hell trying to get parts in and working a few extra hours on jobs, and that was on top of the chaotic thoughts I hadn't been able to quiet down.

I blamed Hannah. Her moving here had thrown me more than I thought it would. Isaac's little sister and I had always gotten along, but there were times she reminded me of Tate. Her drive. The focus she had on her goals. The fact that Hannah had been the only friend Tate had that last summer, and I'd had to compete with her for time with Tate. She also kept texting me to check in, like she was *my* sister. Or a mother. At first it hadn't bothered me, but today, she wouldn't let it go. Every hour or so, I had another text from her, and they all asked the same thing.

Did Isaac call you? Has Isaac talked to you yet? Let me know when Isaac talks to you.

My phone buzzed again, and I pulled it out, listening to Rush as I read another message from Hannah.

Han: *Where R U? You're not at your shop or your house.*

Me: *I'm at the bar with Lane. Why are you at my house?*

Han: *What bar?*

Me: *Not one you should be at. You're 20.*

Han: *I can handle myself. Has Isaac been there? Has he called you?*

Me: *No, he hasn't. What the fuck is going on?*

Rev entered the bar just as Rush got to the meaty part of the story, which I hadn't been paying attention to because of

Hannah's text. He nodded at me, then a grin spread across his face when he saw Lane.

"Nice to see you stooped to our level," he teased, almost shoving Lane off his stool. "I thought you'd try to drag Kellen to some bar with girls dancing in cages and forty-dollar drinks."

"Nah, they don't have those around here. Gotta go to bigger cities for that." Lane tipped his beer at Rush. "They're telling me about Kell's nickname, which you've never mentioned."

"Cause I wasn't there that night." He sat down, tipping his head to Rush who smirked at me before turning back to Lane.

"After Rev, Riot, and Kell got the shop up and running, Kell started giving us discounts and we started letting him ride with us, but no one could think of a name for him. Nothing fit, ya' know?"

Lane nodded, and I could tell he was expecting a wild story about how I'd won a drag race with one of the guys or done something stupid and came out unscathed. The impulsive, reckless shit he was used to me doing, coupled with what everyone assumed about bikers. We were all supposed to be menacing, ready to kick someone's ass within five minutes of meeting them, and our road names reflected that.

Reality was, we only wanted to kick someone's ass if they deserved it, and most of the road names were inside jokes. "Rev" was short for Reverend, because he was always calm and tended to give almost sagely advice when asked. Rush hated the song "Tom Sawyer" and his road name was close to his real name—Russ. Cas was short for Casanova, because when our bar owning VP smiled, the panties of every single girl and half the guys in the bar got wet. Riot was Riot because he went to prison for inciting one. There was also Looper, Snapshot, Mack, among a dozen other generic nicknames. Everyone called one of the older guys TC. I learned after they'd made me a prospect that it stood for Triple Cat. Because he had three cats.

Inside jokes. Sacred ones. Meant to protect our identities and garner some respect from people who weren't in the club but still came to the bar.

"So, one night, about a month after he'd gotten his prospect patch, Kell gets wasted," Rush went on. "We're talking can't walk straight, might piss his pants before the end of the night wasted."

Lane snickered and Rush glanced at me with another smirk. Even his wife Betsy was grinning from her spot on his lap. I'd forgotten she was there that night, probably because the sight of them together always made me a little jealous. I'd had that.

And I'd pushed it away.

"Some jackass was trying to hit on a girl by bragging about how he could two-step or some shit," Rush explained. "He picked a song, started pushing this girl around on the floor, then out of nowhere, Kell starts yelling."

"'*No, no, no!* You're doing it all *wrong*,'" Cas mimicked from behind the bar, drawing another grin from Lane. "'It's *quick-quick-slow-slow*, you fuckin' *moron*.'"

"He got up off his stool, shoved the guy aside, grabbed the girl." Rush mimed each action, using Betsy as a model. "'Watch,' he says, then, drunk off his ass, he starts dancing with her like he's auditioning for that fuckin' dancing stars show everyone watches."

"It wasn't that dramatic," I muttered.

"Bullshit," Rush countered with a laugh. "By the end of the night, Cas had everyone in the bar calling him Foxtrot."

Lane let out a full body laugh, and I shoved him almost off the stool before swallowing the rest of my drink. Cas refilled it while Lane collected himself and spun on his stool so he could see me better. "Our mom made us take dance lessons for... Jesus, how long was it, Kell?"

My smile faded. "I stopped when I was eleven."

Eleven was the age a lot of things ended. Dance lessons, any interest I had in sports, our father putting any sort of effort into being a parent.

It all stopped because mom disappeared for twelve hours before they'd found her car in the ditch four miles outside of town. Run off the road by some drunk asshole or a speeding car. We'd never figured it out, and no one ever came forward. Hit and run. Boom.

Everything changed.

Lane's eyes met mine, and he pursed his lips, taking a breath before moving back to dance lessons and away from grief. "I started at seven, so you were around three. That's what?" He did the math on his fingers. "Eight years?"

"I guess," I said before looking at everyone crowded around listening. "You want to know the funny thing?"

"What's that?" Cas asked.

"I don't have the first fuckin' clue how to do a Foxtrot."

Laughter filled the room, and someone clapped me on the back before Cas ruffled my hair like I was a little kid. I shoved his arm away while Lane grinned, because that was his fame. We were both grown ass adults now but he insisted on calling me, "Kid" and still did shit like ruffled my hair or punched me in the kidney. It would never end.

Maybe secretly I didn't want it to, but I'd never let Lane know that. Or that part of me liked the bars he went to sometimes. It was a change of pace from my hangout, which was three miles off the main road, in a building that looked like it would kick your ass if you stared at it wrong. The crowd at *Styx* was always noisy and just the right amount of wild. Music blared, the walls were decorated with engine parts, old neon signs, and big posters that said things like *Shut Up and Drink*.

Everything about it was rough, but these were guys who didn't give a shit about my conviction cause they all had one too. The Heartland Heathens had been founded by ex-cons who wanted to help out others in the same position. They understood how hard it was to get a life back on a normal path. Riot got me connections with vendors I would have struggled to get otherwise because I was young and newly released. Cas dragged me out when I was in a sulky mood. Rev helped keep my head on straight when I got pissed.

I fit in here, and I liked that. Lane had 800 friends and was constantly making more, but my friend circle had always been small. I liked my people and that was all I needed. And I'd found them here.

Still, even with this, I thought about Tate and how she would have fit right in alongside me.

Lane started asking about the stories behind other nicknames right when my phone buzzed again. I glowered at it but didn't pick it up, at least not until Cas tried to snatch it away from me.

"You've been getting texts all night," he noted. "Finally hooking up with someone?"

"Not likely," Rev put in. "If it's who I think it is."

"Who is it?" Cas asked.

"Isaac's little sister," I said.

"Oh, *shit*." Cas grinned. "Best friend's little sister? That's the kind of hook up I'm talking about. The sneaking around, wondering if he's gonna kick your ass when he finds out."

"I'd worry more about Hannah kicking my ass than I would Isaac," I said, which made Rev and Cas both laugh. They knew he was a cop, had met him a few times and had no problem with him, but Isaac had only ever been to the bar once and didn't plan on coming back anytime soon. He didn't have anything against any of us, but he wasn't welcome.

Not yet at least. I hoped at some point the guys would learn they could trust him. Isaac wasn't a snitch. He'd looked the other way plenty of times for me.

As if on cue, my phone rang, and I picked it up because I

already knew who it would be. Hannah had been asking if Isaac called all day, and finally at a quarter after 5:00, he did.

"Lane's down this weekend if you wanted to come over," I said when I put the phone to my ear. "You can crash on my couch."

"Maybe, I'll let you know. I've got... things I need to look into."

There was a tone to his voice. Tension. Hesitancy. And my whole body went stiff. Cas and Rev watched me closely, and I turned away from them and put my finger in my ear to drown out the music so I could hear Isaac better.

"What's going on?" I asked, swallowing against a tight sensation in my chest. "Hannah has been texting me all day. She said you were gonna call."

"Yeah. I needed to wait until I got off. Wanted to be able to talk."

A chill slid over my shoulders, like tiny ice cubes sliding over my skin. Isaac rarely called me to "talk." We sent texts unless it was something major like Hannah moving down, or his parents moving to North Carolina. I tried to think of what it could be. Maybe something to do with my dad. Another DUI he was trying to have covered up, or he'd put the house up for sale?

There was only one other reason Isaac might call to talk. And it had been a reason I'd been dreading for a while.

There was an update on Tatum's missing person report.

My jaw clenched, and it took a second before I could work it lose to speak again. "Isaac, what's going on?"

There was a beat of silence, then he sighed. "You in a spot where you can talk for a minute?"

I must have made a noise, or a face, because Cas leaned over the bar and Rev elbowed me. They wore identical concerned expressions, the type that said they could switch to commiseration or backup depending on what I asked of them.

But neither of them could do what I wanted. Unless they could bring someone back from the dead.

I got up from my stool, half-numb as I walked outside the bar. Even the humidity in the air couldn't keep the cold chill from consuming me, and once the door was shut and the music from the speakers dulled to a low thudding pulse, I let out a breath, steeling myself for what I knew was coming.

What I'd known was coming for a while.

"Just get it over with. Where'd you find..." I took a breath, my throat burning when I swallowed, the alcohol in my stomach threatened to come back up. "The body?"

"Didn't find one," Isaac said, his tone calm, but otherwise devoid of emotion. "Tate's alive."

The knot in my stomach clenched, then slowly eased, unwinding itself back into a thin loop of rope. A second later, the breath I'd been holding left my lungs, and I sagged against the railing on the small porch that surrounded the bar.

She's... alive.

Tate's alive.

Tatum is alive...

Isaac let this hang between us, giving me no more information or explanation for what he'd just said. It might have been to let me process the words. Let them bounce around in my head before settling into place.

"She's alive?" I asked, wanting him to say it again. I wanted him to laugh, then drive the two hours up here and produce her from the back of his police car. It didn't feel real. Like the shoe I'd been waiting to drop and crush me decide to walk past and move on to some other poor soul. I pinched myself, wanting to make sure the couple of shots I had weren't fucking with my head.

"Yes. She's alive. She assured me she's safe and left Northshore of her own volition."

I stood up straight, eyes fixed in the distance, like I might be able to spot her from here. "You talked to her?"

"Yes. I spoke to her. And now that we know she's not missing, I'm closing her file and notifying you."

"Whoa, whoa, whoa." I held up my hand, like I was talking to him face to face. "Where is she? When did you talk to her? Did she say why she left or—"

"Kellen." His tone turned cagey, which made me grip the railing tighter.

"What?"

"She didn't explain it to me, and there's no point in arguing."

"Did you see her?" I demanded. "Isaac, did you see her? Or did someone else and they updated the file? How do they know it's her?"

"She had a few identifying marks and confirmed her identity when asked."

He was in cop mode. Every response was scripted and blunt. Case closed. No further questions.

Fuck. That.

"Isaac, tell me where she is. I want to see her, I need—"

"She asked me not to."

I blanked again, taking a few seconds to organize my thoughts into words. "She asked you not to."

"She didn't want to be found, Kell. Went to a lot of effort to make sure no one would find her, including you."

"It's me." I put my hand on my chest, speaking to the empty parking lot like Tatum might be able to hear me. "It's... it's me."

"Doesn't matter. She didn't want me to disclose her location or any contact—"

"Since when do you take orders from her?"

"Since, legally, I can't go against her wishes. She could file a lawsuit against the department if I did. And besides, you didn't file the report. I'm giving you more than I should already."

An angry noise ripped out of my throat and I shoved off the railing, stalking halfway down the small porch then back. The door to the bar opened, and a few guys came outside, Rev behind them. He looked at me, arms folded over his chest. "What's going on?" he mouthed.

"It's about Tatum," I hissed, watching his shoulders drop. He took a step forward, hand reached like he was going to take my shoulder to console me. I waved him off, pointing at the phone. "She's alive."

Rev froze, folding his arms over his chest. He'd heard me talk about her enough to know that I'd honestly thought her dead.

She still was, in a way, if I couldn't see or talk to her.

I switched the phone to the other ear, running a shaky hand through my hair. "Isaac, you have to give me—"

"Kellen, I can't give you anything more than I already am." The words were terse, and he let out an angry sigh from the other end of the line. "Did you tell her off when she came to visit you?"

It was my turn to freeze up, and I glanced at Rev before spinning away again. "I was embarrassed. I didn't want her seeing me like that."

"Jesus, Kell."

"What? It was fucking torture having her in that room week after week, wasting her time on me when she could have—"

"So you told her you were nothing? You called her 'clingy'?"

"*You* called her clingy," I shot back. "You never liked her. You were an asshole to her and I never understood why."

"I didn't like the idea of you marrying the first girl you ever actually dated. It was a recipe for disaster. Sue me." I growled and Isaac made an exasperated in response. "I honestly thought she'd get clingy with you and demand to stick around or want you to stay there after you finished college. Never expected it to be you who lost your head. "

"I didn't lose my head."

"No, not at all." He scoffed. "Three years later, you're still pining. Spending every August torturing yourself, and now I find out it's because she did exactly what you told her to do."

"Fuck you," I snapped. "You don't know what you're talking about. You don't know everything—"

"I'm trying to spare you, Kell. She doesn't want to see you, and you guys will have nothing to talk about."

"Oh, we have things to talk about. Where she's been, why the fuck she hasn't answered any of my texts or let anyone know she's safe."

I clenched my fist so hard my arm trembled, my breathing coming so hard and fast I was surprised I didn't feel dizzy. Rev watched me, unsure of what to do. Like I had an answer.

"Kell, leave it be, all right?" Isaac said after a beat of silence. "You know she's alive. Now you can move on. You've got the shop and your little club. She's just a girl. She isn't special."

I narrowed my eyes, trying to think of how to explain that Tate wasn't just a girl to me. She was a connection to parts of myself I didn't always want to see. She'd been the only girl—the only person—to ever see me. Really see me. The parts I liked, the parts I didn't. She poked holes in my veneer and still liked the messiness she found underneath.

And I'd pushed her away because I'd convinced myself I'd end up ruining her, just like I'd ruined the other chances in my life. Like I was ruining it now by not moving on.

"I gotta go, Kell. I'll be in touch."

Isaac hung up, and I pulled the phone away from my ear. Rev took a few cautious steps forward, his arms still folded over his chest.

"I told you this might happen."

The words weren't meant to be cruel. Honesty rarely was. But they stung regardless.

I dropped my head, and Rev sighed. "I'm not gonna stop you

from looking for her. Maybe if she sees you, she might change her mind."

I turned to look at him, grateful the man was smart enough to glean things from a one-sided conversation, saving me the pain of explaining it again. My hand slid through my hair again as I shoved the phone back in my pocket, about to suggest calling Looper up and seeing if he could do a deeper dive into Tatum. I'd searched her name enough times to know there weren't any hits, but he might be able to unearth something with all his tech knowledge. Guy was basically an ethical hacker, but I was sure he'd put that aside if I asked him to.

Headlights flashed from the parking lot, and Rev and I both turned. My shoes ground into the gravel when I stalked off the porch, already on my way to greet Hannah before she got out of the car. What the fuck. Why hadn't she told me outright? Why did I have to wait for Isaac to call?

She slipped out of the slick little car her parent's had gotten her, eyes tense. "Isaac call you?"

"Tate," I said when I reached where she stood, scowling when all she had to give me was a nod.

"Yeah."

"Why the fuck didn't you tell me on the phone?" I demanded, barely acknowledging Rev when he came to stand behind me. "How long have you known? Did you see her? You know where she is?"

Hannah leaned against the car, her foot tapping against the ground. Her expression was conflicted, but finally she sighed and started talking.

"She really didn't want to be found, Kellen. I almost didn't recognize her. Her hair is longer, and she dyed it black, she's got few piercings that threw me off." She let out another sigh and shook her head. "Christ, Kell. She had contacts in too. I think the only reason I looked twice was because of the tattoo behind her ear."

She gestured toward me, and I reach up and rubbed at the design, wondering if I could have passed Tatum on the street or in a bar somewhere. Like Hannah, I wouldn't have looked twice because of the hair and the piercings. I tried to picture what it might look like. Would it wash her out or make her cheeks look warmer?

And contacts. Jesus, contacts. It made sense if she was trying to change her appearance, but the idea was horrifying. I loved her eyes.

Why had she done all this? What was she hiding from?

Hannah was staring at me, waiting for some sort of a response as my thoughts tried to organize themselves. "Her name never turns up an address when I search it."

"Well, it wouldn't." Hannah hesitated, shifting her stance. "She changed it."

There was a record scratch in my head as my body froze on the spot. "What?"

"She changed her name."

"To what?"

Hannah shook her head, a muscle ticking in her jaw. "I don't know. Maybe... She didn't want me to tell you so maybe I shouldn't."

"*Why?*" I demanded, then my stomach clenched, my heart stilling in my chest. "She's not... she's not fucking *married*, is she?"

"No, no, that's not it. She didn't have a ring or anything."

"Then why the name change? Why won't you tell me?"

"Because she's hurt, Kell. She was not happy to see me, or Isaac."

"Han—"

"No, don't you *Han* me."

She pushed off the car, glaring up into my face like she had since we were kids and Isaac used to yell at her to go away when she'd try to hang out with us. "I'm only telling you this because

I know Isaac can't. I thought you should know." I glared, but she jabbed her finger into my chest. "She told me what happened and you're a complete dick."

"What?" I shouted, "You already knew what happened. That fucking asshole hurt her and then was running his goddamn mouth and I—"

"I'm not talking about that; everyone knows about that. You never told us that you broke up with her when she came to see you."

Her eyes narrowed, nose scrunching like it did when she was angry. I took a step back, the tension in my body twisting into something that made me feel almost sick form embarrassment. "I didn't break up with her. Technically, we weren't together."

"Oh, don't give me that bullshit," Hannah snapped. "You blew off everyone to be with her and she did the same. You were both so wrapped up in each other that I half expected her not to leave town like she did."

"And that's why I did it," I said, rallying against Hannah's angry glare. "I had to, Han. If I hadn't done that, she would have stayed in that shitty town and gone to that barely accredited college and slowed her whole life down. For me!" I jabbed my finger into my chest. "I couldn't let her do that."

"You had to tell her she meant nothing? You had to use those words after knowing everything she'd been through with her parents basically abandoning her? With all the shit she went through with that church and the fucking Nichols, and everyone in town giving her the side-eye because of Davey?"

My whole body tensed, shame and rage running hot through my veins, and I looked to Rev for backup, but he didn't say anything. Most likely he was on Hannah's side since he'd said the same thing to me when we were on the inside. Made me realize how stupid my logic had been. I wouldn't have dragged her down. It would have been her choice to wait. There would have been a pause in her life, but Tatum practically had a certificate in picking herself up and moving forward when things got hard.

Which was exactly what she'd done. What I'd wanted her to do.

But not like this.

Hannah was glaring, her eyebrows raised like she was challenging me to counter her arguments. I shoved my hands in my pockets to hide my fists. "Did she at least say why she changed her name?"

"You're not stupid, Kellen. Figure it out. What could have made her shut down all her social media and leave town?"

I lifted my eyes to hers, watching the irritation on her face shift into worry. Or pity. My jaw was so tight, it made talking a challenge. "Did that asshole keep after her? Did he do something?"

Hannah breathed out slowly, dropping her eyes to the ground before looking at me again. "I don't know. She wouldn't say, but it would make sense. And aside from whatever Davey might have done, everyone our age was calling her Taint. I'd start going by my middle name too if people—"

"Her middle name?" My eyes went wide at the clue, the slip of Hannah's tongue. "Noelle?"

Hannah's mouth hung open, then she gritted her teeth and swore under her breath, kicking at the ground when I stalked forward. "She's going by Noelle?"

I looked to Rev, like he could confirm it if Hannah wouldn't. For a second, he looked confused, like Hannah's head had flipped upside down. Then his expression went flat. Stoic and calm. Probably soaking this all in so he could talk me out of doing something stupid later. I was ready to. I was ready to start driving up and down the streets of the Metro to find her.

Especially if Davey had kept harassing her after I left. That I hadn't planned on. I thought he'd stay away after what I did. If I'd thought wrong, and he'd still gone after her…

My stomach heaved. *No. God, please no…*

"Hannah, I to make sure she's okay. And… apologize. I need to apologize."

"For her? Or to make yourself feel better for fucking up things for you both?"

I opened my mouth to snap at her again, but Rev pulled me back, stepping around me to look at Hannah, who instantly tensed. "He didn't fuck up completely. Yeah, he had a lapse in judgement with that asshole, and he said some shit he shouldn't have to this girl, but he's paid for it. She has too, it sounds like."

He stared down at Hannah, who's angry expression faltered. She scrunched her nose, moving to lean against the car again. "I'm not trying to make you pay for it again, Kellen. But you should think about why you want to apologize before you go after her. She's been through a lot, I think. And that's not your fault, but…"

Pain flashed across her face, and she folded her arms again. "I practically had to beg her to take my number. And we were *friends*. Maybe not close, but still. She has a life now and I'm guessing doesn't want it upended for no reason."

I frowned at the sad look on Hannah's face. "What do you mean for no reason?"

"I mean, if you start looking for her to apologize, do it for the right reason. Do it because it's going to help her, not just because you're desperate to see her again."

Hannah's expression turned stern, then her eyes flicked to the bar as the door opened and music blared out for a few seconds. Lane stumbled out, and I knew without even talking to him that instead of having a few more drinks to process this, I was going to have to babysit his drunk ass. I was the younger brother, but it always ended up this way every time he came to visit.

"Kell, what the fuck? I'm in town for two nights and already you're bailing… oh, *shit!*"

A grin spread across his face, and he walked off the porch, gait a little wobbly as he approached where the three of us stood and gestured to Hannah. "*Shit*, is that little Han? That's *not* Hannah Moore. She's like... ten."

"Try again," Hannah said without missing a beat, a wicked smile crossing her face. "Where are you at now, Lane?"

"Not here. I got the hell out of the state." He leaned against Hannah's car, looking her up and down and letting out a low whistle. "You're a whole ass adult, aren't you? Can I buy you—"

"*No.*" Priest practically growled the word, which caught all three of us by surprise. But he wasn't wrong. I didn't want Lane hitting on her either.

"Yeah, that's enough," I snapped. "She's twenty, dick. Isaac will find a reason to throw your ass in jail if you even think it."

Lane scoffed when I grabbed his shoulder and spun him away, ushering him back to the bar. "Pfft. She's just under the rule, and cute as fuck. Holy shit. Why aren't you after that?"

I rolled my eyes, looking back to see Rev talking to Hannah, her expression cautious as he leaned against her car and hovered over her. I knew he wouldn't give her a hard time, but I wasn't sure what else they'd have to talk about.

But Lane tripped as we went inside, and I had to haul him upright while Cas stood behind the bar and laughed. I decided not to worry about Rev. Or Hannah. She was a big girl and could handle herself.

And I had too many other things on my mind. Even more than my drunk ass brother.

Tate was alive.

And despite Hannah's cautioning, I needed to find her.

Chapter Eight
Noelle

"MAY I SPEAK WITH PAULINE MARLAN?"

I held my breath, phone squeezed between my ear and my shoulder, pen in my hand and paper under my wrist, ready to jot down any information I could gather.

"This is she."

"Pauline, my name is Noelle Collins and I work at *The Journal*. I'm doing some research on unresolved missing cases in the state and your daughter's name came up. Do you mind if I ask you some questions?"

This was the fourth call I'd made since I'd gotten home from class. I'd pitched the idea to Pak that afternoon, complete with an outline on the things I wanted to highlight. The shockingly large number of open missing persons cases, how a disproportionate number of those were women and girls, and how varying things affected whether or not they got media attention. Social class, race, religious affiliation. Whether or not the missing person had a history of addiction or other mitigating factors that could affect interest. He'd been eager to hear more and gave me his full blessing to write it.

I'd left out that I had a personal interest in the matter, since a lot of names on my list were from where I'd gone to high school. Where I'd been transplanted after my own addict parents had left me alone again. For the last time.

"You can ask," Pauline said, and I could hear the irritation in her voice. "But I don't know how much help I'm going to be. Kara was out of our lives long before she took off."

"So, you believe she left of her own volition?"

"I don't have any clue. That girl was wild, we couldn't ever control her."

I winced. I wasn't sure of the relationship between Pauline Marlan and Kara, but the former sounded like she'd washed her hands of the situation. From what I remembered, Kara hadn't been trouble per say, at least no more than other teenagers in Northshore or anywhere else. She'd gotten a ticket for possession our junior year, and by senior year, I knew she was actively and openly having sex, which had been a bigger scandal than the possession oddly enough.

And it made her calling me a slut and taping condoms and lube to my locker a little hypocritical, but on par as far as teenage behavior went. Kara had been mean, and that was her biggest crime against me, but it was nothing that warranted this type of disdain from her own mother.

"Do you think its possible foul play was involved? Did she leave anything behind? A boyfriend? Friends who were looking for her?"

"A friend reported her missing, but I don't know about any other boyfriends. She dated a guy for a few months. Steve Bowens. I thought maybe she was cleaning up her act because he got her to come to church once a week. But they broke up and she started partying again. After that, I knew it was hopeless."

I was scrawling furiously, adding to the notes I'd taken about the other girls and trying to find any sort of connection. So far there wasn't anything good. Nothing I thought Isaac might be able to string together.

"How has her disappearance affected your family?" I asked, even though I knew what I'd get in the end. The answer had been the same for all the cases I'd called on and would probably be the same for the few I'd work on tomorrow. Some people were sad. Others were indifferent. Not everyone had someone who cared if they disappeared.

I knew how that felt. Well, until recently. Hannah had texted me a few times since our run-in, probing me for information about my life. Small talk. How'd I get my internship? Did I like working at *The Journal?* Was I ready to graduate? How were my exams? Mostly innocent stuff I didn't mind answering.

It was only when she asked to hang out that things got tougher.

It was easier to make excuses to the people I worked with. There was a boundary there I didn't want to cross. With Hannah, there was no reason to avoid her. Nor was there any reason I couldn't call the Zentu's and apologize about how I'd left things. I was embarrassed, and guilty. That might ease if I gave the back the money I'd stolen the night I'd ran. But facing what they might say when I called was something I wasn't up for yet.

"The biggest pain has been that we can't get her insurance claims," Pauline said after telling me all about how Kara's grandma had been more distressed than warranted for a girl who'd never been anything but trouble. "I'm paying premiums on a corpse. But since they can't find her, the company won't file a death claim. It's a scam, that's what I think."

I decided to leave that quote off the paper, mostly because it made me wonder if my parents, or Harvey and Marta, would have felt the same if they'd had me insured.

There was a knock on the door, and a second later, I heard

Priest's voice. I glanced out the window then at my watch. It was 8:30 on a Friday night. Usually he was out at this time.

"Thank you for your time, Mrs. Marlan. I appreciate it. May I call you if I have any other questions?"

"If you want. Can't tell you much more than I have."

"Thank you. Have a good evening."

I hung up the phone, stretching before I stood and walked to my door. When I opened it, Priest had his lips pressed together, and there was a V between his thick brows.

"What's wrong?" Immediately, I looked down the hall, my heart rate ticking up. "Did something happen with Macy?"

He blinked, then his posture relaxed. "No, she's fine. Far as I know."

I tilted my head, stepping back to let him inside. "Okay, what's going on then? Thought you'd be out. *Castlevania* is good and all, but it's Friday night."

Priest walked inside, giving me a half smirk over his shoulder. "Why aren't you out?"

"I never go out, you know that."

I shut the door and walked to my table, closing my notebook and gesturing to my laptop. "I'm broke and drinks are expensive. Plus, I was working on a new pitch for my editor about all the open missing persons cases in the state."

Priest was halfway into the chair when he hesitated, his eyebrows drawing together again as he sat down. "Oh yeah? What put that idea into your head?"

"Just some things I heard recently. I thought I'd look into it. See if I could string any connections together." I was being cagey on purpose, but he was used to it. It wasn't like I could reveal my sources or even the content of my articles until they were published.

So I was surprised when he kept looking at me, his green eyes filled with tension. I pulled out a chair across from him and sat down, leaning forward on the table with my hands between us. "Priest, what's going on? Why are you here?"

He rubbed at the thick stubble on his chin, the let out a heavy sigh. "If you're looking into this already, could I add a name to your list? A buddy of mine, my business partner, his girl has been missing for about three years."

"Did he report her?" I pulled out the notepad, ready to jot anything he could give me down. "Where'd she go missing from?"

"'Bout two hours Southeast of here."

Which was right around where Northshore was. "Can I talk to your business partner? Would he be willing to give me an interview?"

"He's a little... private."

"I won't ask much."

I looked up, trying to keep my expression calm instead of pleading. This was growing bigger than I expected, but if I could make any connections that might help Isaac figure this out, I'd keep going.

Because it might bring me some closure, too.

"Do you know the girl's name?" I asked, ready to scrawl the name down and compare it with the others I'd found. Priest rubbed his chin again, then folded his arms on the table, leaning forward, his green eyes locked on mine.

"Tatum Ivers."

My wrist jerked so hard the pen left a deep gouge in the paper. I looked down to examine the damage, but also to get my eyes away from Priest's.

What the fuck?

He said nothing, letting the name—*my* name—hang between us like a weight. A sharpened pendulum swinging over a proverbial pit, and if I didn't move it would cleave me in half. How in the hell had he heard my name? Who would have told him I was missing?

The answer was right in front of me, buried in the oil stains that were all over his hands. Long hours in a mechanic shop, working on bikes. Custom builds, but they I knew he did cars by request since he'd offered to look at mine. We'd never talked about work beyond that. No reason to.

No reason to think that the world would be so small, it was literally caving in on me.

"How old would she be?" I asked, deciding to act dumb. It was a losing game, but I was curious how long Priest would let me play.

He was quiet for heartbeat, fingers drumming a rhythm on his bicep, the movement inviting Haku up to bat at his hands. "About your age," he said, scratching behind the cat's ears casually like this was a regular Friday night between two friends. Nothing suspicious. Nothing at all.

"Do you know anything about their history? How long they were together?" I pressed, keeping my tone light. "Where was he when she went missing?"

"In prison."

His voice was flat, and he lowered his arms, drumming his fingers on the table only to have Haku attack them. I watched my cat, unable to look at Priest's face as I scrawled this all down. Like I didn't already know the answers.

"What for?"

"Aggravated assault. He plead guilty. It wasn't anything to do with her."

"You're sure?" I said, wanting to see if there were any cracks in their relationship. Maybe they were business partners and nothing more, and on the inside they'd never talked.

Yeah, right. Two years in a cell with someone and I'm sure stuff would come out. Besides that, Kellen might have been introverted, but he wasn't cruel. Anyone could tell that by looking at him. Including Priest, who when I looked up finally and met his eyes, was staring at me with a perplexed expression, the usual warmth in his gaze muted.

"Yeah, I'm sure." He gave me another look, almost scolding, and a wave of guilt washed over me for insinuating that Kellen had hurt me, even if it was a ruse. I swallowed, ignoring the growing tightness in my chest.

"I wasn't trying to imply anything," I said sheepishly. Priest stared for a second longer, then he sat back in the chair, drumming his fingers on the table again.

"Kell and I bunked together. He told me everything about this girl, and when we got out and he learned she was missing, he was a wreck. Blames himself for it. He broke things off with her after he went in, and he thinks if he hadn't done that, maybe she'd have been safe. Nothing would have happened to her."

My jaw tightened, a pit forming in my stomach that made it hard to think. The corners of my eyes started to burn, but I held the tears back. I'd shed enough over him already; I didn't want to cry anymore. "I'm sure she doesn't blame him for anything."

Priest raised his eyebrows, and I swallowed before going on. "Wherever she is, if she's okay, I'm sure she doesn't hold any grudges against him. Has he gotten any calls on the report he filed?"

Priest let out a heavy sigh and leaned forward, head tilting as he stared at me. "Noelle."

I met his gaze, my pulse thrumming, body tense like it was preparing to run. My leg was bouncing, and the pen trembled in my fingers.

Stop it, I chastised myself. *You don't need to run. There isn't a threat. Priest isn't a threat. Kellen, technically, isn't a threat.*

My own reassurances met nothing. The flight response was active, stronger than it had been in a while. Priest exhaled slowly, almost like he was preparing. Would he stop me if I ran out the door? Would he leave if I told him to?

"Noelle."

"Yeah?" I finally said, tapping my pen on the paper like I was waiting for him to give me more information. Not waiting for a bomb to explode between us. Priest frowned but didn't lean back. His gaze stayed locked on mine, green eyes soft and sympathetic.

"That's your name?"

"It's how I introduced myself to you, so clearly it's my name."

His shoulder's tensed, that V appearing between his eyebrows again while I tried to think. My body started to twitch, legs bouncing, my heartbeat stuttering into a frantic rhythm while we sat and stared at each other, finally crashing into the impasse I'd been trying to avoid. Priest's expression softened as he looked me over, a tightness settling into his expression. His voice was soothing and soft when he spoke again, trying to calm the bubbles of fury he saw boiling under the surface.

"Noelle."

"Yup, that's my name." I threw the pen down and folded my arms, leaning back in the chair and meeting his soft gaze with an angry one. "You *know* me, Priest. You know me better than I've let anyone else know me in a long time. Which is saying something because I've only lived here a year. Before that, I moved around a whole bunch. As often as I could. I don't like staying in one place too long, you know? Gets stuffy. A change of scenery is always nice."

I stared at his sympathetic face, my façade cracking when I spoke again. "But I *like* it here. I haven't felt like I needed to leave because I've been safe. You come over and kill the spiders that get in the windows. You sit with me after I had a long day. *Priest*." My voice shook, and his stoic expression caved some. "You've seen me after a nightmare. You *know* me. We're *friends*."

"Yes, we are. And that's why when I say you don't have to be scared of Kellen, I hope you believe me." I winced, and he let out another sigh. "You're not hiding from him."

"No, I'm not. But the more people who know where I am, the greater the chance of it somehow getting back to—"

"That Davey guy?"

Priest's expression hardened, and when he leaned back, he somehow looked broader. Stronger. A great Dane with a bite that accompanied his bark. "Has he tried to bother you since you left?"

"Right after I moved down here, I got phone calls, and one letter," I confessed, watching his expression harden. "I broke my lease and moved again. And that's... that's when I changed my name. Got a new number. A post office box. Went dark on social media."

I glanced down at the computer beside my note pad and frowned. "When you saw me log in the other night, that was the first time I'd looked at it in over year, because there's still accounts sending me messages. All these Bible verses and comments about how I need to repent. I still have my old phone and there's *hundreds* of texts on there. It didn't matter how many times I blocked him, he always managed to get a new number and call me."

I watched Priest's shoulders rise and fall, his eyebrows pinching again when I shrugged. "I didn't report it. They didn't do shit the first time I tried, so I never bothered doing it again."

Priest folded his arms and leaned forward on the table. "You know if someone tried to bother you, I'd kick—"

"And get yourself thrown back in prison?" I scoffed. "That's happened to someone I cared about already. You think I want to go through that again? Have someone go to jail because they think they're defending me?"

Priest sat up straight. "Kellen was trying to defend—"

"No, he wasn't. And I'm not going to get into this."

Not with him, at least. Priest wasn't involved, and he maybe did know Kellen, had talked with him for hours, but that still didn't mean he knew our history. He didn't know mine. He didn't know how much it hurt to be left all alone when all I'd needed was someone to hold my hand.

I squeezed my arms around my ribs, like I could prevent the pain from bursting out, or lock my heart behind another wall. I turned away, not wanting to Priest to see the tear that slipped down my cheek. "There's nothing to say. It happened, it's over. I've moved on and I'm fine."

There was a bite in my voice I hadn't heard in a while. Since the last time I tried to talk to Kellen. When the officer on duty informed me the prisoner wasn't going to come to see me.

I inhaled sharply, trying to swallow the choked noise, reaching up to push the tear off my cheek. "You need anything else?" I asked, very aware of Priest's gaze on my hunched shoulders. "I've got some work to do before I go to bed."

He said nothing, but also made no move to leave. Not until I looked at him, then he stood, twisting his lips as he leaned against the table.

"You can't stay holed up in this apartment pretending you're busy all the time, Noelle. This isn't living and you know it." He hesitated, pushing his hair back from his face. "Honestly, you'd do well to have some people around who would have your back in case..."

"Thank you for your assessment, but I'll pass." I looked up just long enough to see his sad expression before I turned away. "I can't remember a time when anyone but me ever had my back, and I've made it this far. I think I'm good."

Priest stiffened, then let out a sigh before he turned to the door. I listened to it click shut behind him, then immediately got up and locked the doorknob, the bolt, and the latch. Then I shoved a chair in front of it for good measure and turned to head into my bedroom, images flying through my head so fast I couldn't process them all. I saw my parents faces, then Harvey and Marta. My classmates laughing. Davey looking pitiful, like a dog taken to the pound after biting its owner. Pastor Mark frowning every time he saw me around town. Brandon Michaels the youth minister avoiding me when I waved. Kevin Pike, who drove me and a few others to camp every summer, shaking his head when he saw me working in the bar. All these people were supposed to look out for me, and after one mistake that I didn't make alone, all they had to offer was disappointment.

Then Kellen's face flashed in my mind. Smiling with his full lips, pulling me under his arm. Tucking my body against his every time I climbed on the back of his motorcycle. When we'd stop, he'd always put his hand on my thigh. A check in to see if I was okay, or simply because he wanted to touch me. Same thing whenever his mouth was on my neck, or his hand started to slip up my shirt. He took care of me. He looked out for me.

Until he didn't.

"Kellen, please."

"Tate, just go." He stood up from the table, fists clenched as he walked past me. *"And don't come back."*

I choked back a sob, clutching a pillow as the grief I barely kept at bay burst through the gates, washing over me like a tidal wave. I wasn't sure if it was for Kellen and what we shared, or if it was for myself.

For Tatum.

And the life she had stolen from her before it ever had a chance to really get started.

Chapter Nine
Kellen

I COULD HAVE STARED AT HER ALL NIGHT.

The movie didn't interest me. I'd seen Spirited Away on cable a few times, but never paid much attention. Seeing it now at the drive-in had been more of an excuse to get away from town for a while. I hadn't expected Tatum to be so engrossed in the film. She had a soft smile on her lips, and her hair fluttered around her face in the light breeze. I wanted to tuck it behind her ears.

She'd put on the hoodie she always had with her, the blue one with the cat, a rat, and a rice ball. Her hands were shoved into the oversized pocket in front, and I slid closer, tucking my hands inside even though they weren't cold. She smirked at me, then her eyes turned back to the screen.

"You really like this movie?"

"I do," she murmured. "I used to watch this all the time. It's still one of my favorites."

I pursed my lips, lacing my fingers into hers. "Weren't you a baby when it came out?"

She shrugged. "I don't remember how old I was when I first saw it. My parents brought me with them to a party and someone stuck me in a room and put it on. I think a woman came in and watched it with me."

The grin faded and she dropped her eyes, staring at the bed of my truck as her fingers tightened in mine. "I kept asking for it, and when they sobered up, they bought it for me. I carried that DVD and a portable player with me everywhere I went. Just in case I ended up some place random again and needed something to watch."

I stilled, watching her expression stay completely emotionless as she described the scene so clearly. I pictured Tatum as a little girl, all chubby cheeked and small, in a house somewhere, alone in a room while her parents did God knew what.

It made me feel sick.

"That happen a lot?"

She shrugged and looked back at the screen. "Yes and no. They started leaving me home alone when I was around five or six, and sometimes they'd sober up and I didn't have to worry about it. Then it wasn't bad."

"So you had good moments with them, too?"

"Those were almost worse than the bad ones."

She paused, and I stayed quiet, fingers laced inside hers as I pulled back, trying to scoot her closer to my chest. Tatum hesitated, then she sighed and let her body sink into mine.

"Those sober moments gave me a taste of what it would be like to have them around all the time, then they took it away." She turned away from the screen, and I hugged her tighter. "It was like never having power then suddenly, for a few hours, it comes back. But you can't really enjoy it."

"Because you know it'll get dark again," I murmured, my lips twisting as she shifted against me, snuggling into my hold. "I feel that," I added, setting my chin against her head. "It's not the same, but when Lane and I finished the barn up, it was only supposed to be so we could have parties there. I didn't plan on using it as an apartment but... it was better than being in the house."

Tate turned to give me a sad smile, then leaned forward to grab her bag and pull out the odd orange hat she always carried with her. The cat ears were bent over, but straightened she tugged it onto her head, adjusting the loose parts of her hair that hung over her shoulders. It was warm outside, but I didn't question it. Sometimes I thought she put that

hat or a sweater on to make herself feel safe. Like those shirts they give animals for anxiety. Tate had just made her own.

"Did you want to move out there? Or did your dad suggest it after you decided not to live in the dorms?"

I shrugged as she sat back against my chest, hands tucked in the front of her sweater, waiting for mine. "I think it was mutual. Dorm life wasn't for me, and he was happy I wasn't wasting more money than I already was on my 'stupid' degree. But his parenting days were officially over according to him and I was fine on my own." She turned to look at me, a frown on her face. "We don't get along."

"I've noticed."

When I raised my eyebrows, because I wasn't sure she'd ever seen my dad, let alone met him, she smiled softly. "Whenever I come over I always see the empty beer cases and vodka bottles. My parents' vices were different, but I know the signs of addiction. I'm sorry."

I shrugged, ignoring the tightness in my chest. "It got worse after my mom died, and he likes to blame me for a habit he'd already established years before that."

She hadn't turned back to the screen, and I looked down to see her frowning, eyebrows pinched together as she gazed up at me. "I was the reason she left the night she died," I explained. "My dad and her had gotten into a fight and it… upset me. So she said she'd go to the store to get me a treat. Ice cream." My jaw clenched, throat tight, the words turning into a cloying, thick sensation before I managed to spit them out. "Never came home. Dad decided it was my fault."

Even though it was dark out, and the only light on her face was from the screen, I could see her expression shift. Her eyes turned sad, and lower lip pushed out in a soft pout. "It wasn't."

"I know that."

She sat up, turning her body so she could look me full in the face. "Do you?" The question was gentle, but there was a probing tone to her voice that made my jaw clench again. "No, really, Kellen. Do you?"

"Of course I do," I mumbled, looking back to the screen, waiting for her to do the same. When she didn't I sighed, trying not to roll my eyes. "I was eleven. *Of course it wasn't my fault. It was whatever jackass drove her off the road."*

"You don't eat ice cream, though. You told me you didn't like it."

I froze.

I hadn't had ice cream since my mom died cause it always reminded me of her, but I didn't realize I'd said I didn't like it.

Tate continued to stare, and I shifted under her gaze, the thrum of my pulse oddly loud in my ears. "Does it matter?"

"It does if you're like… punishing yourself with it or something. Same with staying around here. You want to leave so bad, but you don't."

"I'm not punishing myself." I slid back against the cab of the truck, frowning when Tate followed. "My family wants me to go to some fancy ass college and get a financial degree. They think I'm wasting an opportunity, like I ever asked for one. And Lane did exactly that and they like to say the same thing about him cause he won't take over my dad's insurance shit."

She was kneeling between my open legs, her hands on the top of her thighs, eyes soft even though her eyebrows were still pinched together. "So, you're staying here and getting an auto tech degree to spite them?"

"No," I muttered, draping my arms over my bent knees. Why was she stuck on this? "I want to do that. You know I want to do that. Fuck, Tate, half the time we hang out I'm working on a bike. I love it, so why wouldn't I—"

"I know you love it. But you could do it anywhere. Why here?" She moved closer, setting her hands on my forearms and giving me a soft smile. I scowled, and she smiled, shaking her head as she pushed my hand aside and moved back between my legs. "You're not stuck here, you know. You could leave if you wanted to. You have the means to do it."

"It's not that simple," I countered, thinking about the cost of living in other places, bigger places, along with the fact that if I left my dad might actually drink himself to death. Not that my presence here would stop him, but still. Tate continued to stare at me, then when I scowled she laughed.

"Have you ever seen Howl's Moving Castle?*"*

I tilted my head, then glanced at the screen before looking back at her. "I've heard of it."

"You remind me of Howl. He's the antagonist." She tilted her head and paused for half a second before going on. "Well, not really. You think he is, but he's not. It's hard to explain if you haven't seen it."

"Why am I like him?"

Tate flashed me a wicked grin, and my stomach clenched when she pushed my arms open before I could cage them around my chest. I braced as she crawled onto my lap, her legs settling over my hips. My hands fell to the tops of her thighs and she pushed my hair back, tugging a little to coax my gaze to hers.

"When I first met you, it was random. You appeared and plucked me out of my ordinary life. Made me feel like I was special, like I wasn't alone. Like someone was interested in me." She laughed softly, pushing my hair back and shaking her head in amusement. "And then you were gone. You left me alone."

I frowned. I didn't leave. She'd been in high school, and I was in college. There were four years between us and until this summer, that had seemed like too much. Maybe it still was, but I'd stopped caring, and so had she.

"Is that what he does?" I asked, my hands moving to her hips first, then her waist, like I could soothe away the pain I'd caused.

"In a way," Tate said, shrugging one shoulder. There's a book, but it's so different from the movie. But in both of them, Howl is kind of a coward."

Ouch.

Tatum's fingers were soft in my hair, her expression kind, but I spun that word over in my head like it was a tire I was putting on a car. Coward.

I let out a low breath, trying to reign in my irritation. "I'm not a coward."

"Oh?" Her eyes flashed, and that mischievous grew wider. "Did you ignore me the one year we were in school together because you wanted to spare me a run through the rumor mill, or did you want to avoid dealing

with your friends who would have teased you about our friendship? Same with now." Her back arched, pushing her hips against mine as the hand that wasn't in my hair slid down my chest. My hands tightened around her waist, fingers sliding under the hem of her shirt before I realized what they were doing. "Are we dating? Or are we just friends because you don't want to answer questions. I know Isaac gives you heck about hanging out with me. Hannah said so."

I glared, but she shifted again, her closeness only driving the words deeper. Pointing out the lies I tried to tell myself. Girl was too fucking smart for her own good. Too observant.

Journalism was a good career for her.

"You say you want out, but I think you're happy in your cage." She dragged her fingers all the way through my hair and I had to bite back a moan, my hands seeking the soft skin on her back and stomach as she trailed her fingers over my cheek. They got to my chin, and she tipped it up with her pointer finger, bending to kiss my nose but pulling back before I could catch her lips. "You're safe inside your castle. It's just big enough that you can live without too much risk. You can exist in the world without having to be part of it. Frees you from making more choices people will question, even if they're the right ones for you."

I stared at her, my chest tight, brain reeling from that final shot. Tatum smirked, and I didn't look away as she pushed my hair back again, this time with both hands.

"It's funny. Now that I think about it, you even look like Howl."

I reached up, catching her wrists. "I haven't seen the movie."

It came out as a growl, but I wasn't angry. In fact, part of me wanted her to keep going. Tell me more about how I was punishing myself so maybe I could stop. No one ever called me on my bullshit. Or they did, but I didn't listen.

But I was listening now. Listening to this girl I had no business keeping caged up with me.

Maybe if she ripped me open and made space to crawl inside, the ache would ease and I'd feel good enough for something.

Good enough for her.

"*Yeah, I guessed that,*" she said, chewing on her full bottom lip when it was all I wanted to do. "*We should watch it sometime.*"

"*Maybe. But I'm not… keeping myself trapped here as some sort of penance. I'm not hiding from anything.*"

"*Right,*" she teased, leaning forward and pecking my nose again. "*So, tell me again why you're here?*"

"*Because it's cheap. And because I get…*"

I hesitated, watching her eyes widen as I lifted my hands, tucking her hair behind her ears before I pulled that hat off her head. It was blocking part of her face, casting a shadow over her pretty eyes when all I wanted to do was look into them. Get lost in them like they were a sea and I had no lifeboat coming for me. "*I get to see you for a bit.*"

She smiled, pressing her lips together and rocking her hips softly, laughing when I gripped her and pulled her close. "*You said we weren't that close of friends.*"

I had said that. Because I didn't want to be Tatum's friend. I never had.

I'd always wanted to be more.

"*We're close enough,*" I murmured, letting my hands smooth over her shoulders. "*But even so, you're leaving in the fall. There's only so close—*"

"*What if I didn't leave? I get free room and board right now. I have a job. It doesn't make sense for me to—*"

"*Don't,*" I interrupted, cupping her face, pulling her forehead against mine. "*Don't stay here, Tate. Don't get cozy and settle. Get out while you can.*"

"*Why should I when you aren't?*"

"*Because you're better than I am. You've always been better than me.*"

She took a moment to let this sink in, then leaned in, sealing her lips against mine. Her arms slid around my neck, and I wrapped mine around her waist, greedy and eager to touch any part of her I could. I grabbed her by the waist, holding her to me with one arm as I shoved all the shit in the back of my truck aside. Blankets and tarps and a stupid toolbox. I needed space. I wanted to take her home, put her in my bed and never leave…

"Hey, Fox."

I startled back, the stool I was on moving a few inches away from the counter and the toolbox I was staring at. It wasn't dark outside, there was no movie playing. I was at home, in my garage, working on a bike.

And Tatum was nowhere to be found.

"Kellen?"

I turned, spotting my brother first, then Riot. They were sitting beside one another, Lane dressed in a grungy band T-shirt and Riot in one with the sleeves cut off. Lane had a bottle of beer in his hand while Riot looked at me, eyebrows pinched, his palm extended in wait.

"You gonna hand me that wrench?"

I stared at the toolbox, and the wrench Riot needed to tighten the bolts for the foot peg on his bike. The tools in the box rattled as I shuffled them around, finally finding what I'd moved over here for and tossing it to him. There was a towel on the counter, and I grabbed it, giving my hands something to do that looked natural. Not like I was lost in my head, fixating on memories that replayed themselves on a loop. Riot turned the wrench around in his hand, eyes lingering on me before they turned back to the bike.

"You're distracted as fuck today," he murmured. "This about that phone call Cas said you got last night?"

"Yes."

It was Lane who answered, and I threw him a glare before standing up off my stool and walking to the cooler to get myself a beer. "You can shut the hell up anytime you like," I snapped, flipping him the finger when he rolled his eyes at me. "In fact, you could probably call Isaac and the two of you could go out, catch up, and maybe get laid if it would get you off my ass."

Lane rolled his eyes again and Riot gave me a half smile over the bike. "You could join them. Might do you some good. We don't have to do this today. It's not like we have all the parts anyway."

"I'm getting the tires Tuesday, and the new handlebars you wanted should be in this week. If we get it ready for those, you'll have it by next weekend like I promised."

I popped the bottle cap off and tossed it in the trash before walking back to my stool, shaking my head when Riot continued to stare. "Seriously. I said I'd have it done, and I meant it."

"I'm not in a rush, and it's not gonna change anything if you're a little late with it. You're gonna get patched in no matter what, kid."

"The fuck you calling me kid for?" I asked, glaring at Lane, who laughed while Riot grinned. "I put up with it from him cause I have no choice, but if the rest of you start doing it I'm going to be pissed."

"Relax," Riot said. "It'll last until the next prospect comes along, or you hit thirty. Whichever comes first."

I scoffed and took a drink of my beer. I'd probably hit thirty first. Rush and Cas were very selective about who they let into the club, and they'd let me in only after they'd gone through a list of unspoken requirements with the other members. I'd hit all the marks. Ex-con, check. Had my shit together for the most part, check. Took the nature of my offense seriously and didn't want to repeat it, check. It had been Rev vouching for me that finally got me the prospect patch. Had it not been for him I'd still be on the outside of everything.

"What had you so pissed last night?" Riot asked. "Cas said you got a call, then you were outside forever before this asshole came and got you." He jerked is head to Lane, laughing when my brother flipped him off. "Priest was out there even longer. What was he doing?"

"Talking to Isaac's little sister," I said. "He was the one who called me, and she stopped to check in about it."

Riot raised his eyebrows and passed me the wrench to work on the other side of the bike, smirking when I gave him a look.

"It's not like that. I've known her forever, and besides that, you know I don't hook up."

"Then what's got you so upset that you're out here getting a distraction from your distraction?"

I turned to Lane, but he only gave me a shrug. We'd talked about it last night, and he felt the same way Isaac did. Tate was alive, that was good. But that was it. I needed to move on.

Riot, however, looked patient. Curious. And I wondered if he'd have a different opinion considering he didn't know Tate and he hadn't known me before all this. "Can I ask you something?"

He nodded, reaching down to grab his own beer. "Shoot."

"You ever run into anyone you went to high school with? Or college?"

"All the damn time." His eyes rolled and he took a long drink. "I graduated here and never left, so I'm always running into people. The city isn't as big as people think it is. Mack moved here from Dubuque and he ran into someone he knew last week when we were out riding. Had no clue the guy lived down here. Michaela has seen people she went to high school with in court. The metro is just big enough to be anonymous, but small enough that paths cross easily. Why? You run into someone?"

"Not... exactly." I scuffed at the floor, trying to think of how to explain. "A girl I fooled around with just before I went in went missing, but Isaac found her. She's been living down here. Changed her name, her appearance. Shit, even if I passed her, and I might not have noticed."

"This girl the reason you beat the shit out of that guy?"

I nodded, watching as he ran a hand through his short black hair. "She testify for you?"

"It wouldn't have mattered if she had. I didn't want to risk it at trial, so I plead guilty."

"Plus, he kind of told her to fuck off," Lane interjected, shrugging when I turned to scowl at him. "What? You did."

"You didn't want to see her no more?" Riot asked.

"Little more complicated than that," I said, and he tilted his head. "I didn't want her seeing me like that. In prison, and I didn't..."

I bit the inside of my cheek, the bile that had been slowly simmering in my stomach rising to a full boil. "If she would have stayed there just for me, I'd have hated myself. This girl is smart, Riot. She's fucking tenacious and motivated, and I didn't want her hanging around there waiting for me."

"Because you're not those things?" Lane demanded. "You don't give yourself enough credit, Kell. You let dad fuck with your head, too."

"I didn't want her there." I scowled at Lane, then turned back to Riot. "You get it, don't you?"

He huffed a laugh. "Yeah, I get it. I felt like the shittiest goddamn person on the planet having my girlfriend represent me in court, but Michaela wouldn't hear otherwise. And it was her choice. So, I get it, but..."

I frowned, and he motioned for the wrench when I started fiddling with it. I passed it to him and he went back to another part of the bike as he kept talking. "Were you serious with this girl? Or were you just fucking?"

I hesitated, and that seemed to answer his question, even before Lane spoke up. "He was in love with her."

Riot glanced at me over the bike, waiting for me to deny it. "Rev know about this?" he asked.

"He helped me look for her for a few days before I moved down here."

"Does he think you should go looking for her?" Riot pressed. "You could probably find her name out if you really wanted to. Changes like that are public record. Sometimes they put them in the newspaper."

I blinked, because it couldn't be that easy, could it? If it was, anyone could look it up if they needed to. I looked at Lane and he scoffed. "That's fucked up."

Riot held up his hands. "Hey, I don't make the laws. They publish lottery winners' names, too, and that doesn't make any sense either."

He passed me the wrench again, and I turned this over in my head as he and Lane started talking about ridiculous laws, my brother brining up all the financial loopholes he knew people exploited. I didn't pay much attention to it, my mind was fixated on other things.

Like if I could look name changes up online or if I had to go to an office downtown, which would mean waiting until Monday. I didn't know if I could do that.

I wanted to see her. I needed to see her. Hannah had told me to think about what I might say and I still had no clue, but it didn't matter. I'd find the words once I knew she was okay.

And find out exactly why the hell she'd been hiding from me and everyone else all these years.

Chapter Ten

Noelle

My conversation with Priest left me on edge.

The only way he could have connected the dots between Kellen and me was if Isaac had told Kellen my new name and he pieced the information together. It was hard to hold this thought back when I called Isaac a few days later to let him know about the information I'd gathered on the cases I'd picked out.

"And they talked to you willingly?" he asked, his voice tinny and a little distorted by background noise.

"Are you driving?"

"Yes, you're on my Bluetooth. I'm actually coming down if you wanted to talk in person."

I scoffed. "I'll pass. Especially after you went back on your word and told Kellen my new name."

There was a pause, then Isaac grumbled out a curse. "That wasn't me. I didn't tell him, honest to God, Tate. He might have called Hannah or Hannah might have—"

"Hannah?"

"Yeah, she was there when I ran into you, remember?"

"Why in the hell would she tell Kellen—"

"They've been close since she moved down. He checks in on her when I can't. Invites her over for dinner and stuff."

Oh.

When I didn't have any response, Isaac laughed. "They're not dating, though."

"Why would I care if they were?"

My voice was far too casual to be convincing.

I didn't care if they dated. I didn't care if they got married and had 8,000 babies.

In fact, if Kellen was dating Hannah, it made things that much easier. Gave me no reason to look him up and explain myself. Not like I owed him an explanation or owed him anything.

"Never said you did," Isaac replied. "Listen, I can't write any of this down while I'm driving. Let's meet up for lunch. You can give me all the details you've got and I can check a few things out for you."

I twisted my lips, jostling my legs that were propped up on the coffee table. "Fine. When and where?"

"I don't live there so I don't know what's good or—"

"That coffee shop you went to with Hannah, then. You remember where it is?"

He paused. "You don't want to do lunch? Someplace with actual food?"

"This isn't a date, Isaac. You are a source to me, that's it."

"Christ, okay." There was a hint of defensiveness in his tone, and I heard him laugh softly. "When did you develop that chip on your shoulder?"

"Probably when I tried to report Davey for harassment and got told I was overexaggerating."

Isaac said nothing, and for some reason that irked me more. "That was at Lakeside, by the way. I think the officer on call asked me what I expected, you know, since I'd turned my back on God. He said I didn't have proof, but if it was Davey, he had a right to be mad considering everything."

More silence, but I didn't hang up. Instead, I stood, clenching my teeth as I walked to my kitchen where Haku was pawing at the cupboard, seeking out his treats. I gave him two, then pulled out his catnip toy and threw it, trying to distract myself from how hot my face felt, how tight my chest was. Anger had made all my muscles tense and all I wanted to do was hit something. I settled for rearranging a few blankets and kicking my shoes under my bed, waiting for Isaac to speak again. When he did, it was tempered. So calm and controlled.

That only pissed me off more.

"Things have changed. I'm sorry that happened to you."

"Are you?" I asked, listening to him scoff. "I wasn't sure you would be, considering the entire time Kellen and I dated you scowled at me and told him how clingy I was. Like I asked him to blow you guys off. And I think that time in the coffee shop was the first time I ever heard you call me Tatum and not Taint."

Isaac muttered another curse. "You want me as a source or not?"

I scowled at my empty living room, like if I did it hard enough, he might see. My lips pressed together, and I took a slow, deep breath.

This wasn't his fault.

He hadn't been working there when I reported Davey, and I actually believed him when he said he hadn't told Kellen my new name.

Which meant I owed Hannah a very angry text when I got off the phone.

Haku had taken his toy over to the window and was ignoring it to stare outside at the street, his furry body completely still like he was ready to pounce on a bird or squirrel that ran by. I sighed again, then folded my arms around my chest. "I'm sorry, all right? I've just been on edge."

"I'm not gonna tell anyone where you are, Tate." He still sounded irritated but was letting it go. "For what it's worth, I didn't even speak to Davey. I had someone else call and they left him a message. But Phil and Suzanne thanked us and pressed a bit when I called."

My whole body went rigid, and my last hour in Northshore flashed through my head. How frantic I'd been trying to gather as much as I could and shove it into my car. The panic I'd felt about having no money and no place to go. Then the disgust when I unlocked the door to the bakery and raided the cash register, desperate to for anything that might let me at least rent a hotel room and buy some food since I didn't have a credit card. I'd left Phil and Suzanne a note explaining what I'd done, but not why I'd left. And even though I didn't think about it, the guilt for that act was always there. Like an old ache that flared up with a storm, or a chipped tooth waiting for me to bite off more than I could chew before it finally cracked.

"Pressed about what?" I asked, bracing for him to tell me they were pressing charges. They could. I did steal from their business.

"Just about where you were. If you were okay. They were worried, Tate."

I relaxed slightly, guilt still swirling in my chest. "So, are we meeting at the coffee shop? I do have some info that might be helpful."

"Yeah, we can meet there. 2:30 sound good?"

"Sure. See you then."

The line clicked, and I shot off a quick text to Hannah, letting her know we needed to talk. I glanced at the phone to check the time. 1:30, which gave me enough time to shower and hopefully rinse off the anxiety, irritation, and guilt that clung to my skin like a film.

I stayed too long in the hot water, but I wasn't planning on fixing myself up much. My hair dried fast so I dressed in jeans and a T-shirt, grabbing an old zip up hoodie out of the closet. I was about to slip it on when I noticed the image on the back and froze. A white pony galloping on a black background... One of my last gifts from Kellen. Before everything fell to pieces.

I looked up, catching sight of my reflection in the mirror and frowning. My eyes were a little red and there were dark circles under them. The black hair didn't help. It washed me out, and no makeup or bronzer helped.

It was probably a good thing Kellen hadn't, and wouldn't, see me as I was now. Let him keep the memories of Tatum and her honey blonde hair and eyes he said looked like the sea. Let him picture me as that naïve girl who'd always found bootstraps to pull up and ignored it when the world frowned at her and whispered behind her back. It hurt, but pain tempered her like fire did a sword. Let him picture me like that.

Not like this. Not sallow faced and haunted. Scared to go out in the world because someone might see her.

I tossed the hoodie back in my closet, not bothering to hang it up, and swapped my dressy blouse for a T-shirt with an alchemy rune on the front. After that, I stalked into the bathroom and threw on some concealer, a little bit of powder, and mascara. I stared at my eyes, debating for half a second before deciding that yes, I did want to wear my contacts. If I was going to show Isaac I had every intention of living the life I'd created as Noelle, I needed to commit, no matter how much of a pain in the ass they were.

My hair was dry and I tugged on my orange hat, considering the unnecessary accessory a sort of talisman. I was, after all, hiding my true self, just like the character the hat was modeled after. So it fit my aesthetic, even if it looked ridiculous.

I scowled at my phone. 2:20. It would take me roughly ten minutes to get to the coffee shop from here on a bike. If I could drive my car that would be quicker, but then I'd have to pay for parking. And I didn't know if it would start.

And honestly, I didn't know if I could get inside it without having another attack.

I grabbed my notepad and pen and shoved them in my backpack before slinging it over my shoulders and grabbing my bike. If I rode fast, I'd make it on time. At the very worst, Isaac would need to wait a few minutes.

But when I got outside, I froze at the bottom of the steps that lead away from my apartment. Priest was in the parking lot, standing in a small cluster of people all sitting on or leaning against motorcycles. One guy had on a sleeveless shirt covered in oil, and the guy next to him sitting atop an all-black Harley looked vaguely familiar. His brown hair was cut short, shaved on the sides, a little longer on top but styled neatly. He had on a T-shirt with a picture of a band, but it was clean. Pristine almost compared to Priest and the other man's clothing.

But it wasn't any of these men that made me stop in my tracks. It was the last guy, who leaned against a red and black Harley, arms folded over his chest, messy brown hair hanging around his ears. He turned to look at me at the same time the others did, but Priest's eyes were the first to find mine. The smile on his face dropped like a stack of bricks, and his head whipped toward the guy on the red bike.

To his business partner.

To Kellen.

Chapter Eleven
Noelle

I didn't dare move. I wasn't sure I could. My heart seemed to stutter, and I pulled my hat down, like it might shield me from Kellen's shocked gaze.

He stared at me, eyes wide, lips parted in shock, but he seemed just as frozen to the ground as I was. None of the guys beside Kellen moved either. They looked between the two of us, and everything seemed to come to a standstill. The most pregnant of pauses. We're talking fifth trimester level.

Finally, just as I'd decided I was tired of this staring contest, Kellen stood and began walking toward me. Stalking toward me. His hands were balled at his fists at his sides, that shocked expression still on his face though it was giving way to something else. Anger, maybe? Definitely confusion. My body tensed, and I gripped the handlebars of my bike so tight, my biceps flexed. He didn't keep his distance, walking right into my space even when I moved the bike between us to block him.

"What. The fuck…"

I pulled the bike closer, like it was a shield and if I needed to, I could shove it into him and run the other direction. I'd get back to my apartment before he had time to catch me. I wasn't the skinny eighteen-year-old I had been the last time we'd seen each other. I had some muscle now. Biceps and abs and thighs and if he wanted to hurt me—

Kellen would never.

The voice was a whisper, a soft caress inside my ears that did nothing to calm me even though it spoke the truth. Kellen wouldn't hurt me. Not physically, at least. His pain was something I couldn't fight against. It was on the inside. A bike as a shield and strong legs wouldn't stand up against the emotional assault he could levy on my heart if he wanted.

In fact, the ache that always came when I thought about him already started.

Seeing him made my heart flutter against the bars of the cell I'd locked it in, and the longer Kellen looked at me, his eyes scanning my face, registering every change in my features, the organ pounded against the walls of its prison, determined to break them down. I wanted to scowl. Or at least remain stoic, but the hurricane of emotions raging inside me pushed tears to the back of my eyes, so close to the surface it stung. Still, I swallowed heavily, willing the tears back. I wasn't going to let him see me cry.

He'd ended it. Not me.

He'd chosen this.

When I had nothing to offer but a cold stare, at least I hoped it was a cold stare, Kellen's angry expression shifted to something else. Panic. He whipped around and looked at Priest, face twisting into a sneer.

"Why is she here?" He demanded. "Don't... don't tell me you're *fucking*—"

"I *live* here," I snapped, watching as Priest opened his mouth to say the same thing. I shook my head when he looked at me, a surge of adrenaline dulling the pain enough that I wanted to speak for myself. I needed to speak for myself.

"I've lived here for about a year, Kellen. Priest didn't know who I was until a few nights ago."

Kellen's eyes were like saucers when he looked at me. "A few nights ago?" He didn't give me time to respond, turning back to shout at Priest. "You knew where she was and you didn't think to tell me?"

"She didn't want me to."

"I didn't want Priest to."

Priest and I said it at the same time, a stereo rejection that made Kellen's entire upper body tense. His hands closed into fists, visibly shaking as he turned back to me. This time, his expression was pleading. Still angry, but there was a pain inside it that mirrored my own.

"Why?" he asked. "Tatum, *why?*"

I glared at him, unable to stop the scoff that slipped past my lips. "Why *what?*"

"Why don't you want... Tate, it's *me.*"

"Oh, trust me, it's not just you. I didn't want *anyone* to know where I was. That's the whole point of a name change and all this." I gestured to my appearance, which made Kellen look me up and down again, his eyebrows furrowing in pain before they narrowed and his expression turned angry again.

"You should have told me."

I blinked at him, wholly confused. "Told you what?"

"You should have told me what was going on."

I jerked the bike closer to me, but he grabbed it, trying to get it out of my hands. Like he could stop me from leaving. "Why didn't... you should have told me!"

"How could I have told you?" My voice was so icy it dropped the temperature of the air a few degrees. "The two times I saw you in lock up, you spent the entire time telling me to get lost. You couldn't even be bothered to see me the last time I came to visit."

Kellen flinched, his angry expression faltering for half a second. "I was pissed."

"Right. And guess what? Now I'm pissed."

I snatched the bike back, ignoring his aggravated growl. "Goddamn it, Tate. I thought you were dead! I was scared shitless and worried sick and whatever other cliché you want to use! I was—"

"I'm sorry you thought that, but I'd like you to explain why the hell I should care when you literally told me to leave and not come back."

Kellen stepped back like I'd slapped him. Had he really not expected me to bring that up?

I sneered, my embarrassment, fear, and longing giving way to fiery hot rage. That was good. I needed to hold onto that. I needed to keep that anger because facing Kellen now, seeing him like this, with his windswept hair, broad shoulders, and scruffy face, there was a part of me that wondered how good it would feel to have him hold me again. I wondered what it would be like if I gave in and threw myself into his chest, let him wrap his arms around me and nestle into my hair. And it didn't help that the pictures on his website hadn't done him justice. They hadn't prepared me for how his boyish good looks had shifted into a handsome, more manly appearance. He was so different, but so familiar at the same time. His face had filled out, but he still had that hawkish nose, those stormy gray eyes, those kissable lips.

Seriously. Women paid top dollar for glosses and filler that promised to give him what he naturally had. They spent hours in tanning booths trying to get the bronzy peach tone of his skin. And here I was with bags hidden by concealer and contacts to muddy my blue eyes to brown. I felt... inadequate. Like I didn't have any right to be talking to him the way I was even after all he'd said to hurt me. It was wholly unfair.

"I have to go," I said, pulling the bike up and moving to push past him. Kellen tried to block me, but pushed past him, making sure to check him with my shoulder when I did. "I'm meeting someone for a story. You're interfering with my job."

His expression went stoic, lips rolling together. "When will you be back? We need to talk."

"There's nothing to say."

"The hell there isn't."

"If I remember right, you said everything I needed to hear. Don't stay here, Tate. I don't want you here. We were nothing, okay? I don't—"

Kellen's growl cut me off as he ran to get in front of me, his hands slamming down on my handlebars. "I know what I said," he snapped. "I was pissed and embarrassed and scared because I was going to prison, Tate. I went to prison for *two goddamn years!* For *you!*" He leaned in, pushing into my space as I held stock still. "I did that for you. I did it to try and protect—"

"You went in because you beat the *shit* out of Davey."

"For you!"

I didn't back down. Kellen's expression was twisted. I'd never seen him so angry, so tense. So hurt. But it didn't move me.

Priest and the other guys moved forward, and as they got closer, I recognized the one in the clean band shirt as Kellen's brother, Lane. His eyes were on his brother instead of me, concern etched into his features. Did they think I was going to call the police on him or were they worried he would hurt me?

Neither was going to happen, because I wouldn't be the cause of Kellen's arrest this time, just as I hadn't been last time. He'd done that all on his own. He'd made his choices.

And when I jerked the bike out of his grasp and glared up at him, there was a surge in my chest that felt very much like the old me. The girl that existed before that last night in Northshore, when I'd watched my life flash behind my eyes and knew no one was coming to save me. Certainly not Kellen, because he was already locked up. Tatum had almost died that night, but she'd managed to find the strength to run away and keep herself safe and whole for three years by wearing a mask and keeping her heart in check.

I'd be damned if I was going to lose it now. Not for him. Not for a guy who'd seen all my ugly, scarred, scared parts, and promised to care for them, only to look at me and turn away when I'd needed him the most.

Chapter Twelve
Kellen

SO, THIS IS WHAT IT FELT LIKE TO BE RIPPED IN HALF.

I stared at Tatum, cataloging the images of the girl in my head with the woman I saw now. Even with her narrowed eyes —that were the wrong fucking color—and guarded expression, I still couldn't stop looking at her. If anything, the alterations she'd made to herself had me more intrigued. Tiny studs dotted the lobes of her ears, and her left helix was decorated with a small silver ring that matched the one in her nostril. The tattoo behind her ear, the one that mirrored mine, was visible, but she'd added more. I saw a line of text peeking out from the neck of her T-shirt, and more ink on her wrist. Small drawings of the animals featured in the Chinese zodiac lined the length of her calf.

And the hat she was wearing, the orange one with the cat ears, told me there were somethings about Tatum that would never change.

But all the warmth I felt from seeing these glimpses into who she was now drained when she continued to glare at me, that sour expression making anger flare in my chest. This was not how I'd intended on finding her, and even though I'd told myself I'd find the right words to say when I had the chance, everything that passed through my lips was tainted with rage.

Why was she hiding from me? Me? After everything I'd done, after all I'd gone through, she didn't even want to hear me out? That wasn't the Tatum I knew.

That was someone else.

"Tate—"

"Don't, Kellen."

Her voice was sharp, and she jerked the handlebars of the bike out of my grasp. "Don't you tell me you did that for me. You got in a fight with Davey because he said something stupid and you reacted. You acted on impulse, just like you always did. But nothing you did that day was for me."

The accusation was like a slap. The second one her words had given me. My jaw clenched, and I threw my arms out, trying to scatter the pain inside me like ashes. "Then who the fuck did I do it—"

"If you'd wanted to do something for me, you would have let Davey say whatever he wanted and come upstairs to help me!"

Her voice had risen in pitch, but there was a wobble to the words, a crack in her sharp, thick veneer. Her eyes were shining, but she kept the tears back through sheer will. Girl was just as tough now as she'd always been.

"Did it ever occur to you to push past him, come upstairs, and look at me, Kellen?" She demanded. "Or was it too important to teach him a lesson? Use your fists in some stupid alpha male display of dominance."

I gritted my teeth, the words coming out tight and angry. "That wasn't what—"

"Then what happened, Kellen? What was so goddamn important that you didn't come right up to see what happened to me? I mean, Jesus." She let out a bitter laugh and threw up her hands. "Even Phil and Suzanne. When they heard the bakery hadn't been opened, they ran right there. Neither of them thought to come up and check on me."

I shook my head. "No, they did. They knocked on the door—"

"Once." She held up a finger, and I noticed her hands were shaking. "They knocked *one* time. Didn't even call my name. I'm sure they assumed I was with you, but the fact that they didn't come and check after learning I wasn't..."

She swallowed so hard I watched her throat flex, the heel of her hand swiping at her eyes. "No one bothered to check on how I was. No one cared how I was."

A knife lodged itself into my chest, the tip poking at my heart. She thought there wasn't anyone who saw her that day, but it wasn't true. Everyone in the bakery had seen her when she had appeared around the building. She'd been the only person who dared to try and pull me off Davey. There had been people watching, shouting in alarm, demanding someone call the cops. And when she'd grabbed my arm and stopped me from punching him again, I saw her.

I'd looked at her.

I hadn't thought about her like that in four years, because I didn't want to remember it. I didn't want to remember the bruises on her arms, the dark purple and blue shadows across her cheek, the split in her lip.

The terrified look in her eyes.

And I didn't want to remember how in that moment, I'd pulled away, because my anger was justified. Davey had hurt her, so I hurt him. I hurt him until the cops showed up and dragged me back, throwing me into a car while they attended to him. Someone offered to get an ambulance. Call Pastor Adler. Call someone to help Davey.

No one called anyone for Tate.

The police officers talked to witnesses, and I'd watched Tate follow them around, demanding their attention. They gave it in short spurts, and for a while I thought she might be trying to defend me. The idea made me feel sick because there was no defense for what I'd done. All I'd wanted her to do was stop.

I never considered she might not be fighting for me.

It only hit me now that maybe, in that moment, Tatum had been trying to fight for herself.

She jerked her bike away and climbed on the seat, positioning herself to take off. "I should have known from the very beginning you'd be the same as everyone else," she muttered, and the bitterness in her voice was so strong I could taste it from where I stood. "I was too fucking stupid and lovestruck to remember that as soon as it got hard, as soon as it wasn't easy and fun, you'd bail."

"I didn't bail," I snapped, grabbing her handlebars again. "And I did do that for you! I know I... I should have checked on you, but I went after him—"

"You went after him because it was easier than dealing with what he did to me," she hissed, so close to my face I could feel the heat of her breath. "It's always easier to get angry than it is to deal with what hurt you."

I didn't jerk back this time, but out of the corner of my eye, I saw Rev flinch. How many times had we heard that in those stupid group therapy sessions he dragged me to? That anger was just a disguise. A mask for the pain underneath.

It frightened me to think about how much pain Tate was hiding underneath her rage.

I let go of the handlebars, the heat in my chest dropping heavily into my stomach as I watched her wipe at her eyes. She tucked her backpack higher on her shoulders and took a breath, readying herself to ride away. She moved a few feet past me then stopped, and I braced, wondering what she would hit me with next.

"For what it's worth," she started, and the shakiness in her voice was a twist to the knife lodged in my heart. "I am sorry,

Kellen. I didn't have time to stop by county, where you wouldn't have shown up to see me, to tell you I was running away. It was the middle of the night. I'd made the decision to steal from Suzanne and Phil and I was very torn up about it. The whole thing was, I don't know..."

She turned to look at me and held up her hands, weighing them back and forth before settling on a word. "Rushed. It was very rushed. I think the phrase is running for your life. Not walking."

The heat in my stomach twisted, bile burning at my throat as every muscle in my body tensed. How bad had it been?

Tatum put her foot on the pedal and pushed, coasting out of the parking lot. I watched her go, my eyes following her as she moved into the street. She waited at the crosswalk for a bus to pass, and I thought about chasing after her. Maybe, if I threw myself in front of the bus, it might knock away the guilt that clawed at my spine. The remorse that curdled in my gut like sour milk.

You went after him because it was easier than dealing with what he did to me.

...What he did to me.

My stomach heaved and I wobbled, fucking *wobbled*, on my feet. What did he do to her? God, what did he do to her? Was I going to have to ask? Did I want to ask? Did I want to know?

I hadn't then. All I'd wanted was to hurt Davey for hurting her.

I parked my bike, heartbeat elevated but I wasn't sure why.

When Suzanne called me and said Tate hadn't showed up for work, it made both of us wonder. It wasn't like her to sleep in, but maybe she was sick.

So sick she wouldn't answer the door when Phil knocked?

She'd been fine yesterday. I'd visited her during her afternoon shift at the bar. We'd kissed. We did more than kiss. I pinned her against the wall in the storage room and the bottles of alcohol had rattled from the way our hips crashed into each other. She'd been fine.

Then that jackass showed up.

But he'd left. Davey had come into the bar right as Tate and I were finishing up, and he'd lectured her on working in such a place. It wasn't fitting for a woman of God. For his woman of God. I'd scoffed, but Tate had put a hand on my arm and told him to get lost. She didn't want anything to do with him. It was over. And not that she'd needed to make that clear to me, but she had by taking me upstairs into her bed, where I spent the next two hours erasing any trace of that asshole from her memory.

So why the fuck was he coming down the stairs, hair disheveled, looking at me with a pitying expression?

"Where's Tatum?" I asked.

"She's sleeping," Davey replied. "We had a long talk. We're working things out."

"The fuck you are. She told you to get lost."

"She didn't mean it."

"Who are you to say shit about what she means?" I stalked forward, but Davey blocked my way to the door. I raised my eyes, fingers curling into fists in my pockets. "Where is she?"

"I told you, Kellen. She's asleep. It's been a long night." He sighed and put his hands on his hips, looking a lot like his creep of a father did when he was about to give a lecture. "Tatum was angry, but she's coming around. I'm helping her see what God wants for her life and it's not you. It's never been you. I'm sorry if she tempted you during this time when she lost her way, but that wasn't real."

Yes, it is, I thought. It's been more real than anything I'd ever felt, maybe more than anything I ever would feel.

I loved her.

That much had become clear last night, when I'd been out at a party, surrounded by friends, but all I'd wanted was her. I didn't want her to leave. Or, if she did, I wanted to keep in touch. Maybe in a few months, I could move to wherever she was. I had the means, like she said. We could get a place together. I'd work and she could go to school. We'd make it work because we wanted it to. She wanted me. I knew she—

"Kellen, you need to leave. I know." Davey set his hand on my shoulder, but I shrugged it off. He chuckled at me. Fucking chuckled. "I understand, believe me, what a temptation she is. I stumbled myself, and I know that caused her—"

"You didn't fucking stumble. You had sex with her. You fucked her, and when she didn't like how you fucked her, you decided to humiliate her?" Davey's expression turned stern, but I shoved him, unsettling his balance. "Who the hell do you think you are to talk about what she wants? You didn't listen the first time, why would you start—"

"Because she's meant for me. God brought her here for a reason, into our light for a reason, and I can't let her escape that. It's..."

He looked conflicted, then pressed a hand to his chest. "It's ordained. It's been predetermined that I would find my wife in this town, and when I found her, it felt right. It's my job to bring her back into the light and if I fail, my soul will be at risk. I'm not going to fail. Tatum has to repent and come back—"

"She doesn't have to do a goddamn thing." I shoved him again, and this time Davey actually looked alarmed. He held up his hands, like that would stop me.

"Kellen, don't." He blocked my next push, trying to shove me back only to get thrown to the side. "This isn't right. I'm only following the directions given to me by the Lord—"

"I'm not exactly on speaking terms with God, but I'm pretty fucking sure he's not 'ordaining' anything for you. She doesn't want you. Deal with it. It's not her responsibility to save your soul. If you think you've fucked it up, you deal with it."

Davey's eyebrows narrowed. He looked angry, which was almost comical considering he was the unwanted party here. "God should be talking to you, but I doubt he is. And I pity you for that. Your mother was meant to bring you into the light, and she failed, and now you're... you're so easily led astray."

"Don't you talk about my mother," I snapped, stalking after him as he backed away. "Don't you ever say shit—"

"You need to know the truth. What happened to her is something that could happen to us all if we stray from the light. And I won't let Tatum meet the same demise. She has to repent and be with—"

Davey grunted when I shoved him, grabbing onto his shirt collar and slamming my fist into his nose. "Don't you fucking talk about my mother. Or Tatum. You hear me, Goddammit?" He tried to block me, but I pulled back and swung again, knocking whatever bullshit he was about to say out of his mouth. He yelped, clutching his jaw, at least until I ripped his hand away. We stumbled, and I shoved him back, pressing him into the sidewalk and punching him again.

And again.

And again...

"Kellen."

It was Lane's voice that shocked me out of the memory, his hands on my shoulders, trying to steady me as I swayed. I growled and shoved him off, fists clenched, stomach churning as the rest of the memory continued to play even though I wanted it to stop. God, I wanted it to stop. I should have let him walk away. What did it matter if he ran his fucking mouth? Nothing. It was just words.

But words hit harder than fists. Tatum's rejection, the venom she'd spit at me, proved that.

Lane moved closer, putting a hand on my back. Rev and Riot were with him, both of them wearing identical pitying expressions. I didn't need their pity. I needed her.

"Kell."

"I'm fine." I waved Lane off, running my hands through my hair as I stared in the direction Tatum had gone. Would that be the last time I saw her? Would all those words, all that anger, be the last thing I ever got to say?

No.

No, I wouldn't accept this. I couldn't.

I wanted to tell her I was sorry for what I'd said in lock-up. Tell her that it was a lie, that all I'd ever wanted was the chance to prove to her that I was worthy of her kindness, of her affection. Of her love.

She was the only person aside from Lane to ever see me, to make me feel like I wasn't wasting the chances I'd been given.

Including the ones with her. Because that's all Tatum had ever wanted. A chance for someone to choose her.

She didn't know it, but I had. I'd chosen her that first time we met under that tree, and every time I came home to spend weekends with her whenever I could. It had all been innocent, for so long until it wasn't. Until those hot summer months when we collided like stars until everything exploded and ripped us apart.

We were both here again. By chance. By some twist of fate. And I wasn't going to screw it up again. Not this time.

Not when I had nothing to lose but her.

Chapter Thirteen
Noelle

I WAS THANKFUL FOR THE RIDE TO THE COFFEE SHOP. It gave me time to calm down. I'd taken the most difficult route to get there, riding up the sharp hills and crisscrossing the annoying one-way streets that plagued the downtown area. By the time I reached my destination, I was a little sweaty and out of breath, especially considering I was wearing what was basically a stocking hat. But I didn't take it off when I parked my bike, or when I went into the shop. I needed the strength it gave me, the reminder that underneath all this chaos, I was still me.

At least I hoped I was.

Isaac was sitting at a corner table, eyes on his phone, a notepad and pencil in front of him along with a tall cup of coffee. I expected him to be angry at how late I was, but when his eyes met mine I saw calm in them, though it quickly turned to concern.

"You okay?"

"I'm fine," I lied, hoping it would suffice.

"What held you up?"

I bit the inside of my cheek. "It's not important. Anyway, here's what I found. And before you ask, yes, I gained all of this voluntarily. I said I was with *The Journal* and writing an article on missing persons cases. This is all ethical."

Isaac nodded, listening as I went over my notes on each of the cases. They matched his for the most part, all except Courtney Mackelson. Isaac shook his head when I brought her name up.

"I did some digging, and her file should have been closed out," he said, tapping my notes. "Courtney is living somewhere in New Hampshire. I found a statement she gave to an officer who's no longer at Lakeside."

I vaguely wondered if it was the same officer who'd been so terse with me when I tried to file a report on Davey. "So, she's fine."

"Yes. I called the number she left, and she did tell me about some things Pastor Adler said to her that made her leave. Him and the youth minister Brandon. They talked to her about breaking up with Marcus Betten and said it was a shame and she should think about the consequences of lending her heart out to so many when it was meant to belong to the man God had chosen for her."

I winced. The youth group leader had also been there the day Kellen and Davey got into a fight. After I hadn't been able to pull Kellen off, he'd tried to do the same right before the cops arrived.

"Pastor Adler lectured me on that too, after Davey and I broke up. And Brandon tactfully called me a whore when he saw me working at the bar one night."

I looked up to see Isaac tapping his pencil on the table, his lips twisted in thought. "Brandon was fine to me, but I watched him to be an ass to pretty much every girl in youth group. He hated Hannah because she mouthed off to him." He rolled his lips again, then lifted his eyes to mine. "What about Davey?"

I sighed, running a hand through my hair as I looked out the window. I half expected to see Davey standing there. The side-walk was empty, only a few decorative plants staring back at me.

Seeing Kellen had opened a floodgate I wasn't sure how to close. There were a thousand memories playing in my head and most of them weren't sweet. I was sure at some point the more nostalgic, happier memories would flit through my thoughts.

I hoped the thick walls and locks that kept my heart caged in would hold. It helped that Kellen had yelled at me. That helped fuel my anger with him.

If he'd have apologized, groveled for my attention, I wasn't sure what I'd have done.

"Tate."

Isaac's voice was firm, drawing me back to the conversation at hand. "You need to tell me about Davey. What if what happened between you two gives us a clue in the other cases?"

"You have nothing to compare it to establish a pattern," I pointed out. He gave me a look, but I pressed on. "I'm not saying I won't talk about it, Isaac, but say I give you my state-ment. What can you do with it?"

"At the very least, I can keep it on file in the event one of the other cases show up or we find a body." He paused after he said it, his uncomfortable expression matching mine. "We could compare notes. If we find a pattern, we can look deeper. Right now, Davey's not in contact with anyone, and when I had another officer call—like we had to because he opened the report—they left a message on a general voicemail box. No name or anything information, so we don't even know if it was the right number"

I wasn't sure what my face did, but Isaac held up a soothing hand, shaking his head. "Listen, don't let that unsettle you. If he was down here, someone would know, all right? His dad and a few other people I talked to around town said he was up in Minnesota somewhere, doing work with a non-profit organization or something. They just hadn't talked to him in a while, it doesn't mean he's looking for you."

The breath I'd been holding came out in a slow sigh, but none of the tension in my body went with it. Isaac was right. I *knew* that, but trying to explain this logic to my survival instinct was another story.

Isaac licked his lips and ran a hand over his head, letting out a heavy sigh. "Listen, Kellen told me about the fight from his perspective. But what happened *before* that?" he pressed. "Was Davey with you all night? Did something happen between the two of you that made him—"

"No," I snapped. "Nothing happened between Davey and I that should have ever given him the impression I wanted to get back together. I told him to leave so many times." Isaac frowned, but I scoffed, trying to hold myself back from slapping the table between us. "Why would you ask that? If Kellen told—"

"Kellen said you two were together all afternoon, but then he left. So you're the only person who knows what went on after that. You and Davey."

I let out a slow breath, and Isaac began drumming his fingers on the table. "Kellen said you told Davey off, but I need to check, okay? Sometimes we tell ourselves things happened because it justifies an action. Davey hurt you, Kellen hurt him." When I raised my eyebrows he let out an angry breath. "I'm asking because it's my job, Tate. I have to look at every possible angle. You're not the only one pissed about all this. It wasn't fun seeing my best friend get thrown in jail over you."

I scowled. "It wasn't over me. And it wasn't for me."

"It was because of you."

"That erases any of the personal responsibility Kellen had, which is the exact same thing Davey did when he blamed me for what we chose to do together."

Isaac's expression went stoic, and I laughed. "This is the

second time I've had this conversation today. First with Kell and now with—"

"You saw Kellen?" Isaac interrupted, eyes narrowing. "When? Did you look him up?"

He had an accusatory look on his face, and I raised my eyebrows again. "You really think I would have looked him up? After how I demanded you not tell him where I was, you think I would have gone and looked him up?"

"Sometimes people change their minds." I continued to stare at Isaac, and he began to look sheepish. "Excuse me for looking out for my friend, Tate. He had a shitty run of things, but he's got his life together now. He's doing well and I didn't—"

"You didn't want me to come and mess it up again." When I continued to stare, Isaac looked away. "Is that why…"

"Why what?"

"Why you hated me so much?"

Isaac's face flushed just enough that I noticed, and he drummed his fingers, one of his legs starting to bounce. "I didn't hate you, Tatum."

"Could have fooled me," I muttered. "If it wasn't calling me *Taint*, it was you telling Kellen I was controlling, and clingy. You called him pussy-whipped or something and said I was manipulating him. You scowled at *me* whenever he blew you guys off. You know I didn't ask him to do that, right?"

"He told me as much, but I didn't believe him." Isaac finally looked back to me and smiled. "Scratch that, I didn't *want* to believe him. I didn't want to imagine Kellen settling down with the first girl he ever loved."

I sat still in my chair, hands in my lap, my breath stuck in my lungs. My heart was the only thing that moved and I wanted to curse the traitorous organ for continuing to beat. "I doubt he loved me."

Isaac laughed, and I tilted my head. "Whatever. I know he

didn't say it, but anyone who looked at the two of you could tell."

His eyes met mine, and there was a hint of pity in them that made me bristle. "Even if that was true, why did it bother you so much?"

"Because I thought it was a colossally bad idea. How many people marry the first person they love? Or if they do, how many of those marriages actually last?"

I shrugged. "Often enough that love at first sight is a trope. And there isn't any guarantee that marrying your third or fourth love will work out either."

Isaac's eyebrows bounced. "Fair. Even so." He scrunched his nose at me and gave me a sympathetic shrug. "I didn't like it. Maybe it bothered me since I was in full rebellion mode at that point in my life. I'd been told how my 'urges' were evil but I kept having them, so I figured why fight it? I was screwing everything and anything that would let me and feeling shame half the time when I was done. Kellen wasn't doing that, but when he *did* decide to sleep with someone, he felt no guilt about it. He carried no shame about his desires and how he liked things in bed, and maybe I was jealous because he was wasting guilt-free sex on one girl when he could have been having it with twenty."

"He wouldn't have been able to do that," I pointed out, knowing that Kellen's circle of friends was small, but his collection of lovers was smaller still. Two before me, but I didn't know how many after. He told me he felt no desire without emotional connection, so the idea of casual sex was out.

Which was another reason his assertions that we were just friends with benefits hadn't rung true to me. Or to Isaac, apparently. Maybe not even to Kellen, but it was a lie he chose to tell himself and press upon me, because all he'd wanted me to do was leave that town.

And all I'd wanted was for him to come with me.

I let out a long sigh and patted the table. "Well, if it's of any consolation, Isaac, I have no plans of messing Kellen's life up again or letting him mess up mine. It's over." Isaac looked at me, a grimace on his face while I shrugged again. "Running into him was a fluke. He knows my neighbor, and I saw them talking in the parking lot of my apartment. My lease is up in the spring, and I'll probably be moving. End of story."

Even though I'd said exactly what Isaac wanted to hear, he didn't look pleased when he sat forward, tapping the paper again. "I don't think you'd screw his life up, Tate. You'd probably make it better, if I'm honest. But you've been clear how you feel, and I just don't want to see him hurt."

I wrinkled my nose. "Neither do I. So I'll keep my distance."

"If he'll let you."

Isaac grinned when I gave him a deadpan expression. "I'm just saying. Don't be surprised if he starts visiting this neighbor of yours more often now that he knows your there. Who was it by the way?"

"Priest Callaghan."

"No, shit, really?" His grin grew wider. "I know him. If anything, you should thank him that Kellen is in one piece. He kept him from getting his ass kicked on the inside."

I winced, unsurprised to hear this, but the image of Kellen in a jumpsuit trying to fight someone with an actual criminal record, and Priest—who I'd only ever seen get angry once— pulling him back wasn't a pretty one. I didn't want to think about him like that. I didn't want to think about either of them like that.

Maybe Kellen was right to cut me off. If I'd have stayed, it might have messed up his sentence. Knowing I was outside and free where he was trapped could have messed with his head more than prison already would.

Knowing the logic behind is actions didn't make them sting any less.

"Okay, enough dancing around this. Tell me what happened with Davey that night. For that matter, tell me what happened with him after Kellen went in." Isaac gave me an expectant look, and when I hesitated, he sighed. "Did you report any of it?"

"I told you, I tried two or three times, Isaac. No one would listen." I exhaled heavily and ran my hands through my hair, folding my arms on the table and letting my head fall into them for a moment before I sat up. "I brought in the notes Davey left in my mailbox, pictures of when he keyed my car. They said I couldn't prove it was him and the guy said to come back when I had proof. He didn't even file a report, Isaac."

His shoulders sagged and he blew out a long breath. "And I can't file one now, but you can give me a statement, Tate. I'm on your side, I swear. I'm not going to use this against you. What motive would I have to do that?"

My throat was so tight it hurt when I swallowed, and I thought about mentioning he could tell Kellen the whole story. Use it as a reason for him to stay away from me due to all the obvious trauma.

Not that it mattered, because I wanted him to stay away. I didn't want Kellen in my life. Not even as a friend.

I had to keep up that lie, along with all the other ones I was telling. It was like a ring of dominoes at this point, and I wasn't sure how many more I could line up before the whole thing came tumbling down.

"Okay, fine," I warned Isaac, bracing myself for the sick feeling that was building in my gut, the tension slowly weaving its way into my muscles. "I'm only repeating this once, understand?"

Isaac nodded, tapping his pencil on the paper. "Whenever you're ready."

Chapter Fourteen
Noelle

HE LEFT.

I fisted the sheets, opening one eye, then the other, before finally lifting my head. My lips trembled as I looked around the room, the bottom one swollen and aching. I breathed out a shaky sigh of relief. He was gone. He left...

I had to get help.

I sat up, every muscle screaming. I took an inventory, the memories of last night flashing through my head. Davey showing up literally minutes after Kellen left, so angry he was crying, shouting at me because I was damning him. "You're crazy," I muttered before trying to shut the door in his face.

The rest of it was a blur. A chaotic menage of images and sounds. Davey's shouts, my screams of anger, then fear. His hands slapping me. Backhanding me. The sound of my head hitting the wall. The floor. The bed creaking when he threw me onto it, more screams when he tried to tear off my clothes and I fought him. I was temptation. I was lust incarnate. I was defiled.

I was ruined.

He fought with himself more than me. Wrestling with some demon he thought I'd given him. Why did I make him want me? Why did I decide to *tempt him and make him lose control? He'd hit me until I couldn't fight, tried to get my clothes off only to give up and sob because he couldn't. We had to wait until we were married. When I would submit to him.*

It would never happen.

I crawled out of bed, walking on shaky legs toward where my phone had been thrown against the wall. The screen was cracked, but I could see missed calls. Kellen's name. Phil's. Suzanne's. Missed texts.

You up?

Guess not.

Hey, let's talk tomorrow.

Then they changed from playful to frantic.

Where are you? Tatum, answer me.

And another from Suzanne.

Tatum, is everything okay? You were supposed to open this morning?

A noise outside startled me. Shouts, then screams. I cautiously walked to my door, opening it to find the small hallway that led downstairs empty. The noise grew louder as I descended, louder still when I got outside. My feet carried me around the building. I was moving blindly, almost numb, wondering if someone in the crowd could help me.

But no one gave me any notice, not with the chaos on the sidewalk.

"Stop!"

"Someone call the police!"

I blinked, pushing through the crowd without thinking toward where Kellen was. His fist raised, Davey on the ground underneath him, blood running from his nose, staining his teeth. "Kellen," *I whispered, moving closer and grabbing his arm to stop him.* "Kellen, stop!"

Kellen turned to look at me, his face twisted in rage, gray eyes already wide, but they went wider when he saw me. Pain flashed across his features, his shoulders rising and falling with exertion or panic, I didn't know what.

"Kellen…"

My voice was shaky when I spoke, and his name was more of a plea than a bid to get his attention. Please, don't do this.

But it was too late. Kellen let out a roar and pulled away from me, grabbing Davey's shirt and shaking him.

"What did you do, you psychopath?!" he screamed before hitting him. "What did you do?!"

I tried to stop him again, but there was no chance. Davey fought, but all that running he'd done for basketball, the weights he'd lifted, it was no match for Kellen's innate strength, and the anger fueling him.

Anger over what Davey had done to me.

"Kellen, stop!" I yelled as I was shoved back, people moving me aside out of an urge to protect me from him. Would they believe me if I told them the man on the ground was the danger? The one with the perfect GPA and hundreds of hours of volunteer time? Would they believe it if I told them the guy who'd just got back from church camp was a bigger threat than the guy punching him?

Maybe if Kellen stopped.

I kept screaming his name, my voice lost in the crowd. Sirens wailed. Police poured out of their cars. They seized Kellen by the arms, dragging him back, revealing Davey dazed and visibly injured on the sidewalk. There were calls for an ambulance, and people crowded around Davey, comforting him.

"Officer!" I shouted, trying to grab one of the cops standing around. Kellen was already in the car, and there was no way he was getting out, but I didn't want Davey to get away either.

"Officer—"

"Not now."

"No, listen. Davey Adler, he attacked me last night."

"That's not what this is about." The officer moved away, but another one came to take his place. He looked me over, and I stood still, letting him examine me.

"You say that he did this?" he gestured to Davey. "That's Mark Adler's son."

"Yes."

"He's the Pastor."

"I don't care who he is, Davey attacked—"

"Young lady, I have a hard time believing that when the guy you've been all over town with all summer is the one with the temper." He scowled at me, and I gaped in shock. "Don't think we haven't seen you two riding around. We let you get a pass because you weren't doing any harm, but this is the last straw. Don't try to cover up for him."

"Cover... no!" I shouted. "No, Kellen didn't do this. He wouldn't—"

"Seems like the type who would."

I couldn't believe what I was hearing. The officer scowled at me, then turned away, frowning when I grabbed him. "I want to make a report. You can check my apartment for fingerprints. Davey Adler attacked me—"

"Come to the station and make a statement, we're not taking it now."

He jerked away, jogging over to where someone was trying to help load Davey onto a stretcher. The ambulance had arrived, they were focused on him. The crowd on the street was focused on him. There were officers getting into the car with Kellen, focused on getting him out of here and into lockup.

No one wanted to listen.

No one had time to listen.

No one had time to see...

Chapter Fifteen
Noelle

I FINISHED GIVING ISAAC MY STATEMENT, BUT I didn't go home right away. Instead, I rode my bike down to the lake, where I watched families with their kids and couples out for walks pull in and out of the parking lot. The sun started to set, and the lights on the walkway bridge over the water came on. It was pretty. Whimsical almost. But I never considered walking on it at night, not after Elissa told me it was always covered with spiders.

Just one more thing I'd never do thanks to an unnecessary, uncontrollable phobia. I'd add it to the list, right under going out to a bar again, and getting into a relationship.

By the time I got home, it was nearly dark, and I was starving. My muscles ached as I hauled my bike upstairs, and even though I tried to be quiet I ended up bumping the walls a few times with the handlebars, then the front tire. Grace had never been my strong suit but I'd wore myself out and I knew I was going to regret it tomorrow.

Haku trotted over to greet me when I got inside, circling my legs as I shoved the bike into the alcove alongside my coat rack and sank to the floor, flopping onto my back. He nosed my cheek, purring loudly between soft, pleading meows.

"You're not gonna die. I'll feed you in a bit." I tilted my head, letting him push his cheek into mine. "You think you could return the favor? Order take out for me?"

The cat nuzzled my cheek right when my phone buzzed in my pocket. I'd turned off the ringer and had been ignoring the texts that came in while I rode around, figuring if it was an emergency at work, someone would call me.

I wrinkled my nose and pulled the device out of my pocket, frowning at the messages from Priest, Hannah, and Pak. Pak's was the most recent, and possibly the most important, so I opened it first.

Pak: *You free tomorrow morning? There's a conference E was supposed to cover but she's sick. Thought maybe you could pick it up.*

Me: *Yes. What's the conference and where is it?*

Pak: *Events center. Leading Reformative Change in Ministry. Service starts at 9:00. I can give you a ride...?*

I pressed my lips together and looked up the conference to confirm my suspicions. When Pak said "service" he meant it literally. The conference was described as a gathering of youth and adult ministry professionals who were tackling difficult conversations with their congregations. Part of me hoped there would be discussions on poverty, or discrimination, or other real world challenges their congregants faced.

But when I looked through the list of small group sessions, I found focus groups that discussed sin, specifically sexual sin, purity, and how to guide their congregants toward the "right" decisions. Read: how to encourage teenagers with raging hormones and impulsive brains that everything sexual, including their own bodies, was shameful and even an innocent kiss could lead to damnation, let alone anything else.

Or, maybe not. Maybe they would discuss healthy relationships and how sex could be something joyful and intimate. The messages I received as a teen could have been ones tailored specifically to Twin Valley's congregation in Northshore, but since I'd gotten out I learned it was a common message a lot of people had heard growing up. The rings we were encouraged to put were welcoming gifts. A promise I was making to myself and everyone else that I would do my best to stay pure for myself and for the community I was now part of.

Pastor Adler, Davey's father, had been preaching in Northshore for about ten years when I'd moved there, and his message had largely remained the same even as times and the town changed. He'd stressed the importance of community, and that they needed to keep their village alive through faith. Pastor Adler promised that if we all stayed true to the words he preached, and the lessons given to us from his pulpit, God's blessings and better days would come. Boys were told the importance of upholding God's tenets; girls were reminded that their role was to support their husbands and guard their hearts. Both were told that dating meant giving pieces of yourself away time and time again, and without a full heart, salvation and the blessings that had been promised, could be lost.

But the arrival of those blessings depended on people staying within Northshore, or at least close by, to help it grow. And as it always happened in small towns, people were tempted to leave for larger areas and more opportunity. Jobs, and school, and the allure of the world. Davey had echoed his father's, sometimes using me as an example. I'd come from outside of Northshore and had been exposed to all sorts of demonic things. Secular music and television. I was so lucky to have come there, because without their intervention, I was damned for sure. All the more reason I had to stay. Specifically, why I had to stay with Davey.

As much as I convinced my teenage self that I believed those messages, the truth was always clear. Kellen helped me see that the summer we had together, but even before that, I had my suspicions. I never saw any sign of blessings, and each year I lived in Northshore, it seemed to shrink more and more. And the more citizens the town hemorrhaged, the more it was clear there was no bandage of faith that could keep it alive.

I sighed as I scrolled through the conference webpage, deciding that even if I had to listen to a repeat of that twisted message, having my name on the article would be worth it. The more I got myself out there, the sooner I could be independent.

I looked back to my phone, typing out a reply to Pak.

Me: *Sounds good. I won't need a ride. I can meet you there.*

I sent the message, then grimaced. How many times I could keep deflecting his cautious advances without giving him an outright rejection? I'd turned guys down before, but it was different with Pak. He was nice, and cute in a nerdy way.

But there was no desire. No attraction. And I didn't know if it was because I was genuinely not attracted to him, or too scared to let myself be. Maybe, after having my heart shattered by Kellen, and everything that happened with Davey, I'd never feel desire again.

I frowned, pushing thoughts of my grim future as a paranoid cat lady aside to deal with Hannah's message. I swiped it open, a little surprised by what I read.

Han: *I know you're probably pissed at me for telling Kellen your name. It slipped out. I really didn't mean for it to happen, Noelle. And I had no idea that other guy he was with would actually know you. I'm sorry.*

I frowned, but not because I was angry. I really wasn't. Somewhere in my logical brain, I knew I'd have to tell Kellen I was okay eventually; I'd only wanted to wait a while to let the idea of talking with him again sink in.

I pursed my lips at the text, trying to think of how to reply. Hannah had also called me Noelle instead of Tatum, which meant she was trying. She wanted to get to know me as I was now and didn't expect me to change back to who I'd been before.

But that fact made clear something I hadn't wanted to admit: I'd missed hearing the sound of my name.

My real name.

I hadn't thought about it much when I'd first run into Hannah and Isaac at the coffee shop, but looking back, I'd responded so easily to Tatum, or Tate, even after correcting them. And hearing Kellen say my name this afternoon had been the same way. I hadn't bothered to correct him.

Most people hated their name for one reason or another, but I'd always liked mine. Changing it hadn't been a decision driven out of a desire for self-renewal. It had been survival. I didn't want the name Tatum Ivers on my mailbox, rental agreement, bank accounts, taxes, or anything someone could look up to find me.

But it truly felt like a mask. One I put on every day to hide where I'd buried who I really was.

Me: *It's all right. And you can call me Tate. It's okay.*

Han: *You sure?*

Me: *Yeah. The name change was more for legal purposes than anything else. My co-workers and professors are really the only ones who know me as Noelle.*

I winced, wondering if Hannah would ask about my friends, and then I'd have to explain that I didn't really have any outside of Priest. Maybe Elissa, but that was a work friendship. We'd never done anything outside of the office.

Because I always turned her down when she tried.

Just like I always turned Pak down when he tried.

Like I'd turned down anyone when they tried.

Han: *I'm off next weekend. We should do dinner. Or I can come over and we can order pizza.*

I thought about the pizza I was about to order tonight, how I'd be eating it for the next three days. It would be nice to have someone to share it with for once.

Me: *Yeah, okay. Either option sounds fun.*

Han: *Cool. Just text me. Xoxo.*

She was so casual. There was no pressure to be one person or the other. Hannah just wanted me as... me.

Kind of like Priest, who'd never questioned anything about my life until the other night, and that had only been because of my connection to Kellen, who was also his friend.

I dismissed the texts from Hannah and opened Priest's few messages, finding another apology.

PC: *I didn't plan on the guys coming over this afternoon. That's not how I wanted Kellen to find out I knew you. Wanted to talk to you more about it first. Sorry.*

PC: *You're out later than normal.*

PC: *Assuming you didn't run off since all your shit is still in your apartment. Would have heard it if you moved out. No one is going to bug you, Noelle. Not Kellen. Not anyone. Got it? You don't need to hide. Text me when you get home.*

I smiled to myself, reading an unspoken request for me not to be angry or cut Priest out of my life because of Kellen, which I hadn't even considered.

Me: *I'm not mad. And no, I'm not moving out or running. I couldn't if I wanted to. Honestly, not even sure my car will start.*

I closed out the message, hoping it would suffice, and placed an order for pizza from a place down the street, making sure I picked something I'd be fine eating for the next two days. The place was close so I could walk down to get it, which would save me some money, but delivery was a luxury I was going to indulge in tonight.

I'd tugged on jersey pants and an old T-shirt and was pouring food into Haku's bowl when my phone buzzed. I walked to the table, expecting to see a text indicating my order was ready.

But that wasn't what greeted me when opened the lock screen.

Unknown: *Your car won't start?*

I threw the phone halfway across the table, like it would

explode if I didn't drop it. My hands shook as I leaned over, watching the screen, waiting for another message. All the while, I was hyper aware that my old phone, the one with the cracked screen that I'd stopped charging about six months after I moved, was in a box in my room. There were at least twenty to thirty unopened messages on it. All from unknown numbers. All the same threat.

Unknown: *You must repent or you'll suffer God's wrath.*

Unknown: *You cannot hide from your judgement.*

Unknown: *Those who stray from the light will perish in eternal darkness.*

Unknown: *Temptress*

Unknown: *Harlot*

Unknown: *Deceiver*

The phone on the table dinged, and a second message came through, same number.

Unknown: *It's Kellen.*

My shoulders slumped and I let out the breath I'd been holding, but there was no relief when I inhaled again. I was still on edge from talking to Isaac, recalling those memories bringing everything else I'd been through to the forefront of my mind.

How in the *hell* had Kellen gotten my phone number? And why, after everything I'd said to him that afternoon, would he think I wanted to speak with him? Or tell him anything about my life? Including the status of my car?

Haku curled around my legs, purring while I made a snarling noise and closed out the text, making the executive decision to deal with this on a full stomach. Kellen could wait. He'd made me do it long enough, now it was time to give him a taste of his own medicine.

Chapter Sixteen
Kellen

MY PHONE WAS ON THE BAR COUNTER. THE RINGER ON full volume. I didn't need to stare at it. If Tate texted back, I'd hear it even over the noise in the bar.

But I kept glancing down anyway, nursing two beers then a few shots of whiskey with Lane, who rolled his eyes every time I picked it up to check and see if Tate had texted me back.

"I drive all this way to spend time with you, and here we are, hot girls everywhere, and you're making me watch you pine—"

"No one is making you do anything, jackass," I snapped. "You can get laid all on your own, just throw the goddamn sheets in the wash when you're done."

Cas laughed from behind the bar, pointing a long finger at Lane. "Shit, if you take a girl home, that'll be the most action Fox has seen in over a year, right?"

Lane gaped at me because this idea was foreign to him. We were the same but different. Neither of us formed attachments easily, and whether that was an innate characteristic, or a consequence of our upbringing wasn't clear. But his blasé attitude allowed him to make friends with a simple smile and bring any person who caught his eye into his bed. Meanwhile my sheets

were cold even in the dead of summer, and I preferred it
that way.

There were a few nights I'd tried to warm them. When I'd
found someone to kiss and touch, and go through the motions
because, why not? But when it was over, I'd felt empty. My
desire for sex, for intimacy, had vanished with Tate, and there
were times I wondered if I'd ever feel it again.

Which was why, now that I'd found her, I was going to do
everything I could to keep her, now that I knew what losing her
had cost me.

I checked my phone again, listening to Cas and Lane talk
about his crotch rocket as Riot gave him hell for being a
Weekend Warrior. Lane tried to argue that he rode to work on
the weeks when it was nice out, but neither guy was having it,
and I smiled to myself as I looked to Rev, unsurprised to see he
was still frowning.

"She hasn't texted me back. Worst thing that could happen
is she'll block me."

"Would serve you right. And don't fucking touch my phone
again. You're my friend, not my goddamn secretary." He
narrowed his green eyes, meeting my frown with a stern glare.
"She made it pretty clear she wants fuck all to do with you."

I frowned. "She made it clear she was pissed at me. She
never said she didn't want to see me."

"She said she didn't want to talk."

"I'm not asking her to talk. I'm asking about her car."

Rev scoffed, but it was half a laugh. "I admire your ability to
bullshit your way in and out of stuff."

"The more I drink, the better I get at it," I said, tipping my
glass in his direction. He gave me a look, and I nodded, having
gleaned the warning in his words. I was walking a fine line and
could very well bullshit my way into believing that just because
Tate hadn't specifically said *I don't want to see you*, I might have a
chance when in truth I didn't.

But I meant what I said. She didn't have to talk. Fuck, at this point I'd sit with her in silence. That would be enough. As long as I could see her.

"What did you say to Hannah the other night?" I asked him, watching his eyebrows soften. "Still a little pissed at you for not ever mentioning your neighbor was named Noelle."

"Didn't seem important." He rubbed at the stubble on his chin, the tattoos on his arms flexing. "I didn't scare Hannah if that's what you're asking. I asked her what Noelle looked like. Well, I described what Noelle looked like—"

"Tatum."

Rev levied a scolding look in my direction. "I told Hannah what my neighbor *Noelle* looked like, and we decided it was the same person. Then I talked to *Noelle* and figured it out." I scowled and he raised his eyebrows. "What if she tells you she'd love to hang out, but you have to call her by her new name? You gonna argue then?"

My scowl deepened. He had a point. As much as I liked Tatum's name, I'd call her Noelle or the Queen of France if it meant getting back in her good graces.

I was about to tell Rev he was right, but a tap on my shoulder made me look back at Cas. His eyes were on the front door of the bar, where Isaac was weaving his way through a crowd of people.

"You've got company, Fox."

I nodded, well aware that Isaac was on thin ice because of his profession. There were a few cops who were friends of the club, but Rush and Cas were very selective about them. They had a healthy suspicion of anyone who could nark someone out over a minor offense and get one of the brothers sent back to prison when all of us were working so hard to stay clean.

Isaac had on the same jeans and shirt I'd seen him in earlier this afternoon, when he swung by my house to say hi quick before heading downtown for a meeting. There were a few open positions in the metro's force he was interested in, ones that would mean a shift in his career. No longer a cop, but a detective.

But that came with strings, and those stings turned the head of every guy wearing a cut when he walked in. They didn't say anything because they knew he was my friend, but the tone in the room from the club was tense until Cas whistled, the universal signal for everyone to settle. I nodded at Cas in thanks. Isaac wasn't here to start trouble.

At least I hoped not.

"Thought you were going out with Hannah," I said, watching him roll his eyes.

"I went over to her complex for dinner, but there's only so much I can take of her roommates. Shit, there's only so much she can take of her roommates. They're all working nine-to-five jobs and she's working twelve hour shifts four days a week. They don't get it why she's not up for partying all hours. But that's her business not mine." He sat next to me on the stool, pursing his lips before turning to Cas. "I'm actually not here to socialize. I'm here for something else."

I tensed, and I looked at Cas to see him smirking softly, wiping down a shot glass before he set it in front of Isaac. "Oh yeah? What's that?"

"Wondering if you guys had anyone who could look something up for me. Off the books." Isaac took the glass, spinning it around in his fingers. "Not exactly a legal search."

Cas' grin grew wider. "What info you needing?"

"I need to find someone."

"Who?"

Isaac looked to me, eyebrows pinched together. "David Adler."

"The fuck you looking him up for?" I asked. "Didn't Tate ask you *not* to tell him where—"

"I'm not calling to tell him where she is. Especially not now."

Anger flashed on his face, and I felt my stomach twist. What did he know? What had that asshole done? "But I've tried all my search engines and I can't find where he is. He's still on Facebook, but his location isn't listed, and when I called his dad again he said last he knew Davey was up in Minnesota somewhere, but they haven't spoken in about a year."

"Why'd you call him? What's he got to do with Tate?"

"I didn't call him about Tate. I called to ask him some general question about some other cases."

I sat up straighter, unease swirling in my chest. "Cases?"

Isaac pressed his lips together. "Tate made some calls for an article she's writing. She wasn't the only girl missing from around Northshore and I'm trying to see if there's a connection."

My eyebrows rose, and Isaac mirrored the motion. "Yeah. And based on what she told me this afternoon, I have a few questions for Davey, so I need to find where he is. It might give her some peace of mind if I can confirm where he is, and tell her it's nowhere around here," he added as an aside. I bit the inside of my cheek, staring at him in confusion.

"She was who you met up with this afternoon?" I asked. "I thought you were going to the station."

"I met her before that. We had coffee." My hand gripped the counter, knuckles turning red, and Isaac rolled his eyes. "Jesus, Kell. It wasn't like that. She's using me as a source cause I could pull up information she couldn't."

My stomach twisted, and I drummed my fingers, trying to ignore the tension weaving its way into my jaw. "Did she talk to you?" I asked. "Like... talk? About what happened? Why she left?"

He rolled his lips and blew out a breath. "Some, but I'm not going to tell you what she said. It's not my story to tell, but..."

He looked at me, then looked behind me, jerking his head at Rev. "He keeping an eye on her?"

"Unofficially," Rev answered.

"Good," Isaac replied, and when I looked at him he shook his head. "Just in case. She pokes around too much she might end up finding a bear, and I just want to know someone's around that might help her out."

The alcohol I'd drank had made my thoughts a little foggy, but they cleared up fast. Rev was fine, but if Tate needed help, I wanted to do it. She didn't even have ask. I'd drive back to Northshore and set the damn town on fire if it made her feel safe.

Isaac frowned and looked back to Cas, setting the shot glass he'd been fiddling with on the bar. "So, you got someone that can help me? I'm not gonna nark on them cause this could get me in trouble, too. I'm taking a risk here. I don't have a reason to get a warrant or issue a subpoena, but if he talks to me, I might not need one. I just gotta find him first."

Cas looked at me, but I wasn't any help. It wasn't my decision whether the club helped Isaac. I was still a prospect.

But something in Cas' expression said he wanted my opinion. Because I was involved in this by proxy.

"Looper might be able to help," I suggested. "He's into all that tech shit. Might be able to look him up."

Cas nodded. "He's home tonight cause his wife's morning sickness lasts all day." He pulled out a bottle of whiskey, pouring a shot into the glass in front of Isaac. "Hey, Mack. Come over here. Got something you might be interested in."

Mack got up off his stool, sauntering over, looking as broad as his namesake. Isaac sat patiently, waiting for Cas to introduce them so he could explain himself. I settled in to listen, but my phone vibrated on the bar, ringing loud enough that Isaac and Cas both jumped. I snatched it off the counter, eyes widening at the name on the screen.

Tatertot.

Tate was calling me.

I looked at Rev, who only shrugged and gestured while I plugged one ear and put the phone to the other, stumbling as I got off the barstool. My head was clear, but I was still tipsy.

Keep it together, asshole. Don't blow this.

"Hey."

A caustic, almost sinister laugh tickled my ear. "You have got some nerve, buddy."

Fuck.

This shouldn't surprise me. It didn't surprise me, but I wasn't sure how to respond to her anger. My text had been well intentioned on several levels. I was genuinely concerned about her car. I could fix it. I wouldn't even charge her.

And I'd also wanted her to have my number.

Just in case.

"I wanted you to have my number."

"Against my wishes, apparently."

I winced, and she scoffed on the other end of the line. "Do you have any idea how much that scared me? A text from an unknown number? Asking about my car? Jesus, Kellen. I was terrified until you let me know who it was."

I winced. "I'm sorry," I said, meaning it. "I didn't mean to scare you. But I don't have any idea how much it scared you because you…"

I paused, and she filled in the space. "Because I what?"

"Because you haven't told me why you're so scared."

Tatum growled on the other end of the line. "Why would I? After speaking to you—no, *fighting* with you—earlier today about how I didn't want you to find me, and going back and forth about whether or not it was my fault that you ended up in jail—"

"It wasn't your fault. I never said it was your fault, or thought it was your fault." She made another angry noise, but I pressed on, desperate for her to understand. "Maybe I did it for you, but that was my choice. You're right."

I swallowed, encouraged that she was letting me talk without arguing back. "If I had the chance again, I'd do it differently."

The wooden railing outside the bar creaked when I leaned against it, letting it hold most of my weight as I folded my free arm over my chest. I needed to make her see that this wasn't an attempt to force my way into her life. Well, at least not completely.

"Can we start over?" I asked when she still didn't speak, grimacing at her wry laugh.

"From when, Kellen? This afternoon? That summer? Eight years ago by the tree?"

A soft laugh escaped me as I thought of the tree, and how many times I'd sat underneath it with her. "My dad wanted to cut that tree down a while ago, but I threw a fit. Told him I'd buy the place from under him if he did."

She was quiet again, then I heard the ghost of a laugh. "You got that upset over a tree?

"I like that tree. I have a lot of good memories at that tree."

More silence, then Tatum sighed. "Seems like a waste to have a house down there if you're never there to use it."

"True," I agreed, pursing my lips. "Sort of like it seems wasteful to stay mad at you for making decisions I sort of... forced you to make. Not that I forced you to leave, but you know." I scuffed my toe on the deck, rubbing at the dirt marks and trying to smear them. "I pushed you in the direction I thought was best instead of letting you make the decision."

Tate sighed. "You were looking out for me. Someone had to."

"Probably could have looked out for you better if I hadn't gotten sent to prison."

"What did Davey say to you that day?" she asked after a short beat of silence. "You never gave me the chance to ask."

"He spouted some nonsense about how God had ordained you to be his wife, and I was just a mistake." My fingers curled into a fist by my ribs, and I squeezed myself tighter, digging my toe into a knot in the wood. "He apologized to me for how you tempted me. It was just bullshit."

"And that set you off?"

"No." I swallowed. If I wanted her to be honest with me, to open up, I'd have to do the same. Intimacy was a give and take, and Tate had always given way more to me than I had to her. "He said something about my mom failing me, and that she deserved what happened cause she strayed or some shit."

Tate didn't reply, so I went on, gritting my teeth at the memory. "It pissed me off, but still. I shouldn't have gone after him. I should have come up to check on you. He said you were asleep," I told her, listening to the sad laugh she gave in reply.

"I'd been faking it for a few hours at that point, hoping he'd get bored and leave."

"Bored of what?"

"Not now, Kellen."

Her voice was heavy, and I remembered Isaac said he'd talked to her today, so I decided not to push. Remembering that day had been bad enough for me, I wasn't going to make her do it twice.

"So, tell me about your car?" I asked, changing the subject. "You might remember, I do know a few things about them. Maybe I could help."

She laughed, and I closed my eyes, savoring the sound. "Priest said I needed a new battery. Or a new alternator. Probably both."

"What kind of car is it?"

"Pontiac."

I groaned internally. "Those parts are hard to come by."

"I figured. The car only cost me $1000, though. And I don't drive it much."

There was a tone in her voice that made me think there was more to it than the car just being old and unreliable, but again, I wasn't going to push. She was talking. We were talking. It was a start.

"Take a picture and send it to me. I can see what's out there."

"Or, you could ask Priest about it."

"I could also come by. That asshole owes me dinner or something anyway. We haven't hung out outside of rides with the club and work since he started dating Vicky."

"That's over, though. And thank God." She laughed again, this time with real humor. "I was tired of listening to her fake porn screams."

"How do you know what screams sound like in porn?"

Her breath caught, and I grinned to myself when she made another irritated noise. This one was less angry, more playful. Progress.

"You're a menace. I have to go. I have an assignment tomorrow."

"College or job?"

"Both, actually. So, I need my sleep." There was a pause, and I decided to let her to hang up first. I didn't want to end this, hoping it would send a signal that I didn't just mean the phone call. Tate sighed on the other end of the line, and I wished I was there with her so I could feel it on my neck.

"For what it's worth, Kellen, I'm happy for you. I'm glad you're doing well. You have a good life, and you deserve that."

A tightness settled into my chest, creeping upward to my jaw, making it difficult to speak. "So do you, Tate."

A soft laugh, but there was a sadness to it that made the tightness turn into an ache. *Baby, I'm here,* I thought. *Whatever you need, I'm here.*

"Don't linger on this, okay? I'm fine. I don't need you to worry about me anymore."

"Tate, it's…" Shit. Her name. "I mean, Noelle. It's not about me—"

"You can call me Tate, Kellen. Just… don't plan on calling me often, okay?" she said, her voice tight. "I don't want cause you anymore suffering than I have already."

I shook my head like she could see me. "You didn't make me—"

"I gotta go. Bye."

My mouth was open, words on the tip of my tongue, a plea for her to listen to me. But the line clicked off, and silence filled my ear. I lowered the phone, fighting the urge to kick the ground and swear. I should have known it wasn't going to be that easy. Nothing ever was.

But that only convinced me she'd be worth it in the end.

Chapter Seventeen

Noelle Tatum

PAK WAS WALKING ALONGSIDE ME TOWARD THE EXIT of the Events Center, wearing clothes that put me on edge even though they shouldn't. He blended in with the other attendants of the conference: black slacks and a button down, his hair parted and swept to the side. I'd dressed to blend in as well, wearing a long skirt and a white long-sleeved top, one that I'd made sure covered the bulk of my tattoos. The one on my neck was hidden by a loose scarf and at least a pound of full coverage makeup I'd gotten a at a drug store late last night. The damn thing had given me away already, and I wasn't going to risk it happening again.

"What are you up to the rest of the afternoon?" Pak asked when we got outside.

"Not much. I completely forgot I have an assignment due in Long Form Media tomorrow, and I can't use this article since it'll run tomorrow, which means I have to finish the first draft of the other one I've been researching."

"Yikes, that's a lot of writing."

I shrugged, making my way across the street to where I'd parked my bike on a rack. "I type fast, fortunately. It'll be fine"

"Well at least let me buy you lunch," he offered, eyebrows raised in hope when I turned to look at him. "Seriously, my treat. You took this on as short notice on top of all the other work you've been doing."

My stomach rumbled on cue, giving away the I'm not hungry excuse I'd planned on using. I had no reason to turn him down. If anything, it gave me more time to probe him about the small groups he'd gone to while I interviewed the conference organizers.

"Sure, lunch sounds great."

Pak beamed, and guilt slammed into me like I'd stepped into traffic.

We walked to one of the nearby restaurants, a wooden building that had a purposely run-down feel that complimented its aesthetic. Pak led most of the conversation during lunch, commiserating on how bad finals were and recalling the whimsy he'd felt when he graduated. He'd graduated about two years ago and moved here for a job since he couldn't get in where he lived. Too much competition, plus he liked the cozy feel of the state. That he could be in a big city while also feeling like it was a small town.

If only he knew how true that statement was.

Eventually the conversation turned to me, and I tried to keep things vague, probing him for things I could put into the article instead of giving up info about myself. The only thing I did reveal were my plans for the future. He already knew I wanted to do independent articles, but I was hoping that a staffer position was in my future too. The internship was nice, but I'd need something that paid a little more if I was going to make this work. I really didn't want to get a second job.

"I wouldn't worry too much," Pak assured me, winking just before the waitress arrived with the ticket. "It's all but official at this point, so don't be surprised if Gina calls you into her office sometime soon."

He handed the waitress his card, ignoring the cash I pulled out as he leaned forward on the table. "So, now that I have you alone..."

The words weren't a threat. I knew that. I knew Pak was harmless. We were in public, there was absolutely no threat. And it was such an innocuous statement. He probably meant it to be seductive, which was a problem I'd have to deal with later. But I couldn't focus on it now.

Because my heart rate spiked so hard it made me feel faint. Every muscle in my body tensed, the memory so fresh after talking about it yesterday.

"Get out!" I screamed.

"No!" Davey pushed so hard on the door it moved me back a few inches. "I need to talk to you alone."

"What's it gonna take to get you to go out with us?" Pak asked, a half-smile on his face, completely oblivious to the fact that my hands were clenched in my lap, my legs braced, my whole body ready to run. He drummed his fingers and shrugged one shoulder. "Everyone likes you, and I'd... well, I'd like to get to know you better."

"I'm really not that interesting," I said, my voice tight and a little breathless. Pak laughed, right when the hostess walked by with new patrons. I looked up at them on reflex, doing a quick assessment of them and instantly regretting it. Four men, all dressed in khakis and button downs or polo shirts. They looked to be mid-forties or maybe younger and were clean cut all save for the oldest in the group. I only saw a flash of his face. Of hooded eyes, and a rounded jaw that looked familiar. Too familiar.

Like I'd seen the face staring down at me, only it was younger, and there had been hands wrapped around my throat.

The hostess seated the group toward the back, and my breath was shaky when I looked over my shoulder, trying to convince myself I wasn't seeing what I was. It was only when I noticed the emblem on the sleeve of one man's shirt, two trees with a cathedral between them, a cross positioned where the door would be. The words *Twin Valley Reformed* were written in small text under the design.

My stomach heaved, and I pushed my chair back, trying to stay calm and not make a lot of noise. I looked at Pak, smiling as calmly while slinging my purse over my shoulder. "It's hard for me to get out. Between classes and hours at the office and writing I'm tired more often than I'm not. Sorry, I have to get going."

Pak frowned, but when I made my way toward the door he got the hint. I needed to get out of here. The longer I stayed the more at risk I was. Pak positioned his body behind mine, not realizing what he was doing, but I was grateful for it.

They didn't see you, I told myself. Even if they had, a quick glance wouldn't have been enough to give me away. I'd covered the tattoo, my hair was different, my eyes were different. Hannah and Isaac had even debated for a bit on whether it was me before seeing the tattoo.

It was going to be fine. I was fine. This was fine. Like with Kellen, it wasn't them I was afraid of. But unlike Kellen, or Isaac, or Hannah, one of those men would tell Davey they saw me, and I didn't want to find out how he would react.

"I can understand," Pak said as he followed me back to where I'd parked my bike, not finding anything odd about the pace I'd set. "College is rough, especially at the end. My last semester was hell, so I get it. But, you gotta live a little, too."

He raised his eyebrows, grinning while I gave him a tight smile and unlocked my bike, positioning it in front of me like I'd done with Kellen. The way I'd been using it for a shield lately made me wonder if I should add plating to it. "I know. I'll go out sometime. Maybe if I get hired or a promotion or something."

Pak grinned, accepting this option without any more pressure. Guilt twisted my already tight stomach. I was going to have to break it to him sooner or later. There was nothing wrong with him, but I couldn't make it through a simple lunch without something making my fight or flight response light up like Christmas tree, and that wasn't going to change anytime soon. It was the proverbial cross I had to bear, and I didn't want to share the burden with anyone else.

As soon as I got back to my apartment, I jumped in the shower, letting the hot water run over my skin until it was almost cold and my heart rate finally slowed. My thoughts volleyed between wishing I'd run farther after leaving Northshore and trying to convince myself that everything was fine. It shouldn't have shocked me that the clergy from Twin Valley had attended the conference. It was only a little over an hour drive into the Metro, and despite the evils of "secular" culture, a conference that talked about reigniting faith seemed right up their alley. A slowly dying town held together by the bonds of faith would be doing everything they could to weave those ties tighter.

So tight, they'd strangle if necessary.

The comparison had me touching my neck as I got dressed. I had a box full of jewelry but I never wore the necklaces. When I'd put on the scarf today, I didn't tie it. It had sat loose on my throat, only meant to cover what makeup wouldn't regarding my tattoo. I didn't like to be touched in general, but having anything on my neck nearly sent me into a panic.

Haku was sitting in the window when I walked back into the living room, and it wasn't until I'd gotten a full glass of water that I saw his tail twitching. His body was poised to pounce, and I tracked where he was looking to see a thick black orb with spindly legs.

"I hate these stupid windows," I shouted as looked around for a shoe, heart pounding, but I couldn't keep asking Priest to deal with this for me. If I was planning on living alone for a while, I'd have to figure out how to handle spiders because they weren't ever going away.

But when I got close, the stupid beast skittered up the window right when Haku made a jump for it, and instead of squashing it I ended up screaming, throwing the shoe indiscriminately, and sprinting back to my bedroom. "Ugh, this is so stupid!" I shouted, mostly at myself, grabbing another shoe and stalking back into the living room. It was halfway toward my ceiling. I'd need to get a chair, but when I went to grab it when a knock on the door caught my attention.

"Noelle, you good?" It was Priest, and I let out another angry sigh.

"I'm fine," I said, knowing if I didn't reply he'd likely break the doorknob to get inside.

"Why're you screaming?"

"Because another fucking spider is on my wall, that's why!"

There was quiet, then the doorknob rattled. "I can get it for you. Why didn't you call?"

"Didn't want to bug you." I stalked to the door, twisting the lock and opening it, freezing when I found that it wasn't just Priest on the other side. Kellen was behind him, his hair pulled back in a poor attempt at a ponytail, his shirt and pants streaked with oil.

"Why are you here?"

"Came to mess with my bike," Priest explained as he walked past me into the kitchen, grabbing a handful of paper towels. "Thought we might take a look at your car, too."

I huffed, eyes fixed on Priest's back so I could avoid looking at Kellen, who stayed outside the door like a vampire waiting for an invitation. I was hesitant to give one. My apartment wasn't a mess, but I pictured Kellen living in an apartment somewhere that had posters on the wall and furniture he'd bought at a store instead of picking off the street. Maybe he had pictures of friends or bikes he'd built decorating the walls. That's what the loft he'd lived in that summer looked like. A reflection of his personality.

My little space reflected nothing. I needed it that way. It kept people from lingering too long when I didn't want them there.

"You get other bugs besides spiders?" Kellen asked.

"Moths and flies and ladybugs get in," I said, watching Priest carefully ball the spider up in the towel. I frowned as he approached, moving into the kitchen to stay far away from the thing in his hand. "You confuse me, you know that?"

"How so?" he asked.

"You literally broke down my door once after I screamed, and I watched you threaten the landlord when he tried to raise rent on Macy to get her to move out. But kill a spider? Noooo." I crossed my arms over my chest and stepped back when he passed. "No, you're gonna catch it and let the vile thing outside."

Priest gave me a look, but when Kellen snickered, his eyes narrowed. "Moths, flies, ladybugs. You know what you didn't mention? Fucking mosquitos. Cause these guys eat them." He raised the paper towel and I flinched, watching him walk out the door. "Get some caulk and I'll seal up your windows since that jackass landlord doesn't do shit around here."

Priest walked off, but Kellen stayed in the doorway, his gray eyes flicking around my apartment. "I'm probably moving out in the Spring," I muttered, self-conscious since he was examining my bare walls so intently. "That's why there's nothing here."

"Didn't you just move in?" he asked.

"I've been here since last June, but I don't know what'll happen after I graduate so..."

He nodded, considering this, but he made no move to come inside. I wasn't sure why, but it put me on edge. It didn't feel right to have him so close, but so distant.

Even if it was how I wanted things.

"You're graduating in May?"

I nodded, stepping back and tipping my chin toward the living room, an unspoken invitation to come in. He accepted, hands shoved deep in his pockets as he moved through the door. "Don't think you'll stick around?"

"Depends on if I get a job at the paper or not. That would be ideal, and I think I will, but I don't want to bank on anything one way or the other."

"Keeping your options open is good." He looked over my kitchen, and peered into the small hallway that led to my bedroom as he walked further in. His eyes finally moved to the window, and that's when he paused. Haku was sitting in the windowsill, tail flicking idly, his large blue eyes fixed on Kellen.

"What's his name?"

"Haku."

Kellen grinned over his shoulder, then dropped onto his heels, wiggling his fingers in Haku's direction. "He's not terribly social," I said when Haku continued to stare at him. "It took me a week to get him inside."

He nodded, still wiggling his fingers. The cat regarded him, then turned his nose up, walked back to the cat tree, and jumped to the top stoop, settling into a bread-like position where he could observe Kellen from a distance.

Kind of like I was.

"Is this the stray Priest told me about?" he asked. "The one who kept knocking over his plants?"

"Yes, but I don't let him outside anymore, so it's not an issue."

Kellen stood out of his squat, smiling at the cat again before he walked to the window and touched the frame. "Was this gap here when you moved in?"

"Yeah, I took pictures of it before I signed my lease."

"Good girl."

My arms wrapped tightly around my chest, but not out of fear. It was to keep my heart from breaking out of my ribs. Like

Pak's earlier comment, this was innocent, and I knew what Kellen meant. That taking pictures and documenting the state of the place before I moved in was smart. That way, the landlord couldn't hold onto my deposit when I moved out.

But unlike Pak's words, Kellen's stirred up a very, *very* different memory. They'd been whispered in an entirely different tone. Softer. A moment of quiet praise when I needed reassurance. Like when he'd held my hand when I'd gotten my first tattoo.

Other times, I'd heard those words in a husky, heated voice. Whispered into the space behind my ear, breathed against my lips, murmured into the crease of my inner thigh. *You're such a good girl, Tate.*

A shiver rushed through me, the chill molding into warmth as it settled in my lower stomach. I tensed, shifting from foot to foot, rubbing my thighs together unconsciously.

So, I could feel desire. But why did it have to be for the wrong guy? For the one who'd hurt me so badly?

"You have any vinegar?"

I sucked in a breath, happy Kellen had spoken before more memories had time to pop up and make this even more awkward. "Why do you need vinegar?"

"Says if you spray vinegar on the windows, spiders don't like it." He held up his phone, showing me the website he'd pulled up. "I thought it might help until you get something to fill the gap."

"Right." I nodded, avoiding his gaze as I walked into the kitchen. "I don't know if I have any, but I can buy some."

Kellen tucked his phone in his pocket and resumed looking around the room, clearly searching for something to talk about. I winced, not having anything to offer.

That was a lie.

I had a million things to offer, but I wasn't sure where to start. Or how to now that my heart was pounding against my ribs and my lower belly felt tight and warm. I found myself staring at his biceps. His forearms. The sleekness of his body, despite how broad it was. I knew what it felt like to have that body pressed against mine, to have the scent of his skin all around me. I knew how good it felt to have those arms hold me.

I also knew how awful it had been when they'd pushed me away.

"Priest is probably waiting," I mumbled, gesturing to the door. Kellen shrugged.

"We're just fucking around. Nothing needs fixed." His eyebrows narrowed, then he pointed at my purse on the table. "Unless you want me to look at your car…"

"It's fine. I think it's the battery."

"I can get a battery and put it in for you."

"You work on motorcycles."

He smirked. "And cars. By special request."

"I don't want to bother you."

This made his eyes go wide, and he let out a soft, huff of a laugh and ran a hand through his hair. "Christ, Tate. Bother me. My life is easy. Fuck it up, I don't care. Just be in it again."

His eyes locked on mine, and my heart beat so hard, it almost hurt as the air between us shifted. It grew thick, and the nervousness I'd seen in Kellen's posture seemed to fade, replaced with something much more vulnerable.

Need.

I nodded, not sure of what to say. Kellen was close, but he wasn't in my space. He seemed to be keeping his distance on purpose, and part of me wished he wouldn't. I knew he was leaving the choice to me, and I appreciated that. I truly did.

But I was stuck.

He and I had reversed roles. This time, it was me who was trapped, and he was free, watching from the other side.

When I didn't say anything else, he nodded, and turned to leave, carrying the weight of unsaid words on his back. Words he hadn't said. Words he had but regretted. Words I'd used to carefully construct a wall around myself that I didn't know how to tear down.

I let out a breath when the door shut. The wall was necessary. I needed it to be. Keeping him at arm's length was safer because I knew, most likely, this wouldn't last. We might talk a few more times, exchange niceties in lieu of closure, but I was so different than the girl he'd known. Once he figured that out, he'd leave.

And I didn't know what would be left of me.

Chapter Eighteen
Tatum

KELLEN: *REV SAID YOU'VE BEEN WATCHING* CASTLEVANIA. *WHEN you're done we should watch* Demon Slayer. *He'll will like that one too.*

Me: *I don't have a subscription.*

Kellen: *I do.*

The next text included a list of logins for every single streaming service imaginable. I widened my eyes, shaking my head while my thumbs swiped over the screen to write a reply.

Me: *You realize I have classes and an internship? I can't sit around and watch TV all the time.*

Kellen: *Rev says you work half the time you're watching TV.*

Me: *I've seen* Castlevania. *Watching something new takes commitment.*

And that was exactly what I was trying to avoid.

For the last week, Kellen had been texting me regularly, with a few phone calls here and there. I replied when I had a response, answered when I felt like talking, but otherwise, tried to keep a distance. Wrote the attempts at connection off as nostalgia seeking and tried to play up how busy I was.

I had to keep it together. Graduation was in May, that was less than nine months from now. Pak had said it was only a matter of time before my internship turned into a real job. I had to focus on keeping the surface of my life as smooth as possible despite the chaotic riptides happening underneath.

Texting with Kellen was one thing. It was fine. The phone calls? Awkward at times, but fine. There was a barrier in the form of distance and a screen that I relied on to keep things the way I wanted between us. Casual. Friendly.

I couldn't give him more. The cage I'd locked my heart in aside, I didn't want or need the distraction. And that's what he was: a distraction. With his constantly tousled hair, and that smile that could melt ice caps. Anytime he sent me a picture or FaceTimed me he was covered in grease. It stained his fingers and was always streaked all over his coveralls. It should have been a turn off, but it wasn't. I kept picturing those oil-stained hands smearing black on the outside of my thighs, or across my stomach.

Kellen was a distraction. Pure and simple.

But he wasn't the only one. Hannah had become one as well. She texted frequently while she had lulls in her shifts or when she had some free time, and the day my article on the conference was printed, she called me practically screaming with excitement.

"I honestly assumed no one I knew would pay attention to it," I admitted once she calmed down. "It wasn't front page news, and the whole story wasn't particularly exciting.

"But it's your work! It's a big deal to have something printed, isn't it?" she asked. "You've only ever had stuff on the website before, right?"

"I've had stuff in *Beat* and one small article in the back pages, but yeah. Most of the stuff I've covered has been city council meetings and school board stuff. The only reason I got this assignment was because the girl who usually covers these things was sick."

"But they gave it to *you*," she'd told me. "That means something."

I'd quietly agreed, my own excitement at the sight of my name in print muted by fear. The more people saw my name, the more questions they'd ask about who I was. Being a good journalist involved building a level of trust with the community you wrote for. And building a level of trust required exposure. Something I'd mostly avoided for the last three years.

Pen name, I reminded myself. *You write under a pen name. Legally, your name is Noelle Collins. It's going to be fine.* I repeated this to myself like it was a prayer, and told myself with each article, it would get easier. Exposure therapy. Literally and figuratively.

The Monday after the conference article ran, I showed up to the office to find a meeting request in my inbox. 10:00AM: Gina Halston, News Director. My hands shook when I clicked accept, then I immediately ran to Elissa's desk for a pep talk.

"Pak told you it wouldn't be long," she said, smirking as she passed me the card for the daily coffee run. "Honestly, Noelle. Give yourself some credit. You do consistently good work and you're eager, plus the fact that you're already planning other stories to write? Independently? Of course, we're gonna want to snatch you up. Gotta keep good blood in this place or the paper will die."

"True," I said, giving her a wave as I walked outside to grab my bike and head to the shop. Before I climbed on it, my phone buzzed in my pocket, and I pulled it out to see another text from Kellen.

Kellen: *They remade* Fruits Basket.

Me: *I know. I haven't seen it yet.*

Kellen: *I watched it.*

Me: **gasp* Without me?*

I'd meant the last message as a joke. Of course he'd watched it without me, but I was surprised he'd watched it at all. He'd never seemed interested in reading the manga.

Kellen: *We can watch it together.*

Me: *Maybe. I gotta get coffee now.*

Kellen: *Morning Grind?*

Me: *The life of an intern.*

Kellen: *No, is that the shop you go to? I'm there now.*

Me: *You're there?*

Kellen: *I came down to meet up with Hannah. She said you sometimes run into each other.*

I paused on my bike, tucking the phone into my pocket. It made sense. That was, after all, where I'd run into Hannah and Isaac, and I'd seen Kellen with them there before.

But still, the world felt so small. What were the odds that we'd all collide so easily? Fate either had a very twisted, or a very divine sense of humor.

The shop was busy like always, but for the first time I wasn't terribly concerned with the crowd. As soon as I got there, I spotted Kellen's motorcycle parked by a meter. He was leaning against it, looking more like he was headed for a photo shoot than work. There were several girls casting glances in his direction, interest on their faces as they took in his purposefully messy hair, and that square jaw covered in a thin layer of stubble. His jeans were clean today, and so was the dark T-shirt he wore, part of it obscured by a denim vest with a variety of patches. I recognized it from seeing Priest wear his a few times and felt stupid that I hadn't ever thought to put the connection together. Kellen and I could have possibly reconnected sooner if I had. Maybe in a less dramatic way. Not that I necessarily wanted to reconnect, but seeing him here now, waiting for me...

I'd forgotten how nice it was to have people around. To have... friends.

"Don't you have to go to work? You're gonna get those nice, designer jeans all messy," I said when he spotted me, grinning as he walked over and stepped into the line at my side.

"I have coveralls, and I don't usually go in until noon on the days I meet up with Hannah. Traffic is a pain coming in."

"Coming in from where?" I asked, realizing I didn't actually know where he lived.

"Saylorville," he said. "My house is basically right next to the shop."

I grimaced, trying to pass it off like I was blinded by the morning sun. He'd been in my shabby little apartment when he had a house. A whole house. We were horribly unmatched.

"You didn't have to stay for me if you needed to get back."

He breathed a laugh, flashing me the kind of smile that made me and the other girls staring at him lose our collective breaths. All that oxygen, stolen by a flash of white teeth behind those stupidly kissable lips. "Right," he said, running a hand through his hair to mess it up, or smooth it down. I didn't know, but the action made me want to do the same. "It's not like I've been texting you, practically begging to hang out."

I gave him an apologetic smile. "I don't go out much."

"I didn't say go out. I said hang out."

"Wouldn't that be boring?" I asked, gesturing to his vest, poking the small patch that read *Prospect*. "Don't you have friends with motorcycles and harems of women? That has to be more entertaining than sitting around my shabby apartment."

"It's been a few years. I'm sure we'd find stuff to talk about. Besides, not interested in these harems you speak of. There's only ever been one girl for me."

My eyes widened, breath catching in my throat. Kellen saved me from responding by grinning again and tapping the patch I'd poked. "You'd probably like these guys. They're rugged. Down to Earth."

"You know I'm picky about people."

"You like Priest." He elbowed me softly. "You like me."

"Debatable."

Kellen let out a dramatic gasp, pressing his hand to his chest as we moved forward. "You wound me, Tatertot."

"Oh, please don't start with that nickname," I groaned. "I still hate it."

"You hate the food. The nickname suits you." He laughed when I rolled my eyes. "What? Potatoes are a staple midwestern food. Everyone loves them."

"I'd hope I was a little more exciting than plain, shredded potatoes mashed into little cubes."

"They're more... cylindrical."

I laughed so loud the girl in front of me scowled over her shoulder. "Cylindrical. That's a descriptive word."

"I know a few of them." He grinned down at me, tilting his head to look at my ears, and the tattoo on my neck. "Besides, you're not plain. You'd be a... well-seasoned tatertot."

"How do you figure?"

"Time will do that."

There was a heaviness to the words, but I turned, watching him smile softly he gestured to my ears. "Plus, the piercings, the new hair, the tattoos. All of it is spicy." He looked me up and down, then gestured to the ink on my wrist. "How many do you have now?"

I did a mental check. "Five. You?"

"Going on eight."

"But no new piercings," I said, looking at the small gauges he had in his ears.

"Cas, the club VP, wants to get his tongue pierced and I'm gonna go with him. Maybe get my lip done."

"How long does that take to heal?"

"Few weeks." He smirked, licking said lip before biting it softly. "Should be healed by the time I convince you to kiss me again."

My eyes widened, jaw dropping, and Kellen laughed and

pushed me up to the counter, where I met the barista's eyes with a flushed face and a bemused expression.

"Hey, Noelle. Same order as usual?"

"Uh, yeah," I managed, cheeks hot as the steaming coffee as I passed her my card and avoided Kellen's amused smile. I thought him texting me the first time, after he'd stolen my number from Priest's phone, was bold. This was a little more intense.

I should hate it. Honestly, I should tell him off.

But I didn't.

Having him lay his thoughts on the line without any sort of censorship was... comforting. It didn't leave any room for me to guess his intentions, and it crowded the space where my doubt tried to creep in.

But I'd have to find a way to turn him down.

Did I want to turn him down?

I did. I should...

"The basket is cute," Kellen said when we walked outside the shop back to my bike, and I set the two boxes of drinks inside. "Did you get it for coffee runs?"

"That, and groceries or take out. I take this thing every-where." I jostled the bike and smiled. "Probably would be worth getting a newer, better model, but they're surprisingly expensive."

"Or, you could let me look at your car."

"Nah, this ensures I get my exercise in."

Kellen's eyebrows bounced, and he stayed beside me while I climbed on the bike. "What about in the winter?"

"I still use this. I only take my car if I have to. It's old and I don't trust it."

"Is it that bad?" His expression turned worried. "You act like you're scared to drive it."

My fists tightened on the handlebars, lips pressing together when I put my foot on the pedal. In my head, I could the hear glass shattering, feel the door handle slipping through my fingers, hear Davey's angry cry as he ripped the door open and lunged—

"Hey."

Kellen was in front of me, eyes wide but his expression calm, his hands helping steady the bike when it tilted and I almost toppled off. "Hey. Tate. What's that? What's that look?"

I turned away from his worried expression, pulling the bike upright again. "It's nothing."

"What'd I say?" There was a plea in his voice, and it tugged at my chest. "Was it the car thing? Fuck, I don't care if you take your bike everywhere. It's good for you, you're right. I didn't mean anything by it."

"No, it's..." I held up my hands, plastering a very fake smile on my face. "Listen, next time you come over to Priest's let me know and I'll... I'll let you look at my car. I should get it going, or at least get it checked out in case I need to drive somewhere."

Kellen nodded, releasing the handlebars. He stayed close, like he wanted to grab me if I needed it. Like he wanted to hold me if I suddenly fell apart.

If he did, I might actually fall apart.

"Thanks for keeping me company, but I gotta run," I said, offering a tight smile. "I have a meeting with my News Director in less than half an hour."

His worried expression turned to surprise, then another one of those blinding smiles crossed his face. Warm, hopeful, and God did I want to sink into him. Bury myself into his chest and let him cover me with his body. Like a human blanket.

Why did he always have to catch me off guard like this? It was either me freaking out over a spider or yelling at him in a parking lot. I was a mess, and he was so put together and gorgeous it killed me.

"That's a good thing, right?" he asked. "I read your article the other day."

"You did? You didn't tell me."

"Well, I saw the name Collins and assumed it was you, but..." He rubbed at his hair again. "I figured if you wanted to talk about it, you'd tell me."

I scrunched my nose, fiddling with the handlebars on my bike. He was setting the onus of our interactions on me. It was my replies to his texts that kept him going, because if I didn't, he stopped. And I knew without asking that if I'd told him not to seek me out, he'd stop. Just like if I wanted him not to think about kissing me, he wouldn't mention it again.

He was opening doors, waiting for me to walk through or close them. Giving me the chance to say yes when for the last three years, all I'd ever said to anyone was no.

I wasn't sure I knew how to say yes anymore.

"You should go," he said when I stayed quiet, a slightly disappointed smile on his face. "Text me though, tell me how it went. Okay?"

I nodded, trying hard to fight the smile and another flush of color to my cheeks. "Yeah, I will. Bye."

"See ya, Tatertot."

His grin grew wider when I glared at him, listening to his soft laugh as I pushed the pedal forward, letting the bike coast away while my heart stayed behind. Lingering beside Kellen for a few more seconds before it decided to catch up with me.

I was going to have to put the damn thing on a leash and get a heavier lock for its cage.

Chapter Nineteen
Tatum

"Shut the door behind you."

Gina gestured to one of the chairs by her desk, her keyboard clacking under long fingernails as she finished typing before turning to look at me. There was a soft smile on her face, and I returned it with the brightest one I could offer. I felt like I only had a limited supply of them each day thanks to the constant thrum of tension in my chest, and Kellen had stolen a few. I'd have to tell him he owed me.

"How are you, Noelle?" Gina asked. "It's been a while since I actually got to talk to you."

I took a breath to try and unwind the knot in my chest, reminding myself that this was most likely a good meeting. Pak had told me as much. *Breathe, Tatum. Just be honest.*

"I'm good. Staying busy between being here and going to class."

"How many semesters do you have left?"

"Barring any issues, I have two semesters left. I'll graduate in May."

Gina nodded, reaching to pull some papers off the printer on her desk. She looked up and down, her short brown hair bouncing as she stacked the papers, then turned back to me.

"Remind me, will you have a general communications degree? Or were you more specific?"

"I'll have a Bachelors in Multimedia Journalism, and a double minor in English and Public Relations."

A half smile tugged at her full lips, and she stacked the papers again. "I remember when Pak and I interviewed you. You mentioned Nellie Bly as an inspiration, and it had been so long since I'd heard that name, it stuck with me. Is that the kind of reporting you'd like to do? Investigative Journalism?"

"In a way," I said, trying to think of how to explain my long-term career goals. I didn't have a desire to be the one running into burning buildings to cover a story or attending press conferences for every single event. I wanted the smaller, more personal stories. The exposés that brought to light the struggles of everyday people. The stories that exposed the darker side of real life, that shined a light on stories or people the public didn't always see.

"It's sort of personal to me, but..." I took a breath, noting that Gina had tilted her head and was listening intently. "I spent a lot of my life in situations where I didn't feel like I had a voice, so one of my goals is to write things that give others like that a voice. I want to speak on behalf of those who can't. Give them the space and platform to tell their stories and hope they get attention."

Gina smiled. "That's the goal in the end, and it's difficult to accomplish. But I admire your tenacity. You're the only intern we've had in the last few years who has really put in an effort. The others wanted the instant fame and action, but you've been willing to jump in and take on anything. Pak raves about your work, and rightly so. Everything I've read has been outstanding, even if I haven't been able to get it in print."

She grinned and stacked the papers again before passing the

stack of them to me. "And that's why we'd like to offer you a position in general assignment, part time until you finish college. Twenty-five hours a week minimum, but as you've seen, there's always the chance you could work more."

I let out a shaky breath, smoothing my hands over my shorts before reaching for the papers. My heart was pounding, but it wasn't the anxious thrum I was used to, or the fluttery sensation I'd felt a few times in the last week or so. It was lighter, almost effervescent. It took me a second to recognize it as excitement.

As hope.

"Thank you. I'm... this is a great opportunity, thank you."

Gina smiled and sat back in her chair, gesturing toward the general office area. "I want you to talk to photography about getting a headshot and go ahead and link your socials to your reporter profile. It helps build a rapport with the public."

The smile stayed on my face, but I hoped she hadn't noticed how my teeth clenched together.

This was it.

This could be the thing to hold me back. A final line I'd have to cross. I'd had a professor tell me Twitter was an integral part of being a journalist, and when I'd opted not to create a profile, he docked points from my final grade.

But I didn't want to risk losing this opportunity because I was scared to put myself on the Internet.

It's been three years. Aside from everything that had happened in the last few weeks, with Hannah, and Isaac, and Kellen, I knew there were few people who'd ever known my middle name was Noelle. Collins was a common last name, and there was nothing that connected it to my life in Northshore. I could put everything under my by-line as T.N. Collins, and maybe I could put my picture on *The Journal*'s website but have something else as a picture on whatever social media platforms I'd use.

I could do this. I could *do* this.

I set the papers down on the desk, scooting to the edge of my chair. "Which sites would you suggest?"

Gina tilted her head. "Well, Facebook has the broadest reach still, but Instagram is great for reels and stories. Twitter for live updates." She rocked in her chair before sitting forward. "Don't you have all these set up? Pak mentioned you'd started a blog."

I grimaced. "Yes, I set one up for any independent articles I write. But as far as Facebook and things, I haven't..." I hesitated, trying to think of how to explain my hesitancy without going to deep. "Is social media required?"

"No, but it helps to build a presence and helps you create a network of sources."

"I just haven't... I've been off it for a few years," I admitted. "And even before that, I wasn't on it much. I grew up in a really conservative town and didn't mess with it until after I graduated, and the idea of people having that much access to me makes me... uneasy."

"Well, it's not a requirement.," she said, shrugging one shoulder as she sat back in the chair. "You wouldn't be the first. I know a few other journalists who don't have any social media and do fine. If your blog picks up, you could start a mailing list. There are ways to ease into it, so let's start there, okay?"

I tried not to let my shoulders visibly sag with relief. "Thank you, I appreciate that."

She tapped the papers and smiled. "Take as much time as you'd like to look this over, but I'd like it back by the end of this week. Pak should be able to answer any questions you might have if I'm not available. Will that work?"

"Yes, thank you again. I won't let you down," I said, collecting the papers and stacking them before standing up and offering her my hand. Gina stood and took mine in hers, shaking firmly before sitting back down and returning to her project. I left her office, exhaling as I walked back towards my desk, heart still thrumming in my chest. I couldn't wait to tell someone. Maybe if Kellen was still in town, I could—

"Congratulations!"

The shout almost deafened me, so loud and sudden that I flinched and dropped everything I was holding. My thrumming heartbeat turned to a full-on throb, rattling against my ribcage. Someone moved towards me, and I threw myself back, arms coming up to shield my body.

But there was no attack. It was just the newsroom. I could see Elissa, Pak, and several others I knew. There were balloons, someone had a cake. A banner that read "Congratulations" stretched over my desk. That's what they'd shouted. They were clapping. Palms slapping against palms. Slapping…

Pain lashed my face. Cheekbone to jaw. It stole my breath. The same hands that slapped me grabbed my shoulders, pushing me back. My body arched awkwardly over the center console of the car. I kicked, clawing at the seats as Davey pushed me back, using his bodyweight to hold me in place. His hair was disheveled, eyes panicked. Enraged. I blocked the next slap, bending my arms to shield my face. He grabbed my wrists. "Davey, please stop. Please don't—"

An unholy growl filled the small space, and then there were hands around my throat. Squeezing tight. So tight. "You damned me. You made me do all that stuff because you… you tempted me. You have to repent, Tatum. You have to!"

I clawed at his hands, the edges of my vision going black. Someone had to hear this. The sound of my choking, of his sobbing, his enraged professions. The slapping of my hands against his arms, his chest. My feet kicking the door. Help. Please. Someone help…

"Noelle?"

Large hands landed on my biceps, and I jumped, pushing the person back only to realize it was Pak.

Not Davey.

It was my editor, with big eyes and a confused, worried expression that matched the faces of the people behind him.

I let out a shaky breath. The papers of my contract were at my feet, the eyes of every person watching me wide as excitement drained from their faces.

There were so many people around. The whole office.

Goddammit.

Now everyone knew. Everyone could see. There was no makeup or professional outfits or smiles I could put on to hide it anymore.

I was a mess.

A paranoid, perpetually anxious, mess.

Chapter Twenty
Tatum

IT'S TRULY AMAZING HOW DISTRACTED PEOPLE CAN BE by cake. Especially in an office setting. One of the guys that does sports reports cut into it, plating slices that Pak passed out while I watched from a distance. Elissa sat beside me, a bottle of water in her hand. She offered it to me, and I took it, hating how shaky my hands were. I unscrewed the cap and drank a couple sips, just enough to wet my dry mouth, then screwed the lid back on. I didn't want to spill all over myself. That was the last thing I needed.

"So, um." Elissa leaned forward on her chair, lowering her voice to a soothing tone. "No surprise birthday parties for you, then."

I let out a weary, huff of a laugh. "No, definitely not."

She fixed me with a curious, sympathetic gaze. "Does it have anything to do with why you never go out?"

I frowned and turned away from her, staring at the plate beside me, the one covered in smashed chocolate cake. My stomach was rolling, and I didn't want to risk puking and humiliating myself more, so I'd pushed the dessert around with my fork like a kid who didn't want to eat their vegetables, so they just spread them around on the plate.

I treated myself the same way. Spread around the truth, the story of my life, to make it look like I'd moved on, when really, I was avoiding it all together.

"Noelle, you can talk to me." Elissa's expression was cautious, but sympathetic. "No one can hear us. They're all too excited about getting a snack, and I won't tell a soul, I swear it."

My shoulders sagged, and I pushed a hand through my hair, trying to think of how to explain it in the simplest terms. I thought of Kellen on his bike, waiting for me at the coffee shop, the pleasant feeling of someone waiting for me. Someone wanting to be in my life. Elissa was offering that now. Another chance to say yes.

"When I was eighteen, an ex-boyfriend stalked me." I explained, fighting hard not to lose my nerve when her eyes widened. "First it was text messages and stuff I ignored, then he... it got worse."

She sat up, her expression calm, but I could see the horror in her eyes. Pak must have noticed too, because he came over, eyebrows pinched together. "Everything all right?"

I gritted my teeth, avoiding his worried gaze, then breathing a sigh of relief when Elissa gently shooed him away. "Girl talk. I got this."

He hesitated, but nodded, eyes on me as he walked back to the crowd. Elissa waited until he'd engaged himself back in other conversations before turning back to me. "How much worse did it get?"

I shrugged, rolling my eyes. "It... he broke into my car after I'd gone to an orientation at a local college and..."

I shook my head, swallowing bile as the images of that last night popped into my head. The broken glass, Davey's teary, rage filled expression. The way my vision faded into nothing.

"He almost killed me," I said, stomach lurching. It was the

first time I'd admitted that out loud to anyone other than a therapist.

"Jesus," Elissa said. "Did you press charges?"

"I tried when he was stalking me, but... it's a long story."

I waved my hands dismissively, not wanting to talk about it —the anger I'd felt when the cops had ignored me, tried to blame Kellen for the bruises on my body. It was all too much, and Elissa and I weren't that close. I didn't want to lay all that on her.

I didn't want to lay it on anyone.

"Anyway, I don't like surprises. I also don't like going out. I mean, I do, but it's hard." She frowned and I gave her a wry smile and a shrug. "I moved away, went dark on the Internet. Changed my name."

"You changed your name?" Elissa asked, her eyes comically wide when I nodded. "What was it?"

"Tatum."

Her eyes lit up. "T.N. Collins."

I smiled. "Yeah. I had a hard time letting Tatum go."

"Do want us to call you that instead of Noelle?" she asked.

"I don't know," I said, rubbing my hands through my hair. "I've had a really odd few weeks. I ran into some people I knew from back then and it's thrown me off. I kind of..."

Elissa tilted her head, and I grimaced at her for half a second, then let out a sigh. "I'm really tired now, and I kind of want to go home. Do you think it would be a big deal if I headed out? Finished up my stuff at home? I feel bad."

I gestured to the cake and decorations, but Elissa shook her head. "No, go. It's fine. We know how to get ahold of you if something comes up."

I smiled, standing up to walk to my desk and grab my bag. Elissa followed, playing bodyguard and keeping people from asking any questions. Including Pak, who frowned when she shook her head and escorted me past him.

"Don't be surprised if he texts you to check in," she warned, a little smile on your face. "I don't think he'll be your editor for much longer."

I whipped around to look at her, my eyes wide. "What? Why?"

"Conflict of interest." She gave me a half smile. "Don't tell me you haven't noticed."

My nose scrunched. "I was trying to avoid talking about it."

"He's not going to get upset if you let him down," she said immediately, shaking her head. "He wouldn't do that, Noelle."

I nodded, giving her a soft smile before I headed toward the exit, taking the long way around all the desks to avoid anyone asking questions.

When I got outside, I was still shaky, and it didn't fade even after I got home. Haku was sleeping on his cat tree, and I looked over expecting to see another spider in the window because that would be the cherry on top of everything else that had happened.

But instead, there was a note on the outside of the glass, and the gap between the windowsill and the wall had been filled with caulk. I walked over, pushing the glass open and snatching the note, reading the untidy handwriting as my heart rate ticked up again, but not as bad as it had earlier.

Fixed it for you. No more spiders. – K

I let out a slow breath, anger invading every muscle in my body for a half a heartbeat before it faded away. It should last longer. Kellen climbed on my balcony—probably stepping onto it from Priest's adjacent one—and did something I didn't ask him to do.

To help me.

He did it because he wanted to help me. Not hurt me.

My brain spun in circles, trying to find a reasons to deny him this chance. The standard ones I'd used for the last three years kept popping up, the same ones I'd used every time Hannah wanted to go out, denying myself companionship.

And for what? Because I was afraid of Davey? Isaac had called me the other day and let me know he'd tracked him down for some general questions about the other missing cases. Apparently, he wasn't even in the state. He was up in North Dakota for work, hadn't been back for about six months. From everything Isaac said, he wasn't planning on coming back anytime soon.

And if he did find out where I was, there was no saying he'd even care. I could be doing all this for nothing. Denying myself friendship, or the chance to have a celebration at work without having a panic attack, because I'd convinced myself it was safer this way when I had no real proof it was.

Davey aside, Kellen was technically my oldest friend, and it felt wrong to push him away. Seeing him this morning had made me realize how much I wanted someone in my life. How much I wanted him in my life.

But was I willing to risk letting him see the mess it had become?

I'd kept it compartmentalized this long, hiding bits and pieces from my co-workers until today. If I kept it the same way for him, it would be fine, wouldn't it?

There was only one way to find out.

I pulled out my phone, dialing Kellen's number and taking a breath when he picked up on the second ring.

"Hey." His voice was light, a little breathless, maybe even eager, and it was a little unnerving how a single word brought heat to my cheeks. "How'd your meeting go?"

I hesitated, letting out a long sigh. "It went fine. I, um… I got the job."

"Congrats, Tate! I figured you would. Now I get to brag that I know a reporter."

"Journalist," I corrected, leaning against my counter. "Reporters work on TV."

"Journalist, then." He paused, then the tone of his voice changed. There was a curiousness in it now. Concern. "You sound tense. Did something happen?"

My free arm wrapped around my waist as I thought about my answer. "No, I'm just a little tired."

He paused, then the tone of his voice turned worried. "Is it about the crack? I thought about it when I was riding back, and I didn't want you to come home to more spiders in your window."

I breathed out a laugh. "No, that... that's fine. Thank you."

"Anytime, babe—"

He cut himself off, clearing his throat. "Anything you need, Tate. Just ask."

My lips pressed together, my heel bouncing on the tile. "Did you mean what you said about watching *Fruits Basket* again?"

Kellen paused again, and when he spoke, I almost laughed at how casual he tried to sound. Like it was nothing. No big deal. "Yeah. It was good, I'd watch it again."

I hesitated before asking the next question. I could call Hannah, but she probably had to work tonight. I could ask Priest, but the show wasn't at all up his alley.

Kellen was who I wanted to see right now. Whether that was good or bad, I didn't know.

And I didn't really care.

"Would you want to start tonight?" I asked, wholly ready for him to say no. Maybe he had plans. Something with his bikers' club or extra work. Maybe he was going out with a friend, and it was too short of notice.

But his reply came quick, and there was an eagerness in his voice that made my cheeks heat even more.

"Yeah. Your place or mine?"

"Mine. I don't like to leave Haku alone after I've been gone all day."

Kellen snickered on the other end of the line. "Okay. Give me an hour?"

I squeezed myself tightly, trying to ignore the way my heart fluttered, and the way my stomach flipped. "Yeah, that sounds great. See you then."

Chapter Twenty-One
Kellen

THE LITTLE WINGBACK CHAIR TATE HAD IN HER apartment had no business being so comfortable. It was irritating. If it had been boxy or too hard, I would have been able to say, "Hey, can I sit on the couch beside you?" And she'd have replied, "Sure, I know how uncomfortable that chair is."

But no. It was cozy, and soft, and I had no excuse to not sit in it. No excuse other than the fact that I wanted to be next to her.

When I'd asked where she gotten it from, Tate said she'd found it on the street near the college campus and had paid a moving company to come grab it.

"Why didn't you rent a truck? You can get them for like... less than twenty dollars an hour." I watched her eyes drop down to the Pad Thai in her lap, her fingers curling tight around the square container. "If you didn't feel like driving, Rev would have helped."

She stirred the noodles again and shrugged. "I didn't want to bother him."

That was a common theme. She didn't want to bother

anyone, including me. I mentioned looking at her car again but she brushed me off. "It's getting dark outside," she said.

I looked out the window, noting the orange tint of the partly-cloud sky. "Not that dark."

Another shrug. "Some other time."

And then we'd lapsed back into silence, letting the show play on her tiny TV. Tate smiled at certain scenes, giggled at others, and talked a few times about the subtle differences between the show and the manga. I hadn't read it to compare, but it didn't matter. The show was enjoyable enough for me, and I was mostly here for her anyway. I wanted to check in, to watch her in a place she felt safe.

I wanted to move out of this chair and sit beside her on the couch. Thread my fingers through hers. Put my arm around her shoulders. Kiss the top of her head. Her cheek. Slide my hand along her jaw and hold her still so I could kiss her like she deserved.

But no. I stayed in the stupid ass chair, attention split between the anime and trying desperately not to stare at her. At this point, it was beyond staring. I was practically eye-fucking her every chance I got. She had on the same shorts she wore earlier, but her bare legs were tucked under blanket. If she'd let me sit by her, I could have kept her warm. She could put her feet in my lap. She could sit on my lap, but then I'd have to worry about the semi I kept popping every time she laughed.

Christ. If her laugh did this to me, I was fucked if things ever went further.

I wanted them to go further and holding back was killing me. Patience had never been my strong suit. I'd texted Lane earlier asking for advice on how to keep things casual with someone who needed space, but he had nothing to give. He was never subtle with his intentions like I was trying to be. If Lane wanted someone, they knew it. He told them flat out what he wanted and if someone wasn't interested, he'd move onto another person who was.

I'd tried to move on. For over a year, I'd tried to force myself to be interested in other people. It hadn't worked, and now that she was here in front of me, I wasn't going to back down without a fight. This girl was it for me. I was hers. Had been for as long as I could remember.

But I needed to find a way to make her believe she was mine.

Tate tucked herself further under the blanket, curling up against the arm of the couch. It gave me a reason to ask if I could sit beside her since she was that cold. Body heat would help. I didn't have to touch her necessarily, but it wouldn't hurt...

But my phone buzzed, and I pulled it out of my pocket, frowning when I saw Rush's name on the screen.

Rush: *Church in an hour, kid.*

I sighed, gritting my teeth. Why tonight? We never had church during the week unless something other than a ride out came up. "Shit," I grumbled, sending a quick reply that I'd be there. When I looked up, Tate was watching me, a small, curious frown on her face.

"What's wrong?"

I offered her a tight smile. "We'll have to pick this up another night. I've got church in an hour."

She blinked, then looked outside before glancing down at her watch. "It's 6:30 on a Monday. What church do you go to?"

"No, not..." My laugh made her eyes widen, and internally, I grimaced at the contacts that made her entire iris brown. She was probably so used to them now that not wearing them would feel odd to her.

I guessed I'd have to sing "Brown-Eyed Girl" to her now if she wanted to keep them in.

"Not church like that," I said after I collected my thoughts.

"It's what the club calls a meeting. The Prez texted me, so I have to go."

"Oh. *Ohhh.*" She laughed and rolled her eyes at herself. "That makes more sense. I was confused because you never went to church in Northshore."

"That's because the church there was two sermons and a small militia away from being a cult."

I'd bent down to pull on my boots, but when I looked up, her expression was blank, maybe even sad as she toyed with the blanket covering her lap. "Thanks for coming over," she murmured. "Today was... weird."

I finished lacing my boots but didn't stand. The bar was only twenty minutes from here. I could stay for a bit. "Why was it weird?" I asked.

"My co-workers tried to throw me a surprise party." Her eyes met with mine, and we grimaced at the same time. "Yeah. Didn't go over well."

"Did you yell at them like you did me?"

I meant it playfully, but Tate's expression stayed tense, and she shook her head. "No, I um... I practically jumped out of my skin, dropped everything, and when my editor tried to help me up, I sort of... shoved him."

She continued messing with the edge of the blanket, tugging a small fray along the edge. My legs started to twitch, heels bouncing on the floor as I thought about my first week inside, when reality set in and I lashed out. Rev had pulled me back from getting into a fight and shoved me against a wall, holding me there with nothing but his weight while ordering me to calm down. To just breathe.

"I know what that's like," I said empathetically. "I was jumpy on the inside. Something would happen and I'd just... lose control for a bit."

She twisted her lips, finally looking up at me. "Do you still struggle with it?"

"Sometimes I have nightmares, but it hasn't happened much since I've been out."

"What was it like for you? Being in prison," she asked. It wasn't a prying question. She was genuinely curious. I huffed, leaning back in the chair and pushing my hair back.

"What do you want to know?"

She sat up, shoving the blanket off her lap, giving me her full, undivided attention. "Were you scared?"

"Yes." My heels bounced harder, and I pawed at the back of my neck. "Not a manly thing to confess, but I was."

Tate gave me a look. "Your penis doesn't disqualify you from feeling fear, you know."

I snorted, shaking my head when she grinned at me. "I've missed that."

"What?"

"The way you use words," I said. "The way you can make me laugh or cut with them if you want to."

She ducked her head, hands folding in her lap while I tried to think of how to explain what my life was like for two years. "County was bad," I started, waiting until she looked at me again before going on. "After I plead guilty and they sent me upstate, it was worse. I almost ended up in a few fights the first week when I was still in holding, but I met Priest and he kept my ass out of trouble. It was pure luck that I got moved in with him and one other guy."

"He told me that's how you met."

I nodded. "There were three of us in our bunk: me, him, and another guy named Ruben. It was minimum security, so everyone kept to themselves. But I was... pissed off for a long time."

"Anger is easier than fear."

My eyebrows raised, but Tate only smiled. "After I moved, I went to therapy for a while," she explained. "The woman I saw told me I was more angry than scared. She tried to convince me that going out and living was a way of getting revenge on Davey. He'd wanted to stop me from living, so she said the best thing I could do was live."

I swallowed, tuning her words over in my head. He'd wanted to stop me from living.

It was like a punch, forcing up bile I had to swallow before I could speak. "Did it work?" I asked. "What your therapist suggested?"

Her laugh was sweet, but I could hear a trace of bitterness in her words. "I don't know. The last time I tried, I lasted twenty minutes before I had to leave because I couldn't breathe."

I gave her soft smile and leaned forward on my elbows. "Rev dragged me to group therapy sessions, and they said similar things." She grinned, and so did I even as I rolled my eyes. "I think he saw me as a project. But then when we figured out we had the same interests—bikes, cars, old rock bands—we got to be friends. It was a fluke that we got released around the same time. He was supposed to be in longer but got out on good behavior."

"What was he in for?" she asked quietly.

"He's never told you?"

"I never asked." Tate turned to glance at the door, like she expected Rev to be standing there. "He mentioned he was an ex-con the first week after I moved in. Said he'd had panic attacks too while in prison, so he knew what they felt like."

"He find you in the middle of one?"

"Sort of. I woke up screaming in the middle of the night, and he broke my door down. Had to replace the hinges and every-thing himself."

I laughed. "Yeah, that sounds like him."

"I'm glad you had someone," Tate said, the smile on her face turning sad. "I worried about you a lot."

My laugh was breathy and soft, and I looked at her, tipping my head in her direction. "Feeling is mutual."

She nodded, sitting up and running her hands over her legs, like she was trying to brush off the tension rolling off her body. She looked back to me, expecting something. Maybe for me to get up and leave, but I glanced at my watch. I had time. A few more minutes. Anything to stay with her like this.

"So, how about you?" I asked, watching her expression change from expectation to confusion.

"How about me what?"

"You ever gonna tell me what happened?"

She pressed her lips together, then blew out a heavy sigh and shook her head. "You don't want to know."

"Tate," I said, leaning forward, angling my body toward the couch. "I wouldn't ask if—"

"No, Kellen. You don't want to know."

She sighed heavily, and my jaw clenched as a thousand horrible images flashed through my head. Each one made me want to call Isaac and find out where Davey Adler was so I could put him six feet underground. Tate was watching me, waiting for me to snap, but I took a breath, letting out the tension in a long, slow exhale.

"If you're waiting for me to push you, it's not going to happen," I said, watching her blink at me as I slid off the chair to kneel in front of her. I set my hands on the outside of her thighs, holding back a cheer when she didn't push me away. "You can tell me when you're ready. I'll wait."

"What if I'm never ready?" she asked, the shakiness in her voice making my chest tighten. "What if I can't ever tell you what happened because I still... I don't understand parts of it. It was hard enough explaining it to Isaac. And it wasn't just that day, Kellen. He kept after me when he got out of the hospital."

The food I'd eaten began to sour in my stomach, bile burning my throat as unwanted images popped into my head. Davey on top of Tate. Davey hurting her. I swallowed, and she turned to look at me, a sad smile on her face.

"You should go. I don't want you to go to your thing upset."

"Come with me."

I slid closer to her, my chest against her knees, my hands on the outside of her hips as she stared at me like I'd asked her to join me in robbing a bank. "Seriously. Come with me. Come out."

"Isn't it just for your club?"

"Looper always brings his wife because she's pregnant. And Rush's wife is usually there too. She gets a sitter on church nights. You could hang out with them during the meeting, and afterward, we could have a drink." She grimaced, but I shook my head. "Not a drink drink if you don't want. You can meet the guys, too. They're not going to bother you. Fuck, Tate, you have to know I'd never let anyone hurt you."

My head fell into her lap, completely of its own will. God, she smelled good. Like sugar and sweetness and clean laundry and *fuck*…

Her knees parted just enough to let me in, and before I knew what I was doing I was hugging her, my face buried in her lap, the top of my head resting against her stomach. I had to bite back a groan when she lifted one hand, setting it on the back of my head while the other smoothed up and down my arm. Squeezing her tightly, I bit my lip to keep from begging. *Come with me. Be with me. Let me love you, Tate.*

"I have to work tomorrow," she murmured. "Early. At like 5:00 since I have class at 9:00."

I sighed heavily, hating how valid of an excuse it was. "Can I come over tomorrow? We can watch more."

Her stomach shook with a small laugh, and I nestled in further when she slid her fingers into my hair. "Yeah, that'd be fine. Unless I get called on an assignment or something. They're putting me on the crime beat because of that article I'm writing."

"The one about the other missing girls?" I asked, lifting my head. Her fingers slid into my hair, and I tipped my cheek into her palm, thrilled that there was an amused smile on her face. It was small, but I'd take it. "Isaac won't tell me anything about the cases or your reports."

"I'm still working out the details. There are enough cases that I'm thinking of doing a series and highlighting several, I just have to get the idea approved then get it written, on top of my schoolwork and other articles."

She slid her fingers through my hair, petting softly while I bit back a groan. "That's a lot of work."

"It feels right, though. To say something or highlight it. There's so many, Kellen. Three around Northshore alone."

I widened my eyes, and she hesitated, eyebrows pinched over her nose, lips tight. "Rachael Jefferson is one of them."

I lifted my hand out of her palm. "She was in my class."

Tate nodded. "Kara Marlan was in mine, and Tiff Manchester was a year ahead of me. They all vanished about the same time I left town, and no one's bothered to look for them. There's a few dozen other cases around the state like that, but I don't know if they're connected."

"And there's been nothing? No hints of where they are or anything?"

"Not that Isaac or I can see, and when I've called family or friends, they're..." She winced, shaking her head. "Less than interested."

"That wasn't you, you know." I rubbed the outside of her thighs, trying to soothe away the tension in them. "I tried to find you, Tate. I really did. Ask Rev how crazy I went. Shit, call Suzanne and Phil. The only reason they didn't file a report was because of the note you left. They didn't want Davey hearing about it and..."

I shut my mouth when she sucked in a breath through her teeth and took my hands, pushing them away then wrapping her arms around herself. "I can't call them," she whispered. "I'm so embarrassed. I didn't want—"

"Hey."

I peeled her hands off her arms, squeezing them in mine and shaking my head when she opened her mouth to argue. "They don't care. I've talked to them a few times over the last year when I was looking. They'd like to know your safe. They'd probably be ecstatic to hear about your job." She lowered her head to hide her watery eyes, but I could see her lips trembling. I cupped my hands around the back of her neck, pulling the crown of her head against my lips. "When you're ready, you should call them."

"What if Davey hears about it and finds me?"

I slid my fingers into her hair, gently tilting her head up so I could look in her eyes. "Tate, if that happened, it wouldn't be like last time. I'd be there. You could lean on me for whatever you needed. He'd have to deal with an entire pack of bikers who'd kick his ass for even looking at my girl the wrong way."

She laughed softly, and pulled back, an amused smile on her lips. "Kellen, I'm not yours."

I chewed my bottom lip and laid my head back on her lap, allowing myself a soft groan when she lifted both her hands and set them on my head. I covered the back of her hands with mine, coaxing her fingers back into my hair before I wrapped my arms around her hips, squeezing as tight as I could.

"Maybe not," I whispered into her thigh, hoping she could hear me. "But I'm yours."

Chapter Twenty-Two
Kellen

I STOPPED AT HOME TO GRAB MY CUT BEFORE RIDING to Styx, not caring that I'd be the last to arrive. I'd stayed at Tate's, laying on her lap, letting her stroke the back of my head until the absolute last minute. I knew her touches were meant to be soothing, not something more, but I'd take it. She could have pulled my hair or tickled me and I'd have welcomed it just to have her hands on my body.

"Well, well," Cas bellowed when I walked in the door, a shit-eating grin on his face as he set a shot glass on the bar. "Look who finally decided to show up."

I sat on a stool between Rev and Riot, trying to think of an excuse for why it had taken me so long as Cas poured dark alcohol into the glass, his eyes lifting to mine when he finished. "Any luck?"

"Luck with what?"

"Getting your dick wet," he said, and I turned to glare at Rev, who offered a grin and a single shoulder shrug.

"Saw your bike outside the complex. Noelle call you to come over or did you pester her?"

"Tatum called me," I said. "She had a scare at work and wanted some company."

"A scare at work?" His eyes narrowed, lips pressing into a thin line.

"Not like that," I assured him. "Her co-workers tried to throw her a surprise party because she got a job. A *job* job. No more internship."

His eyes lit up, but then his expression shifted into a glare. "Wow," he said, motioning for Cas to pour him a shot. "You and that blonde girl pop back into her life and now she doesn't tell me shit anymore."

"Well, she's got a chance with him," Cas said, gesturing to me. "Isn't this girl a baby?"

"She's twenty-two," I replied."

"Right, she's a baby. You don't know the rule?

"What rule?" Rev asked.

"The human brain doesn't fully mature until the age of twenty-five, so anyone under that is still a baby. Or, a teenager I guess." Cas grinned and passed Priest his shot before pouring me a second one. "I almost majored in psychology before I dropped out."

Rev rolled his eyes. "Fuck that logic. I grew up a whole lot faster than that."

"Shayla's barely twenty and she's pregnant with Looper's kid. You say this to him and he's liable to punch your ass," Riot warned, but Cas waved him off before looking back at me.

"So, how is it going? Rev tells me you've been texting this girl all week. Showing up late cause you drive to fucking downtown to stand in line with her while she gets coffee." He tapped his watch and widened his eyes at me. "Times ticking, Fox. When do we meet this girl? When do I get another niece or nephew to spoil?"

Riot and Rev laughed along with several other guys when I choked on the shot. "Christ, I thought I was impatient. I don't want to freak her out, all right?" I wiped my mouth on the back of my arm, setting the shot glass back down on the bar. "I'm moving slow. Trying to ease her into the idea. The last thing I want to do is push her."

"If you want my advice," Rev said, tipping his glass in my direction. "I think the girl could use a bit of a push."

I shook my head. "You don't know her like I do. If I push—"

"If you push, she'll push back," he said, eyes raising when I glared at him. "Don't give me that look. I've lived next to her for a year, and that's plenty long to have seen that stubborn streak she has. She's got an excuse for every damn thing I suggest that would get her out of that apartment. She needs a push out of that mental bomb shelter before she suffocates."

"She ride a bike?" Riot asked, smirking at me before he held up two fingers. "She sounds cagey, and you said she's cute. Sounds like she'd fit right in."

Rev tipped his head at Riot as he took another shot, and I didn't say it out loud but I agreed. Tate would fit in once her shell softened, and I knew Rev was right. She probably did need a little nudge.

But I'd pushed her once, and I didn't know if I had it in me to do it again, even if this time I was pushing us together instead of apart.

Rush came down the stairs that led to Cas' loft, eyes scanning the group until he found me. He nodded at Cas, then put two fingers in his mouth and whistled to quiet everyone down.

"Alright. Sorry for the last minute. Betsy's aunt came in from Cali and I had to get the fuck out of there."

Laughter bounced off the wood walls, and I grinned to myself, thinking about how much Betsy would like Tate. "First thing's first," Rev said. "Clear off your schedule for the two days around Halloween, the twenty-ninth and the thirtieth. One for a ride-out, and another for a trick or treat thing Bets is planning. I know, I know," he said, folding his arms over his chest when several people groaned. "I get it. But aside from mine, we've got three other brothers with kids and Looper has one on the way. We can give out tickets to the parents for booze and snacks, bring in some money. It's one night where we have to watch our mouths a little bit then shit goes back to normal."

I'd gotten to know Rush's kids since joining the club. Watched them a few times with Cas when they came to the bar, played with them at cookouts. His wife worked for a non-profit, and she was always throwing us ideas on how we could bring a little extra money into the club along with other community service stuff. I thought about Tate again, wondering if this might be something she'd get a kick out of since she'd always liked Halloween and hadn't been able to do anything for it while we lived in Northshore.

"Second thing: Ride out on Friday, around 5:00. All of us. It's what we do when we have a new member."

New member.

I sat up out of my slouch, looking to Rev who smirked at me before Cas shoved me clear off the stool. Rush gestured as a few people laughed, and I flicked Cas off over my shoulder before walking to where Rush was standing, holding a patch that read *Foxtrot* between his fingers.

"Meant to give you this when your brother was still in town, but other shit came up. You've earned it, kid."

He slapped me on the shoulder, then spun me around and pulled out a knife to cut the *Prospect* patch off the vest. "Should probably plan on working by yourselves tomorrow," Cas said to Rev and Riot as the brothers crowded around. They ruffled my hair, punched me on the shoulder or in the chest while I laughed.

"Yeah, most likely," Riot said, pushing through the crowd to grab me by the neck and shake me. "I think Fox will be too hungover to hold a wrench."

I bit back a laugh, holding still while Rush slapped the new patch in place. It had a sticky glue on the back, but I'd find a way to sew it on to make sure it didn't come off. The whole bar was filled with cheers, and there were shots being lined up at the bar. All of them for me. A sense of relief filled me that this was over. That I'd proven myself to the guys I'd been hanging around with for the damn near eight months. I'd never had to really, but there was a pressure in being the rookie. Now it was gone. I belonged.

And all I wanted to do was call Tate and tell her she did too.

Chapter Twenty-Three
Tatum

IT WAS ALMOST 1:00 IN THE MORNING, AND I HADN'T slept.

I'd tried, but when I couldn't shut off my brain no matter how many metaphorical sheep hopped through it, I'd gotten up. Now I was standing in my kitchen, kneading dough to make cream cheese rolls with the cherry pie filling I found in my cupboard. Tomorrow was going to be awful.

"Maybe not, but I'm yours."

The rolls needed to rise before they could bake, so I ripped off a piece of wax paper and covered them, then put them in the fridge in case I did fall asleep. It would be a rush if I baked them in the morning, but then they'd be warm and gooey to bring to work, though I'd leave some for Priest.

Who would give at least one or two of them to Kellen.

"Maybe not, but I'm yours."

I stalked out of the kitchen and flopped onto my bed, snatching one of my pillows and wrapping my entire body around it. Why had he said that? What was the point? It felt manipulative, but I didn't know why. And I also knew that calling it manipulative was me searching for a reason to dismiss what he'd said since I couldn't write it off on other things. He wasn't drunk, or high, or delirious. He had been of solid mind and body and told me he was mine.

It was an odd feeling. Especially since he used to tell me I was his.

I hugged the pillow tighter as warmth flooded my chest and stomach. My pulse was fast. The sheets were soft and warm, but I couldn't get comfortable. I was restless. Achy. Dizzy but not tired. Haku curled up on the pillow beside me and I wondered what he'd do if I ever filled that spot. If Kellen slept over one night, the cat would need to find a new place to sleep.

"That's it, baby."

My breathing turned shaky, and I didn't even bother trying to fight the memory. *Memories,* I corrected myself. Plural. It was the first time I'd let someone hold me in three years. And now I craved it more than I craved sugar or sleep or the sun after a week of rain. I craved it so much that the space between my thighs felt hollow and achy and as images of Kellen's face in my lap in a very different scenario popped into my head, I squeezed the pillow tighter and rocked against it.

This was all his fault.

"You feel so fucking good, Tate."

His lips were close as he moved, brushing mine but not kissing. Our breathing was too ragged for us to kiss.

I clutched his shoulders and pawed at his biceps, feeling the muscles in his arms flex as he thrust. He fisted the blanket underneath me, his other hand cupping my thigh, coaxing my leg higher on his hip before he hooked his elbow under it. I gasped when he sank deeper, my vision blurring. His hips moved fast, thrust after thrust, and he was so thick and long, I felt him everywhere.

"God," I whined, not knowing if it was a prayer, a plea, or just a mindless utterance. Words were lost to me. Hadn't he told me I was eloquent when I spoke? So much for that. Now it was whimpers and

whines and breathless gasps. He felt so good I couldn't think straight. The only thing I could manage was his name. "Kell…"

"I know, baby."

He pushed in harder, hips kicking into a faster pace. I clawed at his back and his breath hitched, a soft groan getting lost in my neck before he moved his lips to mine. He kissed me hard, swallowing my gasps, breathing words against my lips I so desperately wanted to believe.

"You're mine, Tate. You've always been mine."

Growling, I threw the pillow away and rolled onto my back, mouth dry as I scrubbed a hand over my face and stared at the ceiling.

Letting him come over and sit in that chair was a bad idea. The entire night, all I'd wanted to do was crawl onto his lap. It was like I'd completely forgotten how much he'd hurt me and was ready to forgive him without any sort of apology.

I also knew, for as much as he'd hurt me, he'd been hurt too. And it seemed equally as stupid to hold a grudge against Kellen for trying to protect me. To give him a strike for things that had been largely out of our control.

But it was easy to forgive him. Too easy. I didn't trust it. It wouldn't be the first time I'd let someone off the hook for hurting me. I'd had thirteen years of that with my parents, and I'd learned my lesson the hard way about letting people get too close.

And forgiveness aside, there was a nostalgic connection between us, but I didn't really know Kellen anymore, did I? And he didn't know me. Plus, the way he'd been dressed reminded me of how horribly mismatched we were. Boots that probably cost more than my cell phone. Designer jeans, ones that I'd have to tease him about if he ever wore them again. And he had friends. He had a whole club that he went to hang out with.

You could have gone too.

Yeah, and I'd have been awkward and shy and would've

embarrassed the shit out of myself by having another panic attack.

Maybe that would have been a good thing. If Kellen saw how much of a mess I was at times, he'd lose interest.

"*Christ, Tate. Bother me. My life is easy. Fuck it up, I don't care. Just be in it again.*"

If I believed him, what would that mean? If we tried again, and it ended badly, would anyone have any sympathy, or would they say I should have known better. Maybe Kellen's feelings were rooted entirely in chasing nostalgia and once he got to know who I was now, that would be the end of it. Or, maybe, I'd get to know who he was, and I wouldn't want him.

Either way, one or both of us would end up hurt. Again.

I started to doze; worn out by the number of laps I'd done in my head. Then, my phone pinged. Late night work calls had trained me to be wide awake at that sound, and I groaned, rolling over and grabbing my phone off the nightstand, expecting to see Pak or Gina's name on my screen.

Instead, it was Priest. He'd sent me a couple of videos.

I swiped up on the first one, smiling as I watched a short clip of a guy who looked to be in his early to mid-forties holding Kellen's denim vest off his body as he cut away a patch. He was saying something, but I couldn't hear him or Kellen over the laughing cheers of the other men in the group. Someone kept yelling the word *Foxtrot*, and I gleaned what it meant when another man came forward and slapped a patch with the word onto the center of Kellen's vest. There were more cheers, and I watched him being jostled about before the camera cut off.

The second video was more of the same. Cheering, laughing, and Kellen was standing on a bar with another guy, the latter cheering as Kellen drank straight from a bottle of Black Velvet. I gritted my teeth, unease settling into my stomach for half a heartbeat before it changed to annoyance. Why was I worried? I didn't need to be. It was clear from these videos that Kellen had plenty of people looking out for him.

My chest tightened as I watched the first video again. If I'd have been there tonight, he would have focused on me. He'd have worried how I was faring with the two women he mentioned or fixated on getting back to me instead of being with his friends and enjoying this rite of passage.

I moved to set the phone aside, but another text from Priest lit up the screen.

PC: *Ride out on Friday. He's going to ask you to come.*

Me: *What's a ride out?*

PC: *Exactly what it sounds like. The whole club rides out.*

Me: *Isn't that a club thing?*

PC: *Don't be cagey. You'd have fun if you let yourself have fun, Noelle.*

I twisted my lips, chewing the bottom one before I typed out a reply.

Me: *Tatum.*

PC: *Tatum.*

Me: *I'm supposed to go out with a friend this Friday.*

PC: *Which friend?*

Me: *Hannah. You met her. She looks like she walked out of an advertisement for Midwest Living. Tall. Blonde. Brown eyes.*

PC: *Yeah, I remember. Meet up with her after.*

Me: *Maybe.*

PC: *Don't make Kellen drag your ass out. Or if he won't, I will. Friday. And plan on sticking around after it. I owe you a drink.*

Me: *For what?*

PC: *Don't "for what" me. Kell told me you got hired. Little pissed you didn't bother to text me, but I'll let it slide. Last time though. You can't ditch me just cause he showed back up.*

I rolled my eyes, smiling to myself as I tossed the phone back on the nightstand, grabbing the pillow I'd been hugging earlier and trying not to imagine it was Kellen. He was probably passed out in his bed, safe and warm, and completely capable of sleeping without me.

"Just like I'm fine without him," I mumbled, settling in for a long night where I knew I'd doze on and off but never really sleep.

Chapter Twenty-Four
Tatum

THE NEXT MORNING, I KNOCKED ON PRIEST'S DOOR, A plate of freshly made pastries in my hand. He opened it, and I bit back a laugh at his disheveled hair and greenish-tinged skin. I offered the plate, but he wrinkled his nose and shook his head.

"Not too sure I'm feeling like pastries. And I know Kellen won't want them."

I nodded sympathetically, able to count on one hand the number of times I'd been drunk, but I'd never been sick or been hung over the next day. Maybe it was good genes or the fact that I stayed hydrated.

Or maybe it was because I never, ever, drank enough to let myself go fully.

"Well, they'll save in the fridge," I said, pushing the paper plate into his hands. "Wheat toast and eggs for you both."

Priest's eyebrows bounced up. "Your nurse friend tell you that or you know it from experience?"

I raised my eyebrows back at him. "I know it from being the child of two functional addicts. Sometimes, that addiction was alcohol, and you learn fast what works to make them stop puking and what doesn't."

Priest clicked his tongue. "My parents were the same, 'cept they never tried to cure their hangovers."

"We'll commiserate some other time on our mutual poor upbringings," I said, taking hold of my bike. "I've got to run."

He gave me a nod instead of a wave, and I pushed the bike down the hall, climbing onto it when I got into the parking lot and coasting most of the way into work. When I got there, I dropped off a roll at Pak's desk to make up for basically shoving him yesterday, then went to see Elissa and drop off another.

"Oooh," she said, eyes widening as she unwrapped the pastry. "You start bringing in breakfast it might get you off coffee duty."

I groaned, leaning dramatically into the wall of her desk. "Oh, come on. I thought getting hired would get me out of that."

"Technically, you're not hired until you sign the papers," she pointed out, using her thumb to wipe gooey cream cheese off her lips. "This is the last week you'll have to do it, though. Gina said we're getting another intern and you can pass on your coffee legacy to the next poor soul. Maybe convince them to still give us the discount though? Now that we hired you?"

I rolled my eyes and playfully snatched the card out of her hand. "Fine. I'll feed your addictions for one more week. But you owe me for the time it takes to do this."

"I agree. How about drinks this Friday? Don't give me an excuse, Noelle. We should celebrate."

Elissa stared hopefully at me while I gritted my teeth. "I ran into an old friend a few weeks ago, and she rarely has time off from work and we were going—"

"She can come, too."

"But there's something else. Another friend of mine just got... accepted or whatever into his motorcycle club, and they're going on a ride or something. He's probably going to ask me to—"

"Motorcycle club?" She sat up, eyes alight with interest. "Which one? A friend of mine from high school owns a motorcycle bar, the same one I was going to suggest we go to." She winked and shrugged her shoulder. "He gives me discounts on drinks."

"You get discounts everywhere, I swear to God." Elissa flashed me a smug grin as I pulled out my phone to look up Kellen's website, thinking it would probably be easier to look him up on Facebook. I should get back on there. Gina said it wasn't required, but I wanted to take my job as seriously as I could. And if something happened, I could always pull back. I'd done it before after all.

I pulled up Kellen's website and found a picture of him in the vest. "Heartland Heathens," I said, almost dropping my phone when Elissa laughed so loud a few people looked up from their desks. She snatched the phone out of my hand, and her eyes got even wider when she saw the picture of Kellen.

"How do you know Fox?"

"Fox?"

"Kellen. They call him Foxtrot because he took—"

"He took dance lessons," I finished, unable to hold back my laugh as I wondered how that had come up. Kellen wasn't keen on sharing that part of his life. Even I hadn't known until he'd taken me to the lake after I graduated and there had been an outdoor concert going on. I'd teased him about staying on rhythm, and he'd grabbed me around the waist, deciding right there was a good place to teach me how to two-step.

The memory made me chest warm. My face too. And Elissa didn't miss it. "You do know him. How?"

I sighed. "We were friends in high school."

She rolled her lips, leaning forward on her knees. "So, if you knew him back then, do you know what he got arrested for?"

A protective urge flared in my chest, and I set my hands on my hips. "How do you know about that?"

"It's a requirement. Every guy in the Heartland Heathens has served time," she explained. "That's their thing. It's their... support group, I guess. Jesse—he's my friend and he's the VP or something—was in for reckless endangerment," she ticked off one finger. "Riot, he works with Fox—er, Kellen—was in for inciting a riot at a protest on land rights. Looper was in for statutory, but he and the girl got married right after he got out. That's a long story."

"How do you know all this?" I asked, eyes widening when she flashed me a wicked smile.

"Jesse and I went to high school together." She winked, wiggling her shoulders. "We've kept in touch, and he talks after he comes."

The heat already in my cheeks flared, and the guy in the cubicle next to Elissa leaned around to look at her. She challenged his curious gaze by folding her arms over her chest and straightening her back. "What?"

"Is this the club you tried to do a story about but no one would talk?"

Elissa rolled her eyes. "Yes. The Prez, Rush, has a hard rule about the press, apparently. They like to be low-key about things, which, I get, but still."

She grumbled the last bit, flicking her nails like she was getting rid of the rejection. "What was your story gonna be?" I asked.

"Motorcycle club organizes charity for a domestic violence shelter," she explained. "They raised $10,000 from giving away vouchers for all the businesses they run. The Prez is married to the head of a non-profit organization, so they do a lot of events for charity."

"That would be a good story," I said. "I know getting out of prison can be tough. Plus, they're all bikers, and that's a stereotype on top of a stereotype."

She quirked an eyebrow at me. "Well, if Kellen is gonna ask

you on a ride out with him, maybe he can get you an in. Favor for an old 'friend.'"

She put air quotes around the last word, and I shook my head. "No. Kellen doesn't owe me any favors."

"Do you know what he was in for?" she asked again. "A lot of the guys are open about it, but Fox and Reverend are pretty tight lipped."

I assumed Reverend was Priest, a play on his name, and rolled my lips, a heavy feeling settling into my stomach. The information was public record, but that protective feeling spiked inside my chest again and I bit the inside of my cheek to stifle it. "I know, but I'm not going to tell you, E. It's his business, not mine."

Elissa let that sink in, arms folded over her chest, her dark hair falling over her face. "We're you guys… close friends?"

Honesty seemed like the best option right now, even if it made the tightness in my chest intensify. "By all definitions, Kellen was my boyfriend."

Elissa sat up straight, her eyes widening in surprise then narrowing. "Noelle, he wasn't the guy—"

"No. No, that… that wasn't Kellen."

I shook my head, but her face remained stern. Motherly, even though she was less than ten years older than me. "You'd tell me if it was."

I breathed a laugh. "If it was him, I wouldn't be hanging out with him now."

She tilted her head, but I waved off any more questions. "Anyway, coffee. I'm going to go because I do have to get some work done before I leave for class."

Her eyes narrowed, a suspicious look on her face as she turned to the keyboard. "Fine. We'll talk when you get back. Or on Friday when we go out. I'm inviting Pak and everyone who works with us."

My smile was tight, but it was still a smile. I turned away, shoving the card into my wallet and grabbing my bag, my thoughts straying to Kellen and Priest and their respective crimes. I hadn't ever bothered to look Priest's up because I trusted him. If he didn't want to talk about it, that was fine. I was the same way about things.

Thinking about the two of them also brought the image of Priest's greenish tinged face back to mind, and I pulled out my headphones, shoving the buds into my ears before dialing Kellen's number. He picked up on the second ring, his voice heavy with sleep.

"Tate? S'everything okay?"

I choked back a laugh and put my foot on the pedal, pushing forward. "You sound like you've been hit by a truck."

Kellen groaned, and there was shifting on the line as he moved around. "Not a truck, just enough shots that I lost count."

"Think you'll make it?" I teased.

"Probably not." He took a breath, then his heavy voice became a little lighter. "I think you need to come over. Nurse me back to health."

"Hey, I made cream cheese rolls and gave them to Priest. That's the extent of my nursing skills. You'll have to call Hannah for anything else."

"No, see, cause Hannah doesn't have your hair, or your mouth. Or your hips. And I think that's what I really need."

I snorted. "My hips?"

"Yes. I need them on top of mine so I can grab—"

"I think you're still drunk." My face was so hot, I worried it might be red, and then people would stare at me and wonder if I'd gotten heatstroke. Thankfully, it was close to ninety degrees today.

"Might be." There was more shifting, then Kellen let out a heavy sigh. "You know, if you'd have been there last night, I wouldn't have drank so much."

"Oh no. Don't try to blame me for your poor life choices." He chuckled, and I stopped at a cross walk, waiting for the traffic to pass. "Besides, I'm past my babysitting days."

"I'm not. Rush has me and Cas watching his kids tomorrow afternoon, so I'll be late if we wanna watch TV."

"If you have plans don't worry—"

"No, don't do that." I could almost hear him shaking his head. "I'll be over, just later. Or, you could come to me and maybe when we get done watching TV, I could make you come."

I'd just started pedaling again, and I jerked handlebars in shock. "God, Kellen. Don't say things like that. I almost rode into the curb."

"I've got something you can ride."

I rolled my eyes, fighting back a smile as I reached the shop and put my bike in its usual spot. "I'm hanging up now. Text me when you're not drunk."

"No, I didn't mean it like that," he said, then he paused. "Well, I did. But literally, I do have something you can ride. I got patched in last night."

"I know, congrats." I moved into the short line, lowering my voice. "Priest sent some videos of it."

"He did?" Kellen let out a dramatic groan.

"They weren't bad," I assured him. "Well, the one where you were on top of the bar drinking straight from the bottle had me a little worried."

I could hear the smile in his voice. "Aw, baby. If you were worried you should have come and got me. Gotten me home safe. Came into my bed and made sure—"

"No functioning car, remember?" I pointed out. "Don't expect me to be your princess in shining armor."

"Nah, I'm a midwestern boy, I don't need a princess. I need my Tatertot."

I sighed. On the surface I hated that stupid nickname and ever since I'd eaten so many tatertots growing up, the sight of them made me feel sick. But deep down, my heart fluttered whenever he used it. He was the only person to ever call me that. The only person I ever *let* call me that.

"I gotta go. I'm almost to the counter," I said, not sure if I could handle any more of his flirting. I was tired, and it was hard to fight the urge to flirt back, especially when he was being so blatantly filthy. Another thing I loathed to admit I liked.

"Okay, but we're doing a ride out on Friday, and I want you with me." The hopeful tone of his voice made my stomach flutter. "I'll get you a helmet. It'll be fun." When I didn't say anything, he let out a small groan. "Come on, Tate. You can trust—"

"Alright, I'm in," I said, cutting him off. Again, I didn't know what I would do if he ever groveled in front of me. Or begged me for something. I don't think I could handle it. "But afterward I'm meeting up with Hannah and my co-workers from the paper who want to take me out to celebrate, but one, Elissa Rivers, was planning on taking me to your bar anyway so... it works out."

"Oh shit, I didn't even think about that." His groggy laugh tickled my ear. "You would know E since you work at the paper. Did you tell her you know me?"

"I did. She was surprised." I bit my lip. "She also told me a little about your club. It sounds interesting, I'd like to meet these guys."

There was a click, then my phone vibrated in my pocket. I pulled it out to see Kellen's face on the screen. He'd changed the call to FaceTime, and here I was, looking pale and exhausted with minimal make up, and he looked gorgeous, even hung over. His hair was a mess, skin a little green, but his lips were full and kissable and he was shirtless. Dark gray sheets were wrapped around his chest, and jealousy flared in my stomach. I wanted to be those sheets, curled against his warm skin, lost in his scent.

Just friends, indeed.

"You will. They'll like you. Maybe there will be someone else who randomly knows both of us."

I rolled my eyes. "If you ask me, the world is too damn small."

Kellen shrugged a muscled shoulder. "I'm glad it's small."

"Why's that?"

"Kept you close enough for me to find."

I shook my head at his grin, my heart pounding behind my ribs. This was so dangerous.

But I wasn't going to stop.

"I gotta go. Text me when you sober up."

"Yup."

He made no move to hang up, just stared at me with those stormy gray-blue eyes, his lips curled into a soft smile.

"Bye, Kell."

He bit his lip, giving me a tired wave into the camera. "Bye, Tatertot."

Neither of us hung up.

I chewed on my bottom lip, finally clicking the line shut when it was my turn at the counter. Weren't we too old to play the *You Hang Up First* game? Apparently not.

When I got back to the office, neither Pak or Elissa were at their desks. Instead, I found them lingering near mine, a copy of the paper in Pak's hands.

"I was going to tell you yesterday, but you left before I had a chance." Pak opened the paper to the second page and passed it to me, tapping the article on the upper portion. My eyes widened at Kara Marlan's face staring back at me. Above her picture was the title of the article I'd been working on. The one I'd finished for class and sent to Pak the next day.

Faces Forgotten: Searching for Answers on Iowa's Missing Persons Cases.

"Gina pushed to get this printed today since it's the anniversary of when this girl vanished." He tapped the date, and I swallowed, scanning the words I'd written until I found what I was looking for. Kara Marlan had been reported missing on September 14th, but she could have vanished weeks or months earlier.

"It's on the homepage, too," Elissa said, beaming at me while Pak had a proud grin on his face. My heart was pounding, excitement coursing when I thought about texting Kellen, or Priest, or Hannah to tell them about this. I should call Isaac too, in case the Lakeside PD was flooded with calls about it. That's where the report was filed, and that's where I said people should call if they had any information.

Despite the exhilaration of seeing my name in print again, unease settled into my stomach. *The Journal* extended far beyond the metro to several of the outlying towns. Including Northshore. Maybe seeing Kara Marlan's face inside it would finally lend some clues as to what happened to her.

I just hoped it wouldn't give anyone the idea of looking for me.

Chapter Twenty-Five
Kellen

"I THOUGHT YOU HATED CATS."

I turned away from the toolbox I was organizing to see Cas holding up my phone, pointing at a picture Tatum's gray and white cat nestled on her lap. Crossing the half-empty garage, I snatched it out of his hand. "Stay the fuck off my phone."

Cas grinned. "Why? Don't want me to see your nudes?"

I could hear Riot and Rev snickering from the driveway, where they were organizing all the shit we'd pulled out when our schedule cleared, and I decided I wanted to clean my garage before winter came. Since we worked out of it half the time, they came over to help.

I rolled my eyes as Cas continued to grin, pocketing the phone before going back to the scattered tools on the bench. "Not any you'd be interested in. And I don't hate cats. Tate's is fine. But I would like to get a dog at some point."

Cas smirked as he went back to sweeping the cement floor. "Dog. Cat. When are you getting the picket fence and the two point five kids?"

"You're older than I am. When are you getting the two point five kids?"

Cas tossed the broom to his other hand and jabbed a sharp finger at me. "Fuckin' never. Don't get me wrong. I like Rush's kids, and Mack's. And Looper's baby is gonna be cute as shit, but I don't want any of my own."

"The idea of a little Cas running around is scary as shit," Rev joked as he shoved one of the larger tool chests back inside, parking it next to me.

"What about you, Old Man?" Cas pressed. "I don't see you making a rush—"

"The fuck you calling me *Old Man*," Rev snapped, kicking Cas' dirt pile into the dustpan. "You're thirty-two."

"And you're thirty-five. Isn't there a cut off?"

"No," Riot said as he pushed the other toolbox in "Look at Rush. He's forty and still knocking Bets up."

"Not still. Oliver is almost a year old," I pointed out, looking over my shoulder when Riot scoffed.

"I bet you a hundred bucks he'll have her pregnant a few months after that kid's birthday. Fucker has a breeding kink."

My phone buzzed, distracting me from the conversation as it devolved into Rush and his kids, and how they'd manage to make more with three already running around. I threw the dirty rag I'd been using over my shoulder and swiped up, grateful my back was turned to the guys when I saw the pic.

Tatertot: *These are the other two tattoos.*

I swallowed hard. I'd seen most of her artwork since it was in fairly visible places. Behind her ear, on her wrist, running the length of her calf. But there were two I hadn't seen, and I'd casually asked in a quick text exchange we had this morning.

The first pic was of her in a towel, the phone obscuring her face as she leaned toward the mirror. On the right side of her collarbone was a thin line of script text that read, *"Follow your heart and keep smiling."* At the end of the text was a small cat and the silhouette of a girl with short dark hair topped by a red bow. It was cute, but it wasn't that pic that made me hunch over to shield my phone, my heart pounding so hard I worried the guys might hear it.

Tate had dropped the towel for the second pic. She'd turned to the side, one arm wrapped tight around her breasts, palm cupping and covering the one closest to the camera. There was another line of soft, cursive script surrounded by misshapen blue and white stars. It read, *"A heart's a heavy burden."*

"Fox, what the fuck?"

Cas' question reached my ears just as I'd ripped off my shirt. I closed the text message and opened my camera, angling it until the right side of my chest was in the frame. She knew about the dark red ouroboros tattoo. I've had that one since I turned eighteen. I'd shown her the forest scenery and bike on my right side at some point, but right now, it was what was on the left that I needed her to see. Hers was script while mine was a bold font surrounded by a few lines and swirls, but they read the same. *"A heart's a heavy burden."*

It was the first tattoo I'd gotten after my release. After I'd finally watched the movie Tate told me I reminded her of. I sent the pic, pulling my shirt back on while I waited for a reply.

"You good, man?" Rev asked.

"Yeah. Tate wanted a pic of my tattoos."

That was a lie. She hadn't asked for a shirtless picture of me, but I hadn't asked for one of her either. We'd entered into an unspoken, mutual agreement to send each other unsolicited pictures with partial nudity. Maybe this meant, at some point, we'd move into sending pictures with actual nudity.

No, scratch that. With how often someone grabbed my phone to look at it, I didn't want pictures of a naked Tate on there for anyone to find.

I'd just have to hide them.

If she ever sent me any, that is.

Tatertot: *Nice. Great minds think alike.*

I'd scrolled back up to look at the second picture she sent

when the message came in, studying the way her hand cupped her breast and imagined myself doing the same. Thoughts of how it would feel to hold the weight of it in my palm, brush my thumb or my lips over her beaded, pink nipple. The towel was low enough that I could see there was a little curve to her stomach, some softness around her hips, and all I wanted to do was nestle my face against her skin, memorize every new slope and curve with my hands and my tongue. I wanted her against me, under me, on top of me. Christ, I wanted her anyway I could have her, in ways that would make her blush and sigh and cry out and forget we were ever apart.

I wanted her in ways that that would make her as addicted to me as I was to her.

Me: *Giving me too much credit. My mind is way too dirty to be great.*

Rev pushed another one of the toolboxes back into the garage, giving me a raised eyebrow look that could have said *you good?* Or asked why the fuck I wasn't helping. I closed the screen on my phone, but it buzzed a second later and another text came through.

Tatertot: *What else you got? I saw some trees or something on the other side of your chest.*

Me: *I'll show you later. We still on for tonight?*

There was a pause, three dots flashing on and off the screen before the next message came through.

Tatertot: *Was gonna mention that. I forgot there was a banquet tonight for staff and interns. I won't be home until late.*

Me: *I'll be up if you still want me to come over.*

More dots, and I turned around, leaning against the counter while I waited for a response. The garage was clean, all that was left were the tools I needed to put away. Rev, Riot, and Cas were standing in the driveway, gesturing to the lake and probably discussing the route we were taking for the ride out on Friday, a decision they didn't need me for. I was far more curious about what had Tate hesitating so long in her response.

Tatertot: *Are you busy around 6:00? I'm allowed a +1. Might be nice to have someone other than Elissa and my editor with me.*

I froze, my stomach flipping so violently, it pushed my heart up into my throat. I didn't reply right away, too shocked that she was asking me out. Tatum was actually asking me out.

Me: *Where at?*

Tatertot: *Hilton downtown. I can meet you there.*

Me: *I can pick you up.*

Tatertot: *Dresses aren't so great on bikes.*

Me: *We'll take my truck.*

More dots on the screen, flashing green and white over and over. I walked out of the garage onto the driveway, nudging Rev, phone still in hand.

"Tatum's lived in that complex for a year," I said, watching as Rev raised his eyebrows, then glanced down at the phone.

"Yeah. Moved in late last June, about a month after I did."

"Has she ever actually driven that car?"

His eyebrows narrowed, and he rubbed at his chin. "Must have. It's there, isn't it? She wouldn't have had it towed." He pressed his lips together, one arm folded over his chest as he continued to rub his chin. "I saw her messing with it last winter and she said it wasn't working right, but she never let me really look at it. Why?"

Tate replied right then, and I looked down, already knowing what the text was gonna say.

Tatertot: *I'll just meet you there. It's close to where I live, so I can walk.*

"She's asking me to go to a thing with her," I said, holding up my phone. "Some banquet. But she won't let me pick her up in my truck."

Rev raised his eyes. "Take your bike?"

"She's gotta wear a dress."

"Have her wear leggings or jeans then change at the place,"

Rev suggested, turning when Cas letting out a low whistle as he looked me up and down.

"A banquet? That sounds fancy. What are you gonna wear?"

I grimaced, looking down at my oil covered jeans, the stains on my hands. "I have that suit jacket I bought last spring for the awards thing. I can throw that on over the jeans Lane left."

Cas shrugged, but Riot tipped his beer bottle in my direction. "Probably should put on a tie. I've been to a few things with Michaela, and I always have to wear a fucking tie."

"You know how to tie one of those damn things?" Rev asked, and they started miming the motions, looking my way to see if I was watching.

I was, but my mind was elsewhere, stuck in a loop trying to figure out why Tate was scared to drive, or even ride in, a car.

Chapter Twenty-Six
Kellen

I PARKED MY TRUCK IN THE NARROW, CROWDED parking lot near the hotel at about 5:55, tugging on the end of my suit coat as I got out of the cab. The jeans Lane left for me were custom fit. Deep blue, soft instead of the usual stiff feel of denim. They probably cost hundreds of dollars; I'd never bother spending so much money on clothes. The shirt I had on belonged to Riot, an off-white button down that I'd covered with the only part of a suit I owned. The coat—tan, with a pocket on the chest and buttons to close that I didn't bother fastening. I shoved my keys in my pocket, looking around for Tate as I walked toward the lobby. Men and women dressed in khakis and button downs, or full suits and dresses, lingered outside the doors and inside the lobby. College professors, I guessed, but none like I'd ever had. Mine had always been covered in oil and swore more often than sailors did. Just like the guys I hung around with now.

Just like me.

"Kellen!"

I turned toward the shout, stopping awkwardly when I saw Tate emerge from a small crowd of people. A white dress hugged the curves of her body, caressing them like I wanted to as she walked, her short heels clicking against the pavement. She'd twisted her dark hair into an updo, exposing her long neck and the slope of her shoulders. Her makeup was soft, save for the red she'd painted on her lips; red I wanted to see smeared all over my neck and down my chest.

"Christ." I met her halfway, forcing my hands into my pockets so I didn't grab her and pull her against me in front of everyone. "You look…"

She smiled, but it was tight, her palms smoothing down the front of her dress. "Is it too much? I feel overdressed."

"Well, you're making up for me then cause I'm underdressed."

She laughed softly, pressing her lips together as she gave me an assessing look up and down. "I don't think so. You look good."

"You look like a fucking wet dream."

Her cheeks flushed pink, eyes widening, and I bit back a frown when I saw she was wearing those contacts again. *Get used to it*, I told myself, following when she turned and started to walk back to the hotel, her hands in front of her waist, fingers twisting.

I fisted my hands to resist the urge to take hers. My chest was tight as I felt numerous pairs of eyes studying the two of us together; Tate so poised and beautiful even while she fidgeted, and me in jeans, slightly scuffed shoes, and a suit jacket just long enough to cover the tattoos that ran up both my arms. The collar of the shirt was unbuttoned, and the ink on my chest was visible, same with the ink on my neck. The small taurus tattoo surrounded by small flowers.

The one that matched Tate's cancer symbol that peeked out from behind her ear.

I stayed close to her side as she introduced me to a few colleagues, my eyes widening when Elissa came jogging over to us with a guy who looked about my age. At first I thought they might be a couple, which would interest Cas since he and Elissa hooked up sometimes, but it only took a few exchanged words for me to pick up on who the guy had come here for. He didn't take his dark eyes off Tate, not even when she turned and took me by the arm, gesturing with her other hand.

"Kell, you know Elissa. This is Pak, the head editor. *My* editor technically since I send him all my pitches."

I tipped my chin toward him, taking the guy's hand, surprised by how tight he squeezed.

"Nice to meet you…" he said, dark eyes looking me up and down, narrowing slightly.

"Kellen," I said, meeting his curious gaze, then frowning when his eyes went straight to Tatum again. Couldn't blame the guy, but I didn't like it.

I also knew that if he was her editor, I couldn't say shit since I didn't want to screw things up for her.

Tate stayed next to me while they talked shop, the group slowly moving toward an elevator down the hall. When it opened, they started to pile in and I followed, at least until I saw Tate hanging back.

"Oh, no, we'll catch the next one." Her eyes caught mine, and I immediately stepped back into place at her side while Elissa gestured, squeezing herself in beside Pak and the others.

"No, there's enough—"

"It's fine. See you in a minute," Tate said, a bright smile plastered on her face. It stayed until the elevator doors shut, then she slumped so dramatically I almost reached out to grab her.

"You good?"

Her eyes rolled, and she took a breath, steadying her shoulders and re-straightening her spine. "Yeah, I'm fine. It's just a lot."

"Crowds suck."

She grinned. "Yeah, and elevators don't help. I just need a minute, then I'll be good."

She was clawing at the front of her dress, the lines of her body tight despite the softness of her curves. I reached for her, taking one of her hands in mine. She tensed, but didn't pull away, not even when I lifted her knuckles and pressed them to my lips.

"These things aren't my scene either. I own one pair of khakis, and they're too small."

Her fingers relaxed in mine, and I watched a smile—a *real* smile—curl her red lips. "You look better in jeans."

"Glad you think so." I kissed her fingers again, keeping our hands together when the elevator doors opened. "Ready?"

Tate's shoulders and chest rose on a breath, then dropped again when she blew it out through pursed lips. "Yeah. I need to eat. That'll help."

"Wine might, too."

She shook her head. "No wine. Alcohol makes it worse," she murmured, tugging me into the elevator, our hands staying linked together the entire way up.

TATE DIDN'T NEED THE WINE, BUT I DID. AT LEAST one glass. The conversations were so far out of my league I wasn't even on the field. Discussions on journalism versus reporting, the loss of print media and what that meant for the world as a whole. Topics related to her profession. Her internship. Things I couldn't contribute to in the slightest.

I poked at my food, choking down seasoned chicken and a few vegetables while my stomach twisted. People stopped by the table frequently, congratulating "Noelle" on turning her internship into a career. They commented on her work, asked her about the series she was doing on missing persons cases, how the idea came to her. She left out that, for a while, her name had been among the missing. That for three years a lot of people had thought she was dead.

It made me wonder about the other girls she was researching. If they were out there, hidden in plain sight with new names, or if their fates had taken a different turn.

A few times the conversation turned to me, and I smiled and answered questions. I owned a business. Custom motorcycles and auto repairs. A few of the sports guys recognized my name because I'd built a bike for a local motocross celebrity, but that was about as interesting as it got.

Eventually a few people asked how Tate and I knew each other. She took over then. We'd gone to school together. Grew up in the same town. She called me a friend, but she never said we were "just friends," and no one asked, but Pak paid very close attention. He kept his eyes on Tate, watching her responses, smiling whenever she said anything slightly amusing. My jaw ached, and I wondered if I should get another glass of wine to loosen it. Temper the burn simmering in my chest.

When the speakers finished and they started bringing out dessert, a tall woman in a sharp-looking pantsuit came to collect Tate. She clearly held power because Tate didn't hesitate when called. Elissa and Pak watched her go, whispering to each other.

"Who was that?" I asked.

"News Editor," Elissa said. "She's the boss. She's probably trying to help her make connections." Her fingers drummed the table, and she wiggled her shoulders, a mischievous look crossing her face. "So, when did you and Noelle start seeing each other?"

My eyes flicked to Pak, and I watched him visibly stiffen as he reached for the glass of wine in front of him. "A few weeks ago, I can't remember exactly," I said casually, trying to balance the truth with the lie. We weren't seeing each other. Not yet. Not officially.

But I didn't want to give this Pak guy any leeway. If there

was going to be some sort of an unspoken pissing match, I wanted to win.

I had to win.

I didn't know what I'd do if I didn't.

"I took her out for lunch a week or so ago. After that church conference she covered." Pak finished his drink, setting the glass back on the table. "She didn't mention a boyfriend then."

"She wouldn't," I said. "She's... private."

Elissa laughed, and when Pak frowned, she gave him a sympathetic smile before turning back to me. "I'm surprised you convinced her to come out. When did she tell you about this?"

"Uh, today," I replied. "Said she forgot it was happening until this afternoon."

Pak tilted his head, looking at Elissa, who sighed heavily before glancing to where Tate was standing with her Director, the pair of them engaged in a conversation with a couple of suits and another woman in a short, fitted skirt. "She didn't forget," Elissa murmured. "I reminded her about it yesterday. And Monday. She always avoids events if she can, but I'm guessing Gina talked to her."

"She needs to come to things like this," Pak said, the tone in his voice put me on edge. "Gina told me she hasn't set up any social media and that I should nudge her about it. I tried, but she brushed it off. Wesley even offered to take her picture, but she left before he had a chance." His dark eyes flicked to me, a challenge in them. "Do you know what that's all about?"

I clenched my jaw, trying not to bite out that if Tate didn't want to plaster her face everywhere, no one should make her. She could do this job without it, right? It wasn't impossible.

Before I could speak, Elissa sighed and turned to Pak. "She's got her reasons, Pak. She told me something after we tried to throw her that surprise party that explains a lot."

"What'd she tell you?" he asked.

"If she wanted you to know, she'd tell you," I snapped, and he gave me another challenging look.

"Has she told you?"

The silverware on the table rattled when my knee hit the table leg, every muscle in my body tensing. I bit the inside of my cheek, lowering my hands to my lap and curling them into fists. *Keep it together, asshole. That's her editor. She'll hate you if you fuck things up for her.*

Elissa looked me up and down, drumming her fingers on the table before she looked back to Pak. "She had a stalker. It was bad. Noelle said he tried to kill her."

"Oh my God."

"He what?!"

Pak and I spoke it at the same time, both of us looking at Elissa with wide eyes. He immediately narrowed his, and there was something accusatory in them that reminded me of how the cops looked at me the day I was arrested, when they'd tried to pin the bruises Tate had all over her arms and face on me. This guy was doing the same thing, those dark eyes looking me over, stopping on my shaggy hair, the plugs in my ears, the tattoos peeking out from under my sleeve, the calloused knuckles and scraped hands. I stared back, grimacing at his perfectly styled hair, probably $200 shirt, the fucking khakis that complimented Tate's dress. If this guy and I stood next to each other, I knew who everyone would assume Tate should be with. The same way they assumed I'd hurt her while Davey, with his clean-cut image and hours in a church pew, never would.

"I don't think we should get into this," I said, finally dropping my eyes as the food in my stomach soured. "If she wanted to tell either of us, she would have."

Pak leveled me with a cautioning gaze. "Or maybe, she doesn't want to talk about it because she doesn't feel safe. And maybe she doesn't feel safe because every time someone has looked at her tonight, you get—"

"If I were you, I'd stop talking right fucking now."

Pak opened his mouth, but Elissa glared at him before shoving him back, then she swatted me across the shoulder. "Oh, knock it off. Both of you. I can only imagine how she'd chew both your asses out if she saw this."

Pak frowned, a sheepish expression crossing his face while I folded my arms, glaring back at Elissa with raised eyebrows as she continued. "Kellen's right anyway. If she wanted to tell any of us, she would. So, leave it be. I don't want to make her anymore anxious than she already is by gossiping about her."

My fists clenched on the tops of my thighs, but I nodded, watching as Pak sat back in his chair. "I'm only trying to look out for her," he said. "She's got talent. I don't want to see her career stall because she's afraid to put herself out there. For whatever reason."

"Her career isn't going to stall," I said, more forcefully than I'd planned. "And she's always had talent. I know. I used to read stuff she wrote back in high school." Pak opened his mouth again, but I shook my head and pointed to my chest. "Let me talk to her, all right? I'll... give her a nudge about the fucking social media stuff. Sometimes if you push Tate, she only gets more closed off."

I looked at Elissa for back up, but she was grimacing, and Pak stared between us, bewildered. "Tate?"

My eyes widened, then I let out a long heavy sigh. "Shit." I bumped my fist on the table, cursing myself using every insult I knew until Elissa nudged my shoulder.

"It's okay, Fox. She told me about the name change." When Pak still look bewildered, Elissa leaned close to him, lowering her voice. "She changed her name because of that stalker guy. It used to be Tatum."

Pak blinked, the confusion on his face fading away. His eyebrows narrowed, and he folded his arms over his chest, pressing his lips together as he looked back at Tate with her boss. "Tatum Noelle?"

"T.N.," Elissa confirmed, alarm creeping into her eyes at the same time it seized my body. "Pak, what? Why are you making that face?"

I leaned forward on the table, my heart pounding, both Elissa and I staring at Pak expectantly. He frowned, then pulled out his phone, typing in the pass code before he began thumbing around on the screen.

"I had to filter the comments on her article about the church conference because they started to get aggressive. Didn't think anything of it. It happens. Trolls are everywhere, and this stuff is practically in the job description," he added, looking to me before glancing back at the screen. "But this week, they started to get more specific. There were a few users commenting specifically on Noelle's work. All of it. Even the old ones about city council meetings and stuff."

"What did they say?" I demanded, grabbing his phone when he offered it to me. My stomach heaved, the fancy food I'd just eaten threatening to come back up.

Parker H: *Tatum, you know better than to speak so boldly on things you don't understand.*

Bran K: *Your penance is coming, and soon, Tatum.*

Carson L: *You can't hide forever, Tatum. God sees everything.*

I kept scrolling, my heart pounding as I saw her name—her real name—repeated over and over in the comments. All from various users that could have been anyone. Nothing she'd be able to report or get protection from. Nothing anyone would suspect. Trolls were everywhere. It was part of the job.

"She doesn't know about these?" I asked, handing Pak the phone. He shook his head.

"No, I haven't told her. I didn't..." He frowned, looking at Elissa's horrified face. "I didn't want to scare her when she was just getting started. You saw how she acted when we just tried to surprise her. I didn't want to make it worse."

"Should we let her know?" Elissa asked, looking to me, her eyebrows raising when I shook my head.

"No, I..."

I swallowed, unease twisting my stomach. Was it selfish to keep her in the dark? I didn't want this to be what closed her off again. What made her quit a job she'd worked so hard to get and run, all because some asshole had figured out her name. She couldn't do that again, uproot her life out of fear. She needed to stay.

I wanted her to stay.

I wanted to keep her safe this time.

I had to.

"My friend's a cop, and I know from talking to him that this wouldn't hold up. There are too many names, no specific person to report. Restraining orders—"

"Are really hard to get," Elissa filled in with a scoff. "I've done enough crime reporting to know that. It's just going to upset her and there's nothing we can do."

"She rides her bike to work every day," Pak said, folding his arms over his chest. "I don't want to think about someone attacking her or—"

I held up a hand. "I've got it."

He gave me a placating frown. "You can't watch her twenty-four—"

"I said I've got it."

Pak stared, and I let out a slow breath, relenting on one thing. "But, will you tell me if it gets worse? If it turns into something she can actually report to the police?"

His expression was dubious, but when we heard bright laughter and all looked over to see Tate, hands still in front of her waist, fingers twisted tight together as she and her boss talked, Pak relented and gave me a curt nod.

"Alright. I'll keep my mouth shut. For now."

I rapped my knuckles on the table, smiling when Tate slid into the chair beside me. I grabbed her hand under the table, squeezing it tightly, trying to smile casually when she gave me a curious look.

I wasn't going to let anything, or anyone, take her from me. Not this time.

Chapter Twenty-Seven
Tatum

THE NIGHT AIR WAS COOL WHEN WE GOT OUTSIDE after the banquet ended. Brisk, almost. "Classic midwestern fall," Elissa grumbled as she rubbed her arms, keys dangling between her fingers. "Wasn't it like eighty degrees today?"

"Somewhere around that," I said, trying to hide the fact that I was sucking in deep breaths of air like I'd been underwater for the last three hours. It had seemed that way at times. I didn't mind the table chatter, but when Gina walked me around the room, introducing me to at least twenty people whose names I wouldn't remember, all I'd wanted to do was run.

"So we're still on for Friday," Elissa confirmed, beaming at me when I nodded. "Around 7:00? That's when it usually picks up there."

"I'm guessing that'll work. I don't know how long the ride along thing is."

"Ride out."

Kellen stepped beside me, his hand finding the small of my back. The warmth of his palm bled through the thick fabric of my dress, a small pocket of heat that made the rest of my body feel too cold. It was a presumptive gesture, kind of like the hand holding had been.

But I was so grateful for it I could cry.

When I'd asked him to come with me this afternoon, it had been an impromptu decision. I wanted someone to talk to if the conversation died and I couldn't leave. Kellen was good for that. He was easy to talk to and would make me smile.

But he steadied me in a way I hadn't expected. Gave me something to hold onto when I was grappling for purchase on rocky ledges. Something to ground myself with when I felt like I was slipping.

I should buy him a drink or something. Apologize for using him as a crutch when I should be learning to walk on my own.

Elissa eyed Kellen's hand on my back, then gave me a mischievous smirk before she waved and walked to her car. Pak was a few steps behind her, saying a quick goodbye, his expression pensive. Maybe even upset, but I didn't know what to say.

"You don't need to say anything," Kellen told me, reading my hesitation clearly as we walked to his truck. "Honest, you don't. If you're not into the guy, that's fine."

I licked my lips, tasting lipstick, and tried not to frown. "What about you? If I'm not into you, is it fine?"

He gave me a look, a half-smile tugging on his lips. "Yeah, it's fine. I'll just hang around until you are into me. Kind of like a cat pawing at your window."

I glared playfully. "If you're talking about Haku, I set food and water out for him. Not quite the same."

"You asked me out. It's a little the same."

I shoved him, biting back a smile when he feigned injury and rubbed his stomach. "I'll talk to you later, Kell. Thank you for coming with me."

"Whoa, whoa," he said, reaching out for my arm when I turned away. "No. You're not walking home. Not at 9:00 at night across town."

"I'll be fine," I said, waving off the concern on his face. "I can take care of myself. I used to walk home all the time from—"

"No, it's not happening."

"Kellen."

I met his stern glare with a placating one, looking down at the hand he still had on my bicep. His grip wasn't tight, so I gently pushed him off, and he let me. "I'm fine. It's out of your way anyway. You can get right on the interstate from here and go home."

"It's not that late. You want to watch more *Fruits Basket?*"

I bit my lip. It would be nice, but I'd pushed my boundaries enough for the night, and if let him sit in my apartment, with those jeans that showed off his ass and that dress shirt I'd been itching to get off him, I might cross them all together.

Kellen pressed his lips together, his eyes dropping from mine as he moved closer, one hand trailing along the side of the truck. He patted it, raising his eyebrows as he looked from the vehicle to me. "You know, this is the same truck I had—"

"I know."

I hadn't brought up the truck, or the ride part of his proposal. My feet were already dangerously close to the edge of a cliff, and the heels on my feet weren't steady. A therapist told me that, overtime, exposure could decrease my responses to certain stimuli. Crowds. Cars. Being touched on the neck. I understood the logic but doing more than one at a time seemed like a recipe for disaster.

Kellen patted the passenger door of the truck, that soft smile still playing on his lips. "So, you know there's no reason to be scared of this truck."

I didn't nod, but logically, I knew he was right. I'd ridden in this truck more often than I'd driven my own car, and the memories associated with it were ones I was fond of, even if my chest started to ache as they came rushing back. Parking it at the beach while we went swimming. Sitting in the back watching movies at the drive in. The blankets and pillows Kellen always carried in case we wanted to drive away from the town and look at the stars. The annual meteor shower had been active that year, and sometimes we went out and tried to see the shooting stars. I never did see any. Not in the sky, at least.

"Baby."

Kellen whispered the pet name, and I shivered as he slipped a hand around my waist, tucking me into the warmth of his body. I shook my head even as I melted into his shirt, my hands fisting the material, using him again to try and stave off the memories lurking at the edges of my thoughts. Like shadows waiting to creep in once the light died.

"I'm not your baby," I said, but there was no substance to the protest. The words were hollow, and Kellen knew it. He squeezed me tighter, then I heard the heavy clunk of the door handle being pulled, and the passenger side of his truck opened, revealing faux leather seats I knew. Worn foot mats. A spattering of papers and other general debris picked up as he'd climbed in and out. I looked up and Kellen's expression was sad. Sympathetic. Worried. He didn't ask why I was so scared of his truck, or of my car, or of any car. Had he surmised enough to figure out what happened? Could he read me so well I wouldn't ever have to speak the memory out loud?

"Tate." He spoke into my hair, and I fought so hard not to lean into his lips. "You can't expect me to let you walk home. It's not safe."

I ducked my head, annoyed by how right he was. It wasn't the first time I'd heard this argument either, and each time it came up, I knew how irrational my thoughts were. Statistically, I was far more likely to get hurt on the mile walk back to my apartment than I was in Kellen's truck.

But statistics didn't mean shit once you became one, and I

hadn't been attacked on the street by someone jumping out of the shadows. I'd been attacked in a car. A locked one. Where I thought I was safe.

"Come on."

Kellen's arm stayed around my waist, and he urged me forward, taking my hand to help me step up into the cab. My throat felt like it was swollen shut, burning from the bile creeping into it, my heart pounding so hard it made me feel weak. My heel landed on the step and I slipped, but he caught me, gently pushing me up again. I didn't remember his truck being this tall. Was it always this tall? Or did it feel like that because my world was shrinking? Condensing into a single memory I had no desire to relive. The squeak of my body settling onto the seat made me jump, and the truck had seemed so tall and big on the outside, but inside it felt small. A reverse *TARDIS*, and there was no doctor who could help me now.

"There you go. Good girl."

Kellen was next to me, his hand still on my waist as he reached over my body, grabbing the seat belt. I jolted back, pushing his hands away before he could click it into place.

"No."

He pressed his lips together, then nodded. "Okay. No belt."

I watched him hop down, practically running around the truck to get in the driver's seat. He left the passenger door open. I could run. I could get out of this place and run away. Would he stop me?

The driver's side door opened and I jumped, hitting the dash as Kellen climbed in, keys in his hands. His face was blurry when I looked at him, shadows and light from a streetlamp distorting his familiar face. He leaned over me and I flinched back, a pathetic, reedy whimper slipping past my lips. "Tatum, baby—"

"Just go, *please*."

My voice was raspy and rough, shaking so much I could barely get the words out. The keys rattled, and Kellen started the engine. He was talking to me. Saying something. My name maybe. But it was lost to the sound of shattering glass, the high-pitched tinkling sound as it scattered, falling all over my lap. My body was pushed back, the center console making my spine bend awkwardly as Davey crawled on top of me. His weight made the glass dig into my clothes, into my skin. I drew my legs up curling my body over them, braced against the imaginary fists, the invisible hands closing around my throat...

The door beside me flung open, and I flailed, hands and legs extending, stiffened in defense. But it wasn't Davey standing in the doorway. It was Kellen, his eyes wide, palms splayed in surrender. "You're safe," he murmured, stepping back and gesturing to my building. "You're back home, Tate, look."

I could see my building, the yellow lights glowing softly around the entry way. Kellen beckoned, taking my hands, coaxing me out of the truck. My feet were on the pavement, but when I put weight into my legs they buckled. His arms tightened around me, holding me to his side as we moved. The cold air wasn't refreshing anymore. It burned my throat, searing the inside of my lungs. I couldn't catch my breath.

Kellen supported me as we walked across the parking lot and into the building. We went from cold air and darkness broken by yellow fluorescents to a warmer space bathed in white glaring light. I was dizzy, and his face was still blurry. Stupid contacts. Or was it tears. Was I crying?

"Baby, which key is it?"

I looked down. Kellen had my purse. It was slung over his shoulder, my keys in his hand. "Silver one. Round," I said, the sound of my voice loud in the hallway. He pushed the key into the lock and the door opened, and then his arms were around me again, carrying me inside. Haku was mewling, trotting over to circle my legs as Kellen walked me to the couch. I collapsed onto it, and he grabbed a blanket off the back, draping it over my shoulders. The ends of it pulled around me, tight, tucking into my chest and I flailed again, knocking his hands back.

"No," I managed, shaking my head. "Don't... don't touch me there."

"Where?"

My breath was coming so fast and hard I couldn't speak, but I gestured to my neck, letting my fingers trail over the skin. I felt the pressure of hands that weren't there, the ache that had long since passed...

Kellen's presence vanished, but he returned a second later, a glass of water in his hand. He set it on the table, then resumed his spot in front of me. "I won't touch your neck," he assured, gathering my shaking hands in his. He kissed the knuckles before lowering them to my lap, holding them there with one hand while the other smoothed up and down my arm.

"Tate? Look at me, baby." He waited until I managed to lift my eyes to his, stormy blue-gray locking with green-blue. Or brown. My contacts were still in. "You're safe, okay? Breathe. Can you do that for me?"

I made a valiant attempt to match Kellen's deep inhales and exhales. He had to be bored. Or unnerved. Upset. Why was he still here? Why was he watching me crumble like this? It was humiliating. There was nothing in it for him.

"I'm sorry."

Kellen's soothing hand paused on my arm, his eyes widening. "Sorry? Why are you sorry?"

"That I..."

I gestured to myself. The shaking hands, the tears staining my cheeks. My fingertips felt too warm when I went to brush them away, and I startled when Kellen reached up, doing the same thing with his thumbs.

"Don't apologize to me," he murmured, that pained expression returning as he cupped my face, his thumbs wiping away the tears that were still falling. "Tell me what to do, Tate. Tell me what has you so scared you can't even sit in my truck."

My lip trembled, and I tried to shake my head, but he held me steady, shushing me softly as he moved closer. His face came into focus then blurred, and I grumbled, jerking away from his touch to rub at my eyes.

"Fucking *contacts*."

"What do you need to take them out?" he asked, looking toward my bathroom.

"There's a case in there. It's white."

He stood again, and I listened to him walking as I pushed out the annoying things, letting the lenses fall into my palm. Kellen returned with the case, offering it to me as he kneeled again. When I set it aside and turned back, I watched his shoulders sag, and he let out a soft, breathy laugh when he reached up to cup my face.

"God," he murmured, thumb brushing along my cheekbone. "There she is."

My body stiffened at the words, and I looked away, wrapping my arms around my chest. "Not sure if you've noticed, but she's gone."

He shook his head gently. "No, she's not."

I bit the inside of my cheek, the fear clawing at my insides, exposing another emotion. My chest felt hot. So did my stomach. My legs, my face, my ears. I swallowed against the tightness that lingered in my throat, casting Kellen a quick glance before I turned away.

"I think you should go."

He said nothing, but the gentle hands holding me, slowly smoothing up and down my arms, stilled. I tucked my chin into my shoulder and curled in on myself. Was it crueler to end it now and save us both the pain? Or let this drag on when I knew he'd eventually get tired of it. Because who wouldn't? Who wants to date a girl who can't even ride in a fucking car? Who has to take breaks from the crowd when she goes out? Kellen didn't know it, but I'd walked away from Gina at least two or three times during her round of introductions to use the bathroom, blaming it on the wine I hadn't drank, all so I could go in the bathroom and try steady my breathing.

"Baby—"

"No, Kellen. I'm not your baby. This isn't happening. It can't."

I reached down, unfastening the straps on my shoes and sliding my feet out of them, kicking the heels aside. Kellen backed away, standing when I did, his arms extending to help me when I tried to stand only to have my legs give out again. "*Goddammit*," I snarled, shoving Kellen's attempt at supporting me away. "Please, just go."

"Tate, what did I do?" he asked, his voice tight." Please just... tell me."

I turned my back to him, leaning on the edge of the couch, then a chair by my table as I tried to escape. I didn't want to see his eyes or hear the plea in his voice. The desperation for someone we'd both lost.

"Tatum—"

"I said *go*, Kellen."

"No."

I turned at the word, my eyes wide at his refusal. It was the first time he'd denied a request since... whatever this was started last week, or the week before that. I didn't know. Time had lost all meaning. A circle that tried to loop in on itself, forcing me to repeat the past. Relive moments I'd tried so hard to forget. Kellen's fists were tight at his sides, his shoulders tense, and when I opened my mouth, he stalked forward, shaking his head when I backed away.

"No, I'm not leaving. This isn't how this ends. I didn't find you again to let it end like this."

"It can't end because nothing started," I shot back. "You're chasing a ghost, Kellen. You want the girl I was and she doesn't exist anymore. She died in that shitty car I used to drive, choked out by a psychopath bent on making her submit or killing her to purify his sins." I jabbed a finger at my chest. "I'm what's left. *Me*. And I can't drive or ride in a car without wanting to puke. Without thinking about that night. And that's just one of at least fifteen things I can't do anymore, and you don't want—"

"Don't tell me what I want," Kellen growled. "I know what I want. I've known what I wanted since the moment I saw you. Since before I could want you. I've been yours since we were under that tree together, Tate. I was yours that summer. I was yours for the *three fucking years* we were apart. I'm yours now, and there's not a damn thing you can say or do or feel that will change that."

He moved closer, backing me into the counter, his hands reaching for mine then balling into fists again when I pushed them away. "Tatum, please. I won't hurt you. You know I would never—"

"Except you did," I whispered, voice shaking as I reached to wipe away fresh tears. "You did hurt me, Kellen. Not in the same way Davey did but sometimes... sometimes, I think it was worse."

I covered my mouth to stifle a sob, watching Kellen's beautiful face fall. He made a noise, a choked sound and reached for me again, but I pushed his hands away.

"Tate—"

"No, Kellen. I loved you."

His eyes widened, shining so bright in the dim light of my kitchen. My hand slid from my mouth to my chest, pressing against my racing heart, against the ache threatening to tear me apart from the inside. I'd said it. The truth I'd never told him, the words I'd always bit back because I knew they wouldn't be returned. I'd loved him, and somewhere inside, part of me still did. Part of me always would, because you never forget your first love. People say it's because of the way it cuts you. The bruises it leaves behind, but thinking about it now, it was much deeper than that.

You never forget that first love because it doesn't cut. It flays. It peels away every barrier you've put up and you welcome it. You lay yourself at their feet, skinless and bare, heart exposed in offering regardless of the outcome. Will they take it? Will they leave it and walk away? Will they pick it up and examine it like an interesting curio, then toss it aside because it has no value?

The possibilities are endless, but in the moment you don't care. I certainly didn't. I'd been enamored with Kellen, with his sweet words, the freedom he gave me, the storm that always lingered in his eyes. So enamored that I'd let him rip my heart out and take it with him when he left.

And now he wanted to do it again.

"Kellen, please go."

He looked at me, shaking his head, his lips pressed tightly together before he parted them on a raspy, shaky gasp. "Tatum, I'm sorry. I'm so—"

"You don't need to apologize."

"I do. I am. I'm sorry."

"It doesn't matter if you are. I don't..." I choked back a sob, and he did the same, trying so hard to pull me into his arms. "I don't think I can do it again. You tore me apart. You looked me right in the eyes and you said—"

"I know what I said." His voice was hoarse, eyes shining, hair falling out of the careful style he'd had it in to brush his forehead. "I know exactly what I said, and I've regretted it every single day since. It's all I can think about sometimes because it was a lie. Tate, it was a lie to get you to leave because I didn't want… I didn't want you throwing your life away because of me."

"I know why you said it, Kellen, but that doesn't lessen the damage."

My eyes stung, and I watched him swallow and nod, his own lips trembling. "I know. I know it doesn't. But it won't happen again. I swear it won't happen again."

"You don't even know me now," I argued. "And I don't know you. We're not the same people—"

"Then let me know you," he said, and my eyes widened when he laughed, tears slipping onto his cheeks. "You're right, we're not the same people, and that's fine." He lifted a hand, trailing a finger over the collar of my dress, tugging it aside and touching the ink below my collar bone. I closed my eyes, tears slipping onto my cheeks as his hand lowered, his palm cupping my ribs where the other design sat. The quote I loved so much, the same quote he'd inked into his skin.

"But you're not that different, Tate. I'm not chasing a ghost. I'm chasing you. Everything you were, everything you are now, and whatever you're going to become. I want it all."

His other hand lifted, cupping my face and holding me still as he pressed his forehead to mine. I licked my lips, tasting the salt of my tears, then the salt of his when he leaned in. He pressed his mouth to mine softly. The first kiss I'd gotten in three years, and it happened while I was crying.

It was chaste, the way his lips pressed to mine. Soft, but closed. No hint of his breath, no caress from his tongue. Kellen held me with a light grasp, and when I whimpered, he pulled back, choosing to kiss my cheeks, my nose, then my forehead instead of my lips. I let out a shaky breath, the urge to shove him away and run almost a strong as the desire to pull him in. To beg for more when I didn't even know if I could take it.

"Baby, please trust me. Let me in." The words kissed my skin, trying to work their way into my chaotic thoughts. "You can't keep yourself locked up forever. You are denying yourself hope or a chance to heal and its…"

I looked up to see that he'd grimaced, his eyes sad as they moved over my face. "It's just another form of abstinence, Tate."

My eyes closed at the word and the shame and guilt it conjured up. The feelings of failure, and the danger of indulgence. My life was devoid of them all. No caffeine. No alcohol. No sex. No joy. No hope. I wasn't living. I was caged.

And part of me so badly wanted to be set free.

Kellen kissed my forehead again, his fingers curling around my jaw so he could lift my gaze to his. To where his eyes could stare into mine. His face wasn't blurry anymore. It was clear, and so handsome. So familiar. So safe. If I let myself keep looking, I'd never want to stop. He'd be my vice. An addiction I couldn't control.

And I was so scared it would tear me apart.

"I can't promise you anything, Kellen. I don't know if… if I'm ever going to be okay."

"You're okay now, Tate. You're not broken. You never were. There was nothing wrong with you then, and there's nothing wrong with you now." He dipped his head and kissed me again, quickly. Softly. His lips lingering against mine, breathing more promises into my skin.

"I'll do whatever you need, Tate, I promise. Anything except let you go. I did that once. I'm not fucking doing it again."

He took a shaky breath, his eyes closing, forehead pressing hard to mine as he squeezed me so tight it took my breath away. My shaky hands slid up his arms, finding his shoulders, then looping around his neck. He groaned, burying his face in my neck while mine got lost in his shoulder. Fear and hope twisted inside my chest, tugging at the bars around my heart, simultaneously trying to free it and keep it locked up.

I wanted to believe him, and part of me did, but it wasn't because of the vows he'd made to me. It was his last statement that looped through my thoughts, that loosened the tension in my muscles and made me squeeze him tighter. *Anything except let you go. I did that once. I'm not fucking doing it again.*

That wasn't a promise to me.

It was one to himself.

Chapter Twenty-Eight

Tatum

I WAS SO TIRED THE FOLLOWING MORNING THAT, instead of the tea I usually drank, I had the new intern, an overeager guy named Josh, get me a large coffee. Black. No sugar. The caffeine would wreak enough havoc on my anxiety.

Elissa stopped by right after Josh left, and her first question was whether or not I'd spent the night alone. *Yes*, I told her. Kellen left after I'd assured him I was fine, though we'd laid beside each other on my bed in varying states of embrace before that. Elissa gave me an approving look, then immediately made sure I was still planning on showing up at my celebratory gathering tonight. 7:00 p.m. at Styx, which was located on a long stretch of highway between Des Moines and Saylorville where Kellen lived. She'd given me the address and when I looked it up on a map, I immediately texted Kellen to tell him I understood the name of the bar.

Me: *Out in the Styx. That's a much better name than Boonies.*

He hadn't texted back. Instead, about five minutes later, I'd gotten a FaceTime request and when I answered it, I saw Isaac and Hannah sitting at a table before Kellen flipped the screen around on himself.

"We were waiting for you to show up at the coffee shop, but guessing since you're no longer an intern…"

"My coffee schlepping days are over," I said with a small grin. "For now, at least. You never know when I might need a second job, so don't rule anything out."

He shrugged one shoulder. "I think you'll be okay."

There was a tone to his voice that made me narrow my eyes, wondering how he was so certain of this outcome. An image of Kellen offering to pay my bills popped into my head, and it was mixed with annoyance and relief. I'd never had a roommate, even the few months I'd tried living in the dorms, so the responsibility for everything had always been on me. I didn't know how I'd handle giving up that control.

The screen flipped again and Hannah was leaning forward across the table. "So, I'll see you after this motorcycle rally thing or whatever. Kell said you'd probably be at the bar by 6:30-ish."

She shrugged, but my eyes flicked to Isaac to gauge his reaction. Hannah had always done whatever she wanted, and Isaac always had thoughts. This was no different. His expression was a little sour and I hid my smile behind my hand.

"Sounds good. My co-workers said they'll get there about 7:00, so that'll give me some breathing room."

Hannah nodded, waving when Kellen flipped the screen back around and stood. The background changed from the inside of the shop to the outside. Blue sky with a few clouds, the bright sun making him squint as he held the camera. "You want to do lunch?"

I tilted my head. "Didn't you see enough of me last night? And you're gonna see me this afternoon."

"Baby, I always want to see you."

I rolled my eyes, happy my headphones were in so no one could hear. "I'm not your baby."

"Not yet."

"Kellen." There was no force or heat in my voice.

"God, I love it when you say my name." He grinned when I scoffed, biting his bottom lip. "But really, do you want to do lunch? What time do you actually get done with work? Or class?"

"I get done at the office around 12:00, but I have class at 1:00 and another at 2:00. Lunch is gonna be coffee today."

"Thought you drank tea."

"Usually do, but the caffeine jolt might help me get some work done. It might also help to end this call."

He grinned. "Fine. Text me when you're done. We can grab something before we head out."

"What's your deal with me and food all of a sudden?"

"My deal is I looked in your fridge while you changed last night the lack of food alarmed me. I think Rev has rubbed off on you with his take-out habit."

"I am a broke, over-worked college student with a part-time job that sometimes requires full-time hours. This is normal." He laughed at my defensive tone, and I lowered my voice. "Aren't you a twenty-six-year-old bachelor? Show me *your* fridge."

"Come over some time and I will. I'll even cook for you."

"Will I live if I eat it?"

"You survived that time we ate the entire cake mix instead of baking it."

"Ugh, don't remind me of that," I said, unable to hold back a laugh. "And I'm not sure either of us survived. I was so sick the next day."

"Yeah, me too. I still can't eat chocolate cake."

"What do you get for your birthday then?"

"This last year it was cake vodka and pineapple juice."

I shook my head. "I guess that counts. I've got to go, Kellen."

He grinned, blowing me a kiss through the phone. It made my stomach flip, my weary heart stirring to life in my chest. "Bye, Tate."

The call disconnected, and I let my head fall to my desk,

leaving it there until Josh returned with my coffee. I took a few sips, swallowing the bitter black liquid and regretting my decision to get that instead of tea. At least until about ten minutes later when my heart was pounding, and I was focused enough to finish re-writes on my second article on the missing girls. This one was about a case from around the metro rather than around Northshore, but after I emailed it to Pak, I decided to check in and see if Isaac had gotten any calls about the article on Kara.

"I have. More than I've wanted." He sounded exhausted, and I tapped my pen against the notepad in front of me, one that bore Tiff Manchester's name and a slew of random information concerning her disappearance.

"Has it helped at all?"

"A little. We've been able to pin down a timeline for Kara that makes her disappearance a little clearer, and we know she most likely didn't leave the state. And all the girls you told me about went to Twin Valley Reformed at some point, but that's circumstantial right now because it was one of the only churches in the area. We all went there too, and we're still around."

"Have you talked to anyone affiliated with the church besides Davey? Or his dad?"

"I haven't. There's been a lot of upheaval lately and they all say they're busy."

"Upheaval?"

"Pastor Adler was asked to retire about three months ago. Hasn't taken it well." Isaac sighed, then his voice lowered. "You remember how fixated he was on keeping the church alive, practically through force, and the fixation he and the youth minister had on purity and marriage being a key part of that."

"Yeah, I remember," I said, idly rubbing the third finger on my left hand. "We had a whole purity inoculation meeting right after I moved to town. I wore that stupid ring for four years."

"Hannah threw hers in the trash," he said. "Never told mom and dad about it, and they never bothered to look."

"Didn't you have to go through that?"

"I opted out. They started the whole thing when I was a junior and by then it was too late for me. Anyway. They asked Adler to retire, he's fighting it, so the sermons are split between him and Pastor Michaels now."

"Brandon Michaels?" I asked. "The youth minister?"

"Yeah. They promoted him for now, but they're trying to get another pastor to come in full time. Hasn't been easy. Northshore is slowly dying and no one wants to put down anymore roots."

"Is that why they pushed Adler out?"

"I don't know. My dad told me his sermons started to get very dark. Almost threatening. Davey came back once and spoke, and he said something that made his dad furious. They had it out in the church apparently. Not a good look."

"No, it's not." I tapped the notepad again, looking up when Pak approached my desk. "I have to go, Isaac."

"Hey, do me a solid, will you? Keep an eye on Hannah?"

"Aren't you going to be there for Kellen?"

Isaac's laugh was loud in my ear. "A cop in a biker bar? Think about it, Tate. Those guys tolerate me at best."

I grimaced and nodded, ending the call and setting my phone on my desk, looking at Pak's slightly pensive face. "You've been on the phone a lot today."

My shoulders straightened as I glanced down at the device, flipping it over on my desk. "That was my source for the missing persons articles. I have the second one done. I was about to email it to you."

Pak's eyes flicked to my screen as he sat down on my desk, arms tight around his chest. "Your source. How do you know him?"

"We actually went to high school together."

"Ah, so he knows Kellen."

I clenched my fists on my lap. "It's Kellen's best friend, actually."

Pak's eyes widened, then narrowed in confusion. "So, his best friend is a cop, but he still got arrested for aggravated—"

"How do you know that?"

I'd cut him off because I didn't want anyone hearing. Both questions didn't make any sense anyway. Mine was dumb because you could look the arrest record up online. In fact, Kellen's name came up under the Iowa Courts system before his business did. I'd have to talk to him about search engine optimization at some point.

But Pak's was unnecessary, too, and when I narrowed my eyes at him, he had the decency to look sheepish. "I got curious last night, so I looked him up. That didn't have anything to do with—"

"No," I said, pinching my leg to help keep my head on straight. "Kellen got into a fight with the guy who was stalking me. He plead guilty instead of going to trial."

Pak pursed his lips. "Did he have a defense? Did you testify for him?"

I swallowed. "No. I had to leave town. It's complicated. Why are you asking?" I pressed.

"No reason." He rubbed he back of his neck, looking down at my computer screen. "I know it isn't fair, but when you enter the public eye, they start to pick apart everything." He gave me a pointed look, and I started to fidget, my legs bouncing on the balls of my feet while a knot formed in my stomach. "They latch onto any little detail, no matter how insignificant. And I don't want that to affect your career. You have so much potential." He smiled gently. "I'd hate to see something, or someone, hold you back."

"Kellen owns a business. He was nominated for a *Best Of* award earlier this year." My legs were still twitching, so I smoothed my hands over my thighs, which helped loosen my fingers from my skirt. "But I understand scrutiny, Pak. Why do you think I've been so hesitant to get on social media?"

He gave me a half smile. "I assumed that had to do with... your stalker." He angled his body toward mine, leaning on the wall of the cubicle instead of sitting on my desk. "If it helps at all, we take any sort of harassment very seriously. Comments get filtered, users get blocked. We can't do the same on social media obviously but it's something."

I nodded, my fingers still on the keyboard, no letters appearing on the screen. "I know. And I want my work to get out there. It won't get noticed otherwise."

Pak smiled, rapping his knuckles on the edge of my cubicle. "And it deserves to get noticed. You deserve to get noticed."

He smiled, but it wasn't his praise that circled around in my thoughts. Kellen's words from last night popped into my head. *Another form of abstinence.*

I pulled up *The Journal* website, where my name was listed alongside a blank avatar. There was an email in my inbox from one of the photographers, telling me to stop by his desk whenever I had a second and he could take a quick picture to suffice until I got professional headshots. I picked up the pen, tapping it against the notepad again.

At this point, it wasn't Davey holding me back. Or Kellen. Or any of the excuses I tried to use for avoiding the world.

It was me.

I thought of Hannah, who had a grueling job but still found a few hours for friends. A few hours for me. Priest who came over whenever I asked and sat on my couch and watched TV. Elissa who begged me to go out for an evening, or Pak who wanted me to walk with him to lunch. I knew there was an ulterior motive there, but it was still interaction.

Living didn't mean throwing myself into everything all at once. Little doses would be enough. Exposure therapy. Dipping my toes into the water and pulling back if it was too cold or too hot. Eventually, my body would get used to the temperature.

I clicked on the email to set up a time with the photographer.

I had to try.

Chapter Twenty-Nine
Kellen

I PARKED MY BIKE IN THE LOT OF TATUM'S APARTMENT at 4:00, half expecting to have to go in and convince her this would be fun. Seeing her break down last night made me seriously consider selling my truck, but I needed the damn thing. I glanced at her little car in the parking lot. The rusty edges. The slightly deflated tires.

She hadn't told me what happened exactly, but her reactions and the fact that she'd specifically told me not to touch her neck were enough of a clue. That motherfucker had attacked her in her car. Put his hands around her neck and squeezed. I didn't ask if he'd done anything else, because it honestly didn't matter. Violence was violence and it left her with scars I couldn't see, but I wanted to help heal.

If only she'd let me.

I'd been out front for a minute or so when I sent a text, assuming I'd have to send a few before I could justify going inside, but to my surprise, Tate walked out a minute later. Her shoulders were covered by a short denim jacket, but under it was a black dress with buttons that ran from the top to the bottom. I sucked in a breath, my mouth watering as I looked her up and down, unable to stop thinking about the last time I'd seen her in that dress. I knew how those buttons unfastened, the way they slipped open so easily. The skirt hugged the curve of her waist and hips, but I also remembered how easy it was to hike up, and how it had looked bunched up over her hips.

Her back arched, hands clawing at the sheets, her breasts heaving behind the flimsy bra. She was trembling but that wasn't enough. I wanted her fucking shaking under me, clawing and pleading and begging for me to please her. My fingers slipped back into her pussy, sliding easily because she was so fucking wet.

For me. This was all for me.

Her thighs clenched, her legs trying to close again but I nudged them open, kissing her thighs and listening to her quiet, whimpering moan. "You like it? Talk to me, Tate."

Her lips pressed together, little mewling sounds slipping out as she tried to form words. "Y-yes, I like… I like it."

"Good," *I ducked my head, kissing her clit, sucking it softly, then licking again because I couldn't get enough of how she tasted. Skin, and warmth, and sweetness, and God, I'd do this every day if she'd let me. Every hour of every day.*

"God, you're so fucking sweet, Tate. Tell me what feels good. Tell me how to make you come."

I slipped my fingers out so I could bury my face against her, licking the creases of her thighs, her soft, plush folds, her needy little clit. Her breath hitched, then she moaned softly and clawed at the sheets, the words slipping out of her lips in a shaky, breathless voice.

"I don't… I've never …"

What?

I kissed her clit, lifting my head, trying to keep the incredulous look off my face. "You've… never come?"

Her expression tightened, and she shook her head, shame evident in her blue-green eyes. Fucking shame. Over what? Over her body? The way it could feel? The way I could make it feel? No, not with me. She'd never feel that with me.

"Let me show you what it feels like, huh?" I moved up to kiss her belly, then one of her breasts as my fingers slipped back inside her. "Let me make you come."

Her eyes fluttered, and she bit her lip while nodding. "Yeah."

"Yeah?" I grinned, curling my fingers inside her, watching the way she arched and bucked her hips into my hand. "Good girls ask for what they want."

In the midst of her writhing, she scoffed, opening her eyes to glare at me. "Oh, fuck you."

I laughed, leaning up so I could kiss her panting lips, licking and nibbling them, just like I would her pussy in a second. "I want to make you come so fucking bad, Tate," I breathed, my own voice hoarse with need. "Tell me what you want, baby. Ask for it."

"Does it look stupid?"

I blinked, jerked back to reality by her question. It wasn't the one she'd asked in the memory. Not even close. But I had to answer. *Answer, you ass.*

"No, baby," I said, looking her up and down, smiling at the leggings she'd put on underneath the dress. Smart girl. My smart girl. "You couldn't look stupid if you tried."

"I think you might be biased," she said, playfully accusing. "I thought about wearing jeans, but I have all these dresses and I never wear them…"

"Wear the dress. I'll be sure to glare at any fucker who looks at you too long."

"You gonna glare at yourself in the mirror, then?"

"Might have to," I said, climbing off my bike to dig in the small luggage compartment in the back. "Come here, let me see if this fits."

Tate frowned as she moved closer, fingers twisting in front of her waist. "I hope you didn't spend a ton of money on that."

"Don't worry about it. It's like mine, they both have Bluetooth."

She snorted, shaking her head as she took the helmet from me. "What's funny?"

"Oh, nothing." A mischievous smile played on her pretty lips. "Vintage Harley, scuffed denim vest, your Rolling Stones shirt, and a Bluetooth headset." She reached up, patting my cheek. "Just grow a solid beard and you'd be two-steps away from—"

"If you call me a fucking hipster—"

"I'm just saying." She slipped the helmet over her head and grinned at me. "If the helmet fits..."

"Does it fit?" I asked, reaching to adjust the fit, needing to busy my hands so I didn't tear it off her and kiss her right on her smart mouth. I'd pushed a boundary last night, and when I'd done it, I had been fully aware she might slap me, push me away, then slam the door in my face.

But she hadn't. She'd kissed me back. And if it hadn't been for her tears, I would have kissed her longer.

I would kiss her longer. I just had to be patient. God and I didn't talk much so I'd never bothered to ask him for any, but if I suddenly developed the skill, I might take up praying again.

Tate seated herself behind me after I got back on the bike, placing her feet onto the foot pegs, body close to mine. I stood the bike up, putting my foot on the kickstart and listening to her laugh.

"What's funny now?"

"You know you can get a bike with an electric start."

"This is better. It's more fun."

"If I ever got one, it'd have an electric start."

I turned over my shoulder to look at her. "You've thought about getting a bike?"

She shrugged, her hands trembling slightly as the settled on my waist. "Well, you've seen how well I handle cars, so the thought crossed my mind. Not one like this though."

"Not a fucking crotch rocket."

"I'd have to learn how to ride one."

I grinned. "I can teach you how to ride."

She gave me a look, the helmet hiding part of her face, but I could see how her eyes narrowed, the way her lips pressed together. "Let me guess. You're going to make some joke about riding your dick or something."

"I was going to say face, but that works too."

"What?!"

I didn't respond, choosing instead to kick the bike on and wait for her to hold on tight before I pulled out of the parking lot. Tate's arms wrapped around my waist, and she squealed, then laughed, and when I stopped at a light, I reached back, cupping my hand around her thigh just above the knee.

"You good?"

My eyes were on the stoplight, but when I felt her fingers slip between mine, squeezing softly, I looked back. She smiled at me, a little shy, even more nervous, but her hand clutched at mine, and my heart jumped in my chest while my stomach dropped straight to my knees.

"Yeah, I'm good. This'll be fun."

Chapter Thirty
Tatum

I was going to have to take Kellen up on his offer.

Not on... riding his dick. Or his face...

The one to teach me how to ride a motorcycle. This was freeing. A bit dangerous perhaps, but I loved the feeling. The open air hitting my skin, the rumble of the engine. It could have been because they were sounds and memories associated with the joyful times I'd rode around with him before, but regardless, it was a mode of transportation I could easily get used to. Much better than a car for me. I would have to get used to them eventually, or find a way to ride in one without panic, but in the interim, a bike would suffice.

And during that time, something might shift between Kellen and me where I could entertain the other offers he'd put on the table. Like I hadn't been thinking about it since he'd said it back at my apartment, or every time he cupped his hand around my thigh when we stopped. It excited me as much as it rattled me.

Maybe rattled wasn't the right word, but that touch was far different than the steadying feel of his hand in mine. Or of his palm against my back. Or even his arms enveloping me. It was familiar in an intimate way. That spot on my leg was almost like a talisman to him or something. A grounding point of his own.

I'd said I was going to dip my toes into the water, not dive in headfirst when I had no idea of the temperature or of how shallow the pool was.

Kellen didn't seem to have those concerns. Or any, if I was honest. When we arrived at Styx, a wood building literally in the middle of nowhere that somehow looked rundown but well-kept all at the same time, he wasted no time introducing me as his girl to the rest of the Heartland Heathens. Like when I walked around with Gina, I knew there were going to be plenty of names I'd forget, but Kellen made sure to highlight a few of his closer friends. Looper had a bike nearly identical to Kellen's, and he promptly introduced his wife Shayla who was cradling a small bump between her hips. They were young. Looper barely looked older than I was, and I guessed Shayla was around Hannah's age. Elissa had said something about their tale being a long story. My heart ached as I watched them together. It had been a while since I'd seen a couple so clearly devoted to each other.

Which was why when Kellen walked me away from them, his arm slipping around my waist to pull me close to his side, I didn't question it. I even slipped mine around his in response, letting the girl who'd once craved that type of love come out for a bit.

Riot was another mechanic Kellen worked with, and he'd tipped his head at me with a knowing grin while his statuesque girlfriend smiled beside him. Kellen mentioned she was a lawyer as we walked away, and I'd wondered if anyone had questioned their relationship the way Pak had mine.

When I mentioned Pak was coming tonight, Kellen had made a face and tucked me closer against his body. I bit back a smile, and Kellen pinched my ribs. "What?"

"You have no reason to be jealous."

"Oh, I'm not," he assured me. "But I still don't like how he was looking at you."

"You gonna try and tell me what to wear?" I challenged. "Tell me that putting pictures on the internet is a form of cheating or something stupid?"

"No, because that's dumb and you wouldn't put pictures of yourself on the internet anyway." He glanced down at me, a smirk curling the corner of his mouth. "And wear whatever the fuck you want. It'll all end up on my bedroom floor eventually."

"Wow," I said, heat flushing to my cheeks. "We've just abandoned subtly entirely, haven't we?"

"Fuck subtly." The hand on my waist slid lower, curling possessively around my hip. "I know what I want, why should I hide it?"

Kellen slipped his hand lower, off my back, his palm curling around half of my ass for a split second, long enough for me to gape at him and jerk away before he put it back on my waist. He grinned at me and I narrowed my eyes, poking him in the ribs. "You've been planning that since you picked me up, I bet."

"Baby, that was tame," he laughed, bending to kiss my temple before he put his mouth next to my ear. "I've imagined doing things to you that would make a porn star blush worse than you are right now."

He squeezed me again, the heat of his body nothing compared to the warmth flooding through me from cheek to hip. I wanted to scowl at him, but a part of me wanted to skip the ride and have him take me to some secluded part inside the bar to give me a taste of what he had in mind. I swallowed, rubbing my thighs together as we walked, a little embarrassed at how easily my body threw the plans of dipping my toes into this out the window. Between the touches, Kellen's closeness, and his teasing words, I was wet enough that I might as well be swimming.

The internal flinch to this realization was automatic. Something I wondered if I'd ever rid myself of. I rubbed my ring finger absentmindedly, lectures on purity and lust and the sinfulness of it all rushing back. Pastor Adler's words coupled with Davey's assertions that we had to remain pure even as he blamed me for his "missteps." If I hadn't worn jeans, or sundresses, he'd have been able to control himself. If I hadn't been so wanton with my own desire, he'd have been able to control himself.

I felt wanton now with the way Kellen was holding me, and how my body was responding to it. I edged away, but his arm curled around my waist, tucking me into his side. "Hey, you good? We'll probably leave in a few. There's always a little bit of this before every ride out."

"No, I'm good," I said, letting him pull me around so we were facing each other. He smiled, lifting his hands to push my hair back from my face, leaving them there when he finished.

"I'm glad you're here," he said softly, leaning down, and I was ready for it this time even though my hands were shaking. I rose onto the balls of my feet, meeting his lips halfway, my hands fisting in the T-shirt he had on under the denim vest. This one wasn't as chaste. Kellen murmured softly, inhaling a sharp breath when I tried to push his lips open with mine. His arms wrapped tight around my waist, and he held me close, even when he pulled back, biting his lip and shaking his head.

"Kissing me like that is gonna make me want to take you home, Tate." His voice was playful, but the warning in his words made me shiver and clutch him tighter.

"We just got here."

"Yeah, well, my house is less than a mile from here. You want me to take you there quick? Show you how much I've missed you?"

Yes, I thought, the earlier sermons whipped out by a very different memory popping into my head. One of Kellen in my old apartment, his face close to mine like it was now. Except instead of standing we were lying down, and he was above me, one of his arms around my shoulder and the other hand covering mine as he coaxed it between my legs.

"Show me."

His voice was deep. A hint of a command behind the words. I met his intense gaze with wide eyes, and he frowned and shook his head. "Don't, Tate."

"Don't… what?"

"Don't look so scared. Or disgusted with yourself." He kissed me again, lips hovering over mine as he reached up, guiding my own hand between my own legs. "You know whose body this is?"

I let out a shaky breath, my voice so high pitched it sounded like a squeak. "Mine?"

"Yeah, it's yours. So you can touch it all you like." He shuddered, rolling so I was partly on my back. "And I wanna watch. Fuck, baby, I wanna see…"

I blinked, swallowing the heavy, tight sensation in my throat. "Maybe later," I whispered, and Kellen murmured wordlessly before setting me back on my feet, tilting his head when I let out a shaky laugh. "I forgot how powerless you make me feel. Like I have zero self-control."

"Fuck self-control, baby, but you're not powerless." He kissed my forehead, tucking me back into his side as we walked toward two men perched on the railing that surrounded the bar's front porch. "You want power I'll give it to you. Make me beg. Put me on my knees."

"Thought you liked it the other way around," I teased.

"I want you anyway I can have you, Tate," Kellen said. I looked down at myself to the buttons on the front of my dress that ran from my neck all the way to the hem. It was old. I hadn't thought about it when I put it on. Kellen tipped his head when I tugged at the fabric on the dress

"I didn't think about it when I put it on," I said. "But do you… do you remember this dress?"

I widened my eyes, looking up to see Kellen biting his full, lower one and smiling softly. He grinned, and when his tongue slid over the small indentations in his lip, I felt it between my legs. "Yeah. I remember that dress."

I swallowed as he took my hand, tugging me until I was tucked back into his side. I was so doomed. It was all his fault.

Kellen walked me over to the pair of men on the railing. One looked late thirties to early forties, broad and tall with flecks of gray in his dark hair and on the short beard he wore. The other was younger, and my face heated more than it already was when I looked at him. He had to be one of the most attractive men I'd ever seen. Like a young James Dean, if James Dean wore heavy ripped denim pants, a sport shirt under a denim vest, and had a neck tattoo.

"This is Rush, he's the Prez," Kellen said, giving me a funny look when he gestured to the older man. I offered a shaky hand, clearing my throat, trying to push the unwanted, elicit nostalgia aside. *God, Tate. Get it together.*

"It's nice to meet you."

"Polite. My wife would like you," Rush said, gesturing to Kellen with a grin. "She worries about this one. Says he's too cute and 'good-natured' to be single this long."

"I don't know about the how good-natured he is, but he can be pretty cute sometimes," I said, and Kellen scowled playfully at me, squeezing my waist while Rush chuckled. "Um, I work with Elissa Rivers, I think you know her?"

The man beside Rush grinned when he laughed and jerked his thumb toward him. "He knows her better than I do. Elissa is Cas' fuckbuddy, not mine."

My eyes widened and I let out a soft laugh, my face heating so much it was hard not to avert my eyes. "Right. She mentioned that your wife works at a non-profit?"

Rush tilted his head, regarding me with a curious gaze. "She does…"

"She said you all do charity rides and events." His expression was calm, but there was a hint of suspicion in it. He nodded, but folded his arms over his chest, putting a barrier up I knew not to push too hard against. "That sounds interesting."

"It is," he said with a shrug. "Elissa keeps asking to run a story on us, but I have doubts on if it would be good for us or not."

"I get that. Attention, even good attention, comes with consequences."

Rush tilted his head, and I felt Kellen squeeze my waist, a question in the way his fingers toyed with my dress. I lifted my hand and laced my fingers through his at my side, offering Rush another smile. "People pry anytime something makes the news. Sometimes they get nosy. It's important to keep the integrity you're working to maintain intact and preserve the privacy of people involved. Speaking of."

I squeezed Kellen's fingers and turned to look at him, eyebrows raised. "You need to put SEO on your website."

"I don't have any idea what that is. Rev and I built that with one of those pre-made things you buy."

"It helps you show up in search engines before anything else. Hire someone to work on yours, that way it'll come up first instead of... other stuff."

Rush gave me a half-smile, glancing from me to Kellen. "Been here ten minutes and she's already telling you what to do."

Kellen scowled playfully at me. "Seems about right."

"Betsy would like her," Rush said, raising an eyebrow at Kellen. "Bring her around sometime when she's here."

"Bring her around when she's not here," the other man added, extending a hand to me while Rush laughed and walked away. "I'm Cas, by the way. Casanova. Since Fox wasn't polite enough to introduce us."

I extended my hand, very aware of the way Kellen's arm

tightened on my waist. Cas took my fingers only, and when he tugged gently, lifting the back of my palm toward his mouth, I yanked my hand away and glared. He snickered and Kellen shoved him nearly off the railing he was perched on.

"Knock it off, asshole," Kellen growled.

"Aw, I'm just being nice," Cas pouted, and I raised an eyebrow at him. "E called earlier today, told me to be nice to her. Also to open up a tab in her name as soon as you got here so if you want a drink—"

"I'll wait until I get back," I said quickly. "Isn't this thing for Kellen anyway? I assumed I'd have to find a way to get you home."

"Ah, we have a couple Uber drivers on standby. They'll take care of you." He looked to Kellen, which was good because it helped me hide my flinch. Isaac said Hannah was coming. Maybe I'd handle her car better than I would a complete stranger's. Not that I'd handled Kellen's truck all that well the other night...

"Fox, I booked a spot at Ink Spectacle next Thursday, 3:00. You in?" Cas looked at me, catching my gaze before he bit his lip and gave me another handsome smirk. Guy was a shameless flirt. No wonder he and Elissa got along. "You want me to convince him to pierce his tongue? That could be fun."

He bounced his eyebrows at me, but I wrinkled my nose. "Doesn't that take months to heal?"

Cas shrugged. "About a month, give or take." He looked to Kellen. "You game? Mack says his old lady loves it."

"Nah, I'm pretty good with my tongue already." He gave me a wink. "Think I'll do my eyebrow."

"I thought you said you were gonna do your lip?"

"I was, but if you take me up on that face riding offer from before—"

"Yeah, not happening," I said, shaking my head at Kellen's

smirk and Cas' laughter. "Besides, I've been taking care of myself for three years. I can handle another month."

I regretted the words as soon as they were out, gritting my teeth when Cas' laugh made a few people look in our direction. Kellen made a low, hungry noise before bending and whispering, "I know you can," in my ear. "But it's more fun to play with a friend, right?"

"Oh my god," I mumbled, the memory from earlier came flooding back, racing through my head like a freight train. I felt his breath on the inside of my thigh, the pressure of his fingers inside me as he whispered filthy promises against my lips.

There was a loud, piercing whistle, and I looked over to see Rush on his bike, gesturing to everyone. Cas jumped off the railing, winking at me when he passed.

"Fox, if you're up for it, maybe we can all play—"

"In your fucking dreams, man," Kellen said, a possessive grip on my hand as he walked me to his bike, climbing on first then motioning for me to do the same. Cas laughed as he got on his bike, and I'd been about to ask Kellen if he was just a flirt or if he was serious when Priest pulled up beside us.

"Where the hell have you been?" Kellen asked before I could say a word. Priest took off his helmet, his wild hair tucked into a tight ponytail at the nape of his neck.

"Got caught up helping Macy. Fucking landlord. Her AC has been out all week and she's called him, but no answer. I tried to fix it but I might have to grab Pitch this weekend and see if he can help."

He rolled his eyes, then looked me up and down, smiling at me before looking to Kellen. "You sure got her? Been a while since you've had someone on the back of your bike."

"I've got her," Kellen said, reaching back to cup my thigh at the same time Cas shouted, "Hey, I'll take her if he can't handle it. I'm sure I could handle her *just fine.*"

"Not a chance," Kellen snapped, then he turned back to look at me. "He doesn't mean anything by it. He's just a flirt."

"I think he likes to piss you off," I said, grinning when Priest laughed. He reached across the space between the bikes, giving me a soft punch on the arm.

"Told you you'd fit right in," he said, tugging his helmet back on as multiple bike engines roared to life. Kellen stood and kicked his starter on, settling back in and tucking me close to his body. I held on to his waist, my cheeks aching from the smile stretched on my face, and dull throb low in my belly that the vibrations of the bike only made worse. I dropped my head to Kellen's shoulder, and his voice filled my ears, coming over the speaker in the helmet.

"You good, baby?"

My chest ached, and I squeezed him tighter, knowing there was no way I could fight it. I'd told him the other night that I'd loved him, and that was true, but what I hadn't realized until today with his arm around me, his eyes on me, and the ease in how my heart and body and soul fell into step alongside his, was that I'd never stopped.

"Yeah," I said, smiling when he looked back. "I'm good."

Chapter Thirty-One
Kellen

THE BAR WAS USUALLY BUSY FRIDAY NIGHTS, BUT with everyone in the club there, plus outsiders, it was packed. Tatum's co-workers had taken up one of the larger booths and had three empty pitchers on their table already along with several shot glasses. Tate had taken one, but only because I'd done it with her. I was at the bar now, grabbing her a bottle of water since it was making her antsy to move through the crowd.

"It would probably help if her editor would back off a bit," I grumbled to Rev, but all he had to offer was a grin. "Why are you smiling?"

"Pretty sure you're being a jealous ass."

"Pretty sure you can go fuck yourself. He's making her uneasy."

"He's making you uneasy."

I scowled, because he was right, and I had no reason to be. Tate came here with me. She rode around the lake, over the long bridge, all around the winding roads the club likes to ride on. She'd been holding my hand, and it had been my arm around her waist when Pak had showed up.

But I looked at my hands, at some of the stains I could never get rid of no matter how hard I scrubbed. The callouses. The contrast in our chosen careers. It was clear everyone she worked with adored her. They laughed and she smiled along with them, her hand in mine, but it was just like the other night, and the old doubts I thought I'd buried started to creep in. That eventually, she'd move on. She was meant for bigger things and I would somehow hold her back.

It hadn't crossed my mind until she and Rush had exchanged a few words after the ride out, when she'd reiterated her earlier statement that she understood privacy concerns, and the consequences of public attention. I wondered if someone had said something about me to her. It wouldn't be the first time a woman dating an ex-con had gotten the side-eye.

"It's so cute when you're jealous, Fox," Cas said when he handed me the water, laughing when I flipped him the finger. "I tried and that girl didn't even look twice at me."

"You probably scared her, asshole. And I don't worry about her looking. I worry someone's gonna make her realize she's too good for my ass."

"Nah," Rev said. "You've missed it cause you're too busy worrying about that guy watching her, but she's had her eyes on you all night."

"Well, until a few seconds ago," Cas said, jerking his chin toward the table. "Then that blonde came in, and she's been all smiles ever since. Can't say I blame her." He let out a low whistle. "Good God. Can she introduce me? E swears she's not going home with me tonight and—"

"That's Isaac's little sister." I pointed a finger at him as I stood up from the bar stool. "Stay the fuck away from her, too. Got it? She's not even old enough to drink."

"Then what the fuck is she doing in a bar?" Cas shouted after me, but I ignored him, huffing in offense when I got back to the table and Hannah had taken my spot.

"Hey," she said, eyeing at the pitchers of beer. "You gonna tattle on me if I steal one glass?"

"Depends, what's in it for me?" I asked, looking down when Tate grabbed my hand. She stood up off her seat, gesturing that I should take it. I did, and it put me right next to Pak, which I frowned about until Tate sat down on my lap and resumed conversation like it was the most normal thing for us to do. Like we'd been doing it for years.

Hannah grinned at me, accepting the glass someone poured her without a second thought. "One," I said. "That's it."

"Hush, I can take care of myself. It's not the first time I've had one. I'll still be able to drive your drunk asses home if needed."

"You should teach me how to ride a bike," Tate said, shifting so she could loop her arm around my shoulders. I slipped mine around her back, trying hard not to grab her ass.

"I will, once other stipulations are met."

Her eyes shot to mine, narrowed, but she pressed her lips together, and shifted on my lap, crossing her legs. I set mine on top of her thigh, which didn't go unnoticed by anyone at the table. Hannah rolled her eyes and sipped her beer. Pak frowned beside me and took another drink of his, resigned. But a few other co-workers whose names I couldn't remember shrugged and went back to talking before Elissa tilted her head and flashed me a sly grin.

"So you ever gonna show off your moves, Foxtrot?" She pressed, still grinning. "I mean, you've got a partner now."

"Oh, no," Tate said, shaking her head. "I know you're not talking about me. No way in hell am I getting out there and dancing."

Her hand was on my back, fingers tense, searching for something to play with.

Elissa winced. "You're embarrassed to dance with—"

"That's not what I said," Tate interrupted, laughing as she squeezed my shoulder before standing up. "I'll be right back."

I let her go. Reluctantly, my hands staying on her back and hips as long as they could before she squeezed past Hannah and weaved through the crowd, arms close to her sides, fingers curled into fists.

"She okay?" Hannah asked.

"Yeah." I waved to the general atmosphere. "Crowds."

"I would have gladly had dinner somewhere." Hannah glared at me, reaching down to poke the side of my ribs like she was a fucking kid and not a full-grown adult in a bar of other full-grown adults. "But no. You had to take her out on your stupid bike, and now she's here sitting on your lap, and I'm not gonna get to spend any time with her."

"It's not my fault she likes me better."

I winced when Hannah slapped my shoulder, grateful when Elissa leaned over and started asking Hannah about nursing school and work. Pak was quiet beside me, looking from the table to the door like he was thinking about leaving. I elbowed him, unsurprised when he looked annoyed by it.

"She get any more comments on her articles?"

"Lots," he said coolly. "You should read her work and see for yourself."

"I have. I just don't read the comments. Especially the filtered ones, but you probably figured that out already." He lifted an eyebrow, a challenging expression on his face. One of my fists clenched on my thigh. What I was I supposed to say to this guy? *I know what you think of me, I don't give a fuck, stay away from her? Don't look at her like that while I'm looking at her exactly like that?*

"Look, man," I said, channeling some of the pacifism Rev had unironically brow beat into me, "I've got no issues with you, and the last thing I'm trying to do is make her life harder. She's had enough shit from men that she doesn't need either of us getting into a pissing match over her." His face soured, then relaxed, and he twisted his lips.

"Easy to say that when you're the one winning."

I cracked a smile. "To be fair, I had a leg up. People say you never forget your first love. Not sure what they'd say about me never moving on from mine, but..." Pak huffed a laugh when I shrugged, and he wiped a hand over his short hair and sighed. "If she told me to get lost, I'd listen. Maybe reluctantly, but I'd listen."

"She wouldn't," he said, letting out a heavy sigh. "I actually asked her about you the other day. Probably came off like a stalker, and she was quick to shut me down. It was the first time in the six or seven months I've known her that I've ever seen her look angry. Not tense," he added. "Angry. And you're right, she doesn't need anyone making her life harder."

"Good. So, on that note, has she gotten anymore comments with her real name?" I pulled out my phone. "Maybe we should exchange numbers."

He did the same, showing me his number so I could send a text. "Have you talked to your cop friend anymore? What *is* reportable?"

"Specific threats." Hannah spoke before I could answer, leaning over the table, her eyes narrowed in concern. "Someone else knows her real name?"

"There have been random accounts commenting it on her articles," Pak explained. "We have filters set up to remove any personal information about the journalist. Names, address, phone number. Doxing attempts."

"Aren't those illegal?" I asked, and Hannah shook her head, rolling her eyes.

"I know way more about this stuff than I want to, and no. They aren't. All that information is public domain, including her name change if someone really wanted to find it. But I can't think of anyone who would. Well, except you," she gestured to me, then her lips pulled into a frown. "And Davey."

Heat flashed in my chest. Not the pleasant kind. And thinking about the pleasant kind mind made me look around the bar, wondering what was taking Tate so long. I spotted her by the bar, talking to Rev, Cas, and Rush, but her expression was odd. It wasn't playful or happy, or tense. She was sitting on a barstool, legs crossed, back straight, her full attention on the three of them. Mostly on Rush. Pak and Hannah were talking, something about public forums and the gross comments people left in them, so I didn't feel bad for pushing back out of my chair and crossing the bar to see what my girl was up to. Cas looked up as I approached, flashing a sly grin.

"...names and faces in print," Rush was saying when I got to the bar, moving to stand behind Tate. He took a shot, his eyes on her, not once looking at me. "It doesn't matter to some people that they've moved on and are trying to do better."

"Punishment in perpetuity," Tate said, and I realized she had a napkin on her lap, and a pen. She was writing things down. "No, I understand completely. And if your wife wanted to talk to me about it or if you wanted to some more, I'd keep names private. I'm not too keen on having my picture printed either, but," she shrugged, letting out a wry laugh. "I can't imagine doing anything else, so I'll figure out how to handle it."

I set my hand on her waist, giving her a heads up that I was behind her. She turned over her shoulder and smiled at me, inching back so her body was pressed to mine. Rush looked at me, tipping the bottle in his hand.

"I'm gonna shoot you a text next time we get a sitter and Betsy can come around. She'll like her." He took a drink, waving when someone shouted his name and nudging me as he walked past. Tate finished her scrawling, then tucked the napkin into her purse, letting out a deep sigh.

"I will actually take that shot you offered."

"Yeah? Atta girl," Cas goaded, setting four glasses down on the bar. "What am I pouring?"

"God, I don't even know. This is too much pressure."

"Tequila then," Cas said, and he looked at me and winked. "You can lick the salt off—"

"I know you've got better jokes than that. I'm disappointed." Tate frowned while Cas laughed, eyeing the shelf behind him. "That. The peanut butter whiskey."

"Gross," Rev grumbled, but he didn't push his glass away when Cas grabbed the bottle and filled the glasses. "I hate peanut butter. I ate too damn much of it growing up."

"I feel the same about tatertots." Tate said, and she held up her glass toward him. "I think you and I need to sit down and discuss our mutual childhood trauma."

"Might need a few more shots for that," Rev said, waiting for Cas and me to grab our shots. He lifted the glass, eyeing me with a smile before turning back to Tate. "Here's to me for being right."

"About what?" she demanded.

"About you fitting in." He clinked his glass against mine when I laughed, and I watched Tate shake her head, cheeks flushing again when she tipped her head back and downed the alcohol, wincing at the burn. I did the same, but almost choked when I watched Rev gag at the taste and immediately ask for a chaser.

"I guess I know not to bake anything with peanut butter in it now," she said, turning to squeeze my hand. "I'll be right back."

"Where are you going now?" I asked, and she titled her head. "Bathroom?"

"Weren't you just there?"

"Well yeah, but I need to go again." She hopped off the stool, but I followed, ignoring Cas' whistle as we disappeared into the small hallway at the back of the bar. Tate gave me a funny look over her shoulder, stopping just outside the women's restroom.

"Don't tell me you're gonna follow me in here. That's not a kink I'm into."

"What kinks *are* you into?"

"Distraction, right now." Her smile stayed on her face, but there was a tightness in her eyes, and she bit her lip, gesturing to the crowd and the noise at my back. "It's a lot."

"So, do you actually need to pee or do you just need to hide for a minute?"

A flush came to her cheeks. "The latter."

"Thought so." I reached behind her, opening the unmarked door and gently pushing her inside. There was a soft glow from a few lamps Cas always left on, along with a few couches and chairs. It was a room Rush used for club business, but Cas had let me crash here a few times when I'd gotten too drunk to ride home.

Tate glanced at the couch, then at me, an eyebrow raised. "What's this?"

"Just a room for people to crash."

"You mean you didn't bring me in here to show me your moves?"

She was smirking, the flush on her face from earlier muted but still visible. Her hands were twisting in front of her waist, but not as fast as they did when she was anxious. I licked my lips, reaching back to lock the door behind me, angling my body toward hers. "You wanna see my moves?"

"Maybe." Her wide eyes lifted to mine, pupils dilated. I hadn't noticed it until now, but she'd left out her contacts. I stared at them, studying the bright mix of blue-green and the small spot of brown, watching her tongue dart out to wet her bottom lip. "I'm curious if you've picked up any new ones."

"I have, but the old one's work, too." My body pressed against hers, backing her into the wall for some reason when there was a couch less than five feet away.

"Maybe you should show me."

"Maybe you should ask nicely."

I grinned, hands drifting down to her hips, one of my legs pushing between hers. Her face was centimeters from mine, giving me a front row view to the way her eyes fluttered, how her lips parted and tipped toward mine, aching for me like I was her. Tate whimpered, and I laughed softly, cupping her face with one hand and her ass with the other.

"You know how to ask."

"Please don't make me beg."

I groaned, letting my lips meet hers for a quick second, tasting whiskey and sugar and almonds before I pulled back. "I don't want to scare you away," I confessed. "I don't want to push—"

"Push me," she said breathlessly, and when her eyes fluttered this time, I saw a tiny tear slip out of them. "Please, Kellen, push me." She practically clawed at my T-shirt, trying to drag me closer. "I've been pushing myself alone for years, I want someone else to do it for once."

She tipped her lips to mine, the arm she'd looped around my neck preventing me from teasing her anymore. "I want you to do it for once."

"Well since you asked nicely," I said, the quip lost in her mouth as our lips collided. *Finally. God, finally,* I thought before all comprehension was lost and she consumed every single sense I had. Logic. Morality. Sight, smell, taste, scent, touch. It was all her.

We pawed at each other like we weren't twenty-somethings with jobs and lives and supposed rational thought. I wanted to consume her. Take in the changes to her body and face that I'd missed over the last three years. The way her thighs and hips had filled out, soft in all the right places, giving me something to grab onto as I pushed my hips into hers. I was so fucking hard it ached, and when her hands left my shoulders to claw at the top of my jeans I groaned like I was a fucking teenager.

"I don't have a condom on me."

"Well, that's just poor planning."

"You think I won't fuck you anyway?" I asked, savoring the way her eyes closed, the way her breath washed over my face. "I've got a mouth and ten fingers I can use to make you come."

"God." She whimpered when I shoved her hands away from my pants, grabbing onto me when I lifted her and began hiking up her dress, getting a quick look at her pale, peach colored panties. I slipped my hand between her parted thighs, listening to the way her breath hitched, relishing the way her fingers tightened as she gripped my shirt. "God, please."

"I thought you said you'd been taking care of yourself," I teased, trying to keep my wits about me when I felt how wet she was. I tugged the fabric aside, unable to stop the smile that crossed my lips when she gasped and her head fell back, her hips rocking into my touch. Her chin tipped back, that smile still playing on her lips as I softly kissed her neck.

"I've tried," she finally said, threading her fingers into my hair as she rocked, my fingers sliding over her clit. "I even got a vibrator. You gonna be jealous of that thing too?"

"Not at all. I like someone I can tag in if my fingers get tired."

I slipped said fingers inside her, groaning and pushing my hips into hers. "God, you're so wet for me, Tate. You know what that does? How fucking hard it makes me?"

She moaned softly, reaching down to the front of my pants, my breath hitching when she palmed my cock through my jeans. "Show me."

"Greedy little thing, aren't you?"

"Kellen, I want you." She kissed me, pressing her lips together. Her expression tightened, then she pulled me closer with the hand that was in my hair, whispering into my ear. "I want you so bad."

"What do you want me to do?" I teased, grinning when I felt

her growl of irritation against my cheek. She bit the lobe of my ear softly, her lips caressing it when she finished.

"I want you to fuck me."

The noise I made was downright embarrassing, a low desperate moan as I thought about how tight she'd be, how familiar, how new. Soft and wet and warm. I wanted to feel her hips grinding against mine, push into her so hard and deep she wouldn't think about anything but me ever again. I ground my hips into hers again, and she laughed softly, her breath tickling my neck. "I mean it. Please, Kellen. I want you to fuck me right here."

"Don't say shit like that," I growled, and Tate frowned, rubbing the heel of her hand up and down.

"So, you can talk all kinds of dirty to me but I can't—"

"Oh, you can, but save it," I breathed into her next kiss, working my fingers faster inside her. "Save it for when I get you home and get this fucking dress and your panties on my floor, and I can give you what you want so badly."

"I want it now, please." Her begging was going to undo me. Those little sighs, the way she was grinding against my pumping fingers. Christ. "I'm clean. I've still got an IUD and—"

The loud bang against the door startled me, and Tate actually yelped, wiggling out of the hold I had her in. She quickly shoved her dress down, expression mortified while I glared at the door.

"It's me. Cas. I didn't think—"

"Kellen? Is Tate with you?"

Tate straightened at the same time I did, both of us glancing at each other. I opened it, finding Isaac standing in jeans and a T-shirt while Rev and Cas lingered behind him in the hallway. Rev looked like a bouncer, but instead of guarding the entrance, he was guarding the bathrooms.

"The hell are you doing here? You said you weren't coming out."

"I wasn't, but..." His eyes moved from me, settling on

Tatum, lips pressing together in a hard line. "Something came up, thanks to your article."

I stiffened, the arousal and adrenaline still racing through my body cooling rapidly. Tate's shaky hands immediately began to fidget, and she looked at me again before swallowing heavily and turning to Isaac. "What was it?"

Isaac let out a heavy sigh, looking resigned. "Someone called about a body. The coroner thinks it's Kara Marlan."

Chapter Thirty-Two

Tatum

I WOKE UP TO SUNLIGHT POURING OVER MY FACE through a slit in the curtains, and when I opened my eyes, they stung. Haku's normal spot beside me was messy and rumpled, the comforter tucked around my shoulders, my hair swept back from my face. I stared at the pillow adjacent to me, studying the dent in it, the distinct Kellen-shaped impression in my blankets.

I could hear murmuring outside my bedroom. Soft laughter. The tinkling of a tiny bell and quiet meows. I sat up, for once appreciating the way my studio apartment was set up. There was a divider wall over part of the bedroom, but I could look out and see my kitchen, along with part of the living room, where Kellen was sitting on the floor, shirtless, wearing pants a little too big for his frame. He'd asked Priest for a pair since he hadn't wanted to sleep in his jeans after we'd rushed back to my apartment because the news Isaac had dropped was too much for me to handle. Which made me feel stupid. I'd pulled the key from the grenade; I should have known an explosion was imminent.

I crawled out of bed and padded my way to the kitchen, where I not only found Kellen with a cat toy, but I smelled chocolate and sugar. "Traitor," I mumbled, walking to the kitchen and opening the bakery box to find crescents filled with chocolate and topped with almonds. My stomach rumbled, my mouth watering as I took one out of the box. Kellen stood, tossing the toy away into the living room before he turned to face me.

The right side of his chest was inked with branches and long feathery leaves hanging off them. Behind it was a landscape, fields and a fence, a bike parked by the base of the tree. It was scenic, like a photograph, and I wanted to stare at is as much as I did the planes of muscle on his chest. Toned but soft, with a spattering of dark hair across his pecs and his stomach. His abs flexed as he walked toward me, the sweatpants riding low, the line of his hips and the trail of hair drawing my eyes down to where it disappeared under gray cloth.

God, he was gorgeous. Every part of him was so familiar to me, but so different. Changed in the slightest of ways to make him into a man rather than the boy I'd grown up crushing on, and the desire that had flashed through me like lightening last night was still there, but it smoldered now, warming my belly. I wanted to feel his rough hands and hear him breathe those dirty words as much as I wanted him to hold me close, whisper in my ear like he had last night, telling me whatever happened it would be okay.

Giving more to me when all I'd done so far with him was take.

"Crescents take like three days to make."

Kellen moved close, backing me into the counter as he reached into the box and grabbed a pastry, not backing away as he took a bite. My lips trembled, and I hid them behind the crescent, wrapping my arm around my waist so I had something to hold onto. I'd clutched him last night, hyperventilating. Clawing at his skin and clothes until I'd exhausted the surge of adrenaline and shed so many tears they'd soaked the denim collar of his cut.

"You barely have eggs in your fridge, Tate. It's alarming."

"Broke college student, remember?" I said, snatching a bite to feed the rising chaos inside me. Maybe it would hold off on consuming me for a bit. "I have milk for cereal and... a few other things."

Kellen's expression was a little scolding as he took another bite, one hand settling on my hip and ducking under the hem of my shirt. His palm was warm, thumb slightly scratchy as it smoothed over my skin. "Tell me what you want from the grocery store. I'll add it to my delivery order."

"Kellen, I can do my own shopping."

"Well aware of that." He finished chewing, kissed my forehead, and reached behind into the cupboard for a glass. "Make a list anyway. You get busy between classes and work. I just have work. And if I can't bring it down for some reason, Rev can. He already offered."

I grimaced, hiding it behind the crescent again while Kellen pulled out a few glasses and a mug. He filled two with water, the third he put it in the microwave. My stomach turned as it hummed then dinged, and he grabbed a tea bag and dropped it inside. Relaxed. Calm. Unruffled. This was a normal morning to him. Run of the mill. Like we'd been together for months instead of a few days. The crust of the pastry crumpled in my hand, one of the almonds falling off and landing on the top of my foot. Kellen watched it fall, then he drew in close, tucking his hands back under my shirt to hold my waist.

"Get it out, baby." He spoke the words into my forehead, his lips leaving a warm spot on my cool skin. I swallowed, throat flexing, eyes stinging as tears flooded my eyes.

"You don't have to do this."

Kellen's palms stroked up and down my sides. "I know."

"I made you leave last night. They were celebrating you."

"You didn't make me leave. The ride out was the celebration.

And honestly, they wouldn't care if I left early anyway. Cas will probably erase my tab in congrats for getting laid."

"But you didn't."

"Doesn't matter."

"Kellen, it does."

"No, it doesn't." Anger flashed across his face. Half a heartbeat, then it was gone. He took my hips, fixing his eyes on my face. They looked more blue than gray in this light, a break in the quiet storm, the clouds giving way to clear sky. "Things changed, and that's fine. We have time. I'm not going anywhere."

"But—"

"I'm not going anywhere." The pads of his fingers pressed into my flesh, holding me still, his eyes never leaving mine. "You told me to push you. I'm gonna stay around and push you."

His head dropped against mine, the weight of it matching the tightness in my throat, the sensation rattling into my chest. The pendulum, swinging back and forth, making its way to where I was bound. But this time his body was in front of mine. He would take the brunt of it, and I'd escape like I had before.

Like Kara hadn't.

"Baby," Kellen whispered when I let out a shaky breath, his hands coming up to swipe away my tears. "Baby, talk to me."

"I feel like it's my fault."

"What is?" Recognition filled his eyes, and he shook his head. "Kara? No, Tate. No, and it might not even be her. They haven't confirmed—"

"No, just listen. You told me to get it out, let me get it out."

His lips flattened, but he kept his hands on my body, letting his palms drop to my shoulders. They squeezed softly, and I wanted them everywhere. I wanted him to drown out the noise, siphon away the ache, spread out the tension so it was less intense. He was a vice, something I could easily get addicted to as a way to numb the pain.

"I'm selfish," I said, looking away when Kellen's eyes widened. "I am. Jesus, look at how I acted last night. A few kisses and I was all over you."

He let out a confused breath of a laugh. "Tate, if you think that bothered me, you are deeply mistaken."

"It should. Kissing you won't fix me. Sleeping with you won't make this magically disappear. It's just a distraction and deep down I'll still be—"

"You're not messed up," he growled. "And I'm not expecting sex to 'fix' you because you don't need to be fixed, Tatum. You never have. I want you and fuck it if you're selfish sometimes. You deserve it."

"Don't you realize that if we'd never... gotten close, you wouldn't have ended up in prison? Or that if I hadn't hidden, you wouldn't have waisted all that time upset because you thought I was dead? When really, I was just selfish, scared. I didn't want to fight anymore so I just ran. I ran away because—"

"Because you had to stay alive."

"I could have told Suzanne and Phil. I could have demanded the police talk to me. I could have..." My voice broke, and I reached up to cover my mouth. "God, Kellen. I keep saying I want to tell people's stories, but I can't even tell mine. Women get up and testify against their attackers. Children get on the stand and testify, Kellen, but me? No, I run away. I run away and change my whole identity and live a lie because I was scared. And Kara, or whoever this...girl is," I didn't want to say body, "she never even got the chance. I did, and I didn't take it. Because I'm weak. Kellen, I'm weak and I'm scared and you don't—"

"Tate, stop."

Kellen took my face in his hands, shaking his head before he let out a disbelieving laugh. "*Weak*? Jesus, weak my ass. You're not weak because you didn't keep reporting it over and over when no one would fucking listen, and you're sure as hell not weak for keeping yourself alive. Do you see yourself at all? Do you have any clue what the world sees when they look at you? What I see when I look at you?" He paused. "You did what you had to do to stay alive. You came down here with nothing and look what you have."

"My fridge is empty."

He laughed, leaning and kissing me so hard my racing heart threatened to beat right out of my chest and take root in his. It seemed like a safer environment right now. "Yeah, but you have a fridge. And an apartment you pay rent for. You're gonna graduate college, you have a fucking job as a journalist. Do you know how many people actually get to do what they've dreamed about, Tate? Not a whole fucking lot." He glanced down at our feet, where Haku had wandered, his tongue scratching my skin as he tried to lick the almond on my foot. "You took in this guy and you kept him alive."

"I can barely keep myself together some days," I said, wiping away my tears and gesturing to my face. "I mean, look at me."

"I am. Christ, I can't stop looking at you. And I don't see weakness. That's bullshit. I don't ever want to hear you say that again, understand me?"

"You're gonna get tired of it."

"I can't keep my shit together somedays either. Ask Rev. I throw shit around, and so does he. Half the guys in that club have trouble keeping their shit together. Why do you think they all hang out with one another?"

"I assumed it was the bikes," I mumbled, searching for levity. Kellen smiled, leaning in to kiss my nose.

"Yeah, it's the bikes, but it's also cause you need people. Going it alone doesn't make you any stronger. You don't have to prove you can do it all by yourself, Tate. I know you can. Everyone knows you can. You're the strongest person I know.

It's why I love you so much. It's why I've always loved you so much."

I closed my eyes, more tears falling that Kellen quickly swiped away. He whispered it again, three little words. I craved them, but I feared them at the same time. Because whenever I'd had them said before, it didn't last. There was no follow through.

But Kellen's lips were on my cheek, his thumbs swiping away the tears. I hadn't earned this devotion. I'd pushed and blocked and cried.

And he'd stayed.

"I've pieced together what happened," Kellen murmured, still cupping my jaw in his warm palms. "Davey attacked you in your car?"

His thumbs smoothed a steady path on my cheeks as I nodded. "Yeah, I uh… didn't listen to you entirely when you told me to leave," I said, trying to ignore the stitching ache in my chest when he flinched. "I'd gone to Tri-Harbor Community for an orientation that night, and when I came out, he… he was waiting for me. Broke the window when I wouldn't open the door, then he crawled in and choked me."

"And no one came to help?"

He didn't ask if I screamed, because he knew I would have. Isaac had said his questions were protocol when I'd told him, but it had felt like a test. Did I scream loud enough to alert help? Did I thrash hard enough to warrant someone stepping in? Were my protests strong enough that Davey should have known to stop? If they checked all the boxes, did that make it a crime? Was I a good enough victim to warrant justice? I'd never know. I hadn't wanted to ask and be told no.

"There was no one around," I said as an excuse. "It was late. I'd stayed after the orientation to talk to one of the advisors. The parking lot was empty."

Kellen let out a breath, his eyes closing, shaky hands sliding down my arms to settle back on my waist. "So, what happened then?"

I licked my lips, giving him a weary shrug. "Honestly? I'm not sure. I passed out, and when I woke up, I was in the church."

Kellen's eyes went wide, fingers tensing on my back, eyes wide as he waited for more of the story. "I was in the entry way, and there were people in the other room talking. Davey was freaking out about it, saying he'd killed me and his dad was trying to calm him down. It was all muffled, but I remember them saying something about women resisting the will of God and punishment. They kept telling him it was an accident."

"An accident?" Kellen's indignation was so palpable Haku trilled at our feet and trotted away, not wanting to be around when the storm broke loose.

"I don't know. I didn't stick around to listen. As soon as I could get up and move again I ran out of the church and back to my apartment," I explained, the memory rushing back to me. Davey had taken my shoes off for some reason. I'd still been dressed but I'd wet myself. It was only when I brought this up to a therapist that I learned loss of bladder control could have been because my body was shutting down.

"He'd driven my car back to my apartment for some reason. Probably trying to hide what happened, make it look like I'd gone missing. The keys were there and everything, so I grabbed as much as I could and left." I clenched my jaw, wiping away more tears. "When I realized I didn't have enough money to get anywhere, I stole—"

"From Suzanne and Phil," Kellen filled in, his voice heavy.

"Yes."

The word was almost a sob. Breathy and hitched. Kellen wrapped me in his embrace, burying his face in my neck.

"I told you they don't care. They didn't when I talked to

them last. We checked in with each other to see if there were any hits on your missing persons report."

I stiffened, clutching his biceps because I needed to hold onto something. They were hard, the muscles taut under my fingers. He squeezed me tighter, letting me feel how they flexed, reminding an instinctual part of my brain that he could hurt me if he wanted.

Or he could keep you safe...

"Have you told them?"

"No. I thought I'd leave that to you. You were upset enough about all of us finding out, I didn't want to spread it further." I ran my hands up his arms, leaning in when he kissed my forehead. "You should tell them, Tate. They want to see you, but I know you don't want to go back there. Don't blame you for that."

"Davey's not even there right now."

"Still. Shit, my dad still lives there, but he's selling his house, and after that I'll have no reason to go back."

I winced, remembering that was something Kellen and I had in common. He too had an addict for a parent, only his was functional. "You still don't talk?"

He shrugged, rolling his eyes. "I check in every few months. Make sure he hasn't drank himself to death or cut down the weeping willow."

I smiled, running my fingers over the branches of the tattoo on his chest. "Shame you can't replant that thing."

He grinned, looking down to watch as I traced the design. "Oh, believe me, I've looked into it."

"We never carved our initials into it. We should do that before he moves."

"Need a reason to go back. I checked on my dad a few weeks ago, not eager to do it again."

"I could see Suzanne and Phil, and we could stop by Tri-Harbor. Isaac mentioned me coming in."

"He already has your statement. You don't need to give it again."

"No, but if it'll help, I will. Plus..." I leaned into his chest, eyes staring past his body to my bedroom and the unpacked boxes. Specifically, the one on the very bottom of the stack. "I might have something else I can give him besides a statement."

"What's that?"

"The phone I had when I left Northshore. The one with all the voice messages Davey left after I ran." I shrugged when his arms tightened around my waist, his eyebrows narrowing. "They don't have any connections yet, but having that piece of information couldn't hurt."

Chapter Thirty-Three
Tatum

"WE JUST GOT A NOTICE FOR A PRESS CONFERENCE. It's about the body found over the weekend. Noelle, can you make it? You don't have class?"

I looked up from my desk, giving Gina my full attention. I'd expected this, part of me had even hoped for it, but I tried to stay calm. Isaac had texted me early this morning to give me a heads up. The notice had gone out to all news outlets about the conference, and he told me what I'd hear. The body found belonged to Kara Marlan, identified through some articles of clothing and dental records. "No, I'm good. Where is it?"

"About an hour from here. Lakeside PD. I'm sending Pak with you, it's good to have two people at these things. He said he's got you if you need a ride."

"I've got one. Can I borrow a recorder? My cell phone is old and doesn't…"

"I'll have Pak grab one." She titled her head, leaning down and lowering her voice. "You know, you can write a phone off as a business expense, Noelle. Especially since you're doing independent work."

"Yeah, I need to do that." I also needed to save money for

one. After Isaac texted me, specifically asking me to come to Lakeside PD and give a formal statement and give him the phone, I'd taken out the bulk of my savings so I could pay back Phil and Suzanne. They may or may not take it, but offering it was something that felt right.

I finished up my typing, then reached into my purse for my phone and sent a quick text to Kellen.

Me: *You sure you can drive me? Pak offered to give me a ride.*

Kellen: *I'm taking you. Do you think you could handle the truck or do you want the bike?*

Me: *Bike. We'll work on the truck.*

Kellen: *Be ready in an hour. Want to swing by Northshore after?*

Me: *Might as well. Two birds and all that.*

Kellen's reply was a thumbs up on my message, and I tucked the phone away, looking up when Pak appeared at my shoulder. He was smiling, looking far more eager than he should for this sort of thing.

"Your first press conference. Do you think you can get the write up done tonight?"

"I should be able to get something up quick after the conference. I can write a longer article tonight after I get home."

"This is right around where you're from isn't it?" he asked. "Kellen mentioned something about the town once."

I grimaced. "Yeah. I actually knew Kara. We went to high school together."

Pak paused, his easy smile turning to a frown. "Is this gonna be a problem for you? Elissa can go, or one of the others—"

"No, I want to do this," I said firmly. "Kellen's giving me a ride, and while we're there I'm going to take care of a few things I've been... meaning to deal with for a while."

Pak pursed his lips but didn't ask any more questions. There was no iciness in his interactions with me, but when Kellen showed up to the station on his bike, complete with a bag of things from my apartment where he'd been staying over the weekend, I noticed a distinct coolness. He was nursing an injury I hadn't meant to give him, and knowing that gave extra power to the guilt that had been gnawing at me for days.

We got to Triharbor about forty minutes before the conference was set to begin. Pak parked in the lot, but Kellen parked his bike away from the station, which made me wonder if he wanted to avoid the questions or he was giving me space because I needed the walk to loosen my nerves. He stayed close to my side, even when we went into the station and I asked Isaac where the bathrooms were.

"Down the hall, right side." He looked tense, and the uniform didn't help. Kellen was stiff, too. He scanned the room, eyes narrowed, the fingers he had threaded through mine twitchy and tight. I tugged gently, kissing his shoulder, then touching his cheek when he turned to face me.

"Hey, are you okay?"

He blinked, then swallowed and shuddered, shaking off some memory. "Yeah, I'm good. Didn't think about being back here."

His eyes darted behind me, to where Isaac stood, talking with a few other guys in uniform. They stole glances at me, then glances at Kellen, and the hair on my neck stood up when they looked him up and down and frowned. Isaac was scowling, muttering words I couldn't hear as the officers sized Kellen up, seeing through the man he'd become to focus only on the past.

"Hey." I cupped my hand around his jaw, making a show of pressing myself against him, pulling his mouth to mine for a quick kiss that caught him off guard. His hand slipped around my waist, fisting the material of my blouse. "You can leave if you want. You don't have to stay."

"I'm fine."

"You sure?" I looked away from Kellen, glaring daggers at the one officers watching us, his face flashing through my memory as the one who'd looked at me and walked by, ignoring the bruises because he'd decided I deserved them. "Don't give two thoughts to any of these guys, all right? You're not—"

"I know what I'm not."

"Do you?" I asked, cupping his jaw harder. "You said I was the bravest person you knew, but I think you need to look in the mirror more often."

Kellen laughed softly, shaking his head as he dug into his pocket. "I got you something."

"What? Why?"

"Because I wanted to get you something." He pulled out a small package, ripping it open and pulling out a silver band.

"Looper's girl told me about it when I bumped into her over the weekend," he said, which meant it had to have happened yesterday. It was the only time Kellen had been away from me for a few hours. "She has a fidget ring, gives her something to toy with when she gets antsy. You're always rubbing at your finger where that other stupid ring was. I thought this might be better."

He took my hand, slipping it on to my finger, and a very different set of images flashed in my head. The ceremony at church, when I'd been too young to grasp the full meaning of the silver ring I'd been gifted, blended with images that hadn't happened yet, scenes I'd imagined but never knew if they would come to fruition. I rubbed the ring with my thumb, spinning the smooth beads, trying to ignore the tightness in my chest. "Kellen, I... You didn't have to get me something."

"I wanted to." He tilted his head, laughing softly when I grimaced and stared at the ring. "Baby. You rub the skin on that finger raw. You twist your fingers whenever you get tense. If this helps I'd buy you 800 of them. Besides, I gotta get you used to wearing one on that finger again," he added, grinning when my eyes widened. "What? I thought we said 'fuck you' to subtly."

My jaw dropped. "Jesus, Kellen. It's been a week."

"It's been three years." He kissed my forehead, pulling me

close to his body for a quick embrace. "I told you, Tate. I never stopped wanting you, and I'm not going anywhere now."

It would be so easy to believe him and dive headfirst into what he was offering, but I worried there was a hidden quarry under this lake, and if we stayed too long it would suck us into the vortex and we'd both drown.

Kellen squeezed me tightly, kissing my forehead again, then surprising me by giving my ass a soft slap. "Go change. You gotta get your seat. Plus I want to see you how hot you are in a little black skirt."

"Oh my God, stop," I hissed, but it was all warmth and no anger. I dug around in my purse, pushing past the skirt and make up to grab the extra phone I'd brought with me. The one I hadn't charged in years. It felt like a weight when I took it out, and even Kellen grimaced when I offered it to him.

"Can you give this to Isaac while I change? I don't want to stay here any longer than we have to either."

"Yeah, I'll give it to him. Is there anything on here you want?"

"God no. They can do whatever they want with it."

Kellen pursed his lips. "Is this the only place he messaged you? Have you ever logged into your old Facebook or Instagram accounts?"

I wrinkled my nose. "I did for a second a few weeks ago, and yeah… there are messages there too. I'll have to get those to him."

"I'll let him know. They might be able to pull them somehow if you don't want to log in."

His expression was a little sad, but I didn't have time to ask why. Pak peered at me from the second row of chairs, waving to show he'd saved us a spot. Kellen smiled and nodded at me as he walked toward Isaac, offering the phone to him like it was infected in some way.

It hit me then that there were texts from him on that device. Sweet ones, filthy ones. Pics I'd meant for Kellen's eyes only.

Did I want to lose those?

Did I really want to shed everything from my past? Was it really the weight I'd thought it was? A heaviness keeping me from a future?

Or was it something stolen from me for a while that I was just now getting back. Like my heart. Like my courage. Like my life.

Like Kellen...

I pressed a hand to my chest, ducking into the bathroom and taking a deep breath, remembering the reason I was here. A girl had died. Someone had stolen her life before it had ever had a chance to really begin. She was cold and ageless, and I was breathing and safe, still keeping parts of myself caged out of fear the same would come for me.

It would, in a different way, if I kept locking myself in this cage.

Chapter Thirty-Four
Kellen

I COULD HAVE LEFT OR GONE OUTSIDE SO I'D BE IN the fresh air instead of this stuffy concrete box. Most police stations unsettled me, but this one was worse. I knew exactly what desk I'd sat at when they'd done my intake and which cell they'd kept me in. It didn't help that a few of the officers recognized me and seemed to be scowling at Isaac, and later at Tatum, for openly talking to someone they considered trouble. They milled around, casting narrowed eyed glances in my direction as they talked to reporters, a few citizens, including the new Pastor from Northshore. Isaac told me Mark Adler was getting pushed out of his position as the church head, and the youth pastor had stepped up in his place since Davey wasn't around to do it. He'd broken the family tradition and chosen another career apparently.

The new Pastor stood next to the Marlans, nodding solemnly anytime someone spoke to them, but there was a noticeable air of disinterest. The woman I assumed was Kara's mother or at least a maternal figure asked how long it would take. Another woman who looked around Tate's age was examining her fingernails and glancing at the door. Their attitude reminded me of Tate's article, and her descriptions of how missing persons cases often go unnoticed after the initial report due to lack of money, notoriety, or simply lack of interest.

I turned away from the scene, looking over a corkboard near the front desk. It was covered in flyers for events and small business cards for various services. I spotted the business logo of the shop I used to work at, my stomach twisting. I'd seen them at conventions, but even though my shop was making a name for itself, the owners had walked away when I'd waved.

They didn't want to be associated with a criminal.

I shoved my hands deep into my pockets, turning my eyes back to Tate in the second row of chairs. She blended in with the blouses and dress shirts, raising her hand and waiting to be called on like a good student. Her dark hair was pulled up into a high ponytail, the end of it kissing the nape of her neck. I'd assumed she'd look hot in the skirt, but I hadn't prepared for how hot, and I entertained a thousand images of keeping her in that skirt just so I could feel her thighs squeeze my hand when I pushed it between her legs. Maybe I could rip that little slit and pull her legs around me, grind my aching cock against her warmth, and if we got lucky, finally sink in.

Where my mind was felt wrong though, considering the atmosphere. But it was a lot more pleasant than the images the Chief of Lakeside PD put into my head. Kara Marlan, age nineteen at the time of her disappearance, had been found in a shallow grave amongst a cluster of trees just outside of Northshore. The kind you pass on the interstate and don't look twice at. Pocket forests that break up the otherwise flat landscape. Kara had been discovered after a community search was organized in response to an anonymous tip, identified by her clothing and dental records.

I'd stayed in the very back of the small office during the whole event and considered getting one of those spinny rings for myself. It seemed to help with Tate's fidgeting habit. Her hands were in her lap, save for when she raised them to ask a question, but her arms weren't flexing like they did when she twisted her fingers so violently it made my joints ache. They were relaxed, calm at her sides, and when she looked back a few times to check on me, there was relief on her face.

I'm here baby. I'm not going anywhere. Let me love you like you deserve, without all the guilt.

Guilt and I were well acquainted, and it was a cloying sickness in my stomach as I sat next to her in an interview room after the press conference and listened to her detail everything that had happened with Davey. Every intimate detail. How the night before I'd beat him up, he'd tried to rape her, but had stopped himself because sex outside of marriage was a sin. How he'd squeezed her neck so hard in that car, the bruises lasted for weeks, and for months, she couldn't laugh or talk loudly without pain.

By the time we left, all I wanted to do was get her home. I wanted to get her something warm to drink, something healthy to eat, then I wanted to take her into my bed or hers and kiss her until I was the only thing she could think about.

"When are you planning on running the next story on these missing persons cases?" Pak asked after we walked outside, lingering on the sidewalk while I eyed my bike. Tate had changed back into jeans and a shirt and looked much more relaxed than she had in the skirt and blouse she'd worn for the conference.

"I have one written up on a girl from up North, but there's another case of a girl from around this area so I'll run that soon."

Pak had given her a look, his eyes flashing to mine for half a second. "Are you sure you're okay with this? It seems very close to home considering they're from—"

"I'm staying impartial. If at any point I can't, I'll step back."

She spun her ring while Pak looked at her, concern etched into his features. "To be honest, it's helping me a bit. This isn't the outcome anyone wanted obviously, but it's one step closer to getting justice for her. For them. At least they're looking for the girls now."

"Very true," Pak said, giving her a reassuring smile even when his eyes turned to mine. I needed to text him to check in on the comments again, even if in the end, neither of us could do anything about them.

After Pak got in his car, Tate let out a long sigh and looked up at the cloudy sky before shaking herself off violently. "Okay. That's done now. I'm ready."

I'd grinned, pulling her against my side, kissing her forehead as we walked. "Atta girl," I murmured, hoping this would help Tate instead of push her back behind the walls I'd been working to tear down. I didn't mind that they were there, but I wanted a way in, so I could pick at them from the inside and help set us both free.

Zentu Bakery was in downtown Northshore, the only active building in a long line of decaying brick and old faded signs. The cream and violet paint scheme reminded me of an Easter egg, but it drew everyone's attention, which meant more business. Not that they had many places to go to in town, but still.

Phil and Suzanne Zentu couldn't have cared less about me. They were all about Tatum, and as they embraced her then escorted her to a table, gushing over her piercings, the change in her hair—which was slowly fading from black to her brown at the roots—and the few tattoos they could see. I wondered how different her life would have been if they'd been her parents instead of Harvey and Marta Nichols, then reminded myself that they almost were. After her foster parents kicked her out, they'd taken her in. Tate was more than just an old employee to them, she was practically a daughter.

"I never wanted to think like that," she said when I'd pointed this out after a rush of afternoon customers called both Phil and Suzanne away for a bit. "Thinking about someone taking care of you puts an expectation on them, and expectations come with pressure. I didn't want to do that to them when I could take care of myself."

"No one doubts that."

"I know."

"Do you?" I asked, throwing her earlier words to me back at her. She scowled, reaching over to poke me in the side just as Suzanne came back over with a few pastries and some coffee for me, and tea for Tate.

We sat and chatted. Tatum tried to pay them back the money and Phil flat out refused. They asked about that night in hushed voices, about the years after. I got up to take the plates and cups to the counter, not wanting to interrupt the flow of conversation. Instead, I looked at the corkboard here, twisting my lips at how empty it was. A few flyers for local businesses, mostly home run. Tupperware. Candles. A flyer for church. Some handwritten notes from older families, but no drawings from small children. Last I'd heard, Northshore Elementary was being pushed to consolidate again. The class size had dwindled from the thirty or so I'd graduated with to half that. The town was dying, and despite Pastor Adler's flyer saying that the church was strong and everyone needed to be at service to keep it that way, I had a feeling no amount of faith could slow the decay.

I was about to go back to my seat when I felt pressure on my shoulder; like a shadow was weighing down on me. I turned toward the door, eyes connecting with one of the men coming in to shop. He was middle-aged, with thick brown hair that had been colored to try and cover up the gray. He stared at me, thick eyebrows furrowed while I raised mine in challenge. I didn't look that out of place. Nice jeans, black boots that matched my leather jacket, and a heavy, navy Henley shirt. He stared so hard it was uncomfortable, and I was tempted to flip him the finger, but I held back. Widening my gaze, I stared back, even after he turned away and looked toward one of the other men. I watched, eyes narrowing as his lips formed a single word. A name.

Bishop.

Well fuck.

I glanced at the table behind me, at Tate's dark hair, the piercings, her T-shirt and jeans. She looked just different enough that unless someone looked closely, they wouldn't suspect it was her. She'd been thirteen when she'd come to Northshore and didn't have parents and a brother like I did who'd shared teachers and daycare providers, who had broad cheekbones and a too long nose. The guy beside him looked at me, eyes widening as he glanced back outside. Phil caught their attention from the table, moving past me to get behind the counter. The men shuffled forward, ordering as their heads turned back and forth between where I stood and the counter.

I turned around, stomach uneasy as I approached the table where Tate was relaxed with Suzanne. She looked up when I leaned on the back of her chair, smiling softly.

"Are you bored?"

"Never," I said with a forced, casual grin. "But the afternoon rush will start soon, and I'd like to miss it if we could."

"Oh, but you'll come back?" Suzanne asked, taking Tate's hand. "Or can we come visit you? We come to the Metro once or twice a week. I'd love to take you out for dinner, Tatum. Or both of you."

"I'd like that very much," Tate said, gathering the bag she'd brought onto one shoulder, her face relaxed. Peaceful. *Hold onto that, baby,* I thought, glancing back over my shoulder where the men were exiting the shop with their coffee and bag of pastries, the whole group turning to look at me. I took her hand, turning my body so it blocked hers from view. Suzanne chuckled, covering her lips with the tip of her fingers between pointed between us.

"I thought you said you weren't dating."

"We're not," Tate said automatically, her cheeks turning pink as she looked at me. "I mean, we met up a few weeks ago, and we've been seeing each other, but it's nothing official. Is it?"

I raised my eyebrows and Suzanne patted my shoulder, giving me a knowing smile. "Right. Well, for being nothing, you two are awfully sweet together." She gave Tatum a hug, kissing her on the cheek. "Don't be a stranger. Call us, Tatum. Especially when you announce the pregnancy."

Tate's eyes went comically large, which made Suzanne and me laugh. "Don't hold your breath for that one." She glanced at me, a playful scowl on her face when I leaned in and kissed her hair, then she waved goodbye to Suzanne and Phil.

Warm autumn air slammed into us when we got outside, but I tucked her body against mine anyway, my eyes on the small crowd a few parking spaces down, all loitering around a single red sedan. I practically pushed Tatum in front of me when their murmurs grew louder, rushing her toward my Harley.

"You're really in a hurry to get out of here," she said, giving me a confused look as she tucked her bag into the small baggage area under the seat. "Did you get a text or something?"

"We should just get on the road. Rush hour is hell and people don't watch out for bikes. If we can avoid—"

"Mr. Bishop?"

Tate's body went rigid, her hands jerking back from the seat she'd been about to climb on as she backed up. I turned, eyes narrowing as they fell on a man walking forward. Not one of the guys who'd come into the shop and stared at me. It was someone else.

Davey Adler.

He must have been waiting in the car, or outside talking. I looked him up and down, noting his small increase in height and bulk, but the brown hair, the heavy hooded eyes, and the square jaw were all the same. I'd wondered if it would look misshapen at all, considering I broke it.

Davey took a step forward, hand lifting to run through his hair as he sized me up warily, then looked past me when Tatum gasped. I heard her shuffling, and when he tried to bolt around me, I jumped into his path and put a hand on his chest, bracing when he tried to shove me off.

"Oh, Lord. Tatum, is that—"

"Back the fuck off, asshole."

Davey looked at me, at the hand on his chest, then looked past my shoulder. The crowd he'd been with was murmuring, and it was déjà fucking vu all over again. Except Tatum wasn't locked in her apartment and injured this time. She was outside, scared but whole.

And I was going to keep it that way.

I looked over my shoulder to see her behind the bike, arms braced in front of her body, her hands balled into fists. She was shaking visibly, her eyes wide, lips pressed together so hard it looked painful. Davey's expression twisted and he tried to push past me again.

"Tatum—"

"Hey man, she doesn't want—"

"No."

Tate's voice cut like a shard of glass through the warm air, filling with so much tension, it threaded into me. Davey gaped, then threw my arm off his chest only to have both my hands replace it as I shoved him back. "She said no, asshole. You need me to spell it out for you again?"

He ignored me, holding his hands up, palms facing out. "Tatum, I need to speak—"

"Are you deaf?" I snapped, getting back in his face. "Get the fuck out of here. You've done enough to-."

"I haven't done—"

"The fuck you haven't!"

He looked at me, desperate, and gestured to Tate and where she'd moved on the other side of the bike. "I want to see her. I'm not going to hurt her, Kellen. She's not—"

"Not your fucking concern. Never was jackass. Now leave."

"Kellen."

"This is a public street, and I have a right—"

"I said leave!"

"Kellen!"

Tate's voice was shaky but sharp, and closer than I expected. Her hand slipped into mine and it triggered the words she'd said in the parking lot that day. *No one bothered to check how I was. No one fucking cared how I was.*

I shoved the urge to punch Davey down, turning to meet Tate's eyes. "Let's go, yeah? Let's get out of here."

She nodded, following when I began to guide her back to the bike, ignoring the urge to turn and throttle the body attached to the footsteps that followed. "Tatum, please," Davey pleaded, his gravelly voice almost whiny. "I need to speak with you. We need to talk about—"

"No!" Tate peered around me, clinging to the arm I had around her waist, her body shaking so hard I thought she might collapse. "I have nothing to say to you, and don't you dare try to contact me."

I glanced back to see Davey's face twisting; pain etched into his features. "Tatum, I'm so—"

"You should be in prison," she snarled, then she pointed to where we'd come into town from Triharbor. "Is that why you're here? Because of Kara? You used to lecture me about confessing my sins, have you come to confess yours?"

He stilled, and the color drained out of his face even though his eyes turned hard. Defensive. "I had nothing to do with this. I swear to God I had nothing—"

"Was it an 'accident?'" Tatum's voice was so heavy with

venom I winced. "Did whoever was in the church that night convince you I was a mistake? A lapse in judgement? When you couldn't finish the job you moved onto the next—"

"I lost control—"

Tatum laughed. Wild and malicious. "*Lost control?* I'll say. Let's ask the doctor I finally saw a few days later at the ER about your level of control."

She glared at him, and Davey's shoulders sagged as he raked a hand through his hair. "Tatum, please, you have to listen to me."

"She doesn't have to listen to shit." I pushed Tate behind me when Davey stalked forward again, and when he tried to push me aside, I grabbed his collar and threw him back so hard he fell to the ground. I kept my eyes locked on Davey's even as his little friends came rushing over for back up, even as Tate grabbed my arm and tugged me back. Some guy helped Davey to his feet, and he held his hands toward me, surrendering. I jabbed my finger in his direction even as I walked toward the Harley with Tate tucked against me.

"If you start any shit with her, and I mean any shit— messages, phone calls, comments on articles, fucking air dropped letters I don't care—I will end you. You hear me?"

"Kellen, I'll take that as a threat, and if you come near me—"

"Take it as gospel for all I care. The only reason I'll come near you again is if you give me a reason to. You or any of your little cult friends come for her, and I'll find a way to put you so deep in the ground not even God will find you when I'm done."

I spun away from him, grabbing my helmet and Tate's, my hands steadied by rage as I helped her fasten it then lifted her onto the bike.

"It's gonna be okay," I said, climbing onto the bike in front of her. "Nothing's going to happen to you. I won't let it."

I kicked the bike to life and turned out of the spot, almost peeling out as I took off in the opposite direction. I'd take the back roads home, less chance of someone following us. I wanted to get her out of this hellhole and never bring her back. I wanted to get her somewhere safe.

I wanted to get her somewhere where the world didn't feel like it was collapsing in on us.

Chapter Thirty-Five
Tatum

I DON'T KNOW HOW I DID IT, BUT I KEPT THE TERROR of seeing Davey again locked up through the entire ride, holding it in until I got into my apartment. There, it broke loose. I dropped my stuff on the floor, ignored Haku's purring trot into my space, and ran to the bathroom to throw up everything in my stomach. Kellen followed, his hands cool as they brushed my neck and pulled my hair out of my face. When I heaved again, I shoved him away.

"Please."

"It's okay. I don't care."

"*I do!*"

My voice was a whip, and when it cracked Kellen backed away, lingering in the doorway as I tried to breathe. My mouth was sticky, throat burning, and I hauled myself up on shaky legs, shoving the faucet of the handle up and ducking my head under the spigot. Kellen's hand settled on my back, but I shoved it away. It was too much. The heat of his palm, the sound of his breath, the sensation of touch no matter how gentle. It was all too much. I had no solid ground to stand on and try to hold it up. Kellen reached for me again and I groaned, pushing his arm away.

"Don't."

"Tate."

"No, Kellen. I mean it. I feel like I'm suffocating."

I pushed up on my sink, glancing quickly at my pale face, the smudged mascara and eyeliner, before looking away. My lungs burned, heart pounding so hard I was faint but my brain wouldn't shut down. Run, run, run, was all it said, but my legs wouldn't work. They wouldn't carry me.

"I can't breathe," I said, pressing my palm against my chest. "I need space. I need to think."

Silence filled the bathroom, and Kellen backed away slowly. "Okay. I'll be in the other room. Do you want water or—"

"No," I said, and the words spilled out of me before I could stop them or even think about them fully. "I want you to leave."

"Tatum—"

"I need you to leave!" I shot up, pointing at my chest. "I can't even try to sort out my thoughts because you're here acting like a crutch. I'm using you and—"

Kellen blanched. "You're not using me—"

"Yes, I am!"

I don't know what carried me out of the bathroom and toward him. I felt nothing but fight or flight, and Kellen was the closest target. "Everything is happening so damn fast I haven't had time to breathe, or adjust, or even decide if I want this." I gestured between us, and the calm in his expression faltered. His jaw clenched hard, then he opened his mouth, about to argue but I held up my hands. "I don't even know if I can trust myself, Kellen. How in the hell am I supposed to trust you?"

"How can you not trust me?" He pointed at his own chest. "Fuck, Tatum, what do you want me to do? What do you need me to say?"

"I don't know. I'm terrified, and now I don't know what's

going to happen. Is Davey going to come after me again? Should I move? Should I—"

"If he tries to get to you, I'm going—"

"You're going to what, Kellen?" I demanded. "Hurt him? Attack him? Get yourself thrown back in jail? You think I want that?" He closed his mouth, jaw clenched again when I scoffed. "I thought we already learned what it feels like to be without each other, you want to do that again?"

"No!" Kellen shouted. "But I'm going to do everything I can to keep you safe, Tatum. I'm getting to know your co-workers, your friends, so I can be there if something happens. Jesus, Pak has got a fucking crush on you and it makes me insane, but I've been talking to him and making sure no one is—"

"Why are you talking to Pak? I asked.

My sides ached, the muscles working hard to keep up with the rapid pace of my breathing. I waited for a response while Kellen stared, his mouth open, hands at his sides where his fingers were twitching. He dragged a hand through his hair, standing up straight, a sheepish expression crossing his face. "I don't want you to... don't read into this, because I talked to Pak and Elissa and they agreed there's nothing—"

"What did you talk to Pak and Elissa about, Kellen? What's going on!?"

I knew I sounded unhinged, but I couldn't calm down. All I could think was *run, run, run*. The logical side of my brain tried to calm it down, but I was too wired from seeing Davey. His face, those eyes, the memory of them staring down at me.

Kellen's throat flexed, and he ducked his head, staring at the floor like he was being scolded. "The night of the banquet. I accidentally dropped your name—your real name—and Pak told me there'd been comments on your articles. He'd filtered them out, but they were all addressed at you. To Tatum."

I swayed, grabbing onto a chair at the table for support. My name. Someone was commenting my name. Someone had worked out who I was and was commenting my name all over my articles. "Why?" I asked, breathless, hands shoved into my messy hair when I stood up. "Why wouldn't you tell me—"

"Because you can't do anything about it," Kellen said, and he sounded disgusted. "Name changes are public record if you know where to look. Anyone can walk in there and ask—"

"What?!"

He paused, guilt etching his face. "They didn't tell you that? When you filed?"

I wiped a hand over my face. "They might have mentioned it, but I was so desperate I might... not have paid attention."

Kellen nodded, rolling his lips, everything about his stance and his expression distressed. "But there isn't anything you could do about it. Even Isaac said that when I asked if people making comments could be tracked or charged. I didn't want you upset over something I couldn't fix."

"It's not your job to *fix* it, Kellen," I said, closing my eyes. "It's not your job to fix any of this."

"Not fix." He shifted, setting his hands on his hips. "I don't need to fix anything, including you. But I want to keep you safe. I want to help."

"You know you can't do that, right?" I asked, the anger in my voice softening. "You know you can't keep me safe."

"Yes, I can," he growled. "I can and I will. Goddamn it, Tatum. I love you. And it's not because of nostalgia or familiarity or any of that shit. I have to keep you safe—"

"You can't keep me safe, Kellen. I can't keep me safe. He would have come after me even if you hadn't gone to prison. He tried to come after me today."

"And if he fucking tries again—"

"You cannot be with me all the time, Kellen. You have a life and so do I. I could walk out of the office and get hit by a car. I could be caught in a fire. I could get shot while doing a story. I could be assaulted while doing a story. There's an endless list of things that could happen to me, Kellen, and neither of us can do a damn thing to stop any of them."

"Tate, I know. I know all of that, but you can't..." He took a shuddering breath, and I watched as he tried to get control. "You can't blame me for trying."

His eyes locked on mine, hard and shining, his arms flexing as he swallowed hard and moved closer to me. "I love you, okay? I love you and I've never...You are the only person I've ever loved, and I don't know if could ever love anyone else."

"You haven't tried."

"I did," he snapped. "I tried. Twice since I got out, and I could barely touch either of them. I never connected, and it wasn't because I didn't want to. I couldn't because you're it for me. I love you more than you'll ever—"

"Don't say that to me," I said, voice trembling. "Don't you tell me you love me more than I'll ever know. That's such a *stupid* sentiment."

Kellen grimaced, staying still when I drew close to him. "Let me know. Let me know by telling me the truth. By telling me there's a threat even if I can't do anything about it. Don't shut me out of things like that because you're trying to keep me safe or put yourself in front of me because you're trying to defend me. You know goddamn well I can take care of myself. I don't need you to fight my battles. I have to fight them on my own."

"Fight them if you want, but I won't let you do it alone," he said, and before I knew what was happening he'd grabbed me, cupping my face, his fingers practically fisting in my hair. "You want me to let you know? You have to keep me by your side. You want to wield the fucking sword? Do it. But let me be your shield."

His thumbs skated along my cheekbones, smearing wetness, and I reached up, taking his wrists and pulling them away even as his face fell and the cage surrounding my chest threatened to crack.

"You want to be my shield? Then let me decide to pick you up," I whispered, voice trembling. "Kellen, please. You said you didn't want me to make my decisions based off you before, don't force me to do that now. Let me breathe for a minute, let me decide what I... what I need to do. Please."

Kellen's shoulders heaved with his breaths, rising and falling, his eyes closing as the fight went out of his body. He clasped his fingers around mine, squeezing so tight it almost hurt before he leaned forward and pressed his lips to my forehead, letting out a shaky exhale against my hair.

"Okay," he whispered, his hands shaking, like he'd siphoned the tremors out of me, taken them out of my body so he could bear the weight. It made me want to throw myself against him at the same time it made me want to run away. He kissed me again, and I looked up to see his throat flexing as he tried to hold back tears. "Whatever you need."

Chapter Thirty-Six

Tatum

KELLEN LEFT.

He did what I asked, leaving behind a whispered plea for me to call him. Text him. Contact him in some way. His hands were shaking, and I'd half expected him to go to Priest's apartment even if he wasn't home yet, but I'd waited until the sound of his bike roaring to life filled the air outside, then faded into the distance before moving off my couch. Somehow, I managed to write up a brief article about the press conference, making sure to include the most necessary details rather than the gruesome ones, and emailed it to Pak. Then I slapped my laptop closed and stalked to my bedroom.

And let myself pack.

I shoved all my clothes into a suitcase, grabbed Haku's carrier because I wasn't going to leave him behind. I shoved my makeup, shower supplies, anything I could grab into a bag and tossed it on the bed. I put in my contacts. I gathered all my bills up and shoved them in my purse, double checking my cards and the cash I had on me.

Then I went out to my car, threw the door open, and sat down in the driver's seat for ten seconds before throwing myself out again. "Goddammit!" I sucked in a deep breath, clenched my fists, then dropped my body back into the seat and slammed the door shut.

Breathe, Tatum. Breathe. Breathe. Images of shattered glass in my lap, the seat belt buckles and center compartment at my back, and his hands around my throat threatened to overwhelm me. *Breathe. Fucking breathe, you mess. What are you doing? What are you going to do?*

I focused on the words, repeating the question like it was a mantra as the memories muted themselves and my breathing slowed. I opened my eyes, letting the tears slip down my cheeks as I looked around the car. The air was stale. There was a cloudy bottle of water in the cup holder, a few receipts on the passenger seat. Otherwise, it was empty. Clean, save for the dusty film that clung to the center console, the dash, and the steering wheel. I ran my hands over it, the ring Kellen had given me catching the fading sunlight as it melted into the horizon. I let the light fade. Let the shadows creep into the space and darken the gray seats to soft black.

Would he come for me now? Now that he knew I was close? He knew my pen name, had been commenting and spilling my name for everyone to see. And the way he'd stalked up behind Kellen, trying to push around him to get to me, coming even after I'd shouted at him to stop and Kellen had shoved him back. Whoever he was with had just watched the scene and done nothing. They saw how scared I was, how aggravated Kellen was, and had done nothing.

I wanted to know why in the hell he got a pass. Why, when Kellen entered a space, he was scowled at and people moved away, but when Davey came at me like a bull, they just stood there. Why was one man so clearly a threat but they let the actions slide, where the other was a guardian and they tried to lock him away?

My hands slid off the steering wheel and I leaned back, my

breathing slowing down even though my heart rate didn't. My whole body ached with tension, but I forced myself to stay in the car. I wanted to know that if I needed to run, I could.

But I didn't. Not away, at least. I wanted to run, but it was toward a future I'd dreamed about in fleeting moments when no one was looking. One where I had lunches with Hannah, gave Priest hell, and slept beside Kellen in a bed every night. One where I went out with people I was getting to know and made new friends. I wanted a future where I could be happy.

And despite the distance and the years and the pain he'd caused me, this last week had made me realize I wanted that with Kellen. He said he couldn't imagine loving anyone else, and I didn't know if I would either. Not when he was so close, making promises I knew he couldn't keep, but they were promises of something.

There was no guarantee I'd get a happy ending if I went to him now, but there was no guarantee I wouldn't. There was no guarantee that even if I put 800 locks on the door and installed cameras around this hypothetical house I owned something terrible wouldn't happen. There was no guarantee that Davey Adler wouldn't come after me.

There was no guarantee that he would.

There were no guarantees of anything. No promises for a tomorrow, or the day after that. No assurances that Kellen would love me always and be my shield like he offered.

But he'd never get the chance if I didn't give it to him.

I'd said I wanted to swim and dipping my toes in had turned into a full dive. The memory of what to do, how to be with Kellen and love him back, it was all there, but the strokes were impeded by waves and weight and a depth to things I hadn't imagined encountering so quickly. He got me a ring, he said I needed to get used to wearing one again. He said he loved me like it was so easy, the words he'd struggled to come up with three years ago flowing out of him like water now.

But they were sweet as wine, and that scared me more than anything. Because wine was poison if you drank too much, and it left you aching and craving more when it went away. Addicted.

"This is stupid," I grumbled to the empty car. I should be saving my fucking metaphors and comparisons for work and the stories I wrote. Stories that didn't involve me or my life because I was still writing it, and I couldn't let the sudden appearance of the off-screen bad guy derail my path. I hated cliffhangers, so why the hell would I write one if I could satisfy myself with a good ending, or set up a good beginning.

I pulled my phone out of my pocket, but instead of immediately dialing Kellen's number, I stared at the Facebook app I'd put on there the other day but never opened. Pak had pushed me again about a social media presence, saying the public would want a way to follow me, and it was a good way to get tips and make connections. Connections I would need to do my job.

The screen flashed bright white when I opened the app, and I typed my login with shaky hands. It was the same as when I'd looked at it the other day, the only difference was the reduced amount of messages in my inbox. Kellen mentioned Isaac had gotten into my accounts and taken the messages sent as evidence. Documentation of a pattern they might trace if any new evidence came to light.

I opened the message box, finding all the ones from Davey and the random accounts were gone. Cleared out. There were messages from Hannah that were old. Right after I'd left town. *Where are you? Are you okay? Tate, answer someone. People are worried. They think you're dead.* They repeated for a while, but eventually she gave up.

Kellen hadn't.

My fingers shook as I pressed his name, reading the most recent message he'd sent. Back at the end of August. Maybe a week or so before we'd run into each other.

Hey Tatertot.

Yes, I'm still calling you that. I know it pisses you off, but who doesn't love potatoes?

I'm still in Saylorville. Ten minutes from downtown Des Moines. Phone number hasn't changed.

If you see this text me. Or call. Send a smoke signal, I don't care. Anything to let me know you're okay. You don't have to see me if you don't want to. But let me know you're okay.

Love, Kellen.

Or Kellogg. If you still have your phone and I'm in your contacts.

Just call me, okay?

My lips started to tremble as I scrolled up to the next one, which had been sent earlier this year, in April.

The last season of Fruits Basket is out now. I finally read the Manga. I can see why you liked it. I'm gonna watch it. I'd like to wait for you but…

Just call please?

There were tons of messages like this. Little updates on his life. When he got his business license. Pictures when he opened the shop. He told me about Priest. The club. Lane getting a girlfriend, then breaking up with said girlfriend. How he'd tried to move on but couldn't.

It wasn't all sunshine. Some of the messages were angry. Didn't I know how worried he was? Why did this have to happen? His anger wasn't ever at me, but at the world. He raged about being alone even though he wasn't.

He just didn't have me.

Eventually I scrolled to the messages he sent me when he was first out of prison. Frantic ones asking where I was. What happened? Did I know there was a missing persons person report out? There was an agony in his words that made my eyes prick, and tears finally started to fall when I reached messages from late August about a year ago.

. . .

I don't know what to say.

I'm drunk. I miss you like crazy. I have your fucking hoodie and there are days I just pick it up and sniff it.

I'm just as sick as Davey is, right? Maybe? I don't know...

I love you. I love you so fucking much and not seeing you is killing me. Not knowing where you are is killing me. Not being able to say this to your face because I was a coward, just like you said, is killing me. I watched that movie and you're right. I was scared. I am your Howl.

But I love you, Tate. And even if you see this and never contact me, I need you to know that.

I love you.

I love you.

The text repeated over and over again. Different variations of the same three-word phrase. One he'd said earlier. One he'd repeated so many times I was starting to get used to it. I was starting to hear it as it was and not wait for the "but" that should follow, or the issuance of an expectation I'd never be able to meet.

Because Kellen didn't have any. He never would. He just wanted me.

My hands were shaking again when I closed the messages and shoved my key into the ignition, unable to turn it just yet. I pulled up Kellen's number and our recent exchange of texts. It was the better option now. If I called, I'd beg him to come to me, to save me from having to do something should have done months ago. Face my fears. Try to push past them.

And find out if this stupid car still ran.

Chapter Thirty-Seven
Kellen

Fuck.

The word bounced around my head like a ball I'd thrown against a wall. I couldn't say anything else. It was a good summation of how I felt. I'd fucked up. Fucking Davey Adler. I wanted my fucking girl in my arms instead of miles away. Fuck, fuck, fuck.

My chest ached, and my arms were starting to get sore. I moved everything in my garage around, swept, threw a wrench so hard if left a dent in the wall, swore until my voice was hoarse, then moved it all back into place. I went down into my basement where there were weights, and I lifted them until the muscles in my arms and chest and legs burned.

You want to be my shield? Let me decide to pick you up.

How many hours had I sat in therapy and learned about control? Self-control. Lack of control. We were responsible for our actions. That was what we could control, and things that were out of our control were the actions of other people. All we had power over were our choices and how to respond to the constant flux of decisions made around us.

I'd known it from the moment we met, re-met—shit, the

entire time I'd known Tatum—that at any moment, she could decide she didn't want me. She could see what I had to offer, everything I was, and walk away from it.

And there was nothing I could do.

I knew what it was like to push her away. I knew how it felt to wonder if she was gone from this world and I was left behind. But until today, I'd never known her rejection.

And it sucked.

For the briefest of moments, I empathized with Davey, because he'd lost Tatum for reasons that were all his own fault too. So what was going to happen to me now? Would I have to watch her with some other guy, or girl, or anyone else than me? Would I get obsessed? Clearly, it was possible. I had been for three fucking years.

I pictured a nameless faceless person with their arms around Tate, and I wanted to throw them in traffic. Her smile belonged to me. Her eyes belonged to me. Her body and soul and heart...

Belonged to her.

All of it did.

I'd taught her that. I'd tried that summer we were together to give her back her ownership over her body, her choices, and goddammit, she'd done exactly what I taught her to. Exercise agency. Set boundaries that were best for her, one's that might not include me.

At some point I'd made it back upstairs and slumped onto the couch, my eyes fixed at the ceiling when my phone buzzed. First once. Then again. Then a third time. God, please don't let there be church tonight. As much as the guys would help, they'd wonder what the fuck I'd done wrong, and I'd have to tell them it was my own fault. Again.

I pulled out my phone, siting up straight when I saw Tate's name on the screen.

Tatertot: *What's your address?*
Me: *Why?*

Tatertot: *Just give me your address Kellen. Please.*

I typed in the number and street, not daring to hope.

Me: *Baby, can we talk? I'm sorry about the comments. I should have told you. Please, Tate. Just talk to me.*

God, this was pathetic. I was no better than Adler. Whining and begging for her to listen to me instead of giving her time to think for herself. That was what I wanted right?

Heavy self-loathing settled over me, but it was broken by a flash of white coming through the window. Headlights. In my driveway. I narrowed my eyes, standing up to look out the front window at the car sitting in the driveway behind my truck. Small. A four-door with rust stains. My eyes widened when I saw the Pontiac emblem on the front, then the dark-haired girl bolting out of the driver's side.

Tatum.

"Jesus," I charged out the front door. "Baby—"

"It works," she groaned, the words shaking as she stood up, using the side of the car for support. We locked eyes, her shoulders rising and falling with her rapid breaths, but she managed to flash me a smile. It was incredulous, bewildered, and tired. But it was a smile.

"It runs," she said, stumbling as she walked toward my house. "And I... I drove it. Kellen, I drove my car."

I practically jumped off the steps, meeting her halfway down the drive. She slung her arms around my shoulders as I threw mine around her waist, grabbing her ass to lift her up. She circled her legs around me, letting out a shaky moan as she buried her head in my shoulder while I carried her into my house. I kicked the door shut once we were inside, pressing her to the wall. Her breathing was ragged when I sealed my lips over hers, muffling her quiet sob. She clawed at my shirt while kicking off her shoes, her hands shaky when she put them on my face.

"I'm still mad at you."

"I know. I'm sorry. Baby, I'm sorry, I just wanted—"

Her lips cut me off, hands fisting in my hair to pull me close as I worked at her clothing, tearing the button on her jeans open, shoving the denim down her hips. "Kellen, I'm scared. I might always be scared, but I want to be with you. I want to love you and try this for real finally and see—"

The rest of her sentence was lost in a kiss, our lips moving together, her tongue sliding against mine as I stepped on the leg of her jeans and lifted her again, tugging her out of them. I held her with one arm, practically ripping off her shirt before she set to work on mine. My bedroom was down the hall, but I wasn't sure if we'd make it that far. Not at the rate things were going. Her legs were locked around my waist, and I pushed my hips into hers, cupping her thighs, her ass, one of her breasts. She let out a shaky, sobbing cry and clutched me so tight it hurt, her head tipping back when I fisted my hand into her hair, holding her in place so I could kiss her deeply. Ruthlessly. Satisfying a craving I'd been denied for so fucking long.

"*Mine.*"

I bit at her bottom lip, licking the sting away with another kiss. My hand loosened in her hair, but she kept her fingers in my hair. My breath hitched when she closed them into a fist, tugging my mouth back to hers. The ghost of a smile curled her mouth, and she breathed the same word against my lips.

"*Mine.*"

"You're goddamn right I am."

I wrapped an arm around her waist, the other around her thigh, and walked her away from the wall down to my bedroom. We fell onto the bed, and Tate clawed at my jeans while I unfastened her bra. The straps slipped off her arms and I threw it away, burying my face in her breasts. She gave up on my pants for the time being, lacing her fingers back into my hair when I kissed her nipple, sucking the soft peak into my mouth. Her moan was like a catalyst to the lust inside me, a fire that had been simmering for days and she'd thrown kindling onto it.

"Kellen, please."

"Please what?" I rocked my hips between hers, gritting my teeth when she pushed back. "You want me to push?"

"I want you to take," she said, her hands flying back down to my jeans. "God, push and take and love me please."

I growled as I pulled myself away from her, the distance too much as I pulled off my jeans and kicked them onto the floor. Tate lifted her hips when my fingers hooked into her panties, and I bent to kiss her stomach and thighs while my hands went back to her breasts, cupping them when she arched as my head ducked between her legs. Her thighs trembled as I kissed them, and I looked up when she whimpered and tugged on my hair.

"I haven't... been with anyone since... God, I haven't even kissed anyone since we were together. The last time I went on a date I got scared and ended up leaving when—"

"I don't know who that guy was, and I don't fucking care, but you know me," I murmured, kissing and licking the inside of her thighs because I'd die if I didn't taste her right now. "I'm not gonna hurt you. Fuck, baby, all I want is to do is love you. I just want to make you feel good. You'll tell me when I do, right? And just say stop if you need to?"

The last question made her relax, and I watched her nod, her hand cupping mine against her breast. I pulled one of her thighs over my shoulder, kissing the inner crease, teasing her with soft licks until I felt her rocking her hips into my mouth. "Still so sweet, aren't you," I murmured, kissing the top of her mound, then her clit, still hidden even though she was so wet already. She was so soft, so warm, and all I wanted to do was make her hotter.

"God, I missed how you feel." I squeezed her breast and ran my hand over the top of her thigh, palming her soft curves. "I missed how you smell, how you fucking taste." I licked up the seam of her body, burying my face into her pussy, licking every last drop of her, making her squirm and writhe. Soft gasps filled the quiet of my room, the pillows cradling her head like they'd been waiting for her just as long as I had. This was where she should be. Right here with me, spread open, bared and greedy for me.

"Kellen, God," she whimpered when I slipped my fingers inside her, curling them, savoring the feeling of her pussy squeezing around me. I kissed her clit again, sucking it softly until she grabbed my hair and pulled, dragging me up her body as I planted little kisses along the way. "Don't make me beg, please, Kellen. Just fuck me already."

My eyes widened, and I bit back a quiet laugh as I reached for the dresser and the condoms inside, pausing when she grabbed my arm. "I still have my IUD, and I told you I haven't been—"

"Neither have I."

Her panting lips met mine, and I slipped my hand from between her legs so I could grab my cock. I slid myself against her pussy, savoring the soft, wet, warm feeling of her before I notched the tip and sank into her heat. Tate gasped, her head falling back at the same time her legs spread wider, cradling my hips as they started to rock.

"*Fuck*," she whispered, holding tight when I pulled back and sank in again. Over and over, gritting my teeth to stop myself from coming right then. She was so warm and wet and welcoming, her hips rising up to meet mine, no resistance. No hint of pain. Nothing separating us but the space between thrusts.

Mine.

Always mine.

I wrapped myself around her, knees digging into the bed, hands tucked around her supple ass to hold her still for me. She clutched my shoulders, nails biting my skin, her pussy vice-like around my cock, her nipples stiff as they brushed my chest. I buried my face in her neck, moaning as I pumped forward and back, her thighs squeezing me to meet each thrust. She held me like I was her lifeline, like she was afraid I'd vanish if she loosened her grip.

"I'm here," I told her, my fingers digging into her hips before I brought one hand up to cup her face. "Baby, I'm here. I'm not going anywhere."

Her eyes fluttered, and I kissed away the tears that slipped out of them. "Please don't. I can't... I don't want lose—"

"Not fucking happening," I promised, leaning in to kiss her as I felt her start to clench around me. I needed a third or fourth fucking arm at this point to do all the things I wanted to do to her. Hold her close, cup her ass or her tits, rub her clit until she came so sweetly around me. I grabbed one of her hands, pushing it between our bodies, smiling when her breath hitched, and I felt her fingers go to work.

"That's it, baby. Let me feel you come. You're so fucking sweet," I groaned, hovering against her lips, gritting my teeth to keep my pace steady as she tightened, her body tense for half a second before she burst and started to pulse.

"Kellen," she whimpered, her hand reaching around to grab my hips. "Don't stop."

I buried my face in her neck and pulled her thigh higher around my waist. "Never, baby. Never again. You're my girl. My good girl. My perfect girl."

My hand slid out of her hair, grabbing the sheets above her like an anchor. Like if I held tight enough I could bury myself deeper inside her. Tatum's ecstatic pants, her soft moans as she clenched drove me crazy, driving me to thrust harder until I worried my hips might bruise her thighs. My stomach tightened into a knot, pressure building at the base of my spine as pathetic as needy noises slipped out of my lips and landed on hers. She wrapped and arm around my waist, curling her other hand against my cheek.

"Kell, I love you."

She leaned up to seal her lips against mine and swallow my moan, drinking in the obscene noise I made as I came so hard the edges of my vision went blurry. I sank into her deep, letting her thighs frame my hips and pull me closer as my cock throbbed and I filled her with three years of longing. All I could smell was her. All I could feel was her. All I could taste and breathe and hear was her. She was everything, the missing half of me. The piece that completed the puzzle I'd been trying to complete.

She was mine.

Chapter Thirty-Eight
Tatum

BEEP BEEP BEEP

The noise was coming from the floor, and I rolled over, grabbing the offensive device and shutting off the alarm. 6:00AM. I rolled my lips, then quickly typed a message to Pak.

Me: *Working from home today. You get the article?*

Pak: *All good. Already up on the website.*

I sighed in relief, then shot a quick email to my professor for the one class I had this afternoon letting him know I wouldn't be there. They knew I had a job at *The Journal,* so they never asked, and I was good with my makeup work and participation in the online forums. Missing class made me feel twitchy, but I needed the day to think. To catch up on my sanity.

To catch up on other things.

Kellen was asleep beside me on his back, one arm extended into the space where I'd been lying. His shaggy hair had curled at the ends, like it did when he didn't brush or do anything with it. When I rolled over to look at him, my hips and thighs ached in reminder of what we'd done. How my body had been pushed and pulled in positions and ways I wasn't used to. After that first time, Kellen had recovered minutes later and plunged into me again, kissing me and whispering filthy sweet promises as he did. We'd showered after and ended up having sex against the wall and having to rewash when we were finished.

I pushed myself up, leaning so I could drink him in for a bit while he was still. His full lips were parted, chest rising and falling slowly, making the tattoo across it look like it was moving. I ran my fingers over the lines on his stomach, the soft spattering of hair, sliding into the covers so I could press my lips against his skin. The room wasn't cold, but being uncovered and away from his body even for a few minutes had made my skin feel chilled. I nestled against his stomach, kissing and letting my hands roam so I could rememorize him the way he had me last night. This was easily something I could become addicted to, and for the first time I didn't worry what the consequences might be.

Kellen stirred at my touch, his fingers threading into my hair when I'd started to kiss along his hips. He murmured word-lessly, tightening his grasp when I kissed his slightly stiff cock under the tip. It jumped, and I licked the same spot, eyes lifting to see that his were still closed, his expression relaxed.

"Is this okay?"

"Baby, you can do whatever the fuck you want to me."

I smiled, lowering my head and taking him into my mouth so I could wake him up in a way I'd always wanted. My shift at the bakery had started at 5:30, and we'd always stayed up late so morning sex had never been an option when we were together the first time. It couldn't be that different from sex any other time of the day, especially considering the way Kellen stiffened and moaned softly as I slid my mouth along his length, jaw aching after just a few passes because I was out of practice. He was thick, and long. Partly the reason I was sore.

"Fuck, Tate." His voice was tight, the hand gently coaxing me shuddering in my hair. "You gotta stop."

I lifted my head, looking curiously at him. "Why?"

"Because if you don't I'm going to come in your mouth."

"What if I want that?"

"*Jesus.*" He groaned, taking my shoulders and pulling me on top of him, shifting me until my legs were straddled his hips, his cock pressed between my legs. "Some other time." He sat up slightly, bracing on one arm while the other wrapped around my waist. His lips found my neck as he lifted me slightly, then lowered me down on his length. I hissed softly at the quick sting, then moaned as he sank in deep, filling me until all I could think about was him.

"There we go," he murmured, still holding me when I rocked experimentally, testing how to move since I'd never been in this position. Even before. "Just ride me. I don't want to do a goddamn thing today. I just want to stare at how perfect you are."

He laid back, hands coaxing me into a steady rhythm of soft rocking movements, little bounces up and down, his hips rising to meet mine. I braced on his chest, rolling my hips forward and back. "You're so fucking sexy, Tate." His voice was breathless, and mine was completely lost to quiet gasps and moans, words long forgotten as I worked his cock inside me until pressure bloomed between my hips. I ground myself against him, chasing a release I'd had to work so hard to get on my own, but he could bring on so easily. One hand slid to the crease of my thigh, his thumb moving lower until he found my clit.

"That feels good, yeah?"

I nodded, too busy chasing pleasure to say anything but a whispered, "Fuck."

"That's all you need to do, baby." He rubbed my clit softly, grabbing hold of my ass when I fell out of rhythm. "Just ride me. You feel so fucking good. I can't get enough."

He pushed against the bed and rocked his hips up into me, taking over when I stared to whine and wiggle, the rush of heady pleasure almost too much. I squeezed around him, losing my breath. "Kellen."

My back was on the mattress before I had time to process what happened, and Kellen's hips pushed into me over and over, slapping against my spread thighs. He kissed me, a smile curling his lips when I moaned his name again.

"I know, baby." He bent to kiss me as I came apart, smiling against my lips. "Show me how good it feels when I'm inside you. Come for me, that's it. God, that's it."

I clenched around him, able to do nothing more than moan and grip his bicep as it flexed while his fingers worked my clit, his hips slapping against mine at a steady pounding pace until he stiffened, gripping my thigh. His cock swelled inside me, and when he came, he groaned into my neck, his forehead damp, chest slick with sweat as he went slack against me.

I welcomed his weight, the way he curled around me, tucking his head under my chin and wrapping his arms around my back. We laid silently, until our breathing slowed and he softened inside me before slipping out. Kellen lifted onto his elbows, framing my face with his biceps, his hands smoothing over my hair.

"Taking the day off?"

I nodded. "I need to think."

His expression tightened, but I shook my head. "Not about this. About how I'm... going to handle it if things go bad."

"Maybe, if we're lucky, they won't."

He rolled his lips, pressing a kiss to the inside of my wrist when I lifted my hand to trace the side of his face. I slid my fingers into his hair, smiling when he tipped his head into my touch.

"I really hope you're right."

Chapter Thirty-Nine
Kellen

"YOU ARE AN ENTIRELY DIFFERENT PERSON WHEN YOU are well fucked."

I rolled my eyes at Riot, listening to Cas' laugh while I took a sip of the beer in my hand, then set it back on the shelf at the back of my shop. Things were busy today and had been for the last week. It was nearing the end of October. The temps had dropped, and everyone in the club was bringing their bikes in for tune-ups, cleaning, and general prep for the winter. Everyone had cars because we lived in the Midwest, and black ice plus bikes was a recipe for disaster. But we still went on ride outs when it was warm.

"I'm serious. I haven't seen you throw a wrench in weeks," Riot pressed. "If I'd have known orgasms would have made you less of a grumpy bastard, I'd have fucked you myself."

I scowled while Cas practically fell off his stool laughing, and Rev grunted behind me. "He's still an ass. You're not here every day. He's moody on Wednesdays and Thursdays when Tate doesn't let him sleep over cause she has to get up at the ass crack of dawn for work."

"Yeah, cause those are the nights she can't sleep so she ends up baking until God knows when and then is tired all day," I argued, looking over at my shoulder and watching Rev shrug. "I'm telling you. She should sublet her apartment and move in with me. It'd be better for us both."

"Yeah, and then Macy and I would get a new shitty neighbor to deal with," Rev grumbled before sitting down next to me, sliding a drip pan under the bike, something I'd forgotten before I started this task. "Jesus, Fox. She fuck the common sense out of you today or what?"

The others laughed and I twisted my lips, ignoring them because it was the other way around. My mind was on this morning when Pak had told Tate about more comments, and they'd finally figured out a way to put a filter on her email. A week after the press conference about Kara Marlan's body, she'd started getting direct messages sent to her inbox. At first they'd been short, then they'd turned into long tirades about women speaking when they should be silent, and punishment for the wicked who refused to repent. The first few had made her uneasy for a couple days, and that was a kind word for it, but after her boss had stepped in and started monitoring it, Tate was able to relax a bit.

I liked to think that my being around most of the time, stroking her back at night, making sure she ate, fucking her senseless a few times a week, helped too.

We'd settled into a routine and as much as I grumbled about the teasing, Riot was right. I was different. I felt different. Steadier. More settled. And happy. For the first time in three years, I was happy. Things weren't always easy. One of the guys in the club had gotten caught up in a fight, and Rush had to call Riot's girl to step in and help, which put a dent in the funds we used for other things, but he was hoping we'd make it up.

I'd brought Tate around often enough that she'd gotten to know a few people. Riot had introduced her and Michaela formally, and they'd talked about journalism ethics and justice at the last cookout we'd had. Hannah came with her sometimes, mostly because it turned out she worked at the hospital Looper's old lady was delivering at, and they'd talked about what to plan for. Rush had introduced her to Betsy, and in a week Tate had written up an article that would run in the events section about the trick or treat event we were having at Styx. Everyone was nervous about having something about the club go so public, but Rush read the article before Tate turned it over and he seemed fine with it. We trusted him, and I didn't want to admit how much it meant that he trusted her.

It probably helped that his daughter, Lucy, who had only ever latched onto me outside her parents, took to Tate like she'd known her all her life. Maybe it was because Tate had a picture of a cat tattooed on her wrist, or maybe it was because when Lucy cried after her mom left, Tate didn't try to offer her candy or get her to stop. She'd just taken her to the back room where it was quiet and they read books.

When I'd told her she'd be a good mom someday, she'd blanched and immediately changed the subject.

Rev brought over new oil for Cas' bike and my phone buzzed.

Tatertot: *I'm still pissed at you.*

Me: *I'm sorry!*

Tatertot: *You broke my bed, Kellen. And it wasn't even in the fun way.*

Me: *Which is kind of funny. I'm ordering you a new bed.*

The phone rang almost as soon as I sent the text, and I stood up, letting Rev take over while I talked. "I'm ordering you a new bed."

"You don't need to do that." She was breathless, the sound of cars and wind muffling her voice. "I'll figure it out. It just sucks sleeping a mattress on the floor."

"You're gonna stay at my place until you get it fixed, all right? God, don't be so stubborn."

"I'm stubborn?"

"Where are you at?"

"I ran out to lunch with Elissa and dropped off Macy's meds. Hey, is Priest around? Can you tell him to answer his phone? I've been trying to call him for an hour."

"Here, just talk to him now." I passed the phone to Rev, who looked bewildered but took it and wandered to the back of the shop. I sat back down on the stool, pushing the pan of oil over to Riot to dump in the container.

"Fox, you up for getting another piercing?" Cas asked, flicking his tongue ring at me and gesturing to my eyebrow. "I like yours so I think I'm getting mine done."

"Not a piercing, but I'm down for another tat." Tate and I had been looking at designs because she liked my shoulder piece so much, she wanted one done. I'd drawn a sketch of flowers on her the other night to see how she liked it. I looked at Cas, and he frowned down at his tattooed hands.

"Not a whole lot of space left."

"Your whole back is open."

"Because I can't see it," he said. "I like to see them."

I rolled my eyes, taking the phone from Rev when he handed it back. Tate had hung up so I tucked it into my pocket. "What was that about?"

"Apartment stuff. She stopped by to drop off some things for Macy and there was a new car in the lot. No new residents, but Macy said it was probably the new building maintenance guy or something. He'd stopped by Macy's apartment to fix her window and asked when Tate would be back since she had an outstanding request on hers."

"He doesn't have keys?"

"Tate has extra locks on her door."

I nodded, silently making plans to be there when this guy came in to fix Tate's window. She hadn't had a problem with spiders since I'd caulked the edges, but I wanted to see what he would do.

The afternoon went slow. We finished Looper's bike, his girlfriend picked it up with his truck. Cas and Riot gave her hell, and she gave it right back, the swell of her stomach getting a little more pronounced. She was a tiny little thing so I expected her to be bigger, but Hannah mentioned that not every woman looks like she swallowed a beach ball. She worked on the maternity floor so she'd know.

We'd just gotten Mack's bike situated for a tune up when my phone rang again, and this time it was Isaac. "I'm working, what's going on?"

"My transfer went through. You're going to be seeing a lot more of my sorry ass now."

I grinned, holding the phone against my shoulder. "Great, just what I wanted. When does it take effect?"

"A few weeks. Gonna be looking for a place."

I glanced at Rev. "You could sublet Tate's apartment for a while. Rev wouldn't mind having a cop living next door to him."

"He'd probably be quieter at night than you two are," Rev said over my shoulder. "Those walls are so thin; I can hear every fucking thing. Including you breaking the bed this morning."

"It wasn't the fun way. I was messing with the cat and jumped on it, and the frame cracked."

Rev laughed, and over the phone Isaac snorted. "That's not exciting. Hannah is complaining because she barely ever sees or talks to Tate; she says you 'monopolize' all her time."

I raised my eyebrows, deciding to leave out that Tate said the opposite. Hannah would come see her, but she always ended up going home early with someone else. Isaac didn't need to know that, he had enough on his plate.

"Tate tell you she's probably gonna have another press conference to go to?"

I'd been about to take the filter off the bike but stopped,

pulling my hands back so I could hold the phone properly. "She hadn't mentioned anything yet."

"It hit the news junkets about an hour ago. They found another body, this one was about ten miles outside of Northshore, heading toward the Metro."

I jumped off the stool, phone vibrating as another call tried to come through. "They identify it? Was it someone on her list of people she's been doing articles on?"

"No, this one was newer. The missing persons report was just filed a few weeks ago, but she's young. Graduated last year from Beystone."

My fingers closed into a fist at my side. Beystone was even smaller than Northshore. Half the kids had to drive into town to attend school there, and the other half went to Triharbor. It probably had nothing to do with anything, but with the emails and comments still flooding Tate's inbox and all her articles, I was jumpy. On edge again, waiting for to the other shoe to drop.

My phone buzzed again and I pulled it away, surprised to see Tate's name on the screen. "Isaac, I gotta go. I'll call you later. Congrats on the transfer."

"Yeah, see ya."

I hung up and swapped the call, walking out of the garage so I could hear better over the chatter and creak of metal. "Hey, what's up?"

"Kellen, it's Pak. You um... you might want to come down here and get Tatum."

It was like a shock hit my body, freezing me on the spot. "Why? What happened?"

"Someone stopped in earlier, had a package for her. No one thought anything of it because sources send in stuff all the time, and she'd just ordered a new laptop. But it..."

He trailed off, the tone of his voice heavy. "It what, Pak?" I was already on my way back to the garage, grabbing my keys as the guys gave me funny looks.

"It was her yearbooks. Just two of them. But they... they were all stained with something red."

My stomach heaved, and I glanced at Rev, who's eyes were narrowed in concern before I ran to my bike, climbing on before I'd even hung up the phone. "Tell her I'm on my way down. Can she talk?"

"The police are here, she's talking to them."

"Just tell her I'm on my way." I hung up the phone, kicked the bike into gear, and pulled off without explaining to anyone where I was going. I'd text them later. I had to get to her first.

Chapter Forty
Tatum

I HADN'T CALLED THE POLICE. I'D BEEN TOO SHOCKED.

But Gina had. The box had been dropped off on my desk and I didn't think anything of it for a few hours. Elissa and I had gone to lunch, I'd introduced her to Macy when I dropped off meds, and when we came back, I'd decided to open it.

And all hell broke loose.

I'd picked one of the books up before noticing the blood and the dead pigeon stuffed inside the box. Immediately, discussions of "clean" sacrifices came to mind. Elissa had pulled me back and Gina immediately called the police, but it wasn't until they opened the books that the terror really set in.

There were faces scratched out of the class pictures. My face. Kara's face. Tiff's, and a few pages back, another girl I didn't recognize. I didn't connect the two until Pak told me he'd had the intern write up a quick article from a press release we'd gotten earlier that day. Another body had been found, identified almost immediately since the girl had only been missing for a few weeks. Valerie Havaner, age nineteen, from Beystone. Her face stared out at me, marred so much, I couldn't make out her features. There were references to punishment and sin and consequences scrawled throughout the other pages, but I didn't need to read them. I already knew what they said.

"And you say you've been receiving these emails and the comments for a month or so?" Officer Clayberg had a broad chest and belly, heavy arms and thick fingers that held a pen as he scrawled down information for the report. I nodded, taking the stack of papers Pak had printed off for me. All the emails, all the comments, all the usernames that had left them.

"I've turned all this information over to another officer at Lakeside PD. That's where the stalking originally took place."

"And you think it's connected?" The officer pressed, waving the papers. "All this is connected with the yearbooks?"

"And an earlier assault."

"Was the assault reported?"

I shook my head. "No, but I have medical records showing that I sustained trauma."

"But you never made an accusation."

"I tried to file a report at Lakeside, but they told me I didn't... have enough evidence to file a complaint or get a restraining order."

Clayburg's eyes flicked to mine, narrowing as he wrote this down. "And who's the officer at Lakeside that you gave this information too?"

"Now? Isaac Moore."

I gave the officer Isaac's badge number, and his office phone, then as soon as they took the box and all the evidence I hunched over my desk and dialed him.

"Isaac, you *need* to tell Phil and Suzanne," I said after I explained what happened. "I tried to call them, but the line was busy. They might not know. They never go up to that apartment. Someone had to break in and get this, and they could go after—"

"Tate, you don't think there's any way they could have something to do with it?"

"*What?*" My voice was high pitched, utterly aghast. "No. No, this isn't them, Isaac. They were just down here last week. They took Kellen, Hannah, and I out to dinner." I slapped my hand on my desk, fingers curling into a fist. "This is Davey. It has to be Davey, or someone else who knows what happened back then. I don't know."

"He's the first person I'll look at. I'm getting transferred down so I'll ask to see the case from this Clayberg guy, all right? Try to stay calm."

"You stay calm," I snapped. "You didn't just see your face scrawled out of a yearbook. A yearbook covered in blood. Blood, Isaac!"

"The symbolism isn't lost on me, Tate. I'm taking it as seriously as I can." He let out a sigh, and I heard some shuffling in the background. "Do you have a weapon you can carry on you? Any form of defense?"

"I have mace," I said, wondering if any of the guys in Kellen's club knew how to use a gun and would be willing to teach me. "I can see about something else."

"And I wouldn't travel alone if you can avoid it. Just in case."

"There's nothing else you can do?"

Isaac sighed, and there was a commotion behind me, a few people asking someone to stop, and I knew without looking that Kellen had arrived. "File a restraining order. You may not have it granted, but at least there will be a paper trail."

I pursed my lips, thinking if they didn't figure out something quick, there might be more than a paper trail to follow.

Chapter Forty-One
Tatum

"I GAVE MICHAELA YOUR NUMBER. SHE'S PULLING UP paperwork."

Kellen was curled around me, his hands on my back, nose in my hair, while Haku tried to find a place between us. There wasn't much room. Our legs were a tangle of limbs, his over mine, mine over his, denim rubbing against bare skin.

"Are you upset at your boss?" Kellen asked cautiously, and I sighed, rolling onto my back and looking at the ceiling. Right before Kellen took me home for the day, Gina pulled me aside and said I was off the crime beat and general assignment until this blew over. It was a safety precaution, not a punishment. I could still submit whatever independent articles I wanted to Pak or her or whatever publication would accept them, but until everything was resolved, my position was now associate editor.

It was good experience. Editing was something that would always be needed. I could focus on my remaining classes, do work on demand to keep up on what was going on at *The Journal*. But no matter what positive spin I put on it, the reassignment stung.

"I'm not mad at her, it just sucks. I'm pissed because it feels hopeless, like there's nothing I can do and this will go on forever."

"It won't." Kellen sat up, adjusting so his face loomed over mine. When I gave him a dubious look, he shook his head. "No, I'm serious. Everyone in the club keeps their noses clean, but that doesn't mean they aren't willing to get their hands dirty. You know anyone who comes for you comes for me, and if they come for me..."

"But I don't want that." I cupped his face, forcing him to look in my eyes. "The last thing I want is anyone in trouble because of me." He frowned, leaning in to kiss me, his lips pulling the tension out of my body like a thread. Kellen's hand slid under my shirt, his fingers slipping around my back to work on my bra.

"Sometimes I wonder if Davey was right, or if everything they said about me was true," I mumbled as he unclasped the flimsy thing, giving him access to cup me with no barrier between us. I pulled off my shirt and tossed the bra aside, closing my eyes as Kellen kissed the swell of my breasts. "Maybe I am damned and I'm just prolonging the inevitable."

"You don't believe that." He nuzzled against me, kneading and kissing my breasts, then moving lower to my stomach. "Tate, please tell me you don't believe that."

"I don't but it makes me wonder. Why else would this keep happening? Why would Davey be so... fixated on me after all this time?"

Kellen looked up and gave me a sad smile, pressing his lips to the bottom of my ribcage. "To be fair, I'm pretty fixated on you."

"But you and I were something, and we are something now. Davey and I, all things considered, we were short lived. It was less than a year. Eight months. I don't understand."

"I think it's less obsession and more..." His eyes drifted over my face, then he settled his head against my breasts. "Control. I remember something my mom said about Pastor Adler before she died. We'd stopped going to church, and he'd approached her instead of my dad, saying that she needed to be the strong one and bring us all back."

His hands tightened around my waist, and I ran my fingers through his hair, encouraging him to go on. Kellen didn't talk about his mom much; he'd only ever told me her name and that she gave him his taste for classic rock. Colleen Bishop had loved Kiss and Quiet Riot and late 70's early 80's metal. Kellen had loved all of that plus anything that had drums and heavy guitars since.

"Adler talked about membership dwindling. People were leaving and he was building a covenant or some shit. A direct contract with God to bless the town. Every time someone stopped coming to church, he'd deliver some fire and brimstone speech trying to scare them back." He let out a breath, turning his lips to kiss my stomach. "Obviously, it didn't work."

"He spoon fed that to Davey, too," I sighed. "I can't believe they let him preach for so long."

"They started looking for someone new over the summer, and Brandon whatever his name is took over most of the sermons then." Kellen slid his mouth lower, quickly undoing the button on my skirt and sliding it and my panties off my hips. "People love the drama, and everyone in Northshore likes to feel like they're a leg up on the world. Adler told them they were, and they ate it up. Everyone wants to belong to something."

"You're not like that."

Kellen smiled, kissing me once between my legs to make me gasp. "I belong to you," he murmured as he unfastened his pants, freed himself, and shoved his jeans down just enough that they wouldn't rub my thighs. He sank into me slowly, eyes on my face, his lips hovering over mine as I moaned and wrapped a leg around his hip. "And you belong to me." He pushed his hips until we were flush together, staying still for a moment before he pulled back, and then sank in again. "There. That's better, right?"

"We were having a nice conversation and you have to start shit." I pulled him close, arching into his thrusts, kicking his pants off his legs so I could feel his bare skin against mine. "Always distracting me."

"You're a distraction," he murmured, kissing my neck. "A sweet, beautiful, sexy as hell distraction."

He kissed me, tongue licking into my mouth as I gasped and he pumped steady and slow into me, reminding me there were so many other things I could feel than fear. Lust. Pleasure. Satisfaction.

Love.

THE NEW INTERN WENT WITH ELISSA AND PAK TO THE press conference while I stayed behind at home, watching it on TV. Valerie Havaner had been found buried in a shallow grave in a patch of forest off the highway. Just like Kara. There were other things that linked this case to Kara's as well, but the news glossed over most of them, save for the cause of death. Strangulation. Most likely after she'd been held captive for a few hours.

The similarities were enough for the FBI to be called in and they began searching similar areas. Isaac's new transfer to the Metro meant he was around more as well, and he fed me information that I passed onto Elissa since she was covering my beat, even though she frowned at me every time I mentioned it.

"Do you think it's smart for you to be paying such close attention?"

"I can't help but pay close attention," I said, opening my new email address, one that had not been shared with the public. "They're still monitoring my old email and the threats are still coming in, but since it's nothing specific and I'm walking around just fine, there's not a rush." I sounded bitter, but I understood it. Right now, they had bigger things to handle.

Elissa leaned over my desk, lowering her voice. "I know Gina pulled you off everything, but she didn't want to. It's really for your safety. And since you're going to be there anyway and you did the first article about it, and Rush likes you...I'm going to let you write the article on the Halloween event." She gave me a playful scowl.

"Are you coming?"

"Oh, I'm coming. I want to give Cas hell for his costume. But you can write it up. You're closer to the whole thing anyway."

I tilted my head, drumming my pen on the tablet I was using. "What's the deal with you and him? He's a shameless flirt."

"Which is fine by me. It's nothing serious, never will be. That guy is a bachelor for life, and I'm not looking to settle down now yet. But someday, I will be." She shrugged. "It's fun. That's it. Not like you and Kellen who are living in domestic bliss and going to be popping out babies soon."

I laugh scoffed, shaking my head at her. "Yeah, not happening. At least not anytime soon."

Chapter Forty-Two

Tatum

HALLOWEEN CAME A FEW DAYS LATER, AND I HAD TO laugh because even though I'd been to the bar more than a few times since Kellen and I officially started dating, I'd never seen so many vans in the parking lot. Let alone couples with strollers and kids running around. It was almost comical when you looked at the parents, the children in costumes, and a bunch of guys in denim cuts wandering between them.

A few of the guys had dressed up. Rush and Betsy had on costumes that matched their kids'—red and black superhero uniforms and masks. Cas was wearing a blue suit covered in fur and pink dots, a hoodie over his head with gray horns. Looper and Shayla had dressed up as a priest and a nun, which had several people cackling. I'd found a poodle skirt at the costume shop with Hannah, and convinced Kellen to dress in jeans, a white T-shirt, and a leather jacket. He looked similar to Riot, who had dressed up with his statuesque girlfriend as Zuko and Sandy.

"It's from *Monsters, Inc*," Michaela explained to me when I asked about Cas' costume. "And Rush and his kids are *The Incredibles*. You've never seen either of those movies?"

I grimaced, but Kellen slung his arm around me, pulling me against his side. "Weird restrictive foster parents. Cultish. Remember?"

Michaela pursed her lips. "Speaking of, I've been keeping track of your case, got in contact with Officer Clayberg and Fox's friend Isaac." She gestured across the parking lot, to where Isaac was talking with a group that included Priest, Hannah, Looper and Shayla. "They're trying to track the addresses sending the emails. If we can link it, I'll file the restraining order. Until then, you don't have much unfortunately."

"Isaac said there weren't any prints on the yearbooks," I replied, rolling my eyes as I folded my arms around myself. "It's odd that he'd be so careful now when he attacked me right out in the open in town."

"Crime of opportunity versus one he had to plan," Michaela said, twisting her lips before she squealed when Riot came over, picking her up off the ground and carrying her off toward the bar. Kellen shook his head, planting a kiss on my temple.

"This got a lot more attention than I thought it would."

I smiled. There weren't just people here for candy and costumes. A few had come into the bar for food, and some had come to drop off donations for shelters Betsy had me mention in the article. There were people with blankets and old clothes, a few vans had come with boxes of pots and pans, another white Cadillac had crates of books. Cas had to run interference with a few of his employees, taking some of them inside so he could get them a form they'd need for taxes.

"Probably helps that we did it before Beggar's Night, give the kids a chance to wear the damn things more than once," Kellen said, and I laughed quietly to myself. "What? I looked at the prices when I grabbed all those decorations and they're expensive."

I clicked my tongue. "Just another reason to put off having kids."

He leaned back on his bike, bumping the two buckets of candy I'd hung on the handlebars. Rush joined the group where Isaac was standing, and I watched his kids run buy us. His older girl, Melody, took a few pieces then raced on, and Lucy stopped to hug my leg for a bit before she got brave and chased after her sister. The baby, Oliver, toddled after them, his dark black hair styled into a tall spike on his head. I looked over to see Kellen smiling softly, his eyes fixed on the baby as he passed.

"Oliver was born right before they made me a prospect," he said. "I think, before him, I'd held a baby all of twice in my life. Rush told me within the first week I'd better get used to babies, even if I never planned on having any. Then he handed me the kid, told me he'd be right back, and left for an hour."

"That's one way to break you in," I laughed. "How'd you do? Not too bad, considering he's still walking around."

He grinned at me. "Figured out how to change a diaper on my own. Kid puked on my shoulder after I fed him, but he didn't cry, so I must have been doing something right."

"Lucy likes you, too." I elbowed him in the ribs and gave him a playful pout. "Gotta say, sometimes when she hugs you and wants nothing to do with me, I get a little jealous."

"You should be. Melody says Lucy and I are gonna get married."

I burst out laughing. "Oh, well then. Should I pack up my things now? Not that I have much at your place..."

"You should have more at my place."

My chest tightened, and I had to drop my eyes from Kellen's gaze. It wasn't the first time he'd said it, and the more time passed, the better the idea sounded. But I held back, thinking about the bloody yearbooks and the dead pigeon. The emails still trickling into my mailbox.

"I don't... Kellen, what if I bring all this to you? You have a whole house, and everything in your garage. And the shop." I tugged at the skirt, adjusting all the petticoats underneath so they laid straight. "All I can think about is him escalating. Doing something worse. Like setting fire to the building or just showing up and attacking whoever was there. And it would be all—"

"It wouldn't be your fault, Tate."

"I don't think you realize how bad I'd feel if something happened to someone else because of me."

"It wouldn't be because of you. It would be because Davey is a fucking psychopath and that has nothing to do with you. Clearly it doesn't. He kept escalating after you left. Two bodies, Tate, and there are probably more."

"We don't know he did that," I interrupted, stomach twisting at the idea. "It seems connected, but it could be random or... just a coincidence. I have to think that because if it was him and... and now he's coming after me..."

"He's not going to get to you."

His voice was so hard I looked at his face, my breath hitching when he circled his arm around me and pulled me into his chest, bending so he could bury his face in my hair. "Nothing is going to get to you, Tate. I swear it."

I wanted to tell him not to make promises he couldn't keep, but instead I sighed, wrapping my arms around his waist and squeezing. "Bet you didn't think when you sent me all those messages that when we got back together, it—"

"I didn't think about anything but getting you back when I sent those messages, and I haven't thought about anything other than having you since." He kissed the crown of my head. "You're going to have to get used to it, Tate. You're stuck with me. I think even if you wanted to break up, I'd still have to hang around you. Screen every new guy you dated, make sure they're up to par."

I gave him a dubious look. "Somehow I don't believe you'd be so warmhearted toward them."

"No. I'd probably end up getting arrested again because I can't even stand it when Cas flirts with you."

"I already told you. He's not my type."

"Yeah?" His hands drifted down over my hips, cupping my ass and ruining the fluff of the skirt. "What is your type?"

"Guys who don't ever wear slacks unless it's some sort of event. Only jeans. And always have to have the TV or the radio on in the background. Guys who nickname me after a food I hate and have shaggy hair like my cat. You know it gets in my face sometimes at night?"

"Like you have room to talk. One day I'm gonna wake up with your hair strangling me."

I grinned and leaned up to kiss him again, only pulling back when we heard a scuffle then a cry. I looked down to see Oliver at our feet, pushing himself back up on chubby legs and reaching out for whoever would pick him up. I bent down, but Kellen beat me too it, hoisting him into his arms and wiping off his face. He spoke softly, hugging the toddler against his shoulder before walking off to find Betsy.

I might have questions about my own ability to mother someone, but I had zero doubts Kellen would be a good father.

Chapter Forty-Three
Kellen

TATE WAS IN THE SHOWER, BUT I WAS STILL IN BED, avoiding the sunlight by hiding my face in a pillow, only looking up when she came into the room wearing nothing but black panties, the edges trimmed in lace.

"I hope you're not planning on going too far in those."

She glared at me over her shoulder, then scowled at the bag on the floor. "You're staying at my place next time. I need to do laundry. You're a bad influence. These are my only clean underwear."

"So, I should take them off before I dirty you up?"

Another scowl, this one accompanied by pink cheeks. "Will you stay over tonight so I can do laundry?"

"You can do laundry here."

"My cat misses me."

"I can take care of your pussy."

"Kellen!"

"I'm serious," I said, sitting up to take hold of her hips when she came near the bed. "I'll get a cat tree. We'll put his litterbox near the basement. I can even put in one of those little cat doors."

"Sometimes I think you like him better than me."

"Not possible. This," I kissed her pubic bone, nipping at the panties. "This is my favorite pussy. And you don't have claws. Not sure how I feel about having gouges down my back. Riot is into that, not me."

"No, you're just into having me ride things."

"What can I say?" I murmured, pulling her on top of me as I laid back, smiling when she straddled my hips. "You look good doing it."

She shook her head, surprising me when I went to sit up and she pushed me back. Her hands were timid on my shoulders, and it wasn't until she started to climb higher on my body that I realized why. When she stopped above my chest, I picked her up, settling her over my mouth and tucking my arms around her thighs before she could protest.

"These are in the way."

"They're protecting me," she whispered. "They're keeping you from dirtying me up."

"Baby," I murmured, lifting my head and licking her over the fabric. "You put that pretty pussy anywhere near my face and I'm going to kiss it. A little bit of fabric isn't going to stop me, especially not when I can just," I slid my hand to her inner thigh, yanking the fabric aside. "Do that."

"You might have to," she admitted, a nervous laugh slipping past her lips. "I seriously don't know if I can do this."

I pulled her closer, kissing the inside of her thigh as she tried to settle in, hovering over me, her skin clean smelling and still warm from the shower. Her hands balanced on the mattress as she avoided sitting, trying to figure out a way to do position herself without hurting me. Like she could hurt me. I'd drown in her if she'd let me. My thumb stayed hooked in her panties, her pussy centimeters away from my mouth. Tate moved to scoot back, but I grabbed her thighs, keeping hold of the fabric as I pulled her to my mouth.

"Then let me do it for you."

Her gasp was like a starting gun, and when she arched, I braced my arms around her, keeping her settled onto my open mouth while I licked everywhere my tongue could reach. Her inner thighs, her soft lips, her still hooded clit. I heard her moan softly, then felt her arch, and one of her hands slid into my hair and she closed her fingers into a fist.

"That's it, baby," I praised, a groan slipping out of me when she tugged my hair and pushed her clit into my mouth. "Show me what you like."

"Am I hurting you—"

"You couldn't hurt me if you fucking tried."

She settled onto me more, and I let go of her thighs when she started to move. Soft, sweet little rocks against my tongue as I cupped her breasts, my cock throbbing for attention, leaking against the edge of my boxers. She covered my hand with hers against her tit, the other still buried in my hair. I sucked on her clit and she pulled—fucking pulled—my face against her for a second, then let go, shocked by her own actions. I shook my head, humming in approval, not wanting to talk because my mouth was too busy.

"Fuck." The word was a shaky sigh, and I could feel her quivering, so close to orgasm. I wanted her to come like this, to feel her break apart and writhe like she did, but she was holding back. I could tell by the way her body moved, the way her breaths caught. She let out another moan and I sucked her clit one last time then lifted her back, kissing her as she let out a relieved sigh.

"You did good, baby," I moaned, shoving my boxers down so I could sink inside her. "You always fuck me so sweet."

She laughed, then moaned as I started to thrust, clinging to me like I was her lifeline. "That wasn't sweet."

"Bullshit. Everything you do is sweet, including the way you take my cock."

She gripped my biceps, nails biting into my skin as I pumped deep, giving her what she needed, what she craved as she slid her thighs back, moaning as she rocked with me. I kissed her lips, drinking in the pretty noises she made, the soft whimpers and moans and cries when she came around me, her cunt squeezing me so tight.

"Fuck, I can't get enough of you. I'll never get enough. You're all fucking mine."

She grinned, face flushed as her orgasm fade, her hips arching up to meet mine as I sought my own. "You gonna get me a bike now?"

I laughed, then my body tightened as I came and emptied myself inside her, thinking this was the only way I wanted to start the day.

An hour later, Tate jumped in the shower with me to rinse off while I did a full wash. "So, you're coming to my apartment, right? Please."

"Yes. Might as well try out my spare bed for a night."

"Spare bed?"

"Cause it's gonna go in my spare room when you move in."

"I thought that was my office."

"It can be both."

She grinned and shook her head. "I'll call you when I'm headed home after class."

The shower curtain closed again, and I scrubbed my hair, already close to running late for my own job.

"You really gonna get her a bike?" Rev asked when I mentioned it to him, wanting to get his thoughts on the whole thing. "I'm not against it. She rides well with you, and if she's still afraid of her car, then it's an option."

"She's getting better," I said. "We've taken my truck a few times for things, and she rode to lunch with Hannah the other day."

"Michaela said she rode well with her after they went to

court the other day, too," Riot added. I pursed my lips, remembering that Tate had to show up in court the other day for a preliminary hearing on the restraining order. They granted her sixty days, which was something, but it hadn't stopped the communications so far.

Tate texted me after noon to tell me she wasn't heading home after class, she was going with Elissa to cover a school board meeting or something.

Me: *I'll order take out. Thai again?*

Tatertot: *Yes. And get Priest to come over so we can watch more* Demon Slayer. *I'm into it now. I'm gonna have to get to the bookstore and see if they have the whole collection.*

I smiled, remembering the other night when she'd been in the spare room, the "office," reading through Berserk for the first time. She'd mentioned bringing her collection over to get it out of storage and I'd offered to get her another bookshelf so we could fit them all. Any little piece of her merging her life with mine, I'd take.

I'd started to look at take-out menu's when Rev's phone rang. He pressed the phone to his ear, walking to the other side of the shop to talk when Cas pulled up with Riot. "Fine, taking you up on the tattoo offer. When do you want to go?"

"When can we get in? Tate wants to get her shoulder done."

Cas perked up as he leaned forward on his bike. "What's she getting?"

"Some sort of floral design." I pulled out my phone to show him the few drawings I'd done on her as an example, but Rev came stalking over, tapping me on the shoulder, his phone still pressed to his ear.

"No, she's not home," Rev said from beside the tool bench, his voice low and calm. "I know she's usually back by now, but she got called into an assignment or something. Why, Macy, what's—"

He went stiff, shoulders squaring as he stood tall beside me, then stalked to the other end of the shop to grab his keys. Cas and Riot followed his path, their faces curious, especially when Rev pulled the phone away, made a confused noise, then put it back to his ear.

"Macy, call the police. Now. No one gave the maintenance guy access to her apartment." It was a command, and Rev wasn't the kind to issue them unless he was in bed or shit was going down. "I'll be there in ten. Do not leave your apartment. You understand me?"

I stood up, my body tense as I tried to piece together what he was saying. The maintenance guy had an order to work on Tate's apartment, but she'd never been home to let him in, and oddly, he'd never called to schedule a time.

Rev hung up, scowling at his phone. "Stubborn old woman. She's gonna get herself killed."

"What's going on?" I demanded

"Someone's in Tate's apartment. She says there's been banging and shouting—"

"What?"

"Kell, she's not there. You know she's not there," Rev snapped as he walked past me to his bike, and I immediately went to get the keys to close up shop. "I'm going to head over. Call Isaac or someone cause the other cops are gonna take forever."

"Yeah, I know," I said, already on my phone dialing as I pulled down the garage door and hopped on my bike.

Rev pulled out, Cas and Riot following without saying a word while I kicked my bike to a start and waiting for Isaac to pick up.

"What's up? I was just about to call you and see—"

"Someone broke into Tate's apartment."

Isaac was silent. "What?"

"Her neighbor called. Not Rev, the old woman. There's been

a maintenance guy wanting access to her apartment, but he never scheduled a time."

"Doesn't he have keys?"

"Tate has extra locks, and they have to let her know they're coming anyway." I peeled out of the driveway. "Just get there, Isaac," I snapped before shouting the address and hanging up, just a few minutes behind the guys.

The parking lot was empty save for Tate's car and a white Cadillac, one Cas paused to look at before we went inside. "Is that the maintenance guys' car?" he asked Rev.

"How the fuck should I know? I've never met the guy. He doesn't do shit around here." He stalked down the hall, shouting for the old woman, then pausing when he got to Tate's apartment. Where he froze.

Because the door was gone.

"Cas, that car? What about it?" I asked. "Have you seen it?"

"Yeah, last week," he said. "I unloaded eight crates of books from the back of it. Weird books, too. Apocalyptic shit and—"

I shoved him aside, running out to the lot just to see the car starting up and pulling out of the driveway. There was no way I'd catch him, even on the bike. I yanked my phone out, trying to snap a picture, zooming in on the license plate. "Goddammit," I swore, looking at the blurry photo just as Tate pulled up on her bike.

"What are you doing here?"

"Someone broke into your apartment," I said. "The cop—"

"*What?!*" She didn't wait for an explanation, bolting past me and down the hall while I followed, watching Riot throw out an arm when she reached the doorway. Her hand clapped over her mouth, and when I looked into the room I saw why.

The dining room table was broken, legs bent, chairs thrown across the room. A coat rack in the corner had been thrown over, the mirror she had on the wall shattered on the floor. I looked toward her bedroom, finding feathers and ripped up sheets. The new mattress on her new bed had been shoved off the frame, violent slashes in the box spring underneath. Red spots dotted the fabric, the sheets, the comforter. Matching the red streaks on the floor and the red footprints scattered throughout the apartment. Tatum made a panicked, choked noise while I looked at Rev, letting him speak aloud what I already knew.

"Blood."

"*Haku*," Tatum moaned, pushing past Rev even as we tried to stop her. "Oh, God. Kitty. Kitty, kitty, kitty…"

She was sobbing, her hands shaking as she looked desperately around for the cat. Rev stayed by the door with Riot while Cas came inside, looking just as alarmed as he moved past me and headed toward the bathroom.

"He's under the bed," Riot said, and I watched Tate dive down onto her stomach, a sobbing laugh coming out of her.

"Oh, God, baby. Here, kitty. Haku come here."

I bent down beside her, watching the cat's shining eyes as he crawled forward slowly, pausing to bat at something that skittered across the floor. I froze, then I yanked Tate back as soon as she had the cat in her arms.

"Get his carrier and get—"

"What the fuck?!"

Cas ran, flying through the kitchen, almost knocking Tate over in his rush to get away. She glared at him, and then before I could warn her, she shrieked and followed close on his heels into the hall. She hid behind Rev while Riot came inside, calmly staring at the skittering thing as it moved across the carpet, crawling through the blood.

"Is that a tarantula?" Riot asked, his nose scrunched in disgust. I didn't reply, just looked at Tate cowering behind Rev, tears streaming down her face as she hugged the cat. His paw was bent funny, and he wasn't making a sound. I was so used to his meows and chirps and purrs that it unnerved me almost more than the damage in the apartment.

"The carrier is in the closet, Riot, can you grab it?" I asked, reaching down and grabbing the carton of food Tate kept on a standby the cat's bowl. Another spider skittered out from under her bed, and she shrieked again, making the cat finally meow. Or growl. I hadn't realized cats could growl.

"Kitty, it's okay. I'm here." Her voice cracked, and when I looked up I could see that she was close to losing it, tears rolling down her cheeks, her lips trembling as she smoothed a hand over the cat's back. "Oh, God, what *happened* to you…"

"Cops are here," Cas announced, and I heard the telltale sound of walkie-talkies echo down the hall. Isaac appeared in the doorway, looking at Tate first then to me, his eyes widening as he took in the scene. He scanned the floor, the messy bedroom, the broken table, then his eyes fell on the wall where blood was smeared, a threat etched into the stain.

God will not be mocked. Justice will be brought to those who betray his word.

"Jesus Christ," Isaac said, but I shook my head.

"Pretty sure he's not behind this."

Chapter Forty-Four
Tatum

HAKU SAT CURLED ON MY LAP, THE BLANKET OVER MY shoulders brushing his fur. A splint covered in heavy tape cradled his paw. The vet told me he'd probably broken it jumping off something, trying to run away. It was unlikely anyone laid hands on him considering the way the break looked, but that didn't make me any more comforted.

"Your apartment is an active crime scene. You'll have to stay somewhere else for a while."

Isaac said this to me like he didn't already know I'd be staying at Kellen's. I'd pulled on my orange hat, and the old sweater I had in high school that Kellen kept, trying to find some sense of normal in all this, clinging to any feeling of safety I could find. Isaac sat on a coffee table, a pad in his hand as he wrote down information. So far, there hadn't been any fingerprints, but they were still dusting. Kellen had been allowed to come back after the initial walk through to grab clothes and other things for me. That's where he was now. Priest was in the kitchen along with Cas. Kellen hadn't asked them to stay and neither had I, but I could tell they weren't leaving.

"Tate," Isaac said, taking a deep breath and blowing it out.

"I'm doing everything I can. I want you to know that. I'm looking into this white Cadillac, and I've got your landlords number to call and ask about the maintenance guy. This isn't being ignored. It's bigger now, especially if there's anything they can connect to the two bodies."

I winced, swallowing bile and nodding at him.

"You shouldn't go anywhere alone."

"I haven't been."

"And you've got mace? Do you have any other weapons?"

"It takes too long to get a personal carry license, and I don't know how to shoot a gun anyway." I wiped my face, then smoothed my hand along Haku's fur. "I'm not doing it. I'm sure if I did, it would probably get used against me somehow."

Isaac frowned. "Tate—"

"What?" I snapped. "I'm doing all the right things and this is *still* happening. I'm so sick of it."

He sighed, running a hand over his short hair. "I know you are. I can't blame you. If there was something more I could do, I would."

He stood up from the table, a soft laugh slipping out of him that made me look up. "Kellen hates cats."

"He doesn't hate them," I said. "He hates *mean* cats. No one like mean cats. No one likes mean dogs. Haku isn't mean."

"You know him better than I do."

"The cat?"

"No, Kellen."

I bit my lip. "No, I—"

"I didn't mean that as a bad thing, Tate. You do know him better than I do. You know him *differently* than I do. I've known him almost his whole life, and even with all this going on, I've never seen him so happy." He flipped the pad shut, giving me a soft smile then reaching down and ruffling—*ruffling*—my hair. Like I was Hannah. "This will get taken care of, Tate. I promise.

Some way or another it will. Then you guys can get married and have all kinds of babies—"

"Oh my God." I threw up my hands, soothing Haku when he growled softly and gingerly padded off my lap to curl up on a pillow. "Will you all *stop* with the baby nonsense? I don't even know if I want kids."

"Well you and I are the same on that," Isaac said, flashing another grin in my direction. "I'll check in with you tomorrow, let you know if anything comes up."

I waved goodbye, and when he was gone I flopped down on the couch, only looking up when Cas came over and sat on the table. He held out a small glass full of dark liquid, and I took it without even asking what it was.

"Atta girl," he said, laughing when I winced at the rich, burning taste of the alcohol. "Want another?"

I grimaced, looking up at Priest who was pouring another glass, raising his eyebrows as he came and handed it to me before picking up Haku and settling the cat on his lap. "You're not your parents, Tate. I think a few drinks after everything you've been through is allowed."

He tipped his glass at me, and I sighed, staring down at the glass. "There's one favor I need to ask before we do this."

"What's that?" Priest asked, and I turned, letting out a long sigh.

"Looper? That's his name right. The techie one."

"Yeah, what about him?" Cas asked, frowning when I offered my phone.

"He mentioned looking at my social media accounts to trace things, or my computer, but I got to thinking." I swallowed, offering my phone again. "Do you think there's a way Looper could track this?"

"Like now?" Priest asked, but I shook my head, and his eyes narrowed as he read my thoughts and let out a resigned sigh.

"I mean... could he track it if something were to happen to me, and I had it with me."

Priest sighed, but Cas took the phone, frowning as he stared at it for a bit then pulled out his own. "Let's call him and find out."

Chapter Forty-Five
Tatum

KELLEN DIDN'T JOIN ME IN DRINKING WHEN HE GOT home, choosing instead to have Priest help him install a security system around all the doors. Looper came over briefly, assisting them in getting the system set up, then he put a tracker on my phone while Cas and I drank shot after shot between unhelpful comments and horrible jokes. I was dizzy and wobbly when Kellen tucked me in, and when I begged for my favorite form of distraction, he laughed and kissed me before shutting off the light, holding me until I fell asleep.

When morning came, I remembered vividly why I didn't drink. Addiction or not, the morning after a night of nothing but whiskey and water was awful.

Kellen wasn't beside me. In his place, Haku had made himself a nice little spot and was purring softly. I frowned when I noticed there were already little claw marks in the sheet, then ran to the bathroom to gargle away the taste in my mouth and rinse off the lingering terror.

I couldn't go home.

I wasn't safe in my home.

Kellen had plugged my phone into the charger, and when I looked at it I saw I'd been looped into a group chat with several of the guys in the club. Cas was volunteering to grab me from class or work. Priest was offering to hang out with me on the days he had off and Kellen had to work. Riot had already talked to Michaela and she was getting all the records together, adding them to my case file for the restraining order. It was all so much effort I flipped the phone over and left it on the counter, at least until it buzzed again. When I picked it up, Hannah's name appeared on the screen, and I swiped the answer button.

"Hi."

"Jesus, Tate, are you okay?" she asked, her voice filled with worry. "Isaac told me about what happened. Kellen said you were doing okay, but I wanted to check. Are you? I'd rather hear it from you than him."

"He's not a liar," I said. "I am okay."

She let out a sigh. "I'm so sorry. I feel like all of this... is it my fault? If I hadn't recognized you—"

"No, Han. No, God. It's not your fault." I leaned against the counter, scrubbing a hand over my face. "No, honestly? Piecing things together, I bet what started it was that stupid article I wrote about the church conference that happened here back in August. I saw guys from Twin Valley there and didn't think anything of it."

"And you think that tipped Davey off?"

"If it didn't tip him off, maybe it tipped someone in the church off and it spread from there. Maybe I gave them a reason to go looking and if I would have leaned away from that—"

"They could have gone looking anyway, Tate. We'll never know. But you don't blame me?"

"No, I don't blame you, Han. Not... don't ever think that, please."

"Okay," she sounded relieved, and it put a stitch in my chest.

"Isaac was headed back to Lakeside today for a few things. He's still talking to the officers there about the bodies and all that. I haven't been home since my parents left and now I'm glad. Place creeps me out."

"You and me both," I murmured.

"He said he'd call you if there were updates or any new info right?"

"He did, and I hope he does. I just." I sighed, my shoulders sagging as I leaned harder into the counter. "I want this all to be over with, Han. I just want to move on with my life."

"Is there anything you need?" she asked. "Clothes or anything? Kellen has fucking your brains out covered, right?"

"God, Han."

"What? It helps. That's what kept me sane through my tests last year, but then the guy turned out to be a complete jackass, so fuck him."

"Or, maybe not since he was a jackass."

"True. *Don't* fuck him. But really, do you need anything?"

"If I do, I'll call. I swear."

We hung up, I downed a glass of water, then walked out to Kellen's garage, finding it much cleaner than I expected. There were tools on the wall, and my car was parked on one side of the space, the other filled with chests of more tools and various shelves. Kellen stood toward the front near a counter, his hands messy with oil, some part he was working on in front of him. He had on baggy pajama pants that sat low on his hips, but no shirt covered his chest. I walked into the space barefoot, tiptoeing as I tucked myself into his side and kissed his shoulder, reaching up to touch is eyebrow and the barbell through it.

"Does it still hurt?"

He shook his head and grabbed a towel, wiping his hands. "Nah, not much hits it up there." He turned and kissed my forehead, looking over my face. "You eat anything?"

I grimaced. "Not sure if I feel up to it yet actually." He frowned, but I kissed his shoulder again and looked around the space. "This looks just like your shop from what I've seen." I gestured to the part on the counter. "Is this work or hobby?"

"Both. I work on the weekends sometimes if we get backed up. Priest gives me shit about it, but I used to get bored." He finished wiping his hands, then moved and braced his hands around my waist on the counter. "Less so now."

"No, now you just get to stumble upon break-ins and take in strays."

"Gotta shake things up sometimes."

"I think I could use a little less shakiness."

Kellen hummed into my hair, looping his arms around my waist. "What's going on in that pretty head, baby?"

"My cat is probably clawing your sheets up."

He snorted. "And?"

"And you didn't ask for that."

"Technically, I did." His hands slipped under my shirt, palms warm against my ribs, his thumbs stroking the sides of my breasts. "I've been asking you to move in for weeks. I've been looking at cat trees." He ducked his head into my neck, exhaling a deep sigh when I circled my arms around his shoulders. "I pushed my way back into your life with a battering ram. Scaled all those walls you put up. I think a cat clawing my sheets is a small price to pay."

His lips pressed soft kisses over my cheek, behind my ear and down my neck when I tipped my head back. "I feel like all I've given you back is trouble."

"I like trouble."

I laughed softly, the sound cut off when he moved his lips back to mine, palms splaying out over my ribs. I felt his thumb on my nipple, rubbing soft circles that made me shiver, a dull ache building between my hips. Kellen broke the kiss, his lips hovering close to mine.

"I don't know what's going on in your head, but I want you to stop thinking you've fucked up my life. Or that you're gonna fuck up my life, or anyone else's. I asked for it. They asked for it. And if anything, it's the other way around."

"That's what Hannah just asked me when she called. She wondered if I blamed her for all this since she recognized me, and everything fell apart."

"Do you blame her?"

"Of course not."

"Then why are you blaming yourself?"

I opened my mouth to press my case, but Kellen's lips sealed over mine again, stealing the words and replacing them with his tongue. I moaned, trying to climb up his body as he slid his hand to cup my breast.

"How's this gonna work?" I asked, half teasing when he tugged my shirt off and we stared at the black smudges on my skin. "Your hands are filthy. I'm not gonna let you touch me down there with those fingers."

"S'all right." His hands went to my shorts. "You don't have a problem rubbing yourself off."

I shoved him and he grinned, kissing down my neck as he sank to his knees, hooking his fingers into my shorts and panties. He tugged at them, but I grabbed his hands, looking around with wide eyes.

"Kellen, we're in your garage."

"Yeah?"

"The house is like... five feet away. It's dirty in here."

"So is all that guilt you're lugging around."

He shoved my hands away, his mouth hot and wet as he pressed a kiss below my belly button and tugged the shorts down my thighs. "Feels like a good place to fuck that bullshit out of you."

I moved to push his shoulders again, finding the guilt comforting and far less dirty than the dusty floor he was kneeling on, but he ducked his head, kissing my inner thigh and pulling one leg over his shoulder. I gripped the counter as he grabbed my hips, holding them steady as he pushed his head between my legs, his greedy lips and tongue kissing and licking while I tried not to slip and fall on his face.

"God, baby." Kellen opened his mouth, murmuring wordlessly, his fingers tightening on my hips as he licked and sucked and did whatever he always did to make my legs shaky. My fingers ached from gripping the counter, and he looked up at me when I tried to push myself up, forcefully tugging me back down.

"I meant what I said, Tate. I'll teach you to ride."

I blinked, wondering how the hell he expected me to talk when I was so. "Yeah?"

"Yeah." His eyes turned mischievous, and he gave my aching pussy one last lick before standing, cupping the back of my thighs to hike me up on his hips. "Ride my face again whenever I want and I'll teach you. I'll get you any bike you want."

"I can't do that in here."

"You're gonna ride something in here, that's for fucking sure."

Kellen hefted me up onto the counter, cupping my ass to pull my hips to his, using the counter to position me. I glanced down at it and laughed. "Did you plan it like this? Did you build this thing with this in mind?"

He ignored me, dipping his head for another kiss, still gripping my ass with one hand as he reached down to shove the front of his pants down. "Take it out."

There was no hesitation in his eyes, and his voice was dark and so assured I'd follow his order. I would, and that wiped away the gnawing guilt in my chest, replacing it with something warm and safe. Because that's what Kellen was. Warm and safe, and so desperate to have me no matter where we were or what was going on. For as much as he said he was mine, I was just as much his.

My eyes darted down to his toned stomach, and I licked my lips at the spattering of hair that grew thicker and darker as his boxers were pushed aside, the base of his cock coming into view. He looked at me and I bit my lip, giving him a teasing smile. "It's not mine."

His eyes flashed and I gasped, shivering when he grabbed my hand and shoved it inside his pants. "You said my hands were filthy and you're right. I'm not gonna touch your cunt with them, or touch anything that's going inside your cunt with them." He stared pointedly at me and brought his hand back up to cup my ass. "Now, get my cock out and put it inside you."

I smiled at the order, the second one he'd given in such a short span of time, and tugged him free of the fabric keeping him caged. Kellen watched as I gripped his length, giving it a few unnecessary strokes before shifting, tugging him toward me. As soon as I positioned him, he took over, sinking deep in one stroke then immediately pulling back to thrust in again. That was all the warmup I was going to get.

We stared at each other, his eyes watching my every reaction as I clutched the counter, squeezing his hips with my thighs while he fucked into me. His eyes were dark, flicking down to where our bodies merged every few seconds. He pushed in deep on every stroke, sinking until our bodies were flush together before pulling back. It was an easy glide in and out of me, even with the fast, bruising pace he'd set. The knot in my belly tightened, making me ache to have him closer, crave the feeling of his skin under my hands. I managed to get one arm around his neck, my fingers sliding into his hair, drawing out a groan as he lifted his lips to mine.

"The fuck it's not yours," he growled, fingers digging into my hips while mine tightened in his hair. He moaned when I tugged softly, his eyes fluttering as he somehow managed to fuck me harder than he already was. "I'm yours, and you're mine." My eyes closed when he said it, a phrase I feared but now I couldn't live without it. His breath fanned across my lips as he set his forehead to mine, rising up on the balls of his feet to change the angle of his pumps, his cock hitting a spot deep inside me that made my head fall back on a gasp. He breathed against my neck, pecking little kisses against my skin, growling as he pushed in so deep it ached.

"Better or worse, Tate. No matter how sick either of us get or whatever shit comes our way. I'm gonna keep you, and love you, and fuck you until you forget your goddamn name and I have to give you mine."

He nudged my lips to his and kissed me so hard it upset my balance. The arm bracing my body slipped off the counter, and I yelped into the kiss before grabbing on to him. Kellen caught me, never slipping out as he hiked me up, taking my full weight before he stumbled back and landed on the roof of my unrepairable car. I shoved his shoulders down, straddling his hips and doing exactly what he told me I was gonna do earlier.

"God, baby, fuck me."

Kellen's eyes squeezed shut, his head falling back against the hood as I used his shoulders for leverage, thrusting my hips forward and back, half crazed with need. For the feeling of him inside me, for his hands on my body, for the way he made everything disappear for just a little while.

I rolled my hips, pushing his cock into that spot deep inside my cunt, grinding my clit against him when he pushed up. Meaningless words and prayers and his name flew through my head, but I couldn't speak. I could only make needy, whimpering moans that made Kellen sit up to hold me, his face buried against my neck.

"Yes, Tate. Fucking use me. Make yourself come, that's it."

I felt him smile as the orgasm started, my pussy clenching so tight that it almost hurt to keep going. The pleasure was so intense I couldn't see straight, and I closed my eyes as Kellen gripped my hips, taking over the pace, keeping me steady as I lost control. He followed me a moment later, pushing me down hard and encouraging to rock as he groaned, his cock throbbing inside me.

Kellen's satisfied sounds made me shiver, and I wrapped my arms around his neck as he laid back, hands cupping my thighs that were spread over his hips. I tucked my face into his neck, savoring the blissful peace I'd be allowed before the guilt started to creep in. His chest rose and fell under me, and he reached up to cup the back of my head.

"Don't do it, baby," he murmured into my cheek. "Don't tell yourself those lies. You're not a burden. You're not trouble. I'd let you rip my life to pieces and half the world along with it if it meant I could keep you like this."

"Riding you on top of a car?" I asked, trying for some levity. Kellen laughed then pushed me back, taking my face in his hands.

"In my life. With me. No matter what," he said, giving me a look so sincere my eyes pricked. He leaned up to kiss me, lips curling into a smile. "Riding me on top of a car is a bonus."

I shook my head. "I should know not to fight with you. It's moot. You always get your way eventually."

"Not always." He shifted, grinding himself into me as he kissed me deep and slow, a smile curling his lips when he pulled back. "If I had my way, I'd have a real ring on your finger already and a kid inside you."

My eyes flared wide. "Jesus, Kell."

"Not rushing. But you should know the endgame."

"Not for a few years."

"The kid maybe. The ring as soon as I can get one. A year for the kid."

"Five," I countered.

"Three."

"Four."

"We'll talk about it later."

He stood from the car, keeping my legs around his hips and stumbling once as he carried me into the house, to his bed, where we started all over again.

It was afternoon by the time we finally decided to shower and get out of bed, groaning at the ache in my hips. "I don't want take out," I shouted into the bedroom as I walked back to the kitchen, peering into Kellen's fridge. "Pasta sounds good. Do we have everything?"

"Should," he said, walking in with the cat in his arms. Haku was purring softly, and Kellen set him down by his food bowl while I grabbed my phone off the counter, frowning when I saw the number of notifications on it. I swiped up, heart starting to pound as I read through them.

Han: *Tatum call me.*

Han: *Please, have Kellen call.*

Han: *Tatum please call or have Kellen call.*

There were a dozen more texts. Then missed call. Missed call. Missed call...

"Kellen, have you checked your phone?"

"No, it died last night. And it's been on silent probably, why?"

I swallowed, showing him my screen, watching his eyes narrow as he looked at it. "Hannah needs you to call her. She's... I just talked to her this morning."

Kellen stared, then he stalked back to his bedroom, reemerging with the phone pressed to his ear. "Han, what's wrong? My phone was in my bed—"

He stopped talking, and my pulse skyrocketed as I watched the color drain from his face. One hand was at his side, and it started to shake, then he made a choked noise and slumped into a chair, his free hand coming up to fist in his hair.

"Are they... are they *sure* it's him? I just saw him last night? How..."

He looked at me for answers, but I had none to give. All I had were arms that circled him when he started to growl, letting it turn into a yell, then a sob as he buried his head against my belly and I heard Hannah's weeping voice on the other end of the line.

Chapter Forty-Six

Tatum

POLICE SUSPECT OFFICER WAS MURDERED BY HIS OWN WEAPON, WHICH was not found at the scene of the crime. More details to come as they are released.

It was the first story I'd written in a few weeks, and I only got to write it because I walked into Gina's office and demanded to cover it. Isaac was my source. My boyfriend's best friend. My friend's older brother. *My* friend.

And now he was gone.

It didn't seem real.

Death never does. Whether it comes suddenly, or it's been expected for years, it never seems real. It's an abstract concept, that a person no longer exists but you carry pieces of them with you. In your blood. In your soul. In the presence of the people that life mattered to.

The funeral happened fast, planned around when the Moore's could fly back from North Carolina. They stood with Hannah at the service, holding her hand while she looked numb and cold. Isaac's fellow officers from the Metro police force and Lakeside PD were all there, offering hands, but she turned them away to stick near Kellen and me, and a few of the club guys who'd gotten to know her—and Isaac —through us.

After it was over she crashed on our couch, too unsettled to go back to her apartment and roommates. Kellen and I decided to trash the bed he'd just bought for my apartment and buy a new one for the spare room. Hannah moved her stuff in, promising she'd be gone as soon as she felt like her roommates wouldn't ask too many questions.

"You should take more time off. It's only been a week. Don't you get bereavement from the hospital?" I asked her one morning when she was getting ready for work, eyes bloodshot with dark circles under them.

"It's up. Ten days. And what would I do if I did take time off?" She pulled her long blonde hair up into a messy bun. "I can't... sit around and think about how awful all of this is. Isaac would never forgive me if I did."

I grimaced. I knew that drive to busy yourself, to forget what was happening or pretend it never had happened. It was what I'd been doing since moving in with Kellen. Writing into odd hours of the night until he made me sleep, making Cas drive me to the grocery store when he picked me up from class just for something to do so I wasn't sitting at home. Waiting.

But it was different for Hannah. What drove me to stay busy was the fact that someone was targeting me. Oddly enough, that was less upsetting than thinking of someone I loved being hurt. Or being killed.

My phone buzzed and I picked it up, glancing down at the text from Kellen.

Kell: *I've got interviews for a secretary this afternoon. Finally breaking down and hiring one.*

Me: *Good. I'll go into the office. Gina can grab me on the way in, she's offered a few times.*

Kell: *What about Han?*

Me: *She's going to work.*

Kell: *She should stay home another day or two.*
Me: *Her bereavement is up. I told her the same. She can handle it.*
Kell: *Text me when you get to the office?*
Me: *Will do.*

I sent a heart emoji, then tucked my phone away as I watched Hannah finish getting dressed. "You sure you're going to be okay?"

She nodded. "I might stay at my place tonight, or crash on Priest's couch if I'm too tired to drive back here. He offered when I said I wanted to give you guys space but I don't feel like going back to my apartment."

"You can always come back here. We don't mind, Hannah. Or one of us can come get you."

She smiled, then crossed the room to give me a tight hug, her head settling against my shoulder. "Thanks, Tate. If I need you, I'll call."

Hannah left, and I texted Gina, asking if she could grab me on her way back from lunch.

Gina: *Sure. See you in a few.*

I pulled on a pair of slacks Kellen had picked up when he grabbed my clothes, dropped some food in Haku's dish, and watched out the window for Gina, realizing this was the first time I'd been alone in weeks. It was an odd feeling. Refreshing, but unsettling.

Gina pulled up in her grey sedan and I walked outside, only a flutter of nerves coming over me when I got into the passenger side of her car. She shifted into gear and pulled back, eyeing me between glancing back over her shoulder.

"So, we're not going into the office just yet. Pak sent me a text and said the students at South Central have staged a walkout over a teacher getting suspended. I want to get someone on scene and we're the closest ones. Do you have your camera?"

"Yeah, I've got it, and my recorder and my notebook. Do they have any idea what's going on?"

"Something about a teacher suspension. I don't know the whole story. Nick is gonna meet us there since education is his beat."

She drove through town as fast as traffic would allow, getting us close to the interstate. I pulled out my phone to look at the map. "You could go down to 14th and take that all the way through. It's a bit out of the way now but it might save us time."

Gina nodded, then turned onto a side street to cross over to the path I'd suggested. "I suppose you know the faster routes since you can't bike to work anymore."

I shoved my phone into my pocket and sighed. "I miss that, honestly. It was an easy way for me to get exercise and I think that helped—"

The crunch of metal registered before anything else did.

One second, the road in front of us looked normal. The next, it spun, blurring into trees and sidewalks and houses as the tires squealed on the pavement. My body was thrown forward, pain shooting through my neck as I tried to brace on the dash, which exploded a second later. I was knocked back, bluntness turning to silk as a hiss of air surrounded me, drowning out my agonized pants. The airbag deflated, laying across my lap like a popped silk balloon. My vision was blurred, but I didn't have my contacts in. Tears slid onto my cheeks, and I choked out a gasp, every muscle in my body screaming in agony.

I blinked my eyes open and took in the shattered windshield, the glass scattered across my legs, the front of the car now opened so I could see the empty road ahead of us. Cars zipped ahead on the main street two blocks down, the drivers oblivious to the chaos they were passing. No one was outside the old houses. No one to call for help. I looked around at the surroundings, trying to spot anyone who might be able to call if I couldn't. If my voice wouldn't work. Finally I turned to my left to see Gina slumped over, blood trickling down the side of her head.

"Gina? Oh, God."

I unfastened my seat belt, shards of glass pricking at my skin as I turned and hovered my hands over her. "Gina? Can you hear me?" My fingers pressed to her neck, and I slumped in relief when I felt a pulse. I made no move to adjust her position. You weren't supposed to move someone after an accident right? Unless they're moving on their own? Should I be moving?

"Fuck... What the hell? I've gotta call—"

The passenger door opened and I whipped around, neck aching, to see dark pants covered by a dark sweater outside my door. A hand reached inside, grabbing my arm to pull me out of the wreckage. I winced, groaning in pain as they hauled me to my feet. Behind me was a white Cadillac, one I'd seen in my parking lot a few times. Maintenance? Why did it matter? This asshole hit me. The front headlight was smashed, the side of his rusty car dented. He'd come out of nowhere. Was he drunk? Speeding?

The hand on my arm tightened, and I tried to jerk away, turning so I could yell at him. I was met with a sallow, bearded face, the hair on his cheeks and chin scraggly. Unkempt. Like the brown hair on his head, which was piecey and thin. Hooded eyes glared at me, and it was when I looked at them that my thoughts started to clear. I knew those eyes. I'd seen them on the pulpit for years, had them stare at me in disappointed scorn when I'd refused to get back in a relationship I no longer wanted.

I sank all my weight back, trying to pull my arm away from his iron tight grip as a scream built in my throat. I only got out a sharp cry before Mark Adler's other hand swung and pain burst across my cheek. It was followed up a second later by blow to the same spot, just above my cheekbone, and my vision blurred just as the concrete rose to meet me. I tried to soften the blow with my free hand, but another strike hit me on the back of the head and my cheek slammed into the pavement. A haze settled over me, muffling the sounds of the wind and passing cars in the distance as I exhaled a panicked breath.

Then I was struck again, and this time there was no pain. Only a hazy black curtain slowly settling over my eyes, blurring out the pair of beat-up sneakers standing over me...

I STOOD UP OFF THE STOOL TO SHAKE THE WOMAN'S hand. The *final* woman's hand. The last interview of the day.

Rev had gotten a desk at a discount furniture store, and we'd put a lamp and some office equipment on it to make it look official. It was an office, and we were interviewing for a receptionist. Not full time. Four days a week, four hours a day. They could technically do it from home since a lot of it was answering emails, sending out bills, and scheduling appointments.

"Who'd you like?" I asked Rev once the woman's car was gone.

"I liked taking the calls ourselves."

"That's cause you never have to take them," I pointed out. Rev sighed and dragged his hands over his face.

"I don't fuckin' know. They were all fine. The redhead seemed the most on point, but the chick in the business suit had the most experience. Who'd you like?"

One shoulder lifted in a shrug. "The redhead's name is Katherine Bailey. Kate Bailey," I said, picking up the application from the second to last person we'd talked to. "She said she has another job, too. Part-time. Wouldn't interfere. Listed a few referrals. You want to call them?"

"No."

I glared harder. "I don't want to do this shit either, Rev. But we need to. It's time. I'm getting more and more behind on emails, voicemails, and every other type of mail. We need someone to handle that stuff so we can keep working."

He let out a sigh. "Alright, fine. The redhead. She seemed the most eager. You call her, cause I'm fuckin' terrible on the phone. And I'll do the intake, get her set up in here and all that."

"Deal." I shoved her application into a drawer and gathered up the others to put in a file in case she ended up not wanting it. "We done for the day? I'm about tapped out, and Tate and I need to go to the store."

"Look at you all domesticated and shit," Rev teased, stumbling when I checked him my shoulder as I walked past. "Can she actually cook? All we ever did was order take-out."

"She can, she just doesn't like to do it for herself." I flashed him a smug grin. "Me, on the other hand…"

"Maybe I'll come over to your house more often. I get tired of cooking just for myself."

"Bring something to drink and have at it."

I walked to the shop where my phone was, frowning at the screen when I didn't see a text. Tatum was supposed to text me when she got to the office. She'd sent a message she was going somewhere with her boss, but that was hours ago. It was almost 4:00. She'd be getting off soon.

"Anyone call you?"

Rev sounded confused, and when I looked up he was holding out his phone. "I have about four missed calls from a number I don't know," he muttered, pressing the screen then putting the device to his ear.

"It's probably a scammer. Calling about your car's warranty or some shit."

I turned to the list of projects we had going outside of Riot's rebuild. Snapshot was next. A few people were wanting some custom-built dirt bikes for next spring or summer. I looked at my email, finding requests for services on cars, jotting down the ones I thought we could squeeze in.

"No, I'm her neighbor. Are you looking for—"

I turned to him at the same time he looked at me, eyes narrowed as he raked a hand through his hair. "She still has me as her fucking emergency contact," he said.

"*Who* has you?"

"Tate," he said, then he held up a hand. "Where is she?"

I moved so fast I knocked a chair over, reaching for the phone. He handed it to me and I pressed it to my ear. "Hello? What's going—"

"*Kellen?* It's E." Her words were quick, like she was stressed, or shocked. "I didn't have your number and Pak's not here. He's at the hospital with Gina. She picked Tate up for work and they were headed to the South Side for a story, but they got into a car accident."

I leaned against the counter, biting back a curse. "Is Tate okay? Where is she?"

Elissa let out a sigh, and I swore my blood turned to ice. "We don't know."

I whipped my head to look at Rev, who had his arms folded over his chest. "*What?*"

"We don't. *Know.* Gina woke up and she was gone. Her purse was still there and… there was blood on the pavement, but she was gone. We've called the police and they're—"

"What do you mean *she's gone?*" I demanded, trying to get her to say something different. Anything different. Because this wasn't happening. It just wasn't.

How could she be gone? She wouldn't have gotten up and walked away.

I fisted my hand in my hair, the ache in my chest intensifying so much that I had to lean against the counter, my whole body shaking. First Isaac—gunned down, still no fucking leads or arrest—and now this?

Elissa was talking on the other line, telling me I should come down and give them any information that might help. She talked about a search party. Calling Tatum's friends, getting them out looking.

But all I could do was breathe, the ache in my chest too much to take as I was plunged into hell again, wondering how I was going to survive if I came out of this and she didn't.

Chapter Forty-Eight
Kellen

LOOPER SHOVED THROUGH THE DOOR OF THE BAR, A black case in his hand. I jumped off the stool Rush had forced me into, racing over and practically digging the laptop out of the bag. "Can you find her? If she has her phone can you find her?"

"Did you call the cops?" He snatched the computer away from me and opened it up. "If this is connected to what happened with Isaac, they're gonna want to take this fucker—"

"Yes, we fucking called them!" I snapped. "I went down there; I gave them all the fucking information and they told me they're out looking. They said I should organize a search party so what the fuck do you think—"

Someone grabbed the back of my cut and threw me back, and I felt Rev's arms wrap around my mine to pin them back. "Give him a goddamn minute, Kell."

I tried to get out of his hold, but the asshole had a good grip. Plus, Rush and Cas were both looking at me with identical *calm the fuck down* expressions, which made me want to ask what Rush would do if Betsy was missing. Or one of his kids.

I didn't want to imagine either scenario. It was just as bad as the one I was in.

"Do you know if she had her phone on her?" Looper asked.

"It wasn't in her purse," I said, and Rev finally let me go once he'd himself assured Looper was up and running. The guy worked in tech. I didn't know what he did since it was all independent, but on the screen were maps of the area and what I knew was a DOS box from having to have Tate reset my computer a few times.

A wave of horror hit me again. God, where was she? What was happening to her? What was that asshole doing?

This had to be Davey. There was no way around it. I didn't know how they hadn't been able to pin anything down after Isaac was murdered. It was just like when Tate tried to report him. Nothing could be nailed down. No fingerprints, no ability to poke a good enough hole in his alibi because everyone from his missionary co-workers to the fucking fundamentalist assholes in Northshore covered for him. It was all a big web of lies no one had been able to cut the strings on.

"I'm not pinging her on the South Side, or anywhere in the Metro."

"If they smashed the phone, would it still pick up?"

"As long as they didn't rip out the SIM card I should be able to get something. But I can only check a certain radius at a time."

He pulled up another screen, using Tate's email to login. She'd given him the passwords to everything, which showed how much she had come to trust the club.

A wave of nausea swept over me again and I leaned on the back of the stool.

"Foxtrot, you're rattling my chair," Looper said, giving me a quick look before he went back to the screen. "She say anything about someone following her? What about the car that hit her?"

"It was a white Cadillac," I said. "Probably the same one that was parked outside her place, the one I couldn't manage to get a picture of. I got a partial plate and that wasn't enough—"

"The same one I saw?" Cas asked. "The day her apartment got broken into?"

"Yeah."

"It wasn't a young guy who drove that. At least not when it came here."

I paused. "What do you mean? Who drove it?"

"I mean, I remember that jackass because he unloaded six crates of weird books. Not the Bible, there were like... health books and books about lust and hellfire and shit. Didn't you say you and Tate grew up in a really small town that was—"

"Pretty much run by a cult, yeah," I filled in. "It wasn't actively recruiting or holding people hostage, but they spewed all kinds of crazy shit and had a chokehold on everyone. What did this guy look like?"

"Maybe early fifties? He was well dressed but if it wasn't for that, I would have thought he was homeless or sick with the way he was muttering."

"Do you remember what he was muttering about?" I asked.

"Something about people leaving and covenants. Kept mentioning some book in the Bible. The one where everyone leaves, I can't remember. I haven't been to church—"

"Exodus," Rev and I said at the same time, and I turned to give him a look, watching him shrug. "My parents were religious, too."

Rush tilted his head. "I thought they named you Priest to piss off—"

"It doesn't fucking matter!" I snapped. "What... this guy said something about Exodus?"

"Yeah. He said everyone was turning their back on God. His son, friends, people he knew. But he mentioned the first and he said a name." Cas snapped his fingers. "Colleen. Colleen Rathford. She was the first to walk away from her faith or whatever."

Cas stared at me, waving this off like it meant nothing while all the air was pulled out of my lungs. My stomach heaved, and I braced a hand on the back of the stool closest to me. "Are you... Cas, are sure that's the name he said?"

"Yeah. I have an aunt named Colleen, so that's why it stuck out."

I swallowed, the terror I felt for Tate making room for a different ache.

Grief.

Grief that hit me every now and then like slap, then faded because it had been so long.

"My mom's name was Colleen. She... her last name was Rathford before she married my dad."

Everyone's eyes turned to me and I slumped, leaning into the stool for support. "She was killed in a car accident when I was eleven. Some asshole ran her off the road. It was a hit and run. Didn't know if the person was drunk or reckless or what happened." I wiped a hand through my hair, nausea clenching my stomach. "What did this guy look like again?"

"Not balding, but his hair was thin. Brownish maybe? He looked exhausted. Black circles under his eyes. Thick eyebrows, hooded eyes. Like really hooded, you know? Where the upper lid sits on top of their eyelashes. Elissa's are like that."

"Thought Tate said the guy stalking her was in her graduating class," Rush said. "She's twenty-two. He on drugs? That can age you quick. Or does he have an older brother?"

They were looking at me, waiting for a response. But I was struggling to stay up. The world was spinning, and Looper pulled me onto a stool beside him, looking at me like I'd lost my mind. I think I had. I think it had finally snapped.

"No," I slurred, sounding like I'd drank an entire fifth of whiskey. "Davey doesn't have a brother. But he... he has a dad. A dad who told my mom it was her fault we stopped going to church."

Rev's eyes widened, his expression growing tense while Cas ran a hand through his hair. They looked all looked at me. Pitying. Silent. Looper slapped a hand on the bar, causing everyone in the room to jump.

"Got a ping. About a mile off of I35."

He slid off the stool was already on his phone, and I was halfway through the door when I heard Rush whistle through his fingers and tell the others to rally up. I didn't bother with my helmet, kicking my bike into gear, praying for the first time in at least ten years. *Just let her be safe. Just let someone find her. I don't care if it's me just someone.*

Don't take her away from me again.

Chapter Forty-Nine
Tatum

I WOKE UP SO FAST IT WAS LIKE I'D BEEN SLAPPED. A sharp inhale, my eyes bursting open until the pain in my head made me squeeze them shut. My cheek was throbbing. Everything was throbbing. Like the stereo at a club, full bass and raging guitars. My mouth was dry, and I tried to push myself up only to feel something tugging at my wrists.

They were bound together. Zip tied.

There were ties around my ankles, too, over my boots. I kicked, wiggling my ankles against the bindings. Struggling made the pain worse, so I pushed up, leaning into a tree behind me and taking in my surroundings.

The woods. I didn't know where just... the woods.

He took me.

Not Davey. Mark.

Images of when I was in Northshore with Kellen pop into my head. Davey on the sidewalk, a cluster of well-dressed men around him. He'd wanted to talk to me and Kellen hadn't let him. Rightly so. He'd tried to kill me.

And he'd panicked about it.

"I think she's dead. She... I think I killed her."

"If she is, that was God's plan. You did nothing wrong, Davey, believe me."

Everything clicked into place. The article about the conference, it all started after that. It wouldn't take much to figure out my name, not if someone was really looking. Mark Adler had been at that conference, along with the youth pastor who was taking his place.

Even if that wasn't what happened, Davey had seen me with Kellen. Several people had seen me with Kellen. The comments had started before then, but finding me after seeing us together would have been easier. Kellen had social media. He had a business. He had plenty of info out there and he came to and from my apartment week after week, most of the time with me on the back of his bike.

My head fell back against the tree and I closed my eyes, tears sliding down my cheeks. I should have stayed alone. I should have never put myself out there or gone anywhere with Kellen. I should have run when I had the chance.

No.

The voice inside me was soft, but it was there, whispering the truth over my fearful lies. No, that wouldn't have been an answer.

Even if I died here, I didn't want to take back the little time I'd been given with him again. I wouldn't trade the hours in his arms, with his face in my neck, his hands in my hair, for more hours safe, but utterly and completely alone. He brought me joy, I gave him peace. That was worth it.

This was going to crush him.

Isaac's death was hard, and so recent. It was going to kill him when he found out I was gone.

I leaned against the back of a tree, frowning at the direction my thoughts were going. Why was I talking like my death was a foregone conclusion? I did have some choice in the matter. I was still alive right now. Maybe Adler thought he killed me and just dumped me here. A rush job he'd been wanting to get over with for years and now he could move on to better things.

I looked at the zip ties around my wrists and ankles. The binds on my wrists were tight, cutting into my skin, and I wondered if at some point, I'd tried to hit him. I could barely wiggle my wrists but I tried, flashing back to the YouTube videos on self-defense and safety I'd watched. Zip ties could be broken with the right amount of force, or friction. Maybe then I could get free and run or call...

I twisted and rubbed a hand against my pocket, biting back the laugh of relief that bubbled in my chest. My phone. It was still in my pocket.

I yanked it out, staring at the crushed screen, the bent frame. *Please turn on. Please please...*

The screen lit up and I let out a shaky breath, immediately navigating to the phone icon but freezing when I heard the crunching of leaves. Shit. *Shit, shit, shit.* What had Looper said? As long as I had it on, they could track it.

I swiped away from the phone app and navigated to my camera, turning it onto record before shoving the device back into my pocket. Deep into my pocket. At the very least, if they find my body, they might be able to get something from the audio. My name. His name. Finally be able to stop this chaos. It's a long shot, but it was all I had.

Pastor Mark didn't look surprised to see me awake, but I was surprised to see his exhaustion. The bags under his eyes, the pale tone of his skin. In his hand, he carried rope, a shovel, and an odd-looking saw. Bile burned the back of my throat but I kept it down, forcing my breathing to stay even. Years of trying to keep panic attacks at bay were coming in handy.

Months of being with Kellen having him breathe slowly with me helped, too.

Pastor Mark set his things down and moved to kneel in front of me, and I held still as he put his hands on my bent knees.

"You're going to pray one last time, Tatum. I'll grant you that. I've given all of them that choice." He said all this not unkindly. Just… tired. "Do you remember how?"

My hands started to shake, but I managed a nod. "Acknowledge Gods power. Confess your sins. State your plea, then thank him for his kindness."

He nodded, and I was graced with a small smile. "You always were so smart. It's what made you both perfect for and ill-suited to Davey. Intelligence is fostered by curiosity, but curiosity isn't a blessing. It steals souls. Leads people into temptation. You were born into the world without a strong foundation, and that fostered a curiosity that you struggle with to this day. Your work requires it. I believe that if God had you borne in our sanctuary, none of this would have happened. But I cannot control his plans. I can only act on his will."

"Harvey and Marta brought me in."

Mark's expression turned sad, and he nodded, patting my hands gently.

"They tried their best," I said. "You have to know that. I'm just… I was born evil."

If I play into his delusions, it might give them time to track me.

If they knew to look…

God, I hoped Gina was okay. At least he hadn't taken her, too.

"All of us are born evil, Tatum. Original sin is woven into our blood. But you were made clean, then you broke your promise." He paused, those hooded eyes growing dark. "You made Davey break his promise."

Mark's head dropped and he rubbed the top of his thighs, bracing to get up. I seized my chance, noting the distress in his face as he thought of his son. "How is Davey?"

The question came out in a rush. Anything to keep him talking and try to slow what was about to happen. He kept his eyes on me as he stood, looking more tired than he had seconds ago.

"I wanted to believe that Davey would be able to get you back under his wing. You were flourishing together. Even with that curiosity. He was the reason you were so loved for a while. The reason everyone had hope for your future. He led you toward acts that could have saved your soul had you just been obedient, Tatum. But your sinful nature caused Davey to stray. To stumble."

"He regretted it."

Mark shook his head. "He regretted the wrong sins. The sin of the flesh didn't haunt him, it was his punishment of you that drove him away. His righteous act separated him from his faith and I... I could not help him. My only son and I cannot save him."

He turned his back to me and picked up the shovel before walking a few feet away and driving the tip into the ground.

"If you hadn't been so defiant, it would have all been different. You were always so good and pliant toward our guidance, and even now..." He put his shoe on the edge of the shovel and pushed. "You're calm. Understanding. Ms. Marlan screamed and screamed. Said horrible things. It made me so angry and I had to gag her, so she couldn't say her final prayers. Tiff, and Rachael, and Valerie, they cried to the point of panic and couldn't say them either. I tried my best to save them at the end, but they went into hysterics, and I'm certain they were damned."

My jaw ached, and it's only then I realized I'd been clenching my teeth. Biting down so hard that when I swallowed again, I choked. My stomach rolled, but I held down the urge to vomit and pushed out a one-word question. "Isaac?"

Mark sighed, his foot on the shovel, and I stared at the small pile dirt next to a tree beside him. "That was a mistake. That... why did you bring that up?"

"Did he know?" I pressed. "Did he know that you killed—"

"I haven't *killed* anyone. Righteous wrath," Pastor Mark snapped, his face twisting in shame. "Isaac was a mistake. A rash act. But he would have stopped me. He was coming to too close, asking questions. And even though I'd tried to guide those souls of my flock to the path God has set before them, they've all strayed. They've been led astray and would have stopped me if they knew."

He plunged the shovel into the dirt, face turning red as he dug frantically into the soil. "I've tried to explain it to the ones who are still faithful. I tried to explain to Davey that a loss of life is justified. Our Lord demands that we—the *most* faithful—carry out his will. The wicked must be punished. Those who would spread falsehoods, defy His commands, and bring innocent lambs into harm must be dealt with."

He pushed the shovel deeper with his foot, grunting as he tossed the dirt away. "That is what I have done. I have vanquished the temptresses who've harmed my flock. I made Isaac a sacrifice, like his name always intended, and his death led me to you and allowed me to continue the work I've been assigned. What I've been tasked to do by the Lord."

My whole body was trembling now, breaths rattling as they moved slowly in and out of my nose.

"Pastor Adler, I didn't lead Davey into harm. He's... he's fine. He's still doing God's work, isn't he? He's preaching and volunteering—"

"He's lost his way," Adler spat in my direction before he went back to shoveling. "He refuses to listen. He sees the night you survived as his greatest mistake. As his biggest shame when it was his most righteous act! You deserved to be punished for your disobedience and harlotry, for your betrayal of a godly man."

He stalked toward me, ignoring my raised hands to grab the back of my hair and force my gaze upward, my fearful eyes meeting his crazed ones. "Those other girls did the same. They came into His light and drew men into temptation, then left without any shame. Without any sense of duty for the role they have been born into!"

He shook me so hard my teeth rattled, then shoved me to the ground, putting a knee on my back to hold me in place. "Women who stray from their ordained path regret their choices, and I did those girls a favor by ending their suffering early. How many more men would they have led into sin? How many more souls would have been lost because of their treachery? I'm doing you a favor, because you will earn nothing but contempt from any Godly man that touches you. You are tainted. Ruined. And deserve to burn for your defiance."

He spit on my cheek, shoving my face into the dirt before getting back to his feet and going to work again, still muttering as he dug my grave.

"I've seen it happen too many times to let it go on. I warned the men in my flock that impure women were evil. That their deviance would ruin their lives." He grunted when he hit a rock, or a hard patch of dirt. "None of them listened. They laughed in my face. It was only when I sought justice for those two lost boys and their father that I knew what I had to do. I knew what I'd been called to do."

I rolled to my side, taking the chance while I had it to unlace my boot. Adler was busy, each shovel scoop bringing me closer to my demise. My body ached, but I stretched and pulled the string free, looping it through the zip tie and taking one end in my hands, the other between my teeth. I bit down and held tight as I wiggled my feet hard back and forth. Back and forth. Sawing the lace on my boot through the tie. *Come on… come on….*

The zip tie snapped, my lace pulling tight then going slack as my feet burst free.

Run, run, run!

The voice in my head was so loud, but I had to be logical. I had to be smart. Adler was probably faster than I was, and he had a shovel. A good enough whack with that and he wouldn't need to choke the life out of me.

I sat up, making a show of struggling to tuck my legs under me. Adler was engrossed in his task, buried in the hole up to his knees. "The woman who betrayed you," I started, wanting to keep him talking, trying not to let the growing pile of dirt send me into a panic. "Was she the first one you punished?"

He snarled a series of curses, not looking up as he increased the pace of his shoveling. "Colleen knew what she was getting into when she backed away from her faith and took her husband and boys with her. She knew judgment would fall upon her, and when it did, I think she welcomed it. She was grateful to me for releasing her from her hellish life with that drunkard, but I never asked. She was dead when I got to the car, unfortunately. She also never had a chance to say her final prayers."

I'd grabbed the lace again and was trying to tie one end into one, the other to the other, so I could work on my hands, but I froze and looked up, the fear inside me replaced with a sickening realization. "Colleen…" I breathed, trying to work the name loose from my throat. "Colleen Bishop?"

"Rathford."

Mark stood up from the hole, his face twisted in rage as he stepped up and hauled himself out of it just when I tucked my legs under my body. "I warned her there would be judgment. I gave her the chance to repent, to leave her heathen, drunkard husband and save her children before it was too late, and she shunned my offer. Her death was necessary, it set me on the path that brought me here today so I could rectify the deepest mistake I'd made."

He raked a hand through his hair, looking at me like he was disappointed I wasn't being quiet and obedient while he monologued and dug my fucking grave.

But I couldn't speak now. My mind was reeling.

Colleen Bishop.

Kellen's mother. Who'd loved music and ice cream and had left to go to the store after a fight with Kellen's dad. She never came home.

Because Mark Adler ran her off the road.

I wanted to hurl a thousand curses at him, ask how God could sanction the slaughter of a mother and leave two boys without a parent. What kind of God would want that? What kind of God would command him to slaughter girls—just girls— for breaking his commands? What kind of God would have him kill an innocent man to keep going?

Not one I knew. Not the one I still talked to sometimes when I was angry or questioning the purpose of life.

But there wasn't a chance to say anything, or issue challenges to his bastardized theology. Mark stalked toward me, his face hard, hooded eyes looking darker thanks to the shade of the forest and the setting sun hidden behind the trees.

"You broke a covenant. Defiled your body and caused others to defile theirs, and that sin cannot stand. Not in the world the blessed will inherit."

He tossed the shovel beside us, and I sat up on my knees, raising my bound hands when he knelt in front of me. He grabbed my wrists and pressed my palms together, curling my fingers into fists and closing his over top them.

"You should pray now, Tatum. It's the last chance you're going to have." His face was centimeters from mine, warm breath hitting my forehead. "Ask for forgiveness for your sins, repent for—"

I wasn't sure what came over me. There were a thousand thoughts in my head from the terror over my potential death to the fact that Mark Adler killed Kellen's mother and had gotten away with it. No one ever suspected or researched anyone in town, they'd assumed it was a drunk driver. A speeding car just passing through.

But one of those thoughts made the muscles in my arms

tighten, my stomach brace, and I thought again to the videos I'd watched all over the internet. The nose was one of the spots to hit to truly disorient someone, so that's where I aimed, pushing my fists, which I had folded into prayer position, into Mark's face. He braced at the last second and that lessened the impact, but he released my hands, and I didn't hesitate when I clasped them together again and slammed them into his head.

His scream was enraged, as he toppled over. I dove forward and grabbed the shovel, running solely on instinct as I gripped the handle and rose up onto my knees, slamming the blade into his back. I swung again, and again, until he started to crawl away. Then I clambered to my feet and braced, trying to decide what to do next.

The shovel was still in my hands when Mark rolled and righted himself. I went to swing it again, but he grabbed the shaft. I kicked straight up and hit him in the crotch, and he grunted, doubling forward as an inhuman scream that had to belong to me echoed off the trees. I swung the shovel. It connected with his head, whipping his face to the side and making him topple over in a curled-up ball, his hands between his legs.

Run.

I wasn't going to get another chance.

I pitched the tool and took off in a dead sprint in the direction I'd seen him walking when I first came to.

My hands were still bound. One boot laced, the other free and as I ran, it fell off my foot. I bent to pull the shoe off and leave it behind so I could run faster. The trees weren't thick, but there were leaves on the ground, which meant my escape was noisy aside from my frantic breaths. Mark shouted my name. His voice bounced off trees, loud and enraged. Hot tears slid onto my cheeks only to immediately cool in the dusky fall air. My legs burned, the muscles aching from weeks of not being used. I gritted my teeth, trying to hold back my panicked sobs as my name echoed off the trees again. Where the fuck was I? Did this forest ever end? There had to be a path...

"Tatum!"

No, no, no.... I couldn't stop. I'd gotten too far to give up now.

I passed the car that had crashed into Gina and me earlier, the white Cadillac. For a moment I thought about seeing if there were keys, but it was too obvious, and Mark kept shouting my name, so I blew past it and kept running.

The light from the sun was growing clearer as the trees thinned, and in the far, far distance I could see the highway. There were flashing lights, a dozen or so cars. Flashlights cut through the dim evening light. Motorcycles were parked among the cars, clusters of people standing around, waiting...

"Help!"

I'd never screamed so loud in my life. So loud it took the wind out of me, so loud it burned my throat. I nearly collapsed, taking a second to breathe before starting to run again. "Help!"

My ankle rolled when I hit a divot in the ground, but I kept moving, shouting and screaming until I saw bodies turn and the small lights from flashlights face me. There was an uproar, then a group of figures moved toward me as I sprinted into safety.

"Freeze!"

Was that meant for me? Why?

"Freeze! Get your hands up!"

I fell to the ground, socially conditioned obedience to the phrase making me raise my bound hands in the air. The figures approached, then moved past me, only one standing by where I knelt as they others kept shouting.

Behind me, it was chaos, and I turned to see Mark striding out of the woods, shovel in hand. The sun was setting, but I could see his bloody face, tilted funny. Like I'd broken his nose or his cheek or his jaw. He paused at the sight of the police cars and officers, their guns trained on his approaching figure as they shouted and ordered him to stay still. Drop the weapon. I expected him to run, but to my horror he didn't.

Instead, he pulled out a gun from the back of his pants and aimed it in my direction.

The next moments happened in slow motion, but also too fast for me to fully grasp. I curled into a ball, trying to shield myself as the officers closest to me moved and a dozen weapons were raised. The air was filled with contradicting orders, deep male voices filled with rage as they shouted back and forth.

"Get down on the ground!"

"I have done the will of the Lord!"

"Freeze!"

"I have punished the wicked and no man will judge me!" It went on, an endless back and forth.

Then there was a single gunshot and I flinched, braced on my knees, waiting for the pain or more shouting or gun fire.

But it never came.

I turned over my shoulder to see the police stalking forward, weapons raised, though some were being lowered. At the edge of the line of trees, Mark was no longer standing. His body was flat on the ground, and it was then I realized the shot had been far away rather than close.

It had come from his own gun.

A strong hand hauled me to my feet, pulling me away from the chaos toward the road. "Are you Tatum?"

My body was shaking so hard it was difficult to speak. "Yes."

"Get her to a hospital," the officer said, passing me off to another person, who looked at my bound hands and decided he'd deal with them later.

There were half a dozen cars, and part of the interstate was shut off by a blockade. Behind that, I could see more bodies milling around. A search party. Most on foot, some ready to go, seated on motorcycles.

"Kellen?"

"Ma'am, we need to get you to a hospital and get a statement—"

I didn't argue, letting him drag me along as I scanned the group behind the barricade. I spotted Priest first, thanks to the hair, but beside him was Kellen, his arms folded around his chest as he paced back and forth, eyes darting to the area off the road and to the police cars.

"Kellen!"

The officer released his grip but followed when I started walking in the direction of the barricade. *"Kellen!"*

Kellen turned at the sound of my voice, his eyes wide. He hopped over the barrier, shoving past a few officers who raised protests. He moved faster than I ever thought possible and slammed into me, arms looping around my torso as he crushed me to his chest.

"Jesus Christ! Tate?"

His hold on me was borderline painful, but I didn't fight. I only regretted I couldn't hug him back since my hands were still bound. He noticed too, cupping my face then looking down at my wrists then turning to the officers surrounding us.

"What the fuck? Get this off her! Where's an ambulance? Or a blanket!"

He was wearing a jacket and ripped it off, pulling it around my shoulders just as an officer returned to cut the zip tie off my wrists. "She needs to go to the hospital for a statement, you can see her—"

"I'm going with."

"It's not allowed."

"I don't give a *fuck* what's allowed, I'm going with."

"Don't make me give you a warning—"

"A warning for *what*?!"

Kellen's shoulders tensed, and I put my hands on his chest to steady him before wrapping them around his waist. He looped his arms around me, burying his face in my neck. "I'm not letting you go. I'm not fucking doing it."

"It's the hospital—"

"*No.*"

His voice broke, and I looked up to see his face twisted in pain, tears in his eyes. "No. I thought I lost you again. I'm not..."

I swallowed, using my thumbs to wipe away his tears. His shoulders rose and fell, and his breath fanned against my cheek, deep and slow. The cop beside us shifted and the tone of his voice softened. "You can come with, but you're both in the back. Can't have either of you up front. That fine?"

Kellen nodded, pulling back to look me over. His expression was tight as he cupped my face, looking at my cheek at what I assumed was a bruise. "Goddammit. That fucking *psychopath.*"

The word made me wince, and I let out a sigh and buried my face in his chest. "Kellen, I need to tell you something. I got him talking trying to stall him and he... Your mom—"

"Tate." His voice was tight now. Shaking. I gripped his shirt as he nodded, averting his eyes for a second before dropping his forehead to mine. "I already... I know... he... It's a long story. It doesn't matter right now." He took a breath and squeezed me tighter. "I just wanna get you home. I want this to be over."

He buried his face in my neck, and I leaned into him, my chest aching as I realized it was.

I was safe. We were safe.

It was finally, finally over.

"TATERTOT FEELS... ANTI-CLIMACTIC." CAS DRUMMED his fingers on the bar. "We gotta come up with something better."

"How about Tatum? Or Tate? I don't need a road name when I'm not going on the road."

"You will be, though. We've still got a few rides in before it gets freezing out. Even then, bundle up and it's no problem. So you need a road name."

"There's nothing wrong with Tatertot," I murmured, grinning into her shoulder when she made an angry noise.

"There's everything wrong with Tatertot—the primary thing being that I hate them."

My laugh was lost in her hair.

It was early on a Friday night. Tatum was on my lap, arguing with Cas, one of her arms looped around my shoulder and her legs dangling between mine.

I could have let her sit in the stool right next to mine, but I wanted her like this.

It'd been almost a month and a half, and I still wanted her in my arms every second of the day.

There was still an ongoing investigation into how many murders or disappearances Mark Adler had been involved in. He'd spilled quite a bit of his story to Tate, and she'd had the brains to record it, but the loose ends he left by putting a bullet in his head would take a while to tie up.

And the wounds he reopened would take a while to heal.

I'd called Lane the day after it all went down. He'd seen the main story on the news and was already in the car, driving to check in, but he had to pull over when I told him what happened. How Adler had probably followed our mom and ran her off the road, planning on doing to her what he'd done to the other girls. But she had died in the car before he got a chance.

Small blessings.

Lane decided to be the one to tell our dad, but neither of us were sure if he'd believe the story. There was no corroboration for it since none of the people who worked at the church in Northshore had a clue what was going on. They thought pushing Alder off the podium would help ease his obsession, give him time to settle into a new path for his faith.

It'd only fueled his desire for vengeance. Convinced him his mission was right.

A few of Tate's co-workers kept me in the loop about the headlines, but she refused to read about it. There had been countless articles, phone calls, and a few interviews with news outlets much larger than *The Journal*, but Tatum still avoided the spotlight even though the danger was gone.

After it was clear people wanted her story, she'd taken it upon herself to write a personal account of everything and publish it as an editorial. Most people were only interested in her abduction and the scene in the woods, but Tatum went deeper. She talked about the shame levied on her and countless other girls for being normal, developing women, and the burden of responsibility put on them to stifle men's lust, which only added to the guilt teenagers felt over everything from upsetting their parents to changing friendships and other rites of passage. She reached out to get interviews from other girls who'd taken pledges like she had as teens, and shared quotes from them on how it had left them in broken, sometimes dangerous relationships, just like Tate. They'd thought themselves failures, and the church had only confirmed it.

In a move Gina and the others thought was genius, but one that put me on edge, Tate reached out to Davey Adler to do a short phone interview about how the heavy emphasis on purity and the pressure to control and subdue a partner had caused him to break his own faith as he aged and eventually, leave it all together. Davey had felt the same guilt Tate had, the struggle to suppress his own desires, and this compounded over time with his father looming over him. Lectures on damnation and hellfire and the need for men to subdue women who defied them. Protect them when they went astray, lead them on the path to righteousness. Hours and hours of this had left Davey reeling, and that had spilled over into an act he almost turned himself in over. Had Tatum not left town, he would have.

In the end, she'd decided to let the restraining order slide, especially since Davey had mentioned he was planning on moving across the country. Maybe even out of it. He wanted away from the chaos just as much as Tate did.

Which was fine because I never wanted to hear that last name again.

I was grateful she was able to share her story the way she wanted. That she could take control of her destiny and finally move forward. It was healing. There were still the nightmares, and days when she'd lose herself in a memory, but the constant tremor of anxiety she struggled with faded. She'd decided to go back to a therapist and I drove her to appointments, wondering if I should consider it as well. It wasn't like I didn't have shit to work out.

But she was more soothing to me than any stranger ever could be.

The article ended up going viral, and it got her a bit of attention from other news outlets and she was forced to set up a real website instead of a minor blog. Looper helped her with it, then he fixed our site so it popped up before my arrest record in a search.

Hannah texted, and called, and stopped by to check in. She'd began making appearances at the bar after I told her it was a lighter crowd than the ones her friends tried to drag her to.

"I'll ask Hancake to come up with a nickname," Cas said, and I felt Tatum stiffen. She jabbed a finger at him and shook her head.

"You stay away from her."

Cas held up his hands, feigning a completely innocent look. "What?"

"She's not even old enough to drink. She shouldn't even be here."

"She's close enough," I said. "Her birthday is in January."

Tate gave me a look. "You want him hitting on her?" she asked, jerking her head at Cas and grinning when he made an offended noise. Beside us Rev laughed and took a sip from his glass of scotch.

"I think if he did, he'd get an earful. That girl doesn't have a problem holding her own," he said. "Heard some guy giving her hell the other night in the hallway and I walked out in time to see her kick his ass into the parking lot. Then she came back in and went to have tea with Macy like nothing had happened."

"So it's working out well?" Tate asked. "Having her sublet?"

"Good as far as I'm concerned," Rev said. "She did want me to pass on that you need to come get your shit. There's still boxes in the corner of the bedroom."

I squeezed Tate around the waist, pulling her closer to me

and smiling when her head tipped into mine. "Yeah, I know. It's supposed to be warm this weekend. I can use your truck, right?"

"You know you don't have to ask."

She grinned, turning to kiss my head but I tipped my head up to meet her lips, savoring the way she smiled against me before opening her mouth to kiss me deeper.

We stayed long enough to have a few drinks and listen to Rush and Betsy talk about what our holiday plans were for the club. TC was gonna dress up as Santa, we'd be getting more donations for places, raising money with a bake sale and cook off.

It always felt odd to say that, but the business it brought in was good for the club, and baking made Tate happy, so I didn't say much.

Cas gave Tate shit about making better cookies and she grinned at the challenge. I saw hours of decorating in my immediate future and groaned, making the guys sitting around us laugh.

Truth was, I'd decorate a thousand cookies if it made her smile. I'd spent too much time missing it, then worried it was going to be gone for good, I tried to bring it to her face as often as I could.

We walked outside when it got dark and Tate reached into my pocket, stealing my keys before jogging to my bike. She had the hat with the cat ears on, a heavy blue hoodie covering her torso since it had finally started to get cold. I grinned as she straddled the seat and put the key into the ignition, raising an eyebrow at me when I did nothing to stop her.

"Start it."

Her eyes widened. "Seriously? This one? It's your baby."

"Nah, that's you."

"Okay, but this one is your favorite."

"Exactly, which is why it's the best one to teach you on."

She grinned, putting the key in and starting the bike up

before putting her hands on the handlebars. I climbed on behind her, putting my hands on her waist.

"Just put it into gear and pull out. You know the way home."

Tate whipped her head around to look at me. "What?"

I laughed, burying my face in her shoulder before reaching up and setting my hands over hers. "Clutch," I said, squeezing her hand over the grip. "Throttle and brake."

"Clutch. Throttle. Brake." Her shoulders lifted with a breath, then she turned over her shoulder to look at me. "You're really gonna teach me to do this?"

I kissed her cheek. "I promised I would."

She raised an eyebrow. "Gonna make me ride your face again?"

"I mean," I laughed. "I'm not going to object. That's an open invitation. But you can do this. Shit, maybe I'll end up having to build you a bike. We got time, right?"

She licked her lips, that tenacity I loved so much flashing in her eyes when she turned around to kiss me. "Yeah. We've got time."

Epilogue: August
Kellen

"YEAH, THIS TREE IS WHIMSICAL AND SHIT, BUT YOU ever gonna tell me why the fuck you had me ride all the way over here?"

I wiped my face. It was hot today. Even by August standards it was hot. But that didn't matter. We weren't gonna be out here long and the tree did offer a little shade.

Hannah was curled up in the roots of the old thing, wearing shorts and a T-shirt, her blonde hair pulled up in a high ponytail that whipped around her head as she looked at the highway. She'd been quiet since we got here, and it had been a struggle to get her to come. But Tate wanted her here. My dad was selling the house, moving to the East Coast, so this was our last chance to do this and we needed witnesses.

Rev and Hannah seemed like the best options. Tate's friends would be furious and demand some sort of a party, but the brothers wouldn't have any issue about missing a short ceremony. They'd only show up for the keg and whatever else Cas decided to host for us.

Though, I would enjoy seeing the looks on their faces when I came back with a ring on my finger, and Tate showed up in a cut with my name on it.

"So, what are we doing here?" Hannah asked, echoing Rev's question. "Tate didn't tell me a damn thing when we drove up. And why did she drive up with me? She could have ridden with you. She has her own bike now."

I shrugged, the thick button-down I had on feeling heavy on my shoulders. It was also a little tight. So was the white T-shirt I had on under it. Or maybe I was just nervous and it felt tight.

But I wasn't nervous. I'd wanted this for months. Longer than that. It was Hannah and Rev and their questions making me antsy. That and Tate was taking a long time to get out here. She hadn't let me see her this morning, which shouldn't have been a big deal given that I'd seen her face every day the last ten months.

But it was. I'd spent way too much time without it and if I had my choice, I'd see it every single day for the rest of my years on this planet.

That's why we were here. Under the same tree where we'd met. Promising to love each other through thick and thin, sick and well, all that cliché bullshit. The words didn't matter. This whole ceremony thing didn't matter in the end. But it was tradition, and you had to follow a little of that sometimes.

Rev let out a slightly exasperated sigh and leaned against the tree, while Hannah bounced her toes and stared at the highway. I looked over my shoulder, finally spying Tate as she appeared from around the barn, wearing a white dress and the sandals she'd picked out. She jogged slowly, and I grinned and turned back to our friends.

"We needed witnesses. That's why you two are here."

"Witnesses to what?" Rev asked, and I watched Hannah tilt her head, then she shot up so fast it startled Rev.

"*Nooo*," she said, drawing out the word, one long syllable. "No, you're not... Oh, my *God*!"

She clapped her hands over her face, eyes filling with tears as she looked past my shoulders. Rev followed her gaze, his eyes widening, then he turned to me and grinned.

"Betsy is gonna fuckin' kill you man," he laughed. "She loves weddings. She's going to be pissed and if she's pissed, Rush will be pissed—"

"They can blame me. This was my idea. I didn't want a big crowd or to have it in a church."

Tate's voice was right behind me, and my hands were braced at my sides, whole body tight, like a rubber band ready to snap. She laughed and slipped her hand into mine. "You can turn around, Kell. I already know you looked."

I grinned as I turned around, keeping hold of her hand, secretly grateful that Hannah had pulled out her phone and was taking pictures. I wanted ones of us together, not only because people would get a kick out of the goofy ass look I probably had on my face, but because of the way Tate looked right now.

She'd let her hair grow past her shoulders, and it was back to its natural honey brown. Her face was painted with soft colors, pretty lips spread in a wide smile, blue-green-brown eyes bright and shining. She'd picked out a strappy white dress that showed off her shoulders and arms and clung to the soft curves of her body. The flower tattoo she had inked into her shoulder matched the small bouquet she held in one hand. In the other were the papers that needed our signatures, and the signatures of two witnesses, so we could legally declare ourselves husband and wife. Such simple terms for all that we were.

"Tate," Hannah said. "You're so pretty. You look like... Jesus, you look like something out of a poem." She wiped at her eyes, then widened them again. "Wait... are you eloping because you're pregnant?"

I laughed but Tate grimaced and shook her head. "No, God no. Ugh, at the rate everyone is going on about that I'm going to get my tubes tied."

She tucked herself into my side, looping her arms around my waist as I kissed her head. She didn't mean it. We'd talked about it several times and all she ever said was she needed the idea to sink in. To marinate. Motherhood had never been something she'd allowed herself to want considering the way she'd been raised. It wasn't an avoidance of children, or a fear of pregnancy. She wanted to make sure she did it right.

I had no doubts in my mind that she would when it was time. When she chose to.

Tate rubbed at her cheeks and sighed before looking up at me and raising her eyebrows. "We gonna do this?"

"Yes."

I moved toward the tree, helping her hop over the small rotting fence while Rev and Hannah took positions opposite each other. I got a punch to the shoulder that made me grin and Tate got a quick hug, patting Hannah's shoulders gently when she wouldn't let go.

"Hannah, it's okay."

"I know, I know. But you know deep down I'm a stupid girly-girl and this stuff always gets me." She wiped her eyes and released Tate, turning to look at me. "You know Isaac would... he would have been—"

"He'd give me so much shit about marrying my high-school sweetheart."

"We weren't sweethearts in high school," Tate pointed out. I shrugged.

"Close enough."

Hannah collected herself enough to stand behind Tate while we took each other's hands, the rate of my pulse ticking up when she looked up at me.

"I love you," I said. "I didn't take the time to write a note about it and I know you didn't either, because we don't need words on a paper. But I need you. You're my person, Tatum Noelle."

She squeezed my fingers. "And you're mine, Kellen Brady."

"Brady?" Rev asked. "Your middle name is Brady?"

"Yours is worse."

Tate laughed again and let me keep one of her hands as I dug into my pocket and pulled out the rings we'd bought. Simple little things. Slender silver band with a small white stone in the middle for her, and mine matched, a single thread of silver that looped around my finger. I slid the ring onto her finger, and she did the same to mine.

"You good?" I asked, swallowing a lump when I noticed her eyes were wet.

"Yeah, I'm good."

"Can I kiss you now?"

"As long as you promise to never ask again."

I grinned, yanking her forward into my arms. She put her hands on my waist as I cupped her face, leaning down to press my lips to hers. Hannah cheered softly and Rev clapped, punching me on the shoulder again when I gripped Tate harder, kissing her deeper.

"You gonna consummate this thing here too? Cause I'm not sticking around for that part."

The kiss was broken by a giggle, and Tate tucked herself against my chest, handing the papers to Rev first.

"You need to sign this otherwise it's not legal. Full name."

"Considering my age, it's probably the only time I'll sign one of these things."

Hannah waved her hand dismissively at him. "You've still got time. I have some friends I could introduce you to."

Rev raised his eyebrows and handed her the paper. "Pretty sure I can't keep up with them."

"You don't give yourself enough credit," Hannah chirped as she signed her name, then passed the papers back to Tate. "Great, so what now? Do we at least get cake? Tell me we get cake."

"Suzanne made us a cake," she assured. "Angel food. And I got strawberries."

"We gotta have dinner first," Rev grumbled. "There has to be a restaurant or something we can go to. My treat. Then we can come back and have cake and you two can do whatever it is—"

"Yeah, yeah, we'll get to that, but first," I turned to look at him. "You got a pocketknife?"

He gave me a curious look and reached into his pocket. "Yeah…"

I took and turned to Tate, watching her grin up at me as I walked to the tree and popped the knife open. "I think we're safe to desecrate this tree with our initials now, right?"

Her smile could have melted the iceberg that sank the titanic. "Yeah. I think we're safe."

I grinned, meeting her lips when they tipped up into mine as I pressed the tip of the knife into the trunk of the tree. One last tradition to bind us together, before we started making our own.

THE END

ACKNOWLEDGMENTS

To my children - thank you for putting up with late dinners and a distracted mom. I cannot put into words how much you inspire me daily.

To my Editor Susan - thank you for taking my jumble of words and helping me turn them into a story. I appreciate your intelligence, your sharp eye, and that you understood all my references.

To my proofreader/formatter Tori - thank you for putting up with my endless nervousness in our conversations, for catching all the little slips, and for turning these pages into something beautiful.

To Dr. AnneLadyem McDivitt for being an endless well of support.

To Jill Kaczak for being the first person to push me into writing "for real."

To Emily Ewing for reminding me to own my ideas and go for the things I want.

You three are some of the most kick ass people I know and I'm so grateful you're in my life.

To Jacinda - your endless and near daily support, camaraderie, critiques, creativity, and beautiful prose have made my world so much brighter. Thank you for being a part of it, for sharing your work and ideas with me, and letting me share mine with you how matter how wild they get.

To Anne - Thank you for answering every question I could possibly think of regarding a career in Journalism. Your insight and input helped bring Tatum to life and I appreciate your help with that so much.

To anyone in my Flock who reads this. I am so grateful for your continued enthusiasm for my weirdness and appreciation for the randomness that comes out of my mouth.

To the Sparrows who helped me along the way. I would not have done any of this without you.

To the beta readers and ARC readers who gave me the chance to share this with you first.

And to you, the reader, because without your interest in written words I wouldn't have a story to write. I appreciate you all and will see you soon.

Anastasia

ABOUT THE AUTHOR

Anastasia Fenne is an author of contemporary erotic romance and romantic suspense. When she's not dreaming up the emotional turmoil she can put her characters through, she enjoys video games and reading anything she can get her hands on. She resides in the Midwest with her four children, three cats, one dog, and a bewildered spouse.

Want sneak peaks and updates on Anastasia and her work?

Join the Stargazers mailing list

You can also catch sneak peaks, talk about sexy books, and interact with Anastasia in her Stasia's Stargazers reader group, and catch up with her at the following links:

Website

Facebook

Instagram

TikTok

Twitter

Spotify

Pinterest

Made in United States
North Haven, CT
23 May 2022

19452553R00259